Second Innings

The Medicine Men (1975)
Paper Doctors (1976)
Everything You Want To Know About Ageing (1976)
Stress Control (1978)
The Home Pharmacy (1980)
Aspirin or Ambulance (1980)
Face Values (1981)
Guilt (1982)
The Good Medicine Guide (1982)
Stress And Your Stomach (1983)
Bodypower (1983)
An A to Z Of Women's Problems (1984)
Bodysense (1984)
Taking Care Of Your Skin (1984)
Life Without Tranquillisers (1985)
High Blood Pressure (1985)
Diabetes (1985)
Arthritis (1985)
Eczema and Dermatitis (1985)
The Story Of Medicine (1985, 1998)
Natural Pain Control (1986)
Mindpower (1986)
Addicts and Addictions (1986)
Dr Vernon Coleman's Guide To Alternative Medicine (1988)
Stress Management Techniques (1988)
Overcoming Stress (1988)
Know Yourself (1988)
The Health Scandal (1988)
The 20 Minute Health Check (1989)
Sex For Everyone (1989)
Mind Over Body (1989)
Eat Green Lose Weight (1990)
Toxic Stress (1991)
Why Animal Experiments Must Stop (1991)
The Drugs Myth (1992)
Why Doctors Do More Harm Than Good (1993)
Stress and Relaxation (1993)
Complete Guide to Sex (1993)

How to Conquer Backache (1993)
How to Conquer Arthritis (1993)
Betrayal of Trust (1994)
Know Your Drugs (1994, 1997)
Food for Thought (1994)
The Traditional Home Doctor (1994)
I Hope Your Penis Shrivels Up (1994)
People Watching (1995)
Relief from IBS (1995)
The Parent's Handbook (1995)
Oral Sex: Bad Taste And Hard To Swallow? (1995)
Why Is Pubic Hair Curly? (1995)
Men in Dresses (1996)
Power over Cancer (1996)
Crossdressing (1996)
How To Get The Best Out Of Prescription Drugs (1996)
How To Get The Best Out of Alternative Medicine (1996)
How To Conquer Arthritis (1996)
High Blood Pressure (1996)
How To Stop Your Doctor Killing You (1996)
How To Overcome Toxic Stress (1996)
Fighting For Animals (1996)
Alice and Other Friends (1996)
Dr Vernon Coleman's Fast Action Health Secrets (1997)
Dr Vernon Coleman's Guide to Vitamins and Minerals (1997)
Spiritpower (1997)
Other People's Problems (1998)
How To Publish Your Own Book (1999)
How To Relax and Overcome Stress (1999)
Animal Rights – Human Wrongs (1999)

novels
The Village Cricket Tour (1990)
The Bilbury Chronicles (1992)
Bilbury Grange (1993)
Mrs Caldicot's Cabbage War (1993)
The Man Who Inherited a Golf Course (1993)

Bilbury Revels (1994)
Deadline (1994)
Bilbury Country (1996)

short stories
Bilbury Pie (1995)

on cricket
Thomas Winsden's Cricketing Almanack (1983)
Diary Of A Cricket Lover (1984)

as Edward Vernon
Practice Makes Perfect (1977)
Practise What You Preach (1978)
Getting Into Practice (1979)
Aphrodisiacs – An Owner's Manual (1983)
Aphrodisiacs – An Owner's Manual (Turbo Edition) (1984)
The Complete Guide To Life (1984)

as Marc Charbonnier
Tunnel (novel 1980)

with Dr Alan C Turin
No More Headaches (1981)

with Alice
Alice's Diary (1989)
Alice's Adventures (1992)

Second Innings

Vernon Coleman

Chilton Designs

Published by Chilton Designs, Publishing House, Trinity Place, Barnstaple, Devon EX32 9HJ, England

This book is copyright. Enquiries should be addressed to the author c/o the publishers.

First published in the United Kingdom by Chilton Designs in 1999

© Vernon Coleman 1999. The right of Vernon Coleman to be identified as the author of this work has been asserted in accordance with the Copyright, Designs and Patents Act 1988.

ISBN: 1 898146 35 7

All rights reserved. No part may be reproduced, stored in a retrieval system or transmitted, in any form or by any means, electronic, mechanical, photocopying, recording or otherwise without the prior written permission of the author and publisher. This book is sold subject to the condition that it shall not by way of trade or otherwise be lent, re-sold, hired out or otherwise circulated without the publisher's prior consent in any form of binding or cover other than that in which it is published.

A catalogue record for this book is available from the British Library.

Printed by J.W. Arrowsmith Ltd., Bristol

Note

All characters, organisations, businesses and places in this publication are fictitious, and any resemblance to real persons, living or dead, is purely coincidental. Even the existence of the author is in some doubt.

To Donna Antoinette

~ Chapter 1 ~

THE TELEPHONE ON BERNARD BRIMSTONE'S desk made what the manufacturer's brochure described as a cheerful chirping sound designed to 'enliven every day' and guaranteed to turn every telephone call into a 'fun experience'.

Bernard, known to all who knew him as 'Biffo', was a tall, balding, slightly overweight, rumpled-looking man in his mid-forties. Although he hated wearing a suit Biffo had little option for it was a strict company rule that all executives should wear suits, white shirts, black shoes and ties at all times. This rule had only once been relaxed. The office air conditioning system had broken down and a special memo had been sent round instructing executives that they might, if they so chose, remove their jackets while within the confines of their offices. (The memo had made it clear that jackets should be replaced if executives wished to move about in any of the public areas.)

Biffo, dressed according to the rules in a medium blue suit with a wide chalk stripe, stared glumly at the chirping telephone but did not pick it up. Biffo had a rare talent for looking rumpled and the suit he wore was, as usual, badly creased. The plain red tie he wore might have been regarded as a deliberate attempt to match his plain red socks if the two colours had been a little more alike.

'I hate that noise,' he muttered, with quiet resignation. He sighed. 'Why can't we have telephones that go brrr brrr. You know where you are with a telephone which goes brrr brrr.'

Frank 'Streaky' Bacon, the tall, slender, balding colleague to whom Biffo had addressed this comment, slid still further down in his chair until he was very nearly horizontal and rubbed his eyes with his fingertips. Streaky, like Biffo, was a news and documentary producer.

'Worldwide International Global Telephone Communications Inc. sold us eight hundred chirping telephones after convincing our leader that a clear majority of office workers find a telephone which chirps far more restful than one which rings,' he drawled lazily. 'The heady mixture of delightful, youthful impudence and sophisticated *joie de vivre* is supposed to fill us with zest and enthusiasm.'

Streaky had chosen to combine the company's clothing requirements and the needs of his own rebellious personality by wearing a brown silk suit, a blue denim shirt and a pair of patent leather shoes that had never done anything more energetic than press the pedals in his Porsche 911.

'It doesn't fill me with zest,' muttered Biffo, ignoring the telephone. He frowned at something else that Frank had said. 'Who are Worldwide International...er...what was it?'

'Global Telephone Communications Inc.,' said Streaky helpfully.

'Who are Worldwide International Global Telephone Communications Inc.?' he asked. 'I've never heard of them.'

'According to Mavis in the personnel department it's a small company run by Buttress's dishonest and unemployable brother-in-law,' explained Streaky. Ernest Buttress was the boss of Better Television, the company which employed both Biffo and Streaky. 'He operates out of a lock up garage somewhere in North London. He sells office equipment that no one else wants to sell because absolutely no one wants to buy it. I gather he sells almost all his stock to us. Some of it is reputed to be lightly bruised as a result of having fallen off the backs of lorries. My informant tells me that Ernest's brother-in-law has a mysteriously magnetic attraction for goods which have accidentally fallen off the backs of lorries. This may, or may not, have something to do with the fact that many of his friends seem to have broken noses and ears which look rather like bits of diseased vegetable.'

Biffo sighed. 'I don't care where it came from. I hate chirping telephones,' he insisted. 'Almost as much as I hate centrally-controlled air conditioning systems and piped music.' He paused and thought for a moment. 'I hate Buttress too,' he added. The telephone was still chirping.

'If you answered the damned thing it would stop chirping,' said Streaky.

'That would mean admitting that I'd heard it,' said Biffo. 'I'm ignoring it. It's a matter of principle.' He put his elbows on his desk and rested his head in his cupped hands.

'You're not following today's company motto,' said Streaky, waving a finger in admonition.

Biffo, moved a supporting hand, reached across his desk and pulled a small cardboard calendar towards him. The calendar contained an uninspiring photograph of the outside of the company headquarters. A row of small blue vans bearing the company logo were parked in a neat row in front of the main entrance. Underneath the photograph was stapled what remained of 365 pieces of paper. Biffo looked at the motto on the piece of paper he could see: 'Better Television viewers are my friends and it is my task in life to make them happy'.

Biffo read the thought out aloud, paused for a moment, and frowned. 'What's that got to do with chirping telephones?'

'That was our thought for the day at least two weeks ago,' said Streaky with something of a sigh. 'You're not keeping up. Find the thought for today.'

Biffo tore off a series of paper rectangles one at a time. As he tore off each one he screwed it up and tossed it onto the floor next to the waste paper basket underneath his desk. 'What's today's date?'

'The 18th.'

'Oh, dear. I've just thrown it away.' He bent down, picked up each piece of screwed up paper and straightened it out until he found the one dated the 18th. He screwed up the unwanted pieces of paper and tossed them back in the direction of the waste paper basket. Once again each one missed and landed on the floor. As he did this the telephone stopped chirping. Biffo read the message out loud.

'It is my responsibility to rise above all petty troubles. If I am happy then the people with whom I work will be happy too.'

'There you are,' said Streaky. 'You're making me miserable by moaning about your bloody chirping phone.' He sighed. 'I wish I had the courage to walk away from here. Some mornings – no more than nine out of ten – I wake up thinking I'd like to go off and make a complete fool of myself with a 22-year-old bimbo with huge breasts, an outgoing personality and a 1960's attitude towards sex.'

'Who thinks these damned things up?' asked Biffo, waving the crumpled piece of paper in his hand.

'The company has two full-time psychologists on the third floor. It's what they do. I think you ought to get a bigger waste paper basket.'

'Why should I get a bigger waste paper basket?'

'Because that one is clearly too small. You keep missing it.'

Biffo looked down at the mess around his waste paper basket. 'I don't think it would make any difference how big it was. I would still miss it. I'd heard about the psychologists. Do you mean the company employs psychologists to write the mottoes for the firm's calendar?'

'Yes.'

'Is that all they do?'

Streaky shrugged and added another paperclip to the chain he had started making. 'Maybe they also do special mottoes for the Christmas crackers. Since they're psychologists I expect they're both stark raving bonkers. Mavis tells me that one of them used to run an exotic bird shop somewhere in Cornwall. It was called Parrots of Penzance.'

Biffo groaned. 'I hate Mondays,' he said. He screwed the motto into a small ball and tossed it towards the waste basket. He missed and the ball of paper landed on the carpet alongside all the others. Biffo felt he should get up and put the paper into the waste basket. But he didn't.

'So do I.' said Streaky. He abandoned his paperclip chain, crossed his legs and examined a small hole in his left sock. 'I could put up with hating Mondays if the rest of the week was any more fun. But I hate Tuesdays, Wednesdays, Thursdays and

Fridays too.' He sighed. 'The truth is that I hate this job. I don't wish to speak ill of him but Buttress is an evil little sod. I wish he didn't pay me so much.'

'I'm not too keen on Saturdays and Sundays,' muttered Biffo. 'Is that true about one of the company psychologists running a shop called Parrots of Penzance?'

Before Streaky could reply there was a loud knock on their office door, the door opened a foot and a half and a beautifully made up face appeared in the narrow gap.

'There was a call for you, Mr Brimstone!' announced a pair of lips which seemed to have been decorated with several coats of red paint with a high gloss finish. The owner of the face and lips edged into the room. The face was surrounded by a mass of carefully disarranged blonde hair and the body beneath was equipped with impressive looking bumps in all the right places and was supported by a pair of extremely long and delicate-looking legs.

There was no disputing the fact that Ms Voluptua Bradshaw had a pleasing figure, though exactly how much of this was down to genes, nature and a healthy diet and how much was a consequence of a good structural engineering, fine upholstery or the skills of an expensive cosmetic surgeon was a complete mystery to Biffo and Streaky.

Biffo looked up and wearily raised a theoretically querulous but practically disinterested eyebrow. 'Was there?' he asked.

'Good morning, Ms Bradshaw,' said Streaky. 'I'm glad you've popped in,' he added. He pointed to the telephone on Biffo's desk. 'Would you feed that damned thing?'

The beautifully made up face looked puzzled. 'I beg your pardon....?' She brushed a few strands of hair out of her eyes. A split second later they fell back into position.

'It keeps chirping,' Streaky said. 'I think it needs feeding.'

An understanding and condescending smile edged across Ms Bradshaw's porcelain features. A pair of neatly-plucked eyebrows approached one another tentatively. She looked at Biffo and frowned slightly. 'Is he pulling my leg, Mr Brimstone?'

'I wouldn't dream of it, Ms Bradshaw,' answered Streaky.

'He wouldn't dream of it,' said Biffo, wearily.

'Oh, that's good,' said Ms Bradshaw, clearly relieved. 'I was warned that Mr Bacon had a sense of humour.' She smiled and pouted. 'Humour isn't what you might call my strong point,' she confessed. After smiling again and showing Biffo two rows of gleaming white teeth she turned round and started to disappear.

'Did you want to tell me something, Ms Bradshaw?' asked Biffo before their visitor had disappeared entirely.

'Oh yes, silly me!' said Ms Bradshaw, turning at the door and giggling nervously. 'I almost forgot. Mr Buttress's private and personal assistant is asking to speak to you.'

Biffo sighed. 'On this chirpy thing?' he asked, pointing to the telephone on his desk.

'Yes, Mr Brimstone.'

'Thank you, Ms Bradshaw.' The curvaceous young secretary left; her wiggling bottom the last item to leave the room. A minute or so later the telephone on Biffo's desk began to chirp again.

When she had first joined the company there had been some discussion about whether or not Voluptua was the name with which she had been christened. Streaky Bacon's friend in the personnel department, Mavis, had quickly publicised the fact that Ms Bradshaw's two official Christian names were Enid and Cynthia. Rumour had it that she wanted to be an actress.

Biffo picked up the telephone receiver. 'Yes?' he said.

'Mr Brimstone?' asked a young, extremely earnest male voice.

'I think so,' replied Biffo wearily. 'Did you ring his number?'

'Yes.'

'Then that's probably who I am.'

There was a silence. 'This is Roderick, Mr Brimstone. Mr Buttress's personal and private assistant.'

There was a long silence during which Biffo said nothing and Mr Buttress's personal and private assistant listened attentively to the silence.

'Mr Buttress would like to see you, Mr Brimstone,' said Roderick at last.

'OK.'

'Would four minutes past eleven be convenient, Mr Brimstone?'

Biffo paused and looked at his watch. It was nine forty three. 'I think so,' he replied. He carefully put the telephone receiver back onto its plastic cradle.

'Buttress?' asked Streaky.

Biffo nodded.

'I've got an appointment to see him at six minutes to eleven,' said Streaky.

Ernest Buttress had a model railway set permanently laid out on the boardroom table. He ran trains all day long according to a complicated timetable, and always had his appointments arranged to fit in between departure and arrival.

'Do you have any idea what Buttress wants?'

'They're closing down all the news, documentary and arts programmes. We're all going to be making quiz programmes,' said Streaky. 'That's what Mavis told me.'

'Mavis told you that?'

'Who else?'

'They're closing down all of us?'

'All of us.'

'Why didn't you tell me?'

'You didn't ask. Besides it's only a rumour. And you already seemed depressed. I didn't want to tip you over the edge.'

'Where did Mavis hear it?'

'A cameraman she knows heard Buttress's assistant telling his boyfriend about it in the washroom.'

'The private and personal assistant?'

'That one.'

'Ah,' said Biffo, stretching the word out so that it filled the sort of space a sentence would normally occupy. 'So that's it then.' He looked across at Streaky. 'What are you going to do?'

Streaky stretched his neck and pushed back his shoulders. 'I'm going to tell old Buttress exactly what he can do with his damned job,' he said, defiantly. 'I'm certainly not making quiz programmes for him. I had an idea this morning that could make me millions.'

Biffo looked at him and raised an eyebrow.

'The chap who had the idea of sticking little rubbers on the ends of pencils made a fortune didn't he?' asked Streaky.

'I suppose he must have done,' agreed Biffo.

'So what else do people who use pencils need?'

Biffo thought for a moment. 'Paper?'

'Don't be stupid,' said Streaky. 'Pencil sharpeners. I'm going to invent the first pencil with a sharpener stuck on the end of it.' He paused. 'Of course, I've got to work out a way to make the pencil bendy so that you can get the point into the sharpener. But that's just a minor point. It's the idea that counts.'

Biffo threw a handful of paper clips at him.

~ Chapter 2 ~

AT FIVE MINUTES TO ELEVEN o'clock Biffo put down his newspaper, abandoning the crossword puzzle with which he had been struggling, left his office, waved at Ms Bradshaw (who, although puzzled, waved back) and walked down what seemed like a mile and a half of narrow corridor to Mr Buttress's suite of offices.

And at eleven o'clock precisely Biffo entered Mr Buttress's outer office. He felt strangely tired and, in a way which he did not understand, he felt relieved. He had been an obedient servant of society all his life. He had been a cautious and ambitious student and a loyal employee, husband and father. He had learned by rote, lived by habit and common sense and never questioned authority. He had married, fathered children and bought a house he couldn't afford with a mortgage which had for two decades hung around his neck like a millstone. What more could a man do? Why did he feel so disappointed, frustrated and quietly desperate?

Now he felt tired and strangely exhilarated. He knew something was about to change. But he didn't know what or why.

~ Chapter 3 ~

'PLEASE TAKE A SEAT MR Brimstone,' said Mr Buttress's personal and private assistant. 'Mr Buttress won't be a moment.' He glanced at the large digital clock on the wall. 'You are four minutes early.'

Biffo started to explain that he had arrived early so that he wouldn't be late. But he decided that the explanation sounded like an apology and he didn't want to apologise and so he didn't say anything. He sat down.

Two minutes later the door to Mr Buttress's office opened and Streaky Bacon came out. He looked pale and was sweating noticeably.

Biffo rose to his feet and, because he felt that his friend needed support and comfort, reached out and put a hand on his friend's shoulder. But, to his surprise, his friend flinched and moved away slightly, as though the touch of Biffo's fingers had in some mysterious way burnt his skin.

'Mr Buttress won't be a moment,' said the private and personal assistant to Biffo. 'I've just got a few papers for him to sign.' He slipped between Biffo and Streaky, went into Mr Buttress's office and closed the door behind him.

'Well?' asked Biffo. 'How did it go?'

'So, so,' replied Streaky. He seemed embarrassed.

'Was Mavis's cameraman friend right?'

'I'm afraid so,' admitted Streaky. 'Absolutely spot on.' He smiled thinly. 'You can always trust the cameramen to know what is going on.'

'Buttress wants you to produce a quiz programme?'

'That sort of thing,' agreed Streaky.

Biffo frowned. 'What do you mean – that sort of thing?'

'Well, it's a sort of quiz programme,' said Streaky. 'But not just an ordinary quiz programme,' he added quickly and defensively. 'To be honest I think I rather misunderstood what was planned. Buttress isn't a bad sort you know. What he's got in mind is more educational television than anything else. But educational television with a big audience.' Streaky paused. 'He wants me to produce and direct a new weekly programme in which four celebrities visit a local village hall or pub and take on the locals in an educational contest.'

'Ah,' said Biffo, quietly. He paused. 'You said 'yes' to the quiz programme then?'

'It's quite an opportunity,' said Streaky, shuffling uncomfortably from one foot to the other.

'Yes,' said Biffo. There was a long silence. 'I expect so,' he added.

'And it's what the viewers want.'

'It is,' agreed Biffo. He nodded. 'I'm sure you're right.' He felt embarrassed for his friend and embarrassed for himself. He wanted desperately to be somewhere else.

'Besides,' said Streaky, 'at my age what else am I going to do?' He shrugged and looked at Biffo, pleading for forgiveness and understanding. 'There is the mortgage to pay,' he explained. 'And the payments on the Porsche and so on...'

Biffo put his hand out, touching Streaky lightly on the arm. 'I understand,' he said. 'Really,' he added. 'You did the only thing you could. When do you start?'

Streaky looked at his watch. 'In about twenty minutes time,' he replied. He shuffled uncomfortably. 'Do you really think I did the right thing?' he asked, desperate for approval.

'Yes,' lied Biffo. It was, he knew, what his friend needed to hear.

Streaky looked at him and sighed. 'You're lying,' he said. He smiled. 'But that's because you're a good friend.' He put a hand on Biffo's shoulder. 'Thank you.'

Biffo grinned. 'What are friends for?'

'You know, you're the best chum I've got,' said Streaky, suddenly very serious. 'You're going to tell him to stuff his job aren't you?'

'Yes,' said Biffo.

There was a long pause. 'I wish I had your courage,' said Streaky.

'It isn't courage,' said Biffo. 'You are the one who has courage. I'm running away.'

Streaky didn't speak for a moment. 'If there's ever anything I can do for you just yell,' he said at last.

'Thanks,' said Biffo.
'I mean it,' said Streaky. 'Anything.'
'I know.'
The door to Mr Buttress's office opened and the personal and private assistant emerged. 'It's four minutes past eleven,' he said to Biffo. 'Mr Buttress will see you now.'
'Good luck, Biffo,' said Streaky. He was bravely trying to disguise the fact that he felt beaten and utterly demoralised and it seemed unfair that he was failing in this endeavour as well.
'Thanks,' said Biffo. And walked in to see the boss of Better Television plc.

~ Chapter 4 ~

ERNEST BUTTRESS, A SMALL, NEAT man, quite devoid of personality and charisma but skilful at reading a balance sheet, had been the Managing Director of Better Television plc for three months. His main qualification for the job was reputed to be the fact that his lack of weaknesses such as sympathy, empathy and compassion meant that he was ideally suited to firing people without losing sleep over it. He had no previous experience of the television industry but regarded this as an advantage since, as he frequently pointed out, it meant that he had no misconceptions or misplaced loyalties.

He wore a small, neat and almost convincing wig and had false teeth that didn't speak at quite the same rate that he did. His two large and ferocious looking Dobermans, Recto and Verso, sat at his feet slobbering and growling constantly. It was rumoured that the dogs hated their master almost as much as his employees and that although they had attacked him several times they had never attacked anyone else. Streaky had once claimed that if a mugger attacked Buttress the dogs would join forces with the mugger rather than helping their putative master.

During the period that he had been in charge at Better Television Ernest Buttress had made no secret of the fact that he had been appointed solely to make the company more profitable. A specially commissioned, and extremely expensive study of the company's accounts and working practices had shown that the largest expenditure was on programme making. Naturally, therefore, Mr Buttress had chosen to cut costs by making cheaper programmes. Since Mr Buttress seemed to enjoy, and be particularly talented at, making people unhappy he enjoyed his work immensely.

'Ah, Treadmill,' said Mr Buttress, looking up briefly to confirm that the chair he was addressing was, indeed, occupied. 'You're the producer of our arts programme 'The Arts This Week'. Is that right?' He read the title of the programme from a paper in the folder in front of him. He read it as though he'd never even seen it before.

'Brimstone,' said Biffo.

'Is it? I thought it was called 'The Arts This Week'. Are you absolutely sure?'

'I'm Brimstone.'

'Are you?'

'I think so. I usually have been in the past.'

'It says Treadmill here.'

Biffo sighed. 'Then please call me Treadmill if it's easier.'

'Right. Er, thank you. Well I've got some pretty exciting news for you Tread...er...mill. I want you to produce one of our new family quiz programmes. It'll go out every weekday morning. Huge responsibility. Tremendous opportunity. Educational television for the masses.' Buttress beamed like a genial visitor bestowing an extra half day's holiday at a school speech day.

Biffo paused for a few moments. 'A quiz programme?'

'You'll love it,' insisted Buttress. 'And so will the viewers. We are going to have two husbands and two wives in the studio. And the presenter will have copies of their cheque books. Each partner then has to guess what the cheque stubs in his or her partner's old cheque book refer to. Marvellous stuff! When they get an answer correct we give them points towards a holiday in Benidorm. If they get an answer wrong they remove an item of clothing.'

Biffo blanched and hesitated, looking for the right words. 'I've never produced a quiz programme before,' he said.

'Oh, don't worry about that. You'll find this very easy. Nothing at all to it. Just make sure you get lots of close ups of everyone's faces. And when the accusations and counter accusations and tears start coming – zoom right in close! When someone gets down to their underclothing they get drenched in green slime.'

'Green slime?'

'Something the special effects people make up. It doesn't cost much. And by getting the contestants to strip down to their underwear we save on cleaning bills.'

'I'm not sure this is something I'm really qualified to do...' Biffo said. He felt detached from what was going on. It was as though he was floating several feet above himself, looking down and watching someone he knew slightly having this bizarre conversation with this small stupid-looking man.

'Don't sell yourself short, Treadmill! You're going to be really good at this.'

'Oh,' said Biffo. Although this was clearly intended as a compliment he didn't think it was one. He hesitated. 'Don't you think the station is making enough quiz programmes?'

Buttress looked at him and frowned. 'I beg your pardon?'

'Don't you think the station is making...'

'Yes, yes, I heard you,' frowned Buttress, who clearly did not understand. 'How can we possibly be making enough quiz programmes?'

'Isn't there a danger that the viewing public will get tired of quiz programmes?'

Buttress stared at him without understanding. 'The public love quiz shows,' he said. 'They can't get enough of them.'

'Who is going to produce 'The Arts This Week'?' asked Biffo.

Buttress frowned. 'The what?'

'The Arts This Week' replied Biffo. 'That's the name of the arts programme I produce.'

Buttress flicked through the papers in his folder. 'Do you? Arts? Oh no. Oh dear me no. We won't be making that I'm afraid. The viewers don't want that sort of stuff.'

'You're stopping the programme?'

'Oh yes.'

'It's the only arts programme the station produces,' said Biffo, who felt he had a responsibility to defend the programme which had taken up so much of his life for so many years. 'If that goes Better Television won't be producing any arts programmes at all.'

Biffo wondered why he was defending a programme which he truly no longer enjoyed making. He realised that even if Buttress told him that he could continue making the programme he would still want to walk away and say 'No'. He felt he was standing at a crossroads in his life but although he knew which roads he didn't want to take he didn't know which road he did want to follow. He knew he had to make a choice. And he knew there would be few, if any, more chances to make a choice of this magnitude.

He realised, suddenly and with astounding clarity, that all the major decisions in his life had been made either by accident or on a whim.

At school he had chosen to study subjects which were taught by the teachers he liked or which his friends had chosen. He remembered that he had chosen art as his main subject because the art teacher was a young, well-developed female who invariably wore tight sweaters.

Why, he wondered had he applied for a job in broadcasting? He had never thought about any of this before and he found it alarming to realise just how rudderless his life had been.

His whole career had, it seemed, been founded on nothing more important or substantial than the well-built chest of a woman with whom he had never had anything more than a superficial, boy-teacher relationship and whose name he now couldn't even remember.

'There you are. Proves my point. Absolutely no market for arts programmes.'

'But the programme gets quite good ratings,' Biffo heard himself protesting, rather half-heartedly. 'For an arts programme,' he added.

'Too expensive,' said Buttress. 'Far too expensive. All those reporters and cameramen.' He leant forward a little. 'You creative types don't understand finance,' he smiled in a very patronising sort of way. 'Quiz shows. That's the future for television. Quiz shows. The viewers love 'em and they're cheap to make!' He smiled properly at this thought. 'We can make a quiz programme for a fraction of what your arts programme costs. And we get a higher rate from the advertisers.'

Biffo closed his eyes and put his head in his hands. He felt old and tired. He had heard the same argument put forward a hundred times before. He was tired of it. 'You are a bloody philistine, Buttress,' he wanted to say. 'You are ruining a powerful and valuable medium for the sake of quick profits. I loathe you and despise you and I don't want to have anything more to do with your miserable operation.'

But the truth was he really didn't care any more. In his heart he knew that the programme to which he had devoted so much of his life was nothing more than a vehicle for pretentious and untalented individuals with very large egos. They were simply trying to grab some fame and money. He was tired of pandering to their whims. He was tired of his job. He was tired of television. He suddenly remembered another reason why he had applied for that job in broadcasting: one of his lecturers had introduced him to a radio producer who had long hair and a maroon corduroy jacket. He had, he remembered, been impressed by the man's bohemian appearance and apparent intellectual integrity.

'Well, what do you say Treadmill? I haven't got all day.'

Biffo opened his eyes. He suddenly realised that although he invariably worried endlessly about the minor decisions in his life he had rarely, if ever, given much thought or consideration to the big decisions.

He would worry for hours when faced with a decision about which new lawnmower or washing machine to buy. He and his wife Edwina would spend days looking at brochures before buying a new carpet or a new car.

But he suddenly realised that the big decisions had been taken more by accident than design.

He wished he could remember why he had asked Edwina to marry him.

'No time for day dreaming, here, Treadmill!' said the little man behind the desk. Biffo dragged himself back to reality. The little man in the absurd toupee was pounding his tiny fist on the desk in front of him. 'People who pull together arrive at their destination together,' he said.

Biffo recognised the quote and wondered where he'd seen it before. Then he remembered: it had been one of the thoughts for the day that he had noticed a little earlier when he had been flicking through the company calendar.

With a deep sadness Biffo realised that he wasn't just tired of his job; it was far, far worse than that: he was tired of just about everything in his life. There didn't seem to be any point in anything any more. He came to work because it was an escape from home. And he went home because it was an escape from work. The two daily journeys between home had become the highlights of his life.

'My name is Brimstone not Treadmill,' Biffo heard himself saying.

Buttress stared at him and then suddenly looked at his watch and stood up. This was a clear signal that there was a train due in at one of the stations on the boardroom table.

Biffo said and did nothing.

'Do you want the job or not?' asked Buttress, looking at his watch again and edging nervously towards the door which led directly into the boardroom. The Better Television boss still believed that his railway set was a well-kept secret.

Biffo stared back. But he wasn't looking at Buttress. He was thinking back over his life and wondering where he had gone wrong. Without saying another word he stood up and headed for the door.

'Do you want this job or not?' demanded Buttress again. He was trying to look impressive and imposing. He was such a small and insignificant man that he failed miserably.

'No thanks,' said Biffo. 'I don't want the job. I'm leaving. I resign.'

Buttress opened and closed his mouth several times but nothing apart from a few specks of saliva came out.

When Biffo was still several paces away from the door the

door opened as though by magic. Roderick, the personal and private assistant who always listened in on the intercom, was standing in the doorway.

'No one quits this company!' shouted Buttress. 'You're fired Treadmill!'

Biffo didn't say a word. He walked out of the office, out of the building, out into the car park and out of the life he had led for most of his adult life.

Buttress ran for the boardroom but it was no good; the 11.15 was a minute late. The Better Television boss was in a foul mood for the rest of the day. He hated it when his trains didn't run on time.

~ Chapter 5 ~

'YOU RESIGNED!' SAID EDWINA, BIFFO'S wife, for the fourth or possibly the fifth time. He wasn't sure whether the comment was intended to be a statement or a question. 'Why?' she demanded. 'What happened?'

Edwina was medium height but so slim that she looked quite tall. She was an immaculate woman who was so concerned about her appearance that if she had to get up at night to go to the loo she would automatically check her hair before she went into the bathroom. Today her hair was blonde with reddish streaks. She was wearing a beige silk trouser suit and beige high-heeled shoes. She had a pearl necklace around her throat and was wearing pearl drop earrings.

'I resigned,' agreed Biffo, for the fourth or possibly the fifth time. He frowned and tried in vain to remember what had happened in Buttress's office. 'I can't really remember what happened,' he admitted.

He sat down on one of the expensive kitchen chairs which Edwina had bought because they had been made by a carpenter who, if the free colour magazine which came with his daily newspaper was to be believed, sold his work to television celebrities and minor aristocrats.

The chairs looked like the type of modern art that can

only be created with the aid of a hefty government grant. They would not have been out of place in the sort of museum that no one ever visits unless it is raining. The chairs were not designed with the human bottom in mind and were, consequently, desperately uncomfortable to sit on.

Edwina's hobbies were spending money and keeping ahead of the neighbours. Her most arduous activity was sitting at home waiting for men to come and repair her many labour-saving gadgets.

William Morris, the Victorian poet and wallpaper designer, once declared that every artefact should be beautiful or useful or, preferably, both. Generally speaking most people's belongings can be divided into four categories: the practical but ugly, the beautiful but useless, the practical and pretty and the impractical and ugly. Edwina had somehow managed to furnish a whole house with artefacts which fell comfortably and unarguably into the fourth of these categories.

Biffo, struggling to stop himself sliding forwards on the uncomfortable chair, wondered if other people allowed themselves to be buffeted through life by fate. He managed to hold himself on the chair by jamming his feet against the fridge. Maybe, he thought, other people planned their lives properly; choosing career and partner with at least the same amount of thought that they would put into choosing a new pair of curtains or a sweater. Maybe other people had proper plans and did things which they had chosen to do with their lives.

'Why?' demanded Edwina. This time Biffo was in no doubt. This was definitely a question. Edwina had a way with words: she turned them all into weapons. Somehow the short words always seemed to make the sharpest weapons. Biffo tried to think of an answer but was waylaid into trying to remember why he had married Edwina.

He knew he must have loved her once but he couldn't remember what it was about her that he had found loveable.

Tiger, their elderly mackerel tabby cat (so named because of her impressive looking stripes rather than her size or man-eating abilities) rubbed against Biffo's legs. Biffo reached down and stroked the cat's back and neck. She purred and raised her head so that he could tickle her under the chin. The cat had originally been bought for Jasmine (who had had a temper tantrum outside a local petshop until the animal was purchased) but who had lost interest in her in less than a week. Now Tiger was the closest thing Biffo had to a friend. A few years earlier she had been run over by an unknown motorist and she still walked with a limp. Edwina, who never called the cat by her name, disliked the way she left hairs over the carpet and the furniture and had for years fought an increasingly bitter battle to have her put down.

'Why?' repeated a tireless Edwina. It occurred to Biffo that if she were equipped with a small white wig and a black gown she could earn a good living as a prosecuting counsel.

'I've told you,' sighed Biffo wearily. 'Buttress wanted me to produce a quiz programme designed to encourage husbands and wives to have rows with each other over money.'

'And you refused?' Edwina demanded, surprised and outraged. She bent down, peered at Tiger and then recoiled and scowled. 'The cat's got fleas again,' she announced, almost with delight.

'Yes. I think so.' Biffo closed his eyes and tried to think back through the years. What had he ever seen in this woman with whom he had pledged to spend the rest of his life. 'Her name is Tiger,' he added, almost absent-mindedly.

'I know his name is Tiger,' said Edwina. The cat looked up at Biffo who, recognising the look, uncrossed his legs to make a comfortable lap. 'But he's still got fleas.'

'If you know her name why do you always refer to her as "the cat" or "that cat"?' asked Biffo. Tiger jumped up onto his lap, turned round three times and sat down. 'And why do you always call her a he when she is a she?'

'What on earth does it matter?' demanded Edwina, dismissively. 'It's only a cat. I suppose you're too clever and important to produce quiz programmes?'

'It's not what I want to do with my life. I wouldn't be happy producing quiz programmes.'

'Happiness isn't everything,' snapped back Edwina sharply.

Through the mists of a memory overcrowded with experiences Biffo had dragged out a memory of Edwina as a young woman. He remembered her as being rather shy and uncertain. They had, he remembered, met in the university library. There had been an ogre of a librarian on duty that day and Edwina hadn't had the courage to ask her for the book she wanted. Although he too had been frightened of the ogre he had done the asking on Edwina's behalf. She had been pitifully grateful. She had smiled at him and he had asked her if she would like to go for a cup of tea in the university refectory.

He realised now why he had married her: he had felt sorry for her and protective towards her.

It seemed bizarre now to think that he could have ever felt protective towards Edwina.

'You must go straight back and tell him you made a mistake,' said Edwina firmly. She spoke to him as she would speak to a naughty, and slightly backward, child. Biffo realised, as this thought occurred to him, that she had never spoken to their own children in that way.

'I don't want to,' said Biffo. He realised with some horror that he was talking to her as though he was a sulky child.

He idly stroked Tiger as he thought and talked.

After leaving university he had taken a job as a junior researcher at a radio station. That was the job he'd taken because it had meant that he didn't have to find another flat. He and Edwina had, he remembered, been terribly short of money. Their flat was cramped and slightly damp but they'd loved it.

He remembered buying his first car: an old Ford with two gears, no bumpers and a handbrake that came off in your hand if you pulled at it too sharply. Cars didn't have to pass Ministry of Transport road safety tests in those distant days. Edwina had been as thrilled as he had been.

'We agreed that you would work until you were 65. We agreed that early retirement wasn't right for you,' said Edwina.

'You agreed those things,' Biffo corrected her in his mind. But he didn't say anything. He remembered the conversation. Or, rather, the monologue. She had decreed that he should work until he reached his 65th birthday and that for the last decade of his working life they should save as much as they could so that their pension would be well supplemented with extra cash.

It was, he remembered quite distinctly, Edwina who had decided that he should stay at a job he loathed and then, when tired and weary, and when all his hopes and ambitions had faded, he should quietly retire to enjoy some minor and insignificant hobby (not yet selected) and start preparing himself for the grave.

It occurred to him that without his wife his financial needs would be considerably less and that he would be able to live a much more pleasant life. He felt frightened, and slightly ashamed, by the thought. It seemed oddly sacrilegious.

'You have to work until you reach 65 to get a decent pension,' said Edwina, ignoring him, as she invariably did.

Biffo realised that not only did he not love his wife but he didn't even like her. It was a sad realisation. She had become a demanding, greedy, shrewish woman; worst of all, perhaps, she was an enormously selfish woman. Underneath a cruel, harsh, uncaring exterior there was a cruel, harsh, uncaring woman. He wondered if, deep down, she had always been that way or if she had changed over the years. He wondered if it was his fault.

He felt very alone. He wanted someone to hug him, to hold him close, to tell him that everything would be all right, but there wasn't anyone in the world he could turn to. Streaky Bacon was his best friend and Streaky had troubles and worries of his own. Besides, they had never shared their private thoughts or fears.

He could not remember when he had last hugged or even touched his wife. He could not remember when she had last hugged or touched him. He could not remember when they had last made love.

'And just what are we supposed to do for money?' demanded Edwina, still on the warpath.

Biffo scratched his head. He wasn't interested in money or worried about their lack of it. Somehow, it didn't seem important. 'Something will come up,' he said, confidently. He realised, with some surprise, that he meant this; he really wasn't worried about the future at all. He was too busy coming to terms with the fact that his life was changing.

It seemed unlikely but he seemed to remember that he

and Edwina had laughed quite often in the dark and distant past. He tried to remember what Edwina looked like when she laughed properly. It had, he thought, been a long time since she'd laughed. Come to that it had been a long time since he'd laughed. Why, he wondered, didn't they ever laugh any more?

He wanted to laugh. He wanted to have fun. He wanted to throw off the burdens of responsibility which he had carried throughout adulthood. He felt as though he were Gulliver, tied down by a thousand slender ropes. The ropes seemed fragile but they were impossible to break.

'Something will come up!' sneered Edwina, her sharp features distorted by an unpleasant mixture of rage and scorn. 'How am I supposed to manage while we wait for something to come up? I've got a dinner party to cater for next Saturday. How am I supposed to pay my hairdresser? I've got a new dress being made for me by Cynthia De Little. Do you know how expensive she is? I need new shoes. My car is nearly two years old.'

'You've got hundreds of pairs of shoes,' Biffo pointed out. He realised, when he'd said it that this was probably not an exaggeration. 'Why do you need so many pairs of shoes?' he asked, not really expecting an answer.

'Don't be stupid,' snapped Edwina, brushing aside the question as though it did not even merit consideration. 'If you had to go why couldn't you let them make you redundant! You'd have been given redundancy money and I wouldn't have to walk the streets barefoot!'

'It was a matter of pride,' said Biffo, realising as he said it that Edwina would not understand. He wondered if there had been a time when she would have understood. 'I wanted to resign. I wanted to leave.'

'And because of your pride the rest of the family has to starve?' said Edwina. She made the statement into a question by raising her voice at the end of the sentence but it wasn't really intended as a question at all.

'We won't starve,' said Biffo, trying to reason with her. 'We own our house. We own both cars. We don't owe anything to anyone now that we've paid off the mortgage. We have money in the building society.'

'And just how long do you think that is going to last?' demanded Edwina.

'We can make it last six or nine months if we're careful,' said Biffo.

'Hrmph!' snorted Edwina. She snorted a lot these days. 'And what are you going to be doing in the meanwhile? Watching television? Playing golf? Just getting under my feet I expect. Pansy Fletcher's husband lost his job and spent all his time around the house. He drove her quite mad.'

'I don't play golf,' said Biffo. He paused and thought for a moment. 'I'm going to write a novel.' he said suddenly. He regretted saying it the moment the words had left his mouth.

Edwina stared at him as though he had announced that he was going to climb Everest on roller skates. 'You're going to write a novel!' she snorted derisively. 'What do you know about writing a novel?'

'I've always wanted to write a novel,' said Biffo, rather defensively. He felt distinctly uncomfortable. 'I think this will be a good opportunity.'

He wondered what had inspired him to say that he was going to write a novel. He had wanted to write a novel when he had been much younger. But that had been a long time ago. It was a dream he had forgotten he had. And now he wished he hadn't shared the dream with Edwina.

'And when the money runs out? What will you do then?'

'We can always move to a smaller house if I haven't managed to sell my novel or get a decent job,' said Biffo. 'We could sell this place, buy a cottage, put the difference in the bank and live on the interest.'

'Sell the house!' said Edwina, horrified.

'I haven't really thought about it. It's just an idea,' said Biffo, defensively again. 'Just a possibility.'

'But we couldn't possibly do that,' insisted Edwina. 'What would all our friends think?'

'What does it matter what they think?' asked Biffo. 'The important thing is that we can regard this as an opportunity. An opportunity for both of us to decide what we want out of life. An opportunity for us to get to know one another again.'

Edwina remained speechless for a few moments. 'That just about sums it all up, doesn't it!' she said. 'What does it matter what they think?' she repeated. 'We are talking about our friends,' she reminded Biffo. 'We couldn't invite them to visit us in a cottage. And how could I possibly visit them knowing that we were living in some disgusting, damp little cottage? And what about the children?' she asked. 'Have you thought about them?' She snorted again. It was an unpleasant sound.

Biffo stared at her but didn't speak.

'And why do we need an opportunity to get to know one another again?' she demanded. 'I think I know you quite well enough already, thank you very much.' She paused. 'In fact, I think I probably know you rather too well.'

'The children are old enough to stand on their own feet,' Biffo reminded her. 'Toby is twenty two and Jasmine is twenty.'

'Are you suggesting that we throw Jasmine out onto the streets?' demanded Edwina. 'And Toby? I suppose you want him to give up his music career and get a job in a bank?'

'He doesn't have to get a job in a bank,' said Biffo, who considered it extremely unlikely that a bank, or indeed any other employer, would be prepared to give Toby a job. 'But he's old enough to look after himself. It would do him good.'

He realised that he liked his children about as much as he liked his wife. He wondered where he had gone wrong as a father. In his heart he did not feel that he was a bad man. How could he have produced such awful children?

'Are you talking about me?' demanded a youth, suddenly appearing in the kitchen.

~ Chapter 6 ~

ALTHOUGH IT WAS LATE MORNING Toby, Biffo and Edwina's only son and male heir, had clearly only just woken up.

He had shoulder length thick black hair and a straggly, wispy beard and was naked apart from a pair of black socks and a pair of expensive unisex underpants. 'You woke me,' he complained. 'Can I have a cup of coffee, mum?'

'Your father has given up his job,' said Edwina, dramatically. 'We're all going to be in the poor house. You're going to have to get a job in a bank and he's going to put Jasmine and me on the streets.' She moved past Biffo and Toby so that she could fill the electric kettle. When it was plugged into the socket beside the sink she reached into a cupboard and took out a jar of instant coffee and a mug. 'He says he's going to write a novel,' she said. She made it sound absurd, as if he had said he was going to invent a new antibiotic.

'Why can't you wait until you retire to write a novel?' demanded Edwina, talking to Biffo but aiming the words at her son. She slammed the mug and the jar of instant coffee down onto the counter beside the sink and then folded her arms and stared out of the window. Toby yawned, put a hand into the front of his designer underpants and lazily scratched whatever he found in there.

'Don't do that dear,' said Edwina, without turning from the window. 'Not in public,' she said, gently reproving.

'I don't like my job,' said Biffo. It was weakness, he decided, which had made him a poor husband and a poorer father. He had failed because he had allowed Edwina to make too many of the decisions that mattered. He had allowed her to take control because he didn't like arguments.

'Most people don't like their jobs,' said Edwina. 'That's what jobs are. You're not supposed to like them. You're just supposed to do them. That's why they're called jobs.'

'I'll be too tired, too weary and too exhausted to do anything when I retire,' said Biffo. 'I want to do something with my life now – while I'm still young enough.'

'Young!' sneered Edwina derisively. 'Don't kid yourself!'

'I'm not all that old,' said Biffo, defensively.

'You're forty seven!' snapped Edwina.

'Am I?' said Biffo.

'Forty seven!' repeated Edwina.

Biffo thought about this for a moment. 'I'm forty six,' he said. 'I'm not forty seven yet.'

'Forty seven, forty six, forty eight, what does it matter?' said Edwina. 'You're old. I'm old. We're both old. And just what do you want to do with your life?' Edwina demanded. 'Apart from writing some damned silly novel?'

Biffo thought about this before answering. 'I don't know,' he admitted. He felt embarrassed. He wished he hadn't mentioned the novel. 'I want to feel alive. I want to have some fun.'

'Oh my God!' said Edwina. She snorted and waved her arms in the air as though appealing to an audience. 'He's going through a mid-life crisis!'

'Maybe I am,' said Biffo, with a shrug. It didn't seem to matter what anyone called it. Maybe it was a mid-life crisis. Or maybe he had, for the first time, seen his life for what it was.

'I know what it is. It's your hormones,' said Edwina firmly. 'Go and see the doctor. Get him to give you something for it. But before you do that ring up Ernest Buttress and tell him you'll be thrilled to make quiz programmes for him.'

Biffo didn't say or do anything.

'This isn't going to affect my skiing trip, is it?' demanded Toby, scratching his unshaven chin.

'Oh there won't be any more holidays,' said Edwina bitterly, turning back and glaring at Biffo. 'We won't be able to afford holidays.' She made it sound as though Biffo had deliberately doomed them to a life of poverty.

'But I've already told the guys I'll go with them,' whined Toby, with a pout. He slid a hand inside the back of his underpants and scratched down there too.

'There you are,' said Edwina to Biffo. 'I hope you're proud of yourself now. Your only son. And you're telling him he can't go on holiday.' She put a protective arm around her son. 'You've been looking forward to this for ages, haven't you darling?'

'He can't have been looking forward to it for all that long,' protested Biffo. 'He went skiing two months ago!'

'If you don't go regularly you lose all the skills you've acquired,' explained Toby. 'That damned cat's got fleas,' he added, nodding towards Tiger, who was now fast asleep on Biffo's lap.

'He's good enough to be winning medals in the Olympics, aren't you, dear?' said Edwina.

'I don't agree with competition,' said Toby, pompously. 'It's damaging to the inner spirit.'

'Exactly,' said Edwina, who always agreed with Toby, whatever he said. The kettle boiled. She turned and put two spoonfuls of coffee granules into the mug. She then poured hot water onto the coffee granules and handed the mug to Toby.

'What's going on?' The voice belonged to a young woman who appeared in the kitchen doorway. She was wearing a man's shirt and nothing else. She had long black hair and was beautiful. 'You woke John up,' she complained.

'Who's John?' asked Biffo, puzzled.

'John is Jasmine's boyfriend,' explained Edwina. 'If you took any interest in your children you would know that.'

'Has he been sleeping here?' asked Biffo.

'He's moved in for a while,' said Edwina.

'Moved in?' said Biffo. 'Who is he? Why haven't I met him? Are you sleeping with him, Jasmine?'

'Of course she's sleeping with him, Bernard,' said Edwina. Now that his parents were dead Edwina and the nice woman who signed letters for Reader's Digest were the only people in the world to call him Bernard. 'Don't be silly and old-fashioned. He had a little bit of trouble with his landlord so he's staying here for a while. His father is a consultant surgeon.'

'I don't care who his father is,' said Biffo.

'He operated on a member of the Royal Family last year,' said Edwina.

'An Arab sheik, mother,' said Jasmine.

'Well I expect he was a member of the Royal Family,' said Edwina. 'They all are aren't they?'

'By the way, Dad, the cat's got fleas,' said Jasmine.

'Since you're home can I borrow your car, Dad?' asked Toby. 'Some of the guys are going surfing. I said I'd go with them. But we're short of a car.'

'Where are you going surfing?' demanded Biffo. 'There isn't any surf for two hundred miles!'

'Cornwall,' said Toby. 'Or possibly Wales.'

'I thought your boyfriend was called Dominic,' said Biffo, turning and speaking to Jasmine.

'Dominic!' said Jasmine, screwing up her face. 'Give me a break!'

'That was two weeks ago!' said Edwina. 'It really would be nice if you showed some interest in your children's lives.'

Biffo thought for a moment. 'But wasn't it Dominic who stayed here last weekend? Tall, dyed blonde hair?' Not for the first time Biffo felt like a stranger in his own home. He looked down at Tiger, still lying on his lap. Tiger looked thoroughly relaxed. Biffo sometimes felt as though Tiger was the only member of the family with whom he had any real affinity.

'Yes, but that was ages ago,' said Jasmine. 'He wanted to get married.' She screwed up her nose and made a face.

'Can I take the car then?' asked Toby.

'Is that coffee you're making, Mum?' asked Jasmine.

'The kettle has just boiled,' said Edwina.

'John only drinks Colombian Gold with fresh cream and cane sugar and a dash of rum,' said Jasmine.

Edwina moved towards the refrigerator. 'Move your foot,' she said to Biffo.

Biffo braced himself and moved his foot away from the refrigerator. Tiger lifted her head and looked at him. He stroked her back and she settled down again.

'Oh dear,' said Edwina, a moment or two later, looking up from the refrigerator. 'I don't think we've got any fresh cream.'

'Oh, mother!' said Jasmine, pouting. She turned to her father. 'What's all the discussion about? John and I could hear people shouting.'

'Oh yes, here we are,' said Edwina, relieved. She took the cream out of the fridge.

'I've left Better Television,' said Biffo.

'Oh,' said Jasmine, without much interest. 'Congratulations on the new job. Where are you going to work? Have you had a pay rise?'

'He isn't going to work,' said Edwina. 'He hasn't got a new job. Your father has decided that he's going to write a novel.'

'Oh, cool,' said Jasmine. 'Are we going to be super rich? Can I have a car?'

'It doesn't pay at all,' said Edwina coldly. 'Your father has walked out on his job and now he doesn't have a salary. We're going to have to move into a hovel. Probably a council house.

We'll be in the poor house.'

'We will not be in the poor house!' insisted Biffo. 'Anyway, they don't have poor houses any more.'

'What do you mean?' asked Jasmine, frowning. 'How can you not have a salary?' she asked her father.

'I guess I'm just like you and your brother,' said Biffo.

Jasmine laughed nervously and brushed her hair back out of her eyes. 'Is this a joke?' she asked, looking rather desperately at her father and then at her mother.

'No,' said Edwina firmly. 'It's no joke.'

'John wants us to go to Paris next week,' said Jasmine. 'I said I'd go.'

'That's fine,' said Biffo. 'It'll be one less mouth for your mother to feed. Now that we're poor it'll be a help.'

'John's an unrecognised anti-establishment freestyle artist,' said Jasmine. 'I said you'd pay for the tickets and the hotel.'

'I'm afraid not,' said Biffo, shaking his head. He paused. 'I thought freestyle was a swimming stroke.'

'Don't be stupid, Daddy,' said Jasmine. 'Aren't you supposed to be an expert on the arts?' A thought suddenly occurred to her. 'I told John you'd put him into your programme,' she said. 'You will still be able to get him onto television, won't you?'

'This poverty thing isn't going to affect my allowance is it?' asked Toby, suddenly looking very concerned.

Jasmine stared at him and then stared at her mother.

'Maybe you two could try and get jobs,' suggested Biffo.

'And just how do you suggest they do that?' asked Edwina, rather impatiently. 'They don't have the time to get jobs.'

'I thought maybe they could fit something in around their other commitments,' suggested Biffo, with some slight irony. The irony was wasted.

'Sorry, Dad,' said Toby. 'I just don't think that will be possible. I've got band rehearsals twice a week.'

'But you only rehearse in the evenings,' Biffo pointed out.

'But we go on until two or three in the morning and so I can't get up until twelve the following day,' said Toby. He picked up the mug of coffee his mother had made and sipped from it noisily. 'This is too hot, mum,' he complained.

'If you sign on as unemployed you'll get some sort of benefit,' suggested Biffo.

'Oh come on, Dad!' said Toby. 'I couldn't do that. That would be degrading.' He handed the mug of coffee back to his mother who poured out a little of the black liquid and replaced it with cold water. 'Besides, you have to turn up to claim the money. It's strictly uncool.'

'I'm going to have to sign on,' said Biffo.

'I thought you were going to write a novel,' said Edwina.

'I want to,' said Biffo. 'But I think I'll probably have to sign on at the Labour Exchange while I write the novel.'

'I don't think they call it that any more, Dad,' said Jasmine. She clasped her arms around her chest.

'What do they call it?' asked Biffo.

There was silence. No one knew the answer to this tricky question.

'Well, where is it?' asked Biffo. 'Does anyone know where we all sign on?'

There was silence again. It occurred to Biffo that Labour Exchanges and unemployment benefit were not subjects on which the Brimstones would have won prizes if they had been appearing on the sort of television quiz show that Ernest Buttress liked.

Edwina handed two mugs of coffee out to Jasmine who took her arms from around her chest and took the two mugs without thanks. 'Well, just what am I expected to tell John about Paris?' she demanded, sulkily. 'It's not fair. You might have thought of us before you started making big decisions that affect our lives.'

'And what am I supposed to tell the guys about the skiing trip?' demanded Toby. Suddenly, he brightened up. 'I know,' he said to his sister, 'we can use our credit cards!'

'Brilliant!' said Jasmine, delightedly.

'I'm afraid I'm going to have to cancel your credit cards,' said Biffo.

'What?' demanded Toby.

'You can't do that!' said Jasmine, incredulously.

'Well, that's just the end, isn't it,' said Edwina, as though she now knew that there was nothing worse that she could hear.

'We can't risk having unexpected bills coming in,' explained Biffo. 'We have to keep a close eye on our finances from now on.'

'I'm going back to bed,' said Toby, suddenly. He clutched his mug of coffee to him as though it were a good luck talisman.

'Me too,' said Jasmine. 'I'll have to go and tell John that you've said he can't go to Paris,' she said to her father.

'I didn't say he can't go to Paris,' said Biffo. 'I just said I couldn't pay for him to go.'

'He's an artist,' said Jasmine, angrily. 'You're suppressing his creativity. You'll probably ruin his artistic progress.'

'Well I just hope you're pleased with yourself,' said Edwina, when the two children had disappeared.

'It could be the best thing that's ever happened to them,' said Biffo. 'Maybe this will encourage them to take some responsibility for their own lives. And maybe it will be good for us too. It'll be a challenge. It'll be like starting over again. It'll bring us closer together.'

'I don't want a challenge,' said Edwina. 'I don't want to start over again. And why do we want to be brought closer together?'

'I just thought...' began Biffo, miserably.

The telephone rang. They both looked at it for a moment without moving. And then Edwina picked it up.

'Oh, Heather, darling!' she said. 'How lovely to hear from you.' She listened carefully for several minutes, adding only a light scattering of 'Yesses', 'Nos', 'How wonderfuls' and 'Of courses' to the conversation.

'That was Heather,' she said unnecessarily, when she had put the telephone down. 'She's managed to book tickets for the opera next month. It's Don Giovanni. The tickets are £200 each. I said I'd send her a cheque.' She looked at her watch. 'I can't go to the opera without a new dress so I'm going to go into town to see what I can find.'

'Edwina,' said Biffo, wearily. 'Haven't you heard anything I've been saying? We can't afford new dresses and opera tickets. I no longer have a job or a salary.'

Edwina just stared at him. 'I'm not telling Heather Tompkins that you've not got a job,' she told him. 'I refuse to allow you to embarrass me in this way.'

Just then Toby came racing into the kitchen holding his mobile phone. 'I've got Nigel on the line,' he announced. 'He says he'll lend me the money for the skiing trip and you can pay him back in a month's time. OK?'

'No,' said Biffo. 'It's not OK.' He took the telephone from Toby.

'Nigel? This is Biffo. Toby's father. I'm afraid that I've gone bankrupt. Please don't lend Toby any money.' He switched the telephone off and handed it back to Toby who stared at it, and his father, in disbelief.

Edwina opened and closed her mouth twice. 'Was that Nigel Patterson?' she asked Toby. Toby nodded. 'Do you know who the Pattersons are?' she asked Biffo.

'Of course I do,' said Biffo.

'Helen Patterson is the chair of the Church Restoration Fund and Michael Patterson is a merchant banker,' she said. 'He works in the city.'

'I know that,' said Biffo.

'He drives a late model BMW.'

'I know that.'

'An expensive BMW. Not one of the cheap ones.'

'I know that.'

'It has all the extras,' added Edwina.

Biffo wondered when, and from whom, Edwina had acquired her materialistic attitude towards life. It was, he realised, largely because of her that he had spent much of his life doing something he didn't really enjoy solely in order to earn money. And then spending the money on things he didn't need or even want.

'You have deliberately and cruelly embarrassed this family,' said Edwina. 'I am leaving you and going back to my mother.'

'Your mother lives in a two bedroom terraced house on the outskirts of Bolton,' Biffo reminded her accurately. 'The last time you went back to her you stayed in a four star hotel in Manchester and ran up a £1,500 hotel bill.'

It seemed to Biffo that there was a direct correlation between the amount of money he had earned and the amount of misery in his life. He wondered if he and Edwina would have been happier if he had never sought promotion and they had stayed in their small rented flat. Had it been his fault that Edwina had become utterly materialistic?

'You and I are finished,' said Edwina coldly. 'But I'm not leaving this house. You're the one who should go.'

When Biffo heard this he was shocked. Although he didn't like his wife it had never occurred to him to leave her. He had always assumed that he and Edwina would spend the rest of their lives together. But now, suddenly, he knew that what Edwina said made sense. He felt that maybe she would be happier without him. And he felt pretty sure that the only way he could rediscover his life, and rebuild his passion for living, was to be away from her.

He wondered whether it was his fault that Edwina had become obsessed with money. Maybe if he had spent more time at home their relationship would have stayed alive for longer. He would never know.

'You're right,' said Biffo. 'I'll leave.' He gently lifted Tiger from his lap and put the cat down on the floor. Tiger yawned and miaowed and stayed where she had been put.

When he heard himself say this Biffo realised instantly that he meant it and that he had to go now. He went out into the hall, heading for the stairs, and as he did so passed an angry-looking man in a black shirt and a cheap grey suit. The man glowered at Biffo as he opened the front door and walked out. At the top of the stairs Jasmine, now wearing a white towelling dressing gown, was sobbing and leaning on the banisters.

'John has left me,' Jasmine said to her father. 'It's all your fault!'

Biffo, looked at her, started to speak and then changed his mind. He simply couldn't think of anything useful to say. He went upstairs into the bedroom which he had shared with Edwina for more years than he could remember. He took off his suit and replaced it with clothes in which he felt a little more comfortable. He then tossed a few things into a small suitcase before going into the tiny fourth bedroom which he used as his study and collecting a laptop computer, a few notebooks and a small folder of personal papers. When he went down the stairs he was wearing a sports jacket which had one button missing, another button hanging loose and frayed cuffs. Underneath the jacket he wore a pale green, sleeveless sweater and a light blue cotton shirt with a button down collar. Below the waist he wore a pair of faded green corduroy trousers and a pair of very well-worn, comfortable-looking brown brogues.

'What are you doing?' demanded Jasmine, who had followed him down the stairs.

'I'm leaving home,' said Biffo.

'Good,' said Jasmine. 'I never want to see you again. I think you've betrayed us all.'

Biffo looked at her. He could feel tears forming in his eyes. 'Do I get a cuddle?' he asked.

'No,' said Jasmine. 'Why couldn't you let John and I go to Paris?' She burst into tears, turned on her heel, walked back up the stairs into her bedroom and shut the door firmly behind her.

Biffo could not understand what he had done to be treated in such a way.

'What have you got in that suitcase?' demanded Edwina.

'Just a few clothes,' said Biffo.

'And in the briefcase?'

Biffo opened the briefcase so that Edwina could inspect the contents: his laptop computer, the notebooks and so on. Leaving home was, he realised, like passing through customs.

'How much is that computer worth?' she asked, ignoring the other, far less valuable, contents of the case.

'I don't know,' said Biffo. He shrugged. 'You can have the house and everything else in it.' He genuinely didn't want anything from their life together. Now that it had been decided that he was leaving he wanted to go quickly.

'I should think so,' said Edwina. She waved her hand to indicate that Biffo could fasten up his briefcase again. 'I shall consider our bank account and our building society account my own too.'

'That's fine by me,' said Biffo.

'I shall go and visit Damien this afternoon,' said Edwina.

Biffo was puzzled. 'Damien? Who is Damien?'

'Damien Washbrook. My solicitor.'

'Oh,' said Biffo. He hadn't known that his wife had a solicitor.

'You'll have to let me have an address.'

Biffo frowned.

'For the papers. There will be papers to sign.'

'Ah, yes,' said Biffo. 'Papers.'

Toby suddenly appeared. He was still not dressed. He stared at his father. 'Where are you going?'

'Your father is leaving,' said Edwina.

'Job hunting?' asked Toby, sounding pleased.

'He is leaving,' said Edwina quite firmly. 'Permanently.'

'You're not coming back?' asked Toby.

'No,' said Biffo. He held out his hand.

'Oh,' said Toby, ignoring the outstretched hand. He paused and thought for a moment. 'You're not taking your car with you, are you? You know I need it for taking the band to rehearsals.'

Biffo put his hand into his trouser pocket and pulled out his car keys. He threw them to Toby who failed to catch them. The keys clattered on the floor.

'You can have the car,' Biffo said.

'And you can take that cat with you,' said Edwina.

Biffo stopped and turned.

'The cat,' said Edwina, nodding towards Tiger, still sitting on the floor where Biffo had left her. 'I sometimes think that cat is the only thing in this household that you have any feelings for.'

'I can't take her,' protested Biffo. 'I don't know where I'm going. She's too old to be travelling around. It's not fair to her!'

'If you don't take him with you I shall call the vet and have him put down,' said Edwina coldly.

'You can't do that!' said Biffo, horrified. 'And she's a she not a him.'

'Why not?' demanded Edwina. 'You're leaving me to take the responsibility for looking after the children. Besides, you're not going to be here to stop me.'

'But what am I going to do with a cat?' asked Biffo.

'That's your problem,' said Edwina. 'You should have thought of that before you gave up your job.'

Biffo looked at Tiger, whom he loved very much. 'It looks as though you're coming with me,' he said quietly.

The cat miaowed and walked over to where Biffo was standing.

'I need a lead,' said Biffo. 'Otherwise if she's startled by the traffic she may run off and get lost.'

'You're always telling me that cats can find their way home without any difficulty,' said Edwina.

'But she'll come back here,' Biffo pointed out.

'I'll find you some string,' said Edwina immediately. She opened a drawer, rummaged around and pulled out a length of string. 'Will this do?'

'That'll be fine,' said Biffo, he bent down and attached one end of the string to Tiger's collar. He then stood, picked up his case and his briefcase in one hand and held onto the free end of Tiger's temporary lead with the other.

'Goodbye!' he cried, as he struggled to open the front door. There was no answer. The sky, he noticed, was heavy with cloud and rain to come. He hesitated, wondering whether to take a coat. But his mackintosh was in the hall cupboard and he didn't want to go back. He took a brightly-coloured golf umbrella from the stand by the door.

As he left he heard Toby speaking to his mother.

'Can I still go skiing?' he asked.

'Of course you can, my dear,' answered Edwina.

'I'm hungry,' said Toby. 'Have we got any bacon?'

~ Chapter 7 ~

MOMENTS AFTER BIFFO HAD LEFT, before Edwina had even looked in the fridge to see if there was any bacon for Toby's breakfast, the deserted wife was dialling a telephone number she knew so well that she didn't have to look it up.

'Launceston, Holsworthy and Bude,' said the receptionist in a voice Edwina knew well and loathed.

'Damien Washbrook, please,' said Edwina, in her most businesslike voice.

'Is that Mrs Brimstone?'

'Yes.'

'I'm afraid Mr Washbrook is busy in conference,' said the receptionist with not inconsiderable pleasure. Edwina's voice always put her in a bad mood. To make things worse she had been busy painting her nails. She loathed Edwina as much as Edwina loathed her.

'I don't expect he's performing brain surgery on the Queen,' snapped Edwina. 'Tell him it's me and I want to speak to him now.'

Deirdre, the receptionist, was brave but not that brave: she did what she was told.

There was much crackling and button pressing and a short delay while Damien apologised to his clients so that he could take the call in the empty partners' meeting room, but eventually Edwina and Damien were connected by a lot of wires and a good deal of extremely expensive and sophisticated technology.

The receptionist, who had some of this expensive and sophisticated technology on her desk was able to listen to their conversation in perfect privacy.

'Are you all right, my sweet?' asked an anxious Damien.

'Bernard has left me,' said Edwina. She was unable to keep the glee from her voice.

'Left you? What do you mean 'left you'?' asked Damien, sitting forward. The blood had suddenly drained from his face and if he had been standing up he would have probably fainted.

'He's gone. Walked out.' said Edwina, as though explaining something very simple to an idiot, which in a way she was.

'Why? Did you tell him about me?'

'No, of course not. Don't be so stupid. Can't you think of anyone but yourself?'

'I'm sorry, darling,' said Damien, now a little calmer. He liked to think he had a fearsome reputation as a lawyer but that didn't stop him worrying. His big fear was that someone would find out about his affair with Edwina. He really didn't want to read about his sexual misdemeanours in a Sunday newspaper.

The affair with Edwina had been going on for nearly a year and for the whole of that time Damien had lived in constant terror that Bernard would find out. Most of Damien Washbrook's work involved property but he sometimes handled divorce cases himself and he knew just how messy divorce could be.

Damien's fear was so intense that when he and Edwina did manage to arrange a rendezvous (usually at some hotel an hour or two's drive away) he was invariably impotent. Thankfully, Edwina didn't seem to mind his inability to perform the usual functions of a lover. Damien, who was unmarried, continued the relationship because he needed the excitement and the danger to fuel his masochistic need for fear. Fear was the only driving force he understood.

They were held together by his fear and her need to have a secret she could share with her limp-wristed and outrageously camp hairdresser, Charles of Monte Carlo.

(Charles, who had been born in Walsall and who had never been anywhere near Monte Carlo, was terribly discreet and only ever talked about Edwina to those other customers who had their own little secrets and could therefore be trusted to be equally discreet. By and large these were the very women Edwina wanted to impress with her continuing infidelity.)

Edwina wanted a trophy lover (Damien drove a large, late model Mercedes with power steering, twin air bags, air conditioning and an annual insurance premium that would have paid for a family hatchback) and Damien was an adrenalin junkie who needed the thrill of a mistress but who, for practical reasons, needed one whose expectations in bed did not rise too high.

In short, theirs was a perfect, if slightly unconventional, affair.

'He said I can have the house and everything we own,' said Edwina.

'Everything?' said Damien, surprised.

'He took some clothes and a laptop computer,' said

Edwina, dismissively. 'Everything else is mine. I want you to get the papers drawn up before he changes his mind.'

'Did he sign anything?' asked Damien.

'Of course he didn't bloody sign anything,' said Edwina. 'He just walked out.'

'And you didn't tape him when he said you could have everything?'

'No.'

'Pity. Never mind.'

There was a pause.

'Are you sure about all this?' asked Damien, who had suddenly had an awful thought. 'Do you really want a divorce?'

'Of course I want a divorce,' said Edwina. She paused for a moment. 'I think he's going through the male menopause. He walked out on his job this morning.' She paused again. She knew Damien well. She would have smiled if she had been the sort of person who smiled but her brain had forgotten the code to use to summon up a smile – and even if the brain had remembered her muscles had long forgotten how to create a smile.

'Don't get nervous,' she said. 'I don't want to marry you.'

'Oh,' said Damien. He was relieved. He had been married before. He hadn't liked it. 'You don't?'

'No.'

'Oh,' said Damien, who to his intense surprise now found that he was rather disappointed by Edwina's certainty. 'Can you come round to the office at three this afternoon? We can start getting the paperwork all drawn up.'

'Three is fine,' said Edwina.

'Do you know who he'll use as a solicitor?'

'No idea. I'll cook you some bacon in just a minute, darling. I'm sure we've got some. It's probably at the back behind the melon.'

'I beg your pardon?' said Damien, puzzled by this unexpected turn in the conversation.

'I said I've no idea.'

'No, after that. The stuff about the bacon.'

'I was talking to Toby. He's getting a little edgy. He wants some breakfast.'

'Oh. Do you have any joint bank accounts?'

'Yes.'

'Ring the bank and freeze the accounts immediately. Does he have any credit cards?'

'Yes.'

'Joint credit cards?'

'Yes.'

'Ring and get them all cancelled.'

'Good idea,' said Edwina, pleased that she had thought to get professional advice straight away. She would have rubbed her hands with glee if she hadn't been holding the telephone.

'I'll see you at three,' said Damien, his voice suddenly softening. 'We could perhaps go out somewhere for a couple of hours this evening?'

'Not tonight, Damien,' said Edwina. 'But thank you.' She suddenly sounded extremely businesslike. 'I've got rather a lot of telephoning to do.'

~ Chapter 8 ~

WHEN HE LEFT HOME, CARRYING his small suitcase and his briefcase in one hand, and holding Tiger's lead in the other, Biffo had no idea where he was going.

But he had no regrets.

On the contrary, he was happy to be leaving the cold and graceless suburbs of Greyton, the urban sprawl where he had spent most of his married life.

In some ways Greyton was a pleasant enough place. There were plenty of open spaces, the roads were wide, well-built and smooth and there was a large, spacious and comprehensive shopping centre – all under cover. There were plenty of car parks in the city centre and the rows of houses, factories and public buildings were all extremely neat and well cared for. In theory it looked a marvellous place to live and work. There was a railway station with a regular train service to London. Greyton was often described (usually by the local publicity department) as a commuter's paradise.

Greyton was a place where people worked and shopped. It was easy to get to and easy to leave.

But he realised, with some sadness, that he had never thought of it as 'home'. Nor had he ever heard anyone refer to it as home. It would not have been accurate to describe Greyton as an exotic and attractive town. If Greyton were a man it would have worn cheap off the rack suits and would have had a row of cheap pens in its breast pocket.

As he walked past a public telephone kiosk Biffo thought for a moment of calling Streaky Bacon to ask if he could sleep in his spare room for a couple of nights.

But that didn't seem to be any sort of proper answer. He knew that if he spent the evening with Streaky they would talk endlessly about the horrors of working for Better Television. They would complain about Ernest Buttress and they would drink too much. That hardly seemed to offer a real and exciting way forward.

Besides he felt sure that Streaky would be embarrassed at not having had the courage to turn down Buttress's offer of a new career producing television quiz programmes.

Biffo wanted time to think. He had, it seemed, spent most of his adult life working hard and getting nowhere. He wanted a new beginning. He wanted to take back control of his life, regain some of his lost freedom and learn a little more about himself.

When he had talked to Edwina about writing a novel he had surprised himself almost as much as he had surprised his wife. He remembered now that when he had been at university he had started a novel. He had, he remembered, abandoned it after six chapters. But he still felt he could write a novel if he had the time. Maybe he would turn out to be a talented writer. And maybe he wouldn't. Maybe he wouldn't even bother trying to write another novel. It didn't really matter all that much either way. What really mattered was finding out what he wanted to do with his life – and doing it.

After half an hour or so Biffo realised that it had at some time started to rain. It was one of those light almost indiscernible English showers which begin as little more than a mist but which then gradually, ever so slowly, become heavier and heavier until they have, almost unnoticed, become a downpour. It was one of those subtle, ingratiating showers that begin so lightly that even if you are carrying an umbrella you don't bother putting it up. And then, by the time you realise that you should have put up your umbrella, it is far too late; you are soaked and there is no longer much point in trying to keep dry.

Biffo had an umbrella but he didn't have a hand with which to hold it. As the rain steadily got heavier and heavier he stopped to turn up the collar of his sports jacket. It was a rather pointless gesture. As he bent down to pick up his suitcase and briefcase again a car pulled to a sudden halt alongside him.

'Hello, Biffo! Do you want a lift?' called the driver, reaching across and winding down the passenger side window.

Biffo recognised his inquisitor as a neighbour; a man who had a shop, or maybe several shops, somewhere in the town. He realised, with some slight embarrassment that he could not remember the man's name.

'Thank you,' he said. He opened the front door of the car and climbed in, jamming his suitcase and briefcase on his lap. Tiger, who had been walking alongside him without complaint, jumped in and settled on top of the two cases.

'You should have thrown the cases into the back,' said the driver. 'Are you OK like that?'

'I'm fine, thank you,' said Biffo.

'So, you've got custody of the cat then?'

'Er, yes,' said Biffo, assuming that this was meant as a joke.

'Where are you heading?' asked the neighbour.

Biffo, realising that he wasn't quite sure about the answer to this important question, thought hard and quickly. 'The railway station,' he replied.

'I don't blame you for leaving,' said the neighbour. 'In your shoes I'd have done just the same.'

Biffo, totally confused, said nothing.

'If my wife had an affair I'd be off. Sometimes tempted to go anyway.' The neighbour turned and made a grimace. 'Come to think of it I can't imagine anyone wanting to have an affair with my wife.' He shuddered.

Biffo was astonished. 'How do you know that I'm leaving?' he asked.

'Oh word gets around quickly,' said the neighbour. 'Deidre told Audrey.'

'Audrey?'

'The wife,' replied the neighbour. 'My wife. Terrible gossip, as I expect you know.'

'And Deidre?'

'Deidre Jenkins. She works at Launceston, Holsworthy and Bude. Answers the telephone, makes the tea, paints her nails – that sort of thing.'

'Launceston, Holsworthy and Bude?' repeated Biffo, feeling rather stupid. 'Who are they?'

'The solicitors,' explained the neighbour. 'Where Damien Washbrook is a partner.' He peered out through the windscreen. 'It's getting very dark. There must be a real thunderstorm coming. I think I'd better put my lights on.'

'My wife must have rung as soon as I left,' said Biffo, to himself as much as to the neighbour.

'Well, it's not very surprising, is it?' said the neighbour, with a slightly hollow laugh.

'I don't know,' said Biffo answering the second question first. He frowned. 'Why isn't it surprising?'

'Given the fact that they've been having an affair for nearly a year.'

'An affair? Who's been having an affair?'

'Your wife and Damien Washbrook, of course,' answered the neighbour patiently.

Biffo thought about this carefully before speaking. 'My wife and Damien Washbrook are having an affair?' he said eventually.

The neighbour turned towards Biffo and stared. He suddenly seemed very embarrassed. 'You didn't know?'

'No.' said Biffo. 'Watch out!' he shouted, as the neighbour nearly ran into the back of a parked car.

The neighbour swerved and missed the obstacle by an inch or so. 'I'm sorry,' he said. 'I thought you knew. I thought that was why you were leaving...'

'No,' said Biffo. 'I didn't know.'

He realised with some shock that his only emotion on hearing this news was surprise. He could not imagine his wife making love to anyone. She seemed too cold, too clinical and too critical.

He wondered if she was softer and more loving with Damien Washbrook. Or perhaps Damien Washbrook liked cold, clinical and critical women.

He remembered meeting Damien Washbrook several times at dull social events. He was in his late thirties but tried to look younger. Washbrook, he remembered, had dyed blond hair and was suntanned all year round. He wore Italian silk suits and drove a Mercedes convertible.

Biffo was relieved that for the rest of the journey the neighbour, clearly embarrassed, spoke at dull length about the weather, the injustices perpetrated by local government (and, in particular, local planning departments), the failings of the national football team and the difficulty of finding good staff. To all this Biffo listened with unending patience; nodding and making suitable noises at each and every appropriate interval. He still couldn't remember the neighbour's name and had no idea what he sold in his shop or shops. Tiger, curled up on the briefcase on top of the case on his lap slept through it all.

When they got to the railway station the neighbour drew carefully into the taxi rank so that Biffo could climb out of the car under the shelter of the overhanging roof.

'Thanks very much,' said Biffo, politely, clutching his suitcase and briefcase in one hand, holding onto Tiger's lead with the other and trying to close the door with his right knee.

'Don't mention it!' said the neighbour, reaching across the car, grabbing the interior door handle and removing this final, small responsibility from Biffo's remit. 'Do you know where you're going?' he asked.

'No,' said Biffo.

'Good luck,' said the neighbour, regaining his jollity now that Biffo was out of his car.

They smiled their hollow and meaningless goodbyes and then the neighbour drove away leaving Biffo, thoroughly soaked and shivering slightly, at the entrance to the railway station.

'It's just you and me now,' said Biffo, looking down at Tiger.

Tiger miaowed and rubbed herself between Biffo's legs.

~ Chapter 9 ~

There were two platforms, two railway lines and two choices at Greyton railway station. Travellers could choose to travel towards London or to travel away from it. The ultimate destination of trains heading away from London was the distant coastline.

For Biffo the decision was not a difficult one.

In the one direction lay a world of suits, taxis, business meetings, urgency, bustle, pollution and a thousand varieties of glum and humourless determination.

In the other direction lay half-forgotten memories of buckets and spades, surf-edged breakers, golden sandy beaches, children's laughter, rock pools, bathing costumes and ice cream.

It had been a long time since he had been on holiday at, or even visited, the English seaside. Edwina had always insisted that they take their holidays abroad. For the last two years they had shared a large villa in Tuscany with an insufferable group of second-rate lawyers, third-rate architects and fourth-rate politicians. 0

'A single,' said Biffo, bending forwards to speak into the inconveniently-positioned grill which separated him from the sales clerk. 'And a cat,' he added.

'Where to?'

'All the way,' said Biffo.

'Pardon?'

'As far as it goes.'

'Up or down?'

'I beg your pardon?'

'Up or down line.'

'Which is which?'

'Up is to London. Down isn't.'

'Oh,' said Biffo. 'Down.'

'First or second?'

'Second, please.'

The clerk consulted a large and rather tattered book.

'Fifty five pounds,' he said, without looking up. 'No charge for the cat.'

Biffo paused, and thought he must have been misunderstood. 'Just one ticket,' he said. 'A single.'

'Fifty five pounds,' repeated the clerk. 'Do you want the ticket or not?'

'Er, just one moment, please,' said Biffo, embarrassed.

It had been some time since he had bought a railway ticket. He backed away from the partition and examined his wallet carefully. It contained two twenty pound notes, two ten pound notes and three five pound notes. A total of seventy five pounds. He pulled the loose change out of his pocket. He had approximately four pounds in change. If he spent fifty five pounds on a train ticket he would have just twenty four pounds left in the world.

He had also got two credit cards. But he knew that if he purchased a ticket with a credit card it would be easy for anyone to trace his movements. He wasn't entirely sure why but he didn't want anyone to know where he was going. But he did know that he wanted a clean break from his past. It was a world from which he now wanted to escape.

He hadn't brought a cheque book with him but in addition to the two credit cards he also had a cash card. He remembered that there was a branch of the bank at which he and Edwina held their joint account less than a hundred yards from the entrance to the railway station. It would make sense to take out a little extra travelling cash to last him for the next few days until he could decide what to do next.

'How long before the next train to the coast?' he asked the ticket clerk.

The clerk consulted a time table taped to the wall on his left. 'Fifteen minutes,' he replied.

Biffo, who now had Tiger's lead tied around his wrist, picked up his suitcase, his briefcase and his umbrella and left the railway station and headed for the bank. Tiger walked along beside him as though she had been walking, on a lead, along city streets all her life.

Outside the bank Biffo put his card into the appropriate slit in the wall and tapped in his personal code number.

'THIS CARD HAS BEEN REPORTED STOLEN. IT HAS BEEN RETAINED.'

Biffo stared at the small green message in disbelief. At first he was puzzled. And then he realised that Edwina must have already telephoned the bank and cancelled his card. He realised instantly that if she had cancelled his bank card she would have also cancelled his credit cards. He took them out of his wallet and tossed them into a nearby rubbish bin.

Biffo walked back towards the railway station, still clutching Tiger's impromptu lead in one hand and his suitcase and briefcase in the other. The umbrella was once more stuck underneath his arm. Both his bags seemed to be obeying the unwritten law which states that the effects of gravity on objects such as suitcases and bags will be steadily increased the longer they are carried – with the result that a bag which seems easy to carry when it is first picked up will, a few hundred yards later, be insufferably heavy.

As he walked Biffo noticed a street vendor selling flowers. He must have passed the vendor when he had been walking towards the bank but he hadn't noticed him. The vendor had a small stall filled with flowers and he and they were sheltered by a small canvas awning.

'Nice cat,' said the vendor.

Biffo paused for a moment, and smiled. Tiger pricked up her ears, as though she knew she was being praised.

'Not many people take their cats for a walk,' said the vendor, shivering and rubbing his hands to try and keep warm.

'No,' agreed Biffo.

'Bunch of roses, guv?' suggested the vendor, cutting to the chase and pointing to a large bunch of red roses.

'No thanks,' said Biffo, automatically.

'Half price,' said the vendor, quickly.

Biffo automatically hesitated. Unlike many of the flowers sold by street vendors these flowers looked fresh and good for several days in a vase.

Biffo knew about flowers. He had regularly bought flowers for Edwina. She had hardly ever thanked him for them, sometimes she didn't even seem to notice that he had brought them, but he had carried on buying them nevertheless. Perhaps he had been trying to revive the romance in their doomed marriage. Perhaps he had been searching for love and affection and approval.

'There's hardly anyone around,' explained the vendor, staring up at the darkening sky, 'I don't want to be standing here all day. It's going to keep raining.'

Biffo, operating on automatic, was about to reach into his trouser pocket for his wallet when he realised that he had no reason at all to buy flowers. There wasn't a single soul in the world to whom he could give them. This sudden realisation made him feel extremely sad, and very much alone.

'No thanks,' said Biffo, quietly. And there must have been something in his voice that the flower vendor recognised and understood for he stepped back under the protection of his awning and said no more.

Feeling, if it was possible, even more alone in the world than he had felt a few moments earlier, Biffo walked back again to the railway station.

'Would you give me a single to wherever this will take me,' he said to the ticket clerk, putting twenty five pounds onto the revolving disk which enabled travellers and clerk to exchange money and tickets.

The ticket clerk stared at him for a moment without speaking.

'You leaving home?' he asked suddenly and with a perceptiveness which surprised Biffo.

For a moment Biffo didn't answer. 'How can you tell?' he asked. He shivered involuntarily in his wet clothes.

The ticket collector just looked at him. 'I keep meaning to leave mine,' he said. 'She's a real cow. Makes my life miserable. Wish I had your guts.' He pressed the lever which revolved the disk and picked up Biffo's money. He then pressed some buttons on a machine on his desk before pushing a ticket and three pounds in change onto the revolving disk and pulling the lever which sent the ticket and the change back to Biffo. 'Platform two,' said the clerk. 'Six minutes. I've given you a cheap day return.'

'But I only want a single,' protested Biffo, confused.

'A cheap day return is cheaper than a single,' explained the clerk. He shrugged and tried to produce a wink but it looked more like a twitch. 'We're not supposed to tell people.' He bent forward and looked from side to side before whispering: 'Good luck!'

Biffo thanked him, put the change into his trouser pocket and the train ticket into the breast pocket of his sodden sports jacket and walked towards the platform. On his way he stopped briefly at a kiosk to buy a bar of chocolate, an apple and a magazine. In the station buffet, where he bought himself a coffee, he persuaded a shapeless but smartly-uniformed woman with a full moustache to let him take half a dozen tiny plastic containers full of milk for Tiger.

When he saw the train pulling into the station he felt himself suddenly swamped by a mixture of emotions. There was fear mixed with sadness; excitement mixed with hope; and relief mixed with mourning.

He had no idea what the future held for him but he knew that it just had to be better than the past. For too long there had been far too much responsibility and far too little fun in his life.

~ Chapter 10 ~

WHEN BIFFO CLIMBED DOWN FROM the train an hour and three quarters later the rain had stopped and the sun was shining brightly. Whether this was because the weather had changed or because his journey had taken him from bad weather into good he did not know. He had spent most of the entire journey staring into space, quite unaware of what was going on inside or outside the empty carriage in which he was sitting.

Biffo had not even opened the magazine he had bought. Tiger, having emptied three of the small containers of their milk, had spent the rest of the journey sleeping.

The station to which his twenty two pounds had taken him was considerably smaller than the one which he had left. It was a railway station which had probably been fortunate to escape conversion into a bijou holiday residence.

Outside the station there was little to be seen except green fields, trees and hedgerows. On the other side of the railway tracks there were a dozen scattered houses and a small church with a squat stone tower. But on Biffo's side of the tracks there was little sign of human civilisation other than a distant farmhouse, a couple of cottages and a disused stone barn with missing slates and crumbling walls held up by ivy and habit. There was, however, also a single-decker bus and two of Biffo's fellow railway passengers were already climbing aboard and greeting the driver cheerily.

'Hurry up!' said a man in a blazer and a peaked hat, ushering Biffo towards the vehicle. 'Or else you'll miss the bus.'

Biffo had no idea where he or the bus were going but he was content to allow fate to direct his movements and so he obediently climbed aboard the brightly-painted vehicle.

'Oi!' said the driver, while Biffo pushed first his suitcase and then his briefcase into a tiny space intended for luggage. 'You can't bring that on here!'

Biffo looked around before realising that the driver was speaking to him. 'Can't bring what?' he asked, genuinely puzzled.

'That,' said the bus driver, pointing to Tiger.

'Why not?' asked Biffo.

'We don't allow no cats,' said the driver.

'Why on earth not?' asked Biffo.

The driver thought about this for a moment, pushed his hat back and scratched his head. 'I dunno,' he admitted.

'Do you have a rule which says you aren't allowed to carry cats?'

The driver scratched his chin thoughtfully. 'I dunno.'

'I would be surprised if you did,' said Biffo. 'There can't be all that many people travelling with cats.'

'Never seen one before,' said the driver. 'But we don't allow dogs. I do know that.'

'It isn't a dog,' said Biffo. 'It's a cat. Her name is Tiger.'

Tiger miaowed, as if on cue.

'Well there may not be a rule about cats but what if it wants to, well, you know, obey a call of nature?' asked the driver. 'That would be an incident and the company doesn't like incidents.'

'Do you have a lavatory on board?' asked Biffo.

'Of course not!' replied the driver. 'This is a bus, not one of them luxury coaches.'

'So what happens if I want to obey a call of nature?'

'Not the same thing at all,' said the driver.

'Have you ever had an incident with a cat on your bus?' asked Biffo.

'No,' said the driver. 'I told you. Nobody's ever got on with a cat before. But I still don't think you can come on with the cat.'

Suddenly Biffo had an idea. 'Do you have a company rule about what people are allowed to carry in their briefcases?'

The driver thought about this for a moment. 'No. Of course not.'

Biffo took his briefcase back out of the rack and unfastened it. He removed his laptop computer which he put down next to his suitcase and then lifted Tiger up and popped her into the briefcase.

'There you are,' said Biffo.

The driver scratched his head. 'Does that make a difference?' he asked.

'I should think so,' said Biffo. 'Now you can forget all about the cat.'

The driver thought about this for a moment and then sighed. 'OK,' he said. 'Where to, then?'

'Where are you going?' asked Biffo.

The driver recited half a dozen names which meant absolutely nothing to Biffo.

'How far can I go for a pound?' asked Biffo. He paused. 'I'm on holiday,' he explained. 'A mystery tour.'

The bus driver grinned and winked. 'Looking for a bit of adventure, eh?'

Biffo smiled back and nodded. 'Quiet adventure.' he agreed.

'Make it one pound forty pence,' said the driver. 'And I'll tell you when to get off.'

Biffo handed over the one pound and forty pence and put his destiny firmly into the bus driver's hands.

~ Chapter 11 ~

'THAT'S A NICE LITTLE CAT,' said the small, rather frail looking woman next to whom Biffo had chosen to sit. 'What's his name?'

'He's a she,' said Biffo. 'She's called Tiger.'

'Does she like being stroked?' asked the woman, looking at Biffo, but reaching a hand out to stroke Tiger's head.

'She loves a fuss,' said Biffo, looking down at Tiger who had already climbed out of the briefcase and was now sprawled comfortably on his lap.

Tiger purred loudly, and pushed up her head to make the most of the fuss she was getting.

'Where are you going, dear?' asked the old lady.

'This probably sounds odd but I don't really know,' admitted Biffo.

The woman, still stroking Tiger's head, looked at him and raised a surprised eyebrow.

'I'm having something of an adventure,' explained Biffo, with half a smile. 'The bus driver is going to tell me when I get where I'm going.'

The old woman nodded, wisely. 'What are you running away from, dear?' she asked.

'Running away?' said Biffo.

'You've got your bags, you've got your cat and you don't know where you're going,' said the old woman. 'Since you're not much bothered about where you're going I think it's quite likely that the one thing you do know is where you're coming from. And that you want to get away from there as quickly as you can.'

'You're right,' admitted Biffo, with a laugh.

'Do you think there'll be a reconciliation?' asked the old woman.

Biffo, surprised, turned and looked at her and smiled. 'No,' he said firmly. 'There definitely won't be a reconciliation.'

'Children?'

'Two. They're both grown up.'

'That's good.'

'And you've left your job?'

'Yes. How did you know that?'

'I'm seventy six,' said the old woman in reply. 'You get to see things when you get to my age.'

'Ah,' said Biffo, nodding in understanding.

'You don't think me rude, do you?' asked the old woman.

'Rude?' asked Biffo, genuinely puzzled. 'Why should I think you rude?'

The old woman shrugged. 'It's nice to have someone to talk to,' she said.

'Yes,' agreed Biffo. 'Have you been somewhere interesting today?' he asked her.

'Oh, just a funeral.'

'I'm sorry,' said Biffo.

'No, don't be,' said the old lady. 'It wasn't anyone I know.'

Biffo was confused. 'You went to the funeral of someone you don't know?'

'Yes. I do it all the time.'

'Why?'

'It's nice. I like funerals. They are so melancholy. So peaceful. And they always make me feel good.'

'Why do funerals make you feel good?'

'Because at a funeral I feel really confident and good about myself. I'm superior to the grieving relatives. They're sad and I'm not. And I am certainly superior to the centre of the event who is, of course, dead and therefore inferior to everyone.'

'But doesn't anyone ever ask you what you're doing at one of these funerals?'

'Of course not! They just think I'm some mystery woman from the past. An old friend. An old mistress. It doesn't matter. They don't say anything. I go along to the house afterwards sometimes. Have a bite to eat and a glass or two of something to drink. If it's a busy do they don't mind me being there. If it's quiet and there isn't much of a turnout they're pleased to see an extra person there.'

Biffo did not know what to say to this. So, wisely, he said nothing. He wondered if the world was full of people like this. He realised that in London, at the offices of Better Television, he had been rather isolated from the real world.

'I used to talk to myself a lot,' admitted the old woman, suddenly.

'I talk to myself,' said Biffo.

'I don't talk to myself any more,' said the old woman.

'No?'

'I used to argue with myself a lot,' confided the old woman. 'And I started to get really cross with myself. So now I ignore myself. It saves a lot of trouble.' She smiled sweetly.

'That makes sense,' said Biffo.

'Why have you got that umbrella?' asked the old woman.

'It was raining when I left home,' Biffo explained. He shrugged. 'But to be honest it's been more trouble than it's been worth.'

'I like umbrellas,' said the old woman.

'Do you?'

She leant a little closer to him. 'Whenever I go to the city I sell one,' she whispered confidentially.

Biffo frowned. 'Where do you get them from?'

'The railway lost property office, of course,' whispered the old woman. 'Sometimes I go to the bus company lost property office, too.' She winked at him and tapped the tip of her nose a couple of times with a slightly arthritic forefinger. 'You just walk into the lost property office and tell them you've lost your umbrella. They ask you what it looked like and you say it was black and had a handle. Then they bring out half a dozen and you pick out the best looking and most expensive one.'

'And then you sell it?'

'Of course. I take them all to a second-hand shop. I can never be bothered with umbrellas. They're such a lot of trouble. I use the money to buy extra bird seed.'

'You feed the birds?'

'Only in the winter,' said the old woman. 'I collect seeds and nuts during the summer and the autumn. But there's never enough. I have to buy more. The squirrels eat so much you know. I did buy a squirrel-proof bird feeder but no one had told the squirrels it was squirrel-proof.'

'Ah,' said Biffo.

'I don't mind feeding the squirrels,' said the old woman.

'No,' said Biffo. 'They have to eat too.'

'I'm quite potty, you know,' said the old woman, happily.

'You don't sound potty to me,' said Biffo, who was smiling. It was, he realised, a long time since he'd felt like smiling.

'That's because you're potty too,' said the old woman. She reached across and tickled Tiger under the chin. Tiger purred loudly. 'Do you know what you're looking for?' she asked him suddenly.

Biffo frowned, slightly confused. 'I beg your pardon?'

The old woman repeated her question.

'No,' said Biffo, misunderstanding her, 'the bus driver is going to tell me when I've got to my stop.'

'I don't mean that,' said the old woman, shaking her head rather impatiently. 'Do you know what you want out of life? Do you know what you are looking for?'

Biffo thought about this for a while. 'No,' he admitted. 'I don't think I do.'

The old woman moved a little closer to Biffo. 'Until you know what you want you'll never stand a chance of getting it,' she said quietly.

'What do you want?' asked Biffo.

'I want people to leave me alone,' said the old woman without hesitation.

'You're talking to me,' said Biffo.

'I like you,' said the old woman.

'Why?'

'Because you've got a cat with you on a bus. When I saw you I realised you must be a bit potty.'

They were now driving through a small town and the bus driver called out the name which Biffo did not catch.

'This is my stop,' said the old woman, starting to get up. Biffo, holding onto Tiger, moved out into the narrow gangway which ran between the seats and stood up. 'Goodbye,' said the old woman. She leant down so that her lips were close to Biffo's ear. 'Good luck!' she said.

'Thank you,' said Biffo. He handed the old woman his umbrella. 'Would you take this for me, please?' he said. 'And sell it to buy bird seed?'

The old woman took the umbrella from him. 'You'll be all right,' she told him. She spoke with a strange confidence. 'But, remember, you have to find out what you want.'

'I will,' said Biffo.

'If you don't know what you want you'll never find it,' said the old woman, sternly. 'And you make sure you look after Tiger,' she added sharply, looking down as she clambered carefully down from the bus.

'I will,' promised Biffo. As the bus driver let out the clutch and set the bus into motion again he sat down, holding onto Tiger, and waved with his free hand. The old woman, standing on the grass verge beside the road, smiled and waved back to him with his umbrella.

~ Chapter 12 ~

TWENTY MINUTES LATER BIFFO WATCHED the bus which had brought him to his mystery destination rumble off into the distance, leaving behind it a thick cloud of summer dust and an unpleasant smell of diesel fumes. He put his laptop computer back into his briefcase, picked up both the briefcase and his suitcase, and took hold of Tiger's lead. He didn't know where he was or what he was going to do next but he was ready for it.

The road along which the bus had travelled had become steadily narrower and narrower and Biffo had for a while wondered if they would ever arrive anywhere.

They had turned left at 'Loose Chippings', veered right at 'Unsuitable for Caravans' and gone straight on at 'Blasting Daily' but after that he had quite lost track of their route.

Fondling-Under-Water, the village which the bus driver had chosen for Biffo and Tiger, was neat and pretty and, unlike the other villages through which they had passed, it looked exactly the way Biffo had always thought a village should look. (The name Fondling-Under-Water is derived from, and is a modern bastardization of the old English name 'Foundling-On-The-Water', which refers to the fact that many years ago an unwanted child, or 'foundling', was, like the baby Moses, found floating on the local river Ripple in a wicker basket.)

The other villages had been mostly sprawling and rather ill-defined; electoral constituencies rather than places to call home.

But Fondling-Under-Water looked and felt like a proper village. Biffo immediately felt that the bus driver had made a good decision.

Fondling-Under-Water was miles from the nearest traffic lights, pedestrian crossings, street lighting and pavements. It was defiantly remote and gloriously independent.

From the spot where the bus had dropped him Biffo could see a village green, a village store and a half circle of pretty, thatched cottages around a pond upon which swam a dozen noisy ducks.

There was also a small village hall (*circa* 1930) surrounded by a neatly-trimmed yew and laurel hedge and a church (*circa* 1100) with a tower and (although this was a much later addition, paid for by a vicar with a private income, high aspirations and a builder with a squint) a slightly twisted spire.

And, easiest to see of all since it was directly across the road from the spot where Biffo had left the bus, there was a particularly handsome-looking public house called The Gravedigger's Rest.

It had clearly been some time since the pub had been subjected to the sort of care and attention which can normally be regarded as falling within the boundaries of regular maintenance, and Biffo could not help noticing that rather large areas of roof were absent.

The Gravedigger's Rest clearly had character. It had whitewashed walls, criss-crossed with solid, black beams, and a large sign hanging over the door showed a portrait of a grizzled old man holding a foaming tankard of ale in one hand and a large shovel in the other. It was, Biffo thought, the sort of public house which people in cities always think of when they think of rural public houses.

Every roof, apart from the one gracing the church and the incomplete slate roof of the village pub, was thatched or red tiled, and gleaming fresh whitewash on every house and garden wall shone brightly in the early spring sunshine. Back in the middle ages every dwelling in the village had been whitewashed to protect the inhabitants from the plague and no one had ever bothered to update the decorating plan.

But it was the public house, not the thatched roofs or the whitewashed walls, that attracted Biffo's attention; not so much for its outward appearance, but for the beguiling promise of refreshment.

Biffo, still clutching Tiger's lead, picked up his suitcase and his briefcase from the grass verge, walked across the road and entered the pub. Tiger, who had never seemed in the slightest inconvenienced or surprised by the presence of the lead, trotted behind, head and tail held high.

Inside the pub's narrow hallway the walls were lined with dark oak panelling which gave the whole place a gloomy but cosy feeling. Numerous pieces of paper, most of which had clearly been there for a long time for they were browning and curling at the edges, were fastened to the oak panelling with drawing pins. The vast number of other small holes in the panelling suggested either that these were by no means the only pieces of paper to have been fastened to the wall or that The Gravedigger's Rest was host to some particularly enthusiastic and hard-headed woodworm.

Biffo put down his suitcase and his briefcase and opened the door marked 'Public Bar'.

He saw the words 'Mind Your Head' chalked on a beam just in time and so narrowly missed smashing his forehead against the massive slice of timber which threatened to knock out anyone above the height of five foot six inches.

But, even as he was congratulating himself on spotting

the 'Mind Your Head' sign he missed the chalked words 'Mind The Step' and so he entered the public bar with rather more pace, and at a rather more exaggerated angle, than would have been considered prudent by a more cautious guest.

'Are you OK?' asked a feminine, friendly sounding voice coming from a body Biffo could not see.

Biffo, who had knocked over a small table, a chair, and two bar stools as he fell, lay among this scattering of sturdy furniture with a large chunky glass ashtray sticking into his right ribs and a small collection of beer-mats scattered under and around his body.

He raised his head, shook it, blinked and looked around. The bar was welcoming and looked well-used. A vast stone fireplace dominated the wall opposite the bar. Huge piles of logs were stacked on both sides of the fireplace and a mound of grey ash in the hearth confirmed that neither the fireplace nor the logs were there for show.

'There is a sign warning about the step,' said the voice, whose owner Biffo had still not located.

'I saw the notice warning about the low beam,' said Biffo, cautiously moving his arms and then his legs. 'I missed the one about the step.'

'Most visitors only see one or the other,' admitted the voice. 'But to be honest we don't get all that many visitors.'

'Maybe you could combine the two warnings,' suggested Biffo, slowly clambering to his feet and rubbing his elbow. 'Mind Your Head And Watch Out For The Step'. He looked around but still could not see anyone. 'Or Mind Your Step And Watch Out For Your Head.' When he had finished rubbing his elbow he gave his ribs a rub. Rubbing helped, as it usually does.

'I'll suggest that to the landlord,' said the voice.

'Or you could just put a notice on the floor saying 'You Missed The Step, Didn't You?" said Biffo, standing up and bending and straightening his knees a few times to make sure that they were still in working condition.

'Have a drink on the house,' said the voice, which now had a distinct smile in it.

'Thank you,' said Biffo, who was now rubbing his right

shoulder. He looked around and at last discovered the source of the voice.

She was standing behind the bar drying glasses with a plain white cotton tea towel. Biffo was not good at estimating ages – particularly where women were concerned – but she was, he thought, probably within ten or fifteen years (either way) of her mid-thirties. She had shoulder length chestnut hair and unlike most of the women he had met recently she was smiling with her eyes as well as her mouth.

She wore a close-fitting, low-necked dress that ended just below her knees and which clung to her body making it quite clear that she was neither fat nor thin but could perhaps best be described as having what would, in the days before political correctness, have been described as a voluptuous figure. It was a long time since Biffo had been the grateful recipient of a genuinely welcoming smile from a woman; to receive such a smile from such a woman was a bonus. Her fingernails, Biffo noticed, were painted dark red.

'Bernard Brimstone,' said Biffo, introducing himself. 'Everyone calls me Biffo though I can't for the life of me remember why.'

'Laetitia-Anne De Tomatso,' replied the woman standing behind the bar counter. 'Everyone calls me Lettice. What would you like to drink?'

'A pint of bitter would do very nicely, thank you.'

Lettice put down the tea towel and the glass she was drying and picked up a pint glass. 'Any preference?' she asked, waving a hand in the direction of an impressive variety of pump handles.

Biffo shook his head. 'No, whatever you recommend will be fine,' he said. 'Have you seen my cat?' he asked, looking around. 'When I came in here I had a cat with me.'

'Did your cat have a long piece of string attached to its collar?'

'Yes.'

'He's over there,' said Lettice, nodding towards the window sill where Tiger sat licking herself. 'Do you want some milk for him? Is it a he?'

'She's a she. But yes, please, to the milk. Thank you. In a glass.'

'A glass?'

'A wine glass would be fine.'

'Not a saucer?'

'Definitely not a saucer.'

Lettice put down the unfilled beer glass and picked up a wine glass. She bent down, opened a refrigerator underneath the bar and took out a pint of milk. She then filled the wine glass with milk and handed the glass to Biffo. Biffo put the glass down on the window sill next to Tiger. Tiger lapped noisily.

'Does she want anything to eat, do you think? I can offer her cheese flavoured crisps, pork scratchings or peanuts. I'm afraid we're right out of smoked salmon.'

'Do you think the village shop will still be open? Tempted as I'm sure she would be by the cheese flavoured crisps I think I'd better pop and buy her some cat food.'

'The shop stays open until eight unless you get there later. Miss Box once opened up at two in the morning to sell Cheesy Stilton a comb.'

'Miss Box?'

'It's her shop.'

'I don't suppose I should ask why Cheesy Stilton wanted to buy a comb at two in the morning?'

'No. She sometimes claims to be deaf, by the way. Don't believe a word of it. She could hear a bank note flutter to the ground twenty yards behind her. Do you always travel with a cat?'

'This is the first time.'

'I don't suppose you're headed for London, are you?'

'No,' said Biffo, puzzled. 'Why should I be?'

'I thought perhaps you had hopes of becoming Lord Mayor,' said Lettice.

'I'm sorry,' said Biffo, who didn't understand. 'I don't understand.'

'Dick Whittington,' explained the woman behind the bar, taking a pint glass from a shelf behind her. 'Didn't he go to London with his cat? But then he had his belongings tied up in a handkerchief and you've got a Luis Vuitton suitcase and a briefcase with a combination lock.'

'Sorry,' said Biffo. 'It's been a busy day.'

'That's OK,' said Lettice. 'Do you want to use the phone?'

'Er...no, thank you,' said Biffo, slightly puzzled. 'Why should you think I might want to use the telephone?'

'I assumed your car must have broken down,' said Lettice, filling the pint glass with beer.

'No, no. Not at all,' said Biffo. 'In fact I didn't come here by car. I came on the bus.'

Lettice, who looked surprised at this, finished filling Biffo's glass and put it down on the bar counter.

'Thank you,' said Biffo.

'Pleasure,' said Lettice. 'Are you sure you're OK? You had quite a fall.' She picked up her tea towel and continued drying glasses.

'Bit bruised and battered,' said Biffo. 'But I'll survive.' He picked up the beer glass, took a sip, smiled his approval and took a longer drink. He looked at his watch and then looked around at the empty bar. 'Are you always this quiet at five past six?'

Lettice laughed. 'No,' she said, shaking her head. 'Everyone has gone down to the cricket field to see how Constable Hobbling's knee is bearing up.'

'Ah,' said Biffo, as though he understood.

Lettice said nothing, but just carried on drying glasses.

'Who is Constable Hobbling and why is everyone so keen to check on the condition of his knee?' asked Biffo at last. Curiosity can only be suppressed for so long.

'In the winter Constable Hobbling is our village bobby. In the summer he is also fifty per cent of the village cricket team's opening bowling attack,' explained Lettice. 'He wrenched his knee a couple of months ago when he fell off a barn roof.'

'The village takes its cricket seriously then?'

'The men do,' said Lettice. 'They never win anything but they're all cricket mad. I sometimes think that it's the cricket club that holds this village together.'

'But wives, mothers and girlfriends aren't so keen?'

'Actually they are,' Lettice replied. She thought for a moment and then smiled and shrugged. 'At least they know where their husbands are and what they're doing. And quite a few get involved making teas and so on.'

'What about your husband?' asked Biffo.

'My ex-husband wouldn't know his leg before from his caught behind,' she replied. 'He wasn't interested in sport, nature, books, politics or the environment. His world revolved around him – and that was about it. He used to spend several evenings a week on a sunbed at the local country club. The week before we split up he forgot to take his watch off before getting onto the sunbed. He was furious. He ranted and raved and tried to get the club secretary to sack the girl who was in charge of the sunbeds.'

'Why?' asked Biffo, puzzled. 'Does sunlight damage watches?'

'It wasn't his watch he was worried about,' explained Lettice. 'He was upset because there would be a white patch where his watch had been.'

'That worried him?'

'It worried him a lot. He fastened his watch up tighter so that it wouldn't move and show the untanned skin.'

'Why did you marry him?'

'Why do any of us do foolish things? I was young and impressionable and he seemed exciting and romantic. Sadly, I quickly discovered that he really wasn't interested in me. Come to think of it – I don't know why he married me, except that I suppose he felt he needed a wife to make him look respectable. He's a lawyer and, apart from himself, he's only interested in one thing.'

'Which is?'

'Money. He desperately wants to be rich. When I was with him he was always setting up big deals that never quite came off.'

'Oh,' said Biffo. 'I'm sorry.'

'Don't be. I haven't seen him for three years and that suits me fine.'

'He doesn't live in the village?'

Lettice laughed. 'Oh no,' she said. 'I came here when we

divorced. He's strictly a town man. He thinks Islington is rural.'

Biffo sipped again at his beer.

'So, what are you doing here if your car didn't break down?' asked Lettice. 'You don't look like the sort of passenger who normally travels around the countryside on buses.'

Biffo hesitated. 'Bit of a sort of holiday, I suppose,' he answered at last. He thought for a moment. 'Do you do bed and breakfast here?' he asked.

'Puffy charges fifteen pounds a night,' said the woman. 'Or seventy pounds a week. If you're staying longer than that you can negotiate.'

'Puffy?'

'That's the landlord.'

'But why Puffy?'

'That's what everyone calls him. Puffy Harbottle,' the woman replied. 'He's my uncle. His wife, my aunt, used to be the landlady.'

'But why Puffy? It seems an odd name.'

'Yes, Biffo,' smiled Lettice. 'I suppose it is.'

'Sorry.' said Biffo. He could feel himself blushing. 'Do you think he'll mind my cat staying with me?'

'I wouldn't have thought so. Does she catch mice?'

'She has been known to.'

'Then she can earn her keep.'

'Is Puffy down at the cricket pitch too?' asked Biffo, taking another inch or two of beer out of his glass.

'He certainly is,' replied Lettice.

'And your aunt?'

'Oh, Prudence went off with a soft drinks salesman,' said Lettice.

'I'm sorry,' said Biffo.

'Don't be,' said Lettice. 'But Puffy doesn't like talking about it. He was upset for ages but he's gradually getting used to the idea.'

'He loved her a lot, then?' said Biffo.

'No, I don't think so,' said Lettice, after thinking for a moment or two. 'Not for the last few years certainly. But he was pretty miserable about her going off with a soft drinks salesman. He regarded it as a sort of betrayal. I don't think he would have minded if she'd gone off with a malt whisky salesman. Have you got any luggage?'

'Just what I had with me when I came in,' said Biffo, looking around. His suitcase and briefcase were on the floor just inside the door. He drank the rest of his beer. 'That was very good,' he said, putting the empty glass back down on the bar.

Lettice lifted a flap in the bar counter. 'Bring your bags and your cat and I'll show you your bedroom,' she told him.

She led the way up a tight and narrow staircase which seemed to have been built by a corkscrew designer with a twisted sense of humour.

'I assume you don't get many American visitors,' panted an out of condition Biffo, dragging his luggage up the stairs, trying to stop his legs getting entangled in Tiger's lead, and making a genuine attempt not to stare too hard at Lettice's bottom as it swivelled enticingly a few inches in front of his eyes.

'No, I don't think so,' agreed Lettice. 'But how do you know that?'

'The ones I've met have all been far too fat for this staircase – they'd all get stuck,' explained Biffo.

'Actually we don't get many visitors at all,' sighed Lettice, sadly. 'In fact you're my first.'

~ Chapter 13 ~

THE ROOM WHICH LETTICE SHOWED Biffo was not small but there wasn't much room to move about. Most of the floor space was taken up with furniture which looked like the sort of stuff which is usually left over at the end of a house auction. The sort of mismatched, bulky, unfashionable furniture which makes a weak-kneed auctioneer with no available storage space begin to panic.

This was not particularly surprising for the furniture which filled Biffo's room had all been bought at the end of a house auction when a weak-kneed and panicky auctioneer, faced with the prospect of finding somewhere to store massive pieces of furniture which neither dealers nor members of the public seemed to want to buy, had invited offers. He had been relieved to knock down several mismatched items to Mr Harbottle of The Gravedigger's Rest who had offered £5 for the lot.

The bed was, as is not entirely inappropriate in a bedroom, by far the most significant and eye catching item of furniture present. It was considerably wider and much longer than most beds Biffo had ever seen before and had impressive brass railings at both its foot and its head.

'The brass needs a bit of a polish,' said Lettice, rubbing at the nearest piece of brass with her handkerchief. The stretch of brass she had rubbed began to shine. It made the rest of the brasswork look even more as though it needed a polish.

'And I'm afraid Puffy doesn't believe in dusting,' Lettice apologised. 'His philosophy is that if you once start dusting then you have to keep doing it. On the other hand, if you don't dust then the dust will eventually be settling on dust.'

'I guess he's right,' said Biffo.

'He says you're home and dry when that happens,' said Lettice. 'After all, who cares when it's only the dust getting dusty?'

'Er..., yes,' said Biffo.

'I'll put a hot water bottle in the bed later,' said Lettice, changing the subject a little. 'To air it out a bit,' she explained.

On the left of the bed there was a huge, dark oak chest of drawers on top of which stood an old-fashioned water jug and bowl. The chest contained three massive drawers and two smaller ones. Each of the smaller drawers was bigger than Biffo's suitcase and he therefore felt safe in assuming that there wouldn't be a problem finding enough storage space when it came to unpacking. Both the jug and the bowl contained large cracks which cast some doubt on their ability to function successfully as water containers. This possible disadvantage was made irrelevant by the presence of a sink in the corner of the room. It was the smallest sink that Biffo had ever seen, just big enough for a child to wash one hand at a time, but it was served by two incongruously huge brass taps.

On the right of the bed was a huge old pine wardrobe which reached right up to the ceiling and was at least as wide as it was tall.

'How on earth did you get that in here?' asked Biffo, staring at the wardrobe. 'I've seen houses smaller than that!' He stood back admiringly and gazed at the object.

'Puffy and Cheesy Stilton took it apart, brought it in through the roof and then stuck it back together,' replied Lettice as if this was a normal way to furnish a room.

'Through the roof?'

'They removed the slates.'

'Do you have to pay rates on it?' asked Biffo, trying to open one of the wardrobe doors.

'I don't think the doors open,' Lettice warned Biffo. 'Cheesy lost the hinges so he nailed the doors shut. He said it would be safer that way.' She managed to make it sound quite normal to nail shut the doors of a wardrobe.

'I haven't brought that many clothes with me anyway,' said Biffo. He looked at the wardrobe again. It really was huge. 'Actually, I don't think I've got that many clothes!'

'That's exactly what Cheesy said,' said Lettice. 'I'll leave you to unpack and settle in. If there's anything else you need just let me know.'

'Just a box filled with earth,' said Biffo, without hesitation.

Lettice seemed surprised by this request. Although Biffo was the first customer she had met who wanted to stay at The Gravedigger's Rest a box of earth was not an item which she would have expected to feature high on any list of items required by guests.

'It's for Tiger,' explained Biffo, nodding towards his feline companion, who, after a quick exploratory sniff had confirmed the absence of existing cat smells, was already comfortably curled up on the bed.

'Oh, of course,' said Lettice, understanding and smiling in one smooth movement.

When Lettice had left Biffo walked over to the large dormer window at the foot of the bed. There was a fitted window seat in the bay of the window so Biffo sat down, made himself comfortable and looked out.

The window overlooked a small garden immediately behind the pub, then several large horse chestnut trees joined by a thick hawthorn hedge and, beyond the hedge, a large flat green field upon which was situated a small, white cricket pavilion of the type originally designed and favoured by the Victorians and much loved by colonialists for generations.

The pavilion might have been small but it was equipped with all the fancy woodwork which might adorn a much larger erection. At the front of the pavilion there was a white picket fence complete with a small, white gate through which the cricketers could pass on their way to and from the arena before them. Behind the pavilion a broad river could be seen wriggling its peaceful way through the countryside.

The garden, which clearly belonged to The Gravedigger's Rest, contained several large, wooden picnic tables (the sort that have benches attached to them, presumably so that if anyone tries to steal a table they will be grossly inconvenienced by also having to steal a couple of benches) and diners were provided with some protection from both the sun and the rain by a variety of now faded, frail and rather tattered umbrellas which had at one time probably advertised an alcoholic beverage but which now advertised nothing but the fact that they needed replacing.

The cricket field contained a single, solitary, short, round figure. He was bent over a large mowing machine. There was no sign of Constable Hobbling, his troublesome knee or The Gravedigger's Rest regulars.

Biffo watched for a moment or two as the man performed what looked like a primitive dance around the mowing machine, hitting it from time to time with a large metal tool which he was holding in his right hand. It seemed fair to assume that he was not a particularly happy man and even Mr Sherlock Holmes's companion, the slow-witted Dr Watson, would have probably not needed the maestro's advice in order to come to the conclusion that the mowing machine was the major cause of that discontent.

A few minutes later Biffo climbed gingerly back down the narrow, twisting staircase (it was even more difficult going down than going up) and into the bar. He left Tiger fast asleep, and happily chasing rabbits, curled up on top of the bed.

Down below the pub was now considerably busier than it had been half an hour earlier. The absence of Constable Hobbling on the cricket field, and the absence of interested observers was explained, for the cricket spectators had crowded into the bar in force.

'How's the fast bowler?' Biffo asked, having returned to the bar, and nodding towards the large crowd at the far end of the bar, where a good deal of discussion was going on.

'I believe he's in pretty good condition,' said Lettice. 'There were a lot of smiles around when they all came back.' She picked up a fresh beer glass. 'Do you want another?'

'Not just now, thank you,' said Biffo. 'I'm just popping to the shop to buy some cat food,' said Biffo. 'But I wouldn't mind a nibble of something when I get back. Do you have a menu? Do you do food?'

'We have a menu and we do food,' said Lettice. 'But the two don't necessarily have anything to do with one another. I'll see what we can fix up for you when you get back. But I do know we're out of bread. Perhaps you could pick some up from the shop? Mind your head as you go out.'

The warning came a fraction of a second too late.

~ Chapter 14 ~

When Biffo stepped outside The Gravedigger's Rest that April evening the sun was already beginning to set and a couple of early rising bats were searching for breakfast as they swooped and dived through the warm early evening night air. Across the road, in the gardens in front of a neat row of whitewashed thatched cottages, a woman in a pale blue gingham dress and gardening gloves was performing minor horticultural surgery with a pair of sharp secateurs and two small children, a boy and a girl, were playing a game of 'catch' (it would, perhaps, have been more accurate if the game had been called 'drop') with a large inflatable ball.

Biffo turned to his left and began to walk around the village green towards the very traditional-looking village shop.

Above him beech and chestnut trees on the edge of the village green were bursting into leaf. At ankle level, along the bottom of the neat little hedges and walls which separated the highway from the gardens of the thatched cottages overlooking the village green, scores of bright yellow primroses added colour and reality to the springtime promise.

The double-fronted village shop was a riot of colour and looked as if it had been 'dressed' for an early Technicolor movie. The windows were packed from bottom to top with narrow shelves upon which someone had carefully balanced an enormous variety of those non-perishable products which were, presumably, to be found in slightly greater profusion within the shop itself.

Two bouncy rubber balls (one red, one yellow); three coffee mugs decorated with pleasant pastoral scenes; half a dozen toy soldiers; a pack of two pale blue toilet rolls; a box of hair rollers; two small packets of paper handkerchiefs; a tin of humbugs; a pack of notepaper and envelopes; a box of aniseed balls; a doll that, according to the faded writing on a small piece of card pinned to its dress, said 'Mama' when tipped forwards; a selection of birthday, anniversary and congratulations-on-passing-your-driving-test cards; a bright yellow tin of baking powder; two bottles of tomato ketchup (one large and one very large); a small pile of boxes full of drawing pins; a plastic folder full of coloured pencils; a sketchbook; a variety of maps of the area; a collection of paperback novels and, as enthusiastic advertisers are prone to put it, much, much more.

Outside, in front of the two large windows, there were two rows of wooden benches laden with brown and white cardboard boxes full of fruit and vegetables. There were red apples and green apples, green and white cauliflowers, red tomatoes, potatoes still covered in dried brown earth, yellow bananas, orange oranges, dark green cabbages, rusty golden onions, light green lettuces, red and white radishes, huge green cucumbers, blood-red cherries, green pea pods just ready to be burst open and beautiful, ready for biting, early red strawberries which had presumably been imported from a part of the world where the strawberry ripening season was somewhat more advanced.

Lest there were any doubt at all about the nature and purpose of the establishment, there was a large black and white sign above the shop. The sign carried the legend 'The Village Shop' in neat, but nevertheless obviously hand-painted letters. Underneath the sign, in much smaller letters were the words: Est: 1946 Prop: D. Box.

Biffo paused for a few seconds and gazed in admiration at this colourful and attractive display. And then he stepped from the early evening sunshine into the surprising darkness inside the shop, taking great care as he did so for the entrance to the shop had been narrowed by two large wicker baskets. The basket on the left hand side of the doorway was filled with small whitish bundles of neatly-chopped and parcelled kindling. The basket on the right hand side of the door was filled with a large mound of purple and grey beetroot. Kindling and beetroot were clearly either popular items in Fondling-Under-Water or else the proprietor of the shop was endeavouring to disencumber herself of overstockage in the kindling and beetroot departments.

'Hold this!' said a voice out of the darkness, thrusting something into Biffo's arms. Biffo unexpectedly found himself clutching something that felt like a mushroom but was far too large. It was the size of a football.

'And this!' said the same voice, thrusting something else on top of the mushroom disguised as a football. It was, Biffo quickly realised, another mushroom disguised as a football.

'Bring them over here,' said the voice, which Biffo discovered by leaning forwards and peering into the darkness ahead of him, belonged to a plumpish, middle-aged woman who was wearing a knee-length floral pinafore over a purple tweed skirt and a matching cardigan. She wore red rubber gloves and a blue beret and had a distinctive but uncultivated collection of black hair growing on her upper lip in a style that would have merited some commendation as a moustache had it been situated on a male visage. She had a jaw that looked as though it had been carved out of a large block of granite and, generally speaking, she seemed to be about as feminine and delicate as your average bad tempered rhinoceros. She had large ears which stuck out rather a good deal from the side of her head and wore her hair tucked behind them. This, together with her short stature, gave her a curious, rather wide-headed, almost extra-terrestrial appearance. This was, Biffo accurately assumed, either D. Box herself or some authorised representative.

After many years of marriage to a forceful and demanding woman Biffo was accustomed to doing as he was told by members of what is sometimes utterly inaccurately known as the 'weaker sex' and so, unquestioning, he did as he was told and carried the items which had been thrust into his arms over to the indicated site.

'Are you Mrs Box?' he asked, rather hesitantly.

The woman glowered at him as though he had pinched her bottom. 'I most certainly am not. Mrs Box has been dead for twenty seven years. Do I look as though I've been dead for twenty seven years?'

Since the woman who was not Mrs Box had moved away into the darkness and was virtually invisible as she spoke it was difficult for Biffo to produce an entirely satisfactory answer to this question which, he accurately assumed, was, in any case, purely rhetorical.

'Put them in here,' said the woman, gently lowering the three football-sized mushrooms that she was carrying into a large wicket basket. Biffo, stumbling along behind her added his burden to the basket. 'Everything is in chaos today,' said the woman. 'I'm Delphinium Box. Miss Box to you, young man. My father founded the shop. He was Donald Box. He ran it with my mother. She was Hermione Box.'

Biffo introduced himself. It was a long time since he had been addressed as 'young man'. He immediately warmed to the shop owner.

'Hrmph,' was Miss Box's only reply. It was, Biffo was to discover, her favourite reply to almost all questions, comments and answers.

'What on earth are these?' asked Biffo, peering at the football-sized mushrooms overfilling the basket. He reached out a finger, as though to touch one of the mushroom-like creations, but withdrew quickly when his wrist received a firm slap.

'Puffballs!' said the woman. 'Haven't you ever seen a

puffball before? I'm in a state. Did you hear that the damned fool Franklin Minton has fallen off his bicycle and broken his ankle?'

'No,' said Biffo, answering both questions economically. 'What do you do with them? I am sorry to hear about Mr Minton's accident.'

'Eat them,' said Miss Box, apparently accustomed to two tone conversations. 'Don't feel sorry for him. It was undoubtedly his own damned silly fault. Probably drunk. Or not drunk which in his case, would probably have similarly disastrous consequences. He's more stable when he's drunk. Where have you come from?'

Biffo started to tell her.

But, even in the semi-darkness, he got the distinct feeling that his words were not being received by a sympathetic audience. His instincts in this matter were unerring. 'I haven't got time for all that now,' said Miss Box, impatiently. 'You must tell me some other time. What do you want?' She had somehow managed to squeeze in between a huge stack of pickled gherkins in large economy-sized jars and an equally impressively sized display of floral-patterned kitchen rolls and was now standing behind a well worn wooden counter. The counter, a long one, was piled high with tins, packets and boxes. A large, old-fashioned till stood in the middle of the counter and numerous notices and posters had been pinned, glued and taped to the wooden panel on the front. One small notice in particular caught Biffo's eye. 'Genuine Axe,' it read, 'previously the property of George Washington. Offers invited.'

'Do you really have George Washington's old axe?' asked Biffo. 'The one he used to chop down the apple tree?'

'I certainly do,' replied Miss Box. 'We get a few Americans coming through here in the summer. They're usually lost but Americans are always on the look out for antiques – especially New World antiques and very especially if they think they can pick up something at a bargain price.'

'And it's the original axe?' asked Biffo. 'George Washington's axe?'

'Well, I had to have another head put on it and the handle

has been replaced,' said Miss Box. 'But apart from that it's just the way it would have been when used by the great man himself.'

Biffo thought about this for a moment. 'Do you sell many?' he asked.

'One or two,' said Miss Box, cautiously.

'Mmm,' said Biffo. He smiled. Miss Box did not smile back. Biffo felt slightly uncomfortable and swallowed hard. Miss Box did not display any signs of feeling uncomfortable and certainly did not swallow hard. 'Do you have any cat food?' Biffo asked. 'And bread?'

'Do I have any cat food?' said the woman. 'What sort of question is that? Of course I've got cat food! Of course I've got bread. This is a shop isn't it?' She peered at him. 'Just what sort of sandwich are you going to make? Do you know what they put in cat food? I've got some very cheap paté. You'd be much better off with that.'

Biffo started to point out that not all shops sell cat food but Miss Box was talking again. 'Wholemeal? Granary? Cottage loaf? Sliced? Unsliced? Or do you want bread rolls? Crusty rolls? Finger rolls? Soft rolls? Baps?'

'Perhaps a wholemeal loaf?' said Biffo, rather timidly.

'Small or large?'

'Large.'

'Sliced or unsliced?'

'Unsliced.'

The woman reached behind her, pulled a large, unsliced wholemeal loaf off the shelf and put it down on the counter in front of her.

'What sort of cat food do you have?' asked Biffo.

'Turkey, beef, chicken, lamb, duck? Extra jelly? Crunchy dry stuff? What do you like best on your sandwiches?'

'It's not for me, it's for my cat,' explained Biffo.

'Of course it is,' said the shopkeeper, nodding. 'That's what they all say. What does your cat like?'

'Anything expensive,' said Biffo. 'She won't eat cheap cat food.'

'Well that's fine then,' said the shopkeeper. 'All my cat food is expensive. And if it wasn't I'd just charge you more for it to keep your cat happy. The paté from Cranberry Farm is much cheaper.' She led Biffo to the shelves upon which tins and packets of dog and cat food were displayed. 'What would you like?'

'Oh that should go down well,' said Biffo, eagerly pointing to a brand which he knew Tiger liked.

'How many?'

'Half a dozen tins, please. And do you have a toothbrush? And toothpaste?'

'Toothbrushes are behind you, slightly to your left, knee height, between the apricot jam and the horseradish sauce and directly above the toothpaste.'

Biffo carefully followed these instructions, reached out into the darkness and, a moment or so later, was impressed to find himself clutching a toothbrush and a tube of toothpaste.

'And a razor? And some shaving soap?'

'Came away in a hurry did you?'

'Sort of,' admitted Biffo.

'Are the police after you?'

'Good heavens, no!'

'Don't worry so much,' said Miss Box. 'Doesn't matter to me. Razors are in between garlic tablets and ladies' tights. Razor blades are directly below tinned tomatoes and in between the stuffed olives and the children's socks. Shaving soap is to the left of the birthday cards and just above shoelaces.'

Biffo followed these instructions with satisfying success. Miss Box's display system might not have followed any logical order but she certainly seemed to know where everything was.

'Anything else?'

Biffo thought for a moment. 'Er, no thank you.'

Invisible fingers played the keys of an old-fashioned till and then Miss Box announced the result as though she were a returning officer announcing the consequences of a contentious election.

'How long are you staying in the village?' she asked as Biffo pulled out his wallet and handed over an appropriate note.

'I'm not sure,' admitted Biffo. He paused and coughed nervously. 'I'm actually looking for work,' he said.

'Honest?'

'Oh yes. I really mean it. I'm really looking for work.'

'No, you fool. I mean are you honest? Can you be trusted?'

'Oh, yes.'

'You seem a bit stupid,' said Miss Box, who was clearly not a woman who felt herself constrained by normal social niceties. She peered at him. 'Are you?'

Biffo was thrown by this. 'I don't think so,' he replied eventually.

'Can you ride a bicycle?'

'Er...yes,' said Biffo bravely. 'At least I used to be able to...I haven't ridden a bicycle for twenty years. But they do say that riding a bicycle is, er, like, er...well once you've learnt you never forget.'

'When can you start?'

'When would you like...?'

'In the morning,' interrupted the shopkeeper. 'Eight o'clock sharp.'

'Right. Fine.' said Biffo, surprised at how quickly everything was happening. 'I suppose I should ask about wages...'

'Of course there are wages,' said the shopkeeper, speedily dismissing this subject. 'Do you have any trouser clips? Franklin always brought his own.'

Biffo had always been regarded as a skilful negotiator in the world of television. Artists' agents and outside contractors had been known to blanch upon discovering that they had to negotiate with him. He felt that he was not doing particularly well with Miss Box.

'Are those the same as bicycle clips?' asked Biffo.

'The same as what?'

'Bicycle clips. The things you put round the bottom of your trousers to stop them getting caught in the chain,' said Biffo.

'They're trouser clips,' said the shopkeeper. 'Why would anyone want to call them bicycle clips?'

Biffo swallowed. 'I don't, er, have any trouser clips with me,' he admitted.

'Directly behind you and just above your head. They're hanging on a nail. Just above the mixed screws and below the jam pot covers. They're 34 pence each but we only sell them in pairs.'

Biffo turned round, found the trouser clips and took a pair.

'Now that you're a regular customer do you want to start an account?'

'Yes, I suppose so,' agreed Biffo, beginning to think that a little credit might help eke out his meagre wealth.

Somewhere in the darkness the invisible fingers once again played the keyboard of the invisible till. 'I could take it out of your wages,' said Miss Box.

'That sounds like a good idea,' timidly agreed Biffo. 'Er, while we're on that subject, I hope you don't mind my asking, but what, exactly, are, er, my wages?'

'Quite satisfactory,' said the shopkeeper firmly making it clear that this aspect of the conversation was now over. 'You just make sure you're here by eight in the morning. I want your bum on that saddle by one minute past eight at the latest.'

'Of course. Thank you,' said Biffo meekly.

Television executive to grocery delivery boy in one day seemed a fairly substantial career move. Biffo couldn't help smiling to himself as he wondered what Edwina would have had to say about it if she had known.

The shopkeeper thrust a large, stout, brown paper bag into Biffo's arms. 'Don't forget your shopping,' she said. She scurried off into the darkness as soon as Biffo had taken the bag from her.

Outside the sun was beginning to set and the sky over the church was a glorious mixture of red and orange.

~ Chapter 15 ~

WHEN BIFFO WALKED BACK IN through the front door of The Gravedigger's Rest he remembered the step down into the bar just in time. Unfortunately, because all his attention was concentrated on his feet, he forgot to duck and so, inevitably, he cracked his head.

He staggered into the bar, dropping the brown paper bag, and, holding his head in his hands, leant against the wall for a moment while the galaxy of stars he could see slowly dissolved. It had been a long day and all he wanted now was a quiet, pleasant meal and a good night's sleep.

'Don't knock the place about!' called a voice Biffo did not recognise. Biffo looked hard in the direction of the voice which seemed to have come from the far end of the bar. His eyes and brain didn't seem to be functioning too well but the owner of the voice appeared to be a jovial, red-haired, red-faced fellow in a white open-necked, short-sleeved shirt and a pair of grey flannels. 'This is a listed building,' said the red faced man, whose arms and face were generously supplied with freckles. This was Puffy Harbottle, the landlord of The Gravedigger's Rest.

'Listed or listing?' asked a very short, round man who was wearing a pair of oil-stained jeans and an oil-stained shirt. He was so round that he looked as if he would probably roll right over and back up onto his feet if he fell over.

'Are you all right?' Lettice asked Biffo.

'That's seven so far!' called a fourth voice, yet another that Biffo did not recognise. 'Write it down on the slate, Lettice.' Biffo's brain was recovering quickly from the unequal collision with the beam and he could see that the owner of this voice was a fellow who was leaning on the very far end of the bar and who, unlikely as it seemed, appeared to be wearing a green and pink striped jumper.

Biffo bent down, picked up his brown paper bag and tottered weakly over to the bar where Lettice, who had just finished wiping clean a small wood-edged piece of slate with a damp cloth, was busy writing something on the slate with a very small piece of white chalk. Biffo took the loaf of bread out of the bag and placed it on the bar counter. 'I hope this is OK,' he said, leaning on the counter, and looking at the slate on which Lettice had been writing. She had written the figure seven on it.

'Oh, thanks,' said Lettice, picking up the loaf. 'I'll get you the menu. You must tell me what we owe you.'

'Er, excuse me for asking this, and do please tell me if it's got nothing to do with me, but can you tell me why you wrote down seven when I banged my head?' asked Biffo.

'Oh that!' said Lettice, picking up the slate and pushing it under the counter. She was blushing bright red. 'Some of the locals have a bit of a bet on the number of people who will knock their heads on that beam every week,' she explained. 'The regulars don't do it very often, but visitors usually do it once or twice an evening. And since you're the only visitor we've had for a while you're naturally rather the centre of attention. Quite a bit of money rests on how many times you hit your head.'

'Are you staying here long?' the short, round man in the oily jeans asked Biffo. He spoke very quietly and winked when he had asked his question. He wore a toupee which sat on top of his head a little uncertainly. His hands were covered in oil.

'Well, I rather think I might,' replied Biffo. 'It all depends on my finances.'

'Splendid!' said the short, round fellow, rubbing his oil-stained hands together with undisguised delight and scurrying off towards the far end of the bar.

'That's Roderick Hedrubb,' said Lettice, 'and the guy at the other end of the bar – the tall, blonde, curly-haired guy in the striped jumper – is Cheesy Stilton.'

'Ah,' said Biffo.

'And this is Puffy Harbottle,' said Lettice, introducing the red-faced man in the white, open-necked shirt.

The two men shook hands and exchanged greetings. 'The good lady wife is away for a day or two,' said Puffy, rather apologetically. 'Little bit of family business up north,' he added unnecessarily. 'But Lettice is helping me to run a tight ship.'

'Lovely pub,' said Biffo, wondering why Lettice had told him that the landlord's wife had run off with a soft drink salesman. Lettice showed no sign of embarrassment and Biffo said nothing.

Introductions over, Lettice disappeared, clutching the wholemeal loaf to her bosom.

'I'm just going to pop upstairs and feed Tiger,' Biffo called after her. 'Do you have a can opener I can borrow? And a plate?'

'I'll get them for you,' called Lettice.

'Are you dining with us?' asked Puffy.

'Oh yes,' said Biffo.

'Splendid!' said Puffy. 'My wife usually does the cooking but I'm sure Lettice and I will be able to sort something out for you.'

'Great!' said Biffo. 'I'm starving.'

'You've come to the right place!' said the landlord, puffing out his ample chest and giving Biffo one possible explanation for the soubriquet. 'I'm sure you will agree that we've a right to be proud of our international cuisine here at The Gravedigger's Rest.'

'International cuisine!' said the short, round man managing to express considerable reservoirs of doubt and scepticism in those two words.

'Absolutely!' said Puffy, proudly. 'International cuisine!' he repeated.

'And just what's international about the food you sell?' demanded the short, round man.

Puffy thought about this for a moment. 'We have Welsh Rarebit and Yorkshire Pudding,' he pointed out. 'They're foreign.'

The small, round man snorted rather disdainfully.

'And Scotch Woodcock,' said Puffy.

The small, round man dismissed this with a sniff.

'And Scotch eggs!' added Puffy Harbottle. 'Scotland is very foreign.'

'What's Scotch Woodcock?' asked the small, round man.

Puffy opened his mouth and then shut it again before anything came out. He looked to Biffo for help.

'I think its sort of scrambled egg with anchovies on top,' said Biffo. 'Isn't it?'

'Sounds about right to me,' said Puffy. 'Scrambled egg with anchovies on top. Scotch Woodcock.'

'Not exactly international though is it?' said the short, round man, making it clear that he didn't regard Wales, Scotland or even Yorkshire as being foreign parts.

The landlord racked his brain in an attempt to provide more support for his claim.

'Frankfurters!' he said at last, as though playing a trump

card. 'They're quite definitely foreign.' He turned to Biffo. 'They're international aren't they?'

'Definitely!' agreed Biffo, nodding.

'Pshaw!' snorted the short, round man. 'Pfui!' he added as a vocal postscript.

Puffy moved an inch or two closer to Biffo. 'We have difficulty with some of the locals,' he said. 'Not many gourmet palates around here,' he complained. 'Most of them just want a pie and a plateful of chips.'

A moment later Lettice returned, carrying a can opener and a large white plate. Biffo went up to his room and fed a by now ravenous Tiger.

~ Chapter 16 ~

'LET ME KNOW WHAT YOU fancy and I'll tell you if we've got it,' said Lettice, handing Biffo a small red plastic folder. Biffo opened the folder and found a neatly typed menu inside. The menu, which had a date just over three years old typed in the top right hand corner, was extremely impressive.

'Oh, whoops, ignore the date,' said Lettice, 'I think it's been a while since the menus were redone.' She paused and bit her lower lip for a moment. 'Actually, I think these menus were put together when Puffy's wife was doing the cooking.'

'It's very impressive!' said Biffo, examining the menu carefully and preparing to throw caution to the winds now that he had a job and possibly even an income as well. It is true that he might have been a little happier if he had known exactly what the income was, but he was well aware that the employment possibilities for former television executives in the village of Fondling-Under-Water were probably not dropping off trees or even terribly thick on the ground and so he was pleased to have landed on his feet, or, to be more accurate, on Franklin Minton's bicycle.

While Biffo struggled to choose between Aylesbury Duckling A L'Orange, Sirloin Steak Avec Une Sauce Poivre Piquant and Coq au Chambertin the relative peace of the bar was abruptly disturbed by the ringing of a telephone.

Biffo lowered the menu he was reading for a moment and watched as Puffy walked methodically along behind the bar before lifting the chipped and discoloured, old-fashioned black plastic handset from its matching, chipped and discoloured, old-fashioned black plastic receiver. Biffo had seen more modern telephone equipment displayed in antique shop windows.

The landlord listened to the caller with rapidly growing disquiet, speaking only at irregular intervals to add obviously appropriate encouragement ('Yes', 'Yes', 'No', 'Ooh', 'Yes', 'No', 'Ah', 'No', 'Yes' and 'Yes') to what was clearly a spirited and anxious monologue.

When the conversation was over Puffy replaced the receiver with a heavy-handed clatter, and returned to the far end of the bar with a gloomy look on his face. Those to whom he hurried could see that all was not well, and that the publican was the bearer of bad tidings, and they clutched at their pint glasses as though they were children holding tightly to their comfort blankets.

Biffo could not hear what was going on at the other end of the bar but the news Puffy had received through the telephone caused such great consternation that the landlord and Lettice were kept busy pulling fresh pints for all concerned. While they were awaiting their calming pots of foaming brew the customers sat silently on their stools as though they had just been given advance notification of an early date for the end of the world.

'Have you chosen yet?' asked Lettice.

'I think I'll have the Coq au Chambertin,' said Biffo. He nodded towards the far end of the bar 'What's happened?'

'Franklin Minton has broken his ankle,' whispered Lettice back as she wrote Biffo's order on a small notepad.

'So I heard,' Biffo replied quietly. 'I gather he fell off his bicycle. I was very sorry to hear it.'

Lettice's lower jaw dropped open and she put down her pencil. 'Just how did you know that?'

'Well it's a village,' explained Biffo, with a dismissive shrug. 'You know how things get around in villages.'

'Mmm,' agreed Lettice, who did. She nevertheless still looked surprised and impressed. 'He was probably tiddly,' she said. She thought for a moment. 'Although come to think of it he's always tiddly and he doesn't usually fall off his bicycle. Maybe he tried to ride it while he was sober.'

'Mr Minton seems to have a lot of very good friends,' Biffo said, nodding towards the far end of the bar. 'Everyone seems very upset. It's rather touching.'

Lettice looked towards the other end of the bar and then looked back at Biffo. 'Franklin is an important member of the cricket club,' she said. 'And the season has just started.'

While Lettice spoke Biffo slowly became aware that just about every pair of eyes at the far end of the bar was looking in his direction. He noticed this out of the corner of his eye and tried hard not to turn his head and stare back.

'Brace yourself,' whispered Lettice. 'I think you're going to get an invitation any minute now.' She disappeared off into the kitchen.

Biffo, who had not worked as a television executive for many years without acquiring the ability to add two and two together with a good chance of getting the right answer, knew instantly what she meant. Fact one: Franklin Minton had clearly been a member of the cricket team. Fact two: with a broken ankle he obviously wouldn't be able to play. Conclusion: the Fondling-Under-Water village cricket team would be a player short. Solution: Biffo.

Biffo hadn't played cricket since he'd left school and so he had no immediate or easily recallable memories to pollute his distant and romantic recollections of his playing days. He had, he rather seemed to remember, been an extremely promising batsman. He remembered crisply pulling a full length ball to the boundary and hearing his colleagues just over the boundary rope cheering in delight. And he half remembered bowling too – though the memories did not encourage him to believe that he would make his mark by taking many wickets. He seemed to remember bowling so slowly that on one occasion, when dissatisfied with the ball he had sent down, he had been able to race after it, recover it, and bowl it again. On another occasion a team member had, he remembered, commented that if a ball he had bowled had gone far enough it would have probably been a wide.

Despite these slightly less than majestic memories he decided that playing for the local village cricket team could be just the jolt he needed to help him forget his past. He wondered if anyone would have any cricket trousers he could borrow. He hoped he had put a decent white shirt into his suitcase when he had packed his belongings. Slowly he turned his head and looked along the length of the bar. The cricket club members were all still staring in his direction.

'I forgot to ask you if you would like anything to drink with your meal,' said Lettice, who had popped back out of the kitchen.

'Do you have any claret?' asked Biffo, who was beginning to feel that the first day of his new life was worth celebrating.

'I don't know. I'll ask Puffy,' said Lettice. She walked up behind the bar to where Puffy was standing. A few moments later she returned.

'Puffy says we're right out of claret at the moment but that he's got a very nice little wine that is so good that Orson Welles himself wouldn't be able to tell it wasn't claret.'

'I don't expect he would,' agreed Biffo. 'He's been dead for quite a while. His taste buds have probably deteriorated a bit by now.'

'Has he? What a pity. I hadn't heard. Anyway he was a bit of an expert on wine wasn't he?'

'I think he used to do advertisements for sherry.'

'I expect that is what Puffy meant.'

'Fine. I'll have a bottle of the Orson Welles special then.'

Lettice disappeared again.

There was still a good deal of muttering and whispering going on at the other end of the bar. Every few moments someone would stare in Biffo's direction and then quickly look away again. Biffo, who had decided to play it cool, carefully studied the message on a slightly soggy beer-mat. It seemed to be some sort of joke.

'Excuse me,' said Puffy, who had moved along behind the bar so silently that Biffo hadn't heard him coming. 'But do you by any chance know anything about cricket?' Puffy had been accompanied by Cheesy Stilton.

Biffo, who had, of course, been expecting this question, turned, smiled and thought for a moment. 'Twenty two players and a very hard ball?' he said, slipping a question mark onto the end of the sentence by raising his voice for the last word or two.

'Exactly!' said Puffy. 'That's the game. I don't suppose you play do you? How much do you know about the game? Leg before wicket? Googlies? Fast medium bowled round the wicket? Chinamen? Seam up bowled over the wicket? Deep extra cover? Silly point? Au fait with the laws and that sort of thing?'

'Well, I'm probably a little rusty,' admitted Biffo. 'But in my time I have been known to twiddle with a bat.'

'I say,' said Puffy, 'that's pretty good news.' Cheesy Stilton turned and raised a thumb to the waiting crowd at the other end of the bar. This promising indication of good news to come was well received and there was much nodding and smiling and holding up of thumbs in return.

'Are you going to be here on Saturday?' asked Puffy.

'I sincerely hope so,' said Biffo.

'Wonderful!' said Puffy, clapping Biffo on the shoulder with a fist the size of a small goose. 'You see one of the villagers, a vital member of the cricket club, had a most unfortunate accident today. He fell off his bicycle and appears to have rather done himself a bit of a mischief.'

'Franklin Minton,' said Biffo.

Puffy seemed surprised. 'That's right!' he said. 'How did you know?'

Biffo shrugged. 'Oh you know how it is in a village,' he said, dismissively. 'Word gets around quickly.'

'Yes,' said Puffy. 'It does, doesn't it?'

'He was seen standing on his good leg trying to kick the bicycle with his bad leg,' said Cheesy.

'Sounds like road rage!' said Puffy.

'Oh I don't think so,' said Cheesy. 'I expect he was just hopping mad.' He showed no sign of realising that he had inadvertently cracked a joke.

'Ah!' nodded Biffo. He wasn't sure whether or not it would be appropriate to comment on the joke so he didn't.

'And so we rather wondered if you would be willing to

take his place?' continued Puffy.

'I'd be absolutely delighted!' said Biffo, bracing himself as Puffy hit him playfully on the shoulder with the goose again.

And Biffo truly was delighted. He had been in Fondling-Under-Water for considerably less than a day and already he had a job and was a member of the local cricket team. He definitely felt that, if he had anyone to write home to, he could have quite justifiably written home to report that his arrival in the village had been greeted with something approaching rave reviews. (He realised, of course, that if he had had anyone at home to write to he probably wouldn't have been in the village in the first place.)

'Of course you'll have to join the cricket club,' said Cheesy.

'Of course,' said Biffo. 'Willingly. What do I have to do? What are the rules?'

'Rules?' said the other villager. 'What do you mean – rules?'

Biffo was puzzled. 'All clubs have rules,' he said. 'It's just something about clubs.'

'Oh,' said the other villager. He looked at Puffy. 'Do we have rules?'

Puffy frowned for a moment. 'I'm not sure,' he said. 'The only important one I can think of is that no one can be a member unless they join.'

'OK,' said Biffo. 'That sounds fair enough. Do I have to do anything to join?'

'Oh yes,' said Cheesy quickly. 'You have to hand over money.'

'Of course,' nodded Biffo. 'That sounds like a club rule. How much?'

'How much is it?' Cheesy asked Puffy.

'I think it's probably a fiver,' said Puffy.

'Can you put it on the slate for me?' asked Biffo. 'I have something of a cash flow problem at the moment.'

'Of course,' said Puffy, with a sigh. 'I think that's probably the other rule of membership.'

Biffo looked at him and raised an eyebrow.

'That members never pay their membership dues,' explained Puffy.

~ Chapter 17 ~

'I'M TERRIBLY SORRY ABOUT THIS,' said Lettice. 'But it seems that we're right out of Coq au Chambertin.'

'That's OK,' said Biffo accepting this bad news cheerfully and with good grace. He was busy imagining himself playing spectacular on drives through the covers. Or, he wondered, should that be off drives through the covers? Or cover drives through the off side? Or cover drives through the on side? He was getting very confused. Puffy and Cheesy had disappeared.

'Would you like to choose something else?' asked Lettice handing him the menu again.

'I'll have the Sirloin Steak Avec Une Sauce Poivre Piquant,' said Biffo without hesitation.

'I'm sorry if the French isn't quite accurate,' said Lettice, writing down Biffo's new order. 'Puffy got Franklin Minton's grand-daughter to write out the menu.'

'It sounds fine to me,' said Biffo, whose skills as a linguist definitely put him in the unskilled category.

'She's only ten.'

'It's absolutely charming,' said Biffo.

'Would you like anything while you're waiting for your meal?' asked Lettice.

'Perhaps just a packet of crisps?' suggested Biffo. 'I'm a little peckish.'

'And a pint of beer perhaps?'

'Sounds good!' agreed Biffo, who had suddenly become aware that a small deputation of two from the informal meeting of cricket club members had quietly moved to his end of the bar. Puffy was half of the small deputation.

'May I introduce the cricket club captain, Cedric Stickers?' said Puffy. He waved an introductory hand in the direction of a short, round man who was wearing what appeared to be an expensive blue suit which was, sadly, several sizes too large for him. The newcomer was shorter and rounder than Roderick Hedrubb and this surprised Biffo who had regarded Mr Hedrubb's shortness and roundness as pretty well definitive. The trousers of Mr Stickers' suit were slightly too long and were, consequently, rather baggy around his ankles. The sleeves of the jacket were long enough to keep Mr Stickers' hands warm in winter. The suit looked as though it had been bought by a careful parent who expected the wearer to grow into it. In view of the captain's age this did not seem to Biffo to be a realistic expectation. On the other hand, thought Biffo, the upside of this advance planning was that the purchase of gloves would not be a major expense in the household budget. 'Last year Mr Stickers was elected Best Captain Of The Season,' added Puffy.

The captain, who was a decade or two past his prime, had the sort of shape modern car designers like to describe as aerodynamic in that there are no sharp corners but lots of well-rounded curves. However, no one could have ever described him as streamlined. He had a white, pasty, round face and two rather small eyes. Above the neck the general effect, Biffo thought, was rather that of a family-sized steamed pudding into which a penny-pinching chef has tossed a couple of currants.

Lettice quietly put a packet of crisps on the bar counter.

'So good of you to help us out,' said the short man, peering up at Biffo. He wore a toothbrush moustache and had attempted to cover a very large bald patch with seven, or possibly eight, strands of dyed black hair. Despite the almost total absence of head hair the shoulders of his blue suit were nevertheless generously sprinkled with dandruff. Since he was very short the dandruff, like the bald patch, was easy to see.

'Bernard Brimstone,' said Biffo, holding out his hand. 'Biffo. Pleased to meet you.'

'Call me Bill,' said Mr Stickers. 'It isn't my name but it's what everyone calls me.' He frowned for a moment and turned to Puffy Harbottle. 'Puffy, why do they call me Bill? I've forgotten again.'

'Bill Stickers,' explained Puffy patiently. 'It's a sort of friendly joke. It shows that the chaps like you.'

'Of course,' said Bill, still looking puzzled for a second or two but then quickly abandoning his attempt to understand the joke and simply accepting it and beaming with pride. He rather belatedly laughed. At least Biffo assumed that it was a laugh. It sounded rather like a blocked drain suddenly emptying.

'Were there a lot of captains last season?' asked Biffo, innocently.

Everyone looked at him but no one said anything. It was clear that no one understood what he was talking about.

'You said that Mr Stickers had been elected Best Captain Of The Season,' explained Biffo. 'I wondered...'

'Ah,' said Puffy, understanding at last. 'No, Bill was captain for the whole season.'

Biffo thought about this for a while. He wasn't at all sure that he understood. 'But he was the only captain?'

'Oh, absolutely,' said Puffy.

Biffo nodded and tried to look as though he understood, though he did not.

Lettice put a pint of beer next to the packet of crisps that still lay unopened and then hurried off back into the kitchen.

'Bill is also chairman and president of the Fondling-Under-Water Cricket Club,' said Puffy.

'Congratulations!' said Biffo, suitably impressed.

This went down terribly well and it was immediately clear to Biffo that Bill Stickers was very proud of his three positions.

'Bill saved the club,' said Puffy. 'Our cricket ground had been in the hands of the Hepplewhite family for generations but Lord Hepplewhite had a little bit of bad luck recently and had to sell.'

Bill, who looked extremely pleased with himself, straightened first his shoulders and then his tie and tried to make himself look as tall as possible.

'The cricket club would have probably gone to the wall without me,' said Bill. 'There would be bungalows all over it or some farmer would be growing beetroot at square leg by now.'

'Well, good for you!' Biffo said to Bill. He opened his packet of crisps and offered the cricket club president, chairman and captain the opportunity to dip into the contents. 'It's good to see someone using their money wisely.'

'Lottery money,' said Bill, greedily taking as large a fistful of crisps as he could pull out of the bag and pushing them all into his mouth at once.

Biffo was confused. 'You mean the lottery people gave

you the money to buy the ground?'

'Gnheu,' said Bill proudly. 'I crunch crunch crunch lottery crunch crunch year crunch. Crunch crunch six crunch. At the crunch it crunch crunch crunch.'

'I'm sorry,' said Biffo. 'I didn't quite get that...'

Bill swallowed the crisps he was eating. 'I won the lottery five years ago. Seven point four six million. At the time it was the fourth biggest win ever. I was in all the papers.'

'Ah,' said Biffo. 'Congratulations.'

Suddenly, the calm of the evening was shattered as a huge bear of a man in a tattered sheepskin coat burst into the bar carrying a large plastic bag. He marched over to the bar and emptied the plastic bag out on the bar counter. Biffo stared in astonishment at a pile of trophies, silver tankards and plaques.

'These were in with a couple of old pictures I bought yesterday,' said the stranger. He spoke in a strange accent which Biffo couldn't place.

Puffy, examining the silverware, nodded his head appreciatively. 'Impressive!'

'Should fill up the cabinet nicely,' said the newcomer, nodding in the direction of a large wooden cabinet behind the bar. The cabinet, which had the words Fondling-Under-Water Cricket Club stencilled onto it, was half full of trophies and other silverware. Biffo had assumed that the trophies had all been won by the cricket club. He leant over and looked at the trophies which the newcomer had brought. One was inscribed 'Eastern Counties Schools Lacrosse Champions 1953', a second carried the inscription 'Cardiff Region Boys Darts Champion 1946' and a third was engraved with the name of an amateur football club in the West Midlands. There was no indication of the contest in which they had been victorious, though judging by the modest size of the trophy it was probably not the FA Cup.

Puffy opened the cupboard, and gave each of the trophies a cursory rub on his jumper before putting it onto one of the display shelves.

'Did you get all your trophies this way?' asked Biffo, genuinely surprised.

'Of course we did,' replied Puffy. 'You don't think our team could actually win anything, do you?' He pulled a trophy out of the cabinet and showed it to Biffo. It was engraved 'West of England Formation Dancing Association Team Trophy 1951 (Tango).'

'But aren't you supposed to practise and win trophies through hard work,' protested Biffo.

'Probably,' agreed Puffy. 'But it's a hell of a lot easier this way.'

The stranger who had brought the bagful of trophies picked up his now empty plastic bag, screwed it up and stuffed it into his pocket. 'See you later!' he promised, disappearing as rapidly as he had arrived.

'Who was that?' asked Biffo.

'Helmut,' replied Puffy. 'Bill used to be a hairdresser before his big win,' he continued, before Biffo could ask any more questions about the stranger in the tattered sheepskin coat.

Biffo, in a slight state of shock, offered Puffy a crisp. Puffy declined. Biffo breathed a quiet sigh of relief and took another crisp for himself.

'I once cut Paul McCartney's hair,' said Bill, reaching out and, unasked, helping himself to another handful of crisps.

'Really?' said Biffo.

'Crunch crunch crunch actually crunch crunch crunch,' said Bill. 'It was a crunch crunch crunch playing Paul crunch in a crunch about the crunch.' They were very noisy crisps.

'Sorry?' said Biffo who had no idea what Bill had said. 'I'm afraid I didn't quite get that...'

Bill finished crunching the crisps he was eating and swallowed them.

'It wasn't actually the real Paul McCartney,' said Bill, after licking his lips. 'It was an actor playing Paul McCartney in a play about the Beatles.'

'Ah.' nodded Biffo, putting two fingers into his crisp bag and discovering that it was empty. He screwed up the crisp bag and lay it on the bar counter.

'But it was a very good play,' said Bill, half closing his eyes, staring at the ceiling and giving a good imitation of a man in thought. 'I can't remember the title. Did you see it?' He picked up Biffo's pint of beer and drank half of it in one swallow.

'I don't think so,' said Biffo, glumly watching his beer disappear. He was beginning to feel very hungry and wondered just how hungry he would have to be before he went upstairs to his room and started eating some of Tiger's food. He remembered his former television colleague Streaky Bacon once saying that hairdressers are specially trained to be able to talk for hours without saying anything. He had claimed, probably without justification, that they took a diploma in 'inconsequential chit-chat'. Biffo decided that on this occasion he would have preferred it if Bill had chatted more and eaten less.

Bill then began to give a monologue on the history of the potato crisp. The former hairdresser was clearly not only a man who read widely and indiscriminately but also someone who was always eager to share his extensive knowledge with a largely untutored world.

During a pause in the monologue (unlike professional politicians Bill had not yet perfected the art of breathing in mid-sentence in order to stop anyone else getting a word in edgeways) Lettice, who had emerged from the kitchen looking even more flustered, interrupted.

'I'm terribly sorry,' she said. She looked rather dishevelled and was holding the now familiar menu in her hand.

'That's OK,' said Biffo, welcoming the interruption. Bill, who did not seem so pleased, simply glowered.

'I've been right through the freezer,' said Lettice, clearly apologetic. 'And we don't seem to have any sirloin steak in stock.'

Biffo smiled and took the menu from her. 'That's OK,' he said. 'Don't worry.' He checked the menu. 'I'll have the Aylesbury Duckling A L'Orange,' he said. 'Sounds wonderful.'

'Right,' said Lettice, relieved. 'And do you want to stick with the same wine?'

'Yes please,' said Biffo. 'That'll be fine.'

Lettice went back into the kitchen in search of a spare Aylesbury Ducking and, presumably, an unemployed orange.

'Where's he gone?' Biffo asked Puffy, noticing that Bill had disappeared.

'Probably phoning Mrs Stickers to tell her to get the caviar out of the fridge for his tea,' replied Puffy. He nodded in Bill's direction. The lottery winner was standing by the door talking on a mobile telephone. He seemed a little more agitated than one would have expected of a man ordering up his nightly supply of overpriced fish eggs.

'I rather get the impression Bill likes being cricket club president, chairman and captain,' said Biffo.

'Loves it,' said Puffy, rather wearily. 'He's a real pain in the butt. To be honest I don't really think he has much interest in cricket. But he loves the fact that everyone in the village is in his debt.' He leant a little closer. 'I rather think he likes being important,' he confided.

Bill shut his telephone and left the bar hurriedly. He did not say goodbye or hit his head on the beam.

'Odd fellow,' said Puffy. 'Even though he won z point x million I sometimes actually feel sorry for him.'

'Who are the other players?' Biffo asked Puffy, nodding towards the far end of the bar where a small cluster of drinkers, clearly regulars at The Gravedigger's Rest, appeared to be doing their best to make the next beer delivery truck driver's journey well worthwhile. When they had celebrated the fact that their fast bowler's knee was in good condition they celebrated the start of the forthcoming the cricket season and then they celebrated the end of winter. They celebrated the existence of The Gravedigger's Rest and mostly, and most consistently, they celebrated the fact that the public house of that name was blessed with a good supply of excellent beer and a wise landlord who was always happy to give credit to his most valued customers. They liked celebrating.

'I've never before been in a pub where the customers help themselves,' Biffo said, as Cheesy Stilton displayed exceptional and unexpected dexterity by reaching over the bar and refilling his own glass with beer. When he had completed that task to his own satisfaction, and had filled the glass to the point where only the wonders of surface tension prevented spillage, he repeated the performance with a second glass. There was little doubt that if beer drinking had been a recognised Olympic sport the regulars of The Gravedigger's Rest would have all been favourites for medals. Observers would have had little choice but to have been seriously impressed by the amount of training going on.

'We have an honesty book,' explained Puffy. 'The regulars just help themselves and jot down what they owe me in the book.' He paused. 'Once a month I add it all up and write it off as a bad debt.' He sighed. 'Actually, the honesty book has gone missing. I think someone has nicked it.' He brightened up. 'Probably somebody's idea of a joke. I expect it'll turn up.'

'Tell me about Cheesy,' said Biffo.

'Walter 'Cheesy' Stilton,' said Puffy, as though introducing a victim for 'This Is Your Life'. 'Last year he was elected Best Lower Middle Order Batsman Of The First Half Of The Season. He is one of the team's most capable drinkers. A great beer man. Cheesy can drink ten or twelve pints of the best and still drive a car right along the white line in the middle of the road.'

Biffo nodded appreciatively.

'He's a brilliant mimic too,' added Puffy, with undisguised admiration. 'There is no one for miles to touch Cheesy when it comes to imitating farmyard animals.' Puffy lifted up the bar flap as he spoke. 'His cow in labour is sensational. Quite remarkable. He brought the house down at last year's Annual Cricket Club Dinner.' He wandered along behind the bar and helped himself to a large gin. 'And if you ever have any plumbing problems Cheesy is your man,' said Puffy. 'He may not look much out of the ordinary but that man can work miracles with a wrench.'

'A wench?' said Biffo, slightly puzzled.

'A wrench,' said Puffy. 'But, come to think of it he can probably work miracles with wenches too.' He turned to Biffo. 'Can I get you anything?'

'I wouldn't mind another beer,' said Biffo.

Puffy poured Biffo a pint of beer.

Just then Lettice reappeared looking rather embarrassed.

'I don't know how to tell you this,' she said to Biffo.

'No Aylesbury duckling?'

'No duckling from Aylesbury, Wednesbury or anywhere else for that matter.'

Biffo held out a hand. 'So, what else is on the menu?'

'There isn't a lot of point in showing you the menu,' said Lettice, holding tightly onto the menu. 'I've checked. We don't have anything that's listed on it.'

'Let me look!' said a disbelieving Puffy, holding out a hand. Lettice handed him the menu.

'We don't have anything on here,' he announced almost immediately, closing the menu with a loud snap and handing it back to Lettice.

'I'm sorry,' said Lettice to Biffo.

'Do you have any food at all?' asked Biffo. 'Or shall I just have another packet of crisps.' He brightened up. 'I do like crisps,' he assured her.

'We've got some tinned tomatoes,' said Puffy. 'Pru – that's my wife – bought a few cases a couple of years ago. We can't have eaten them all.' He suddenly seemed depressed and looked guilty about something.

'I found the tinned tomatoes,' said Lettice. 'You definitely have lots of tinned tomatoes. You could build an extension with the number of tins of tomatoes you've got.'

'Why would I want to build an extension with tins of tomatoes?' asked Puffy, puzzled. He still looked guilty.

'And bread,' said Biffo. 'I know you have bread because I brought a loaf back from the shop.'

'I could do you tomatoes on toast,' offered Lettice, with some relief.

'Sounds great to me,' said Biffo.

'Do you still want the wine?' asked Lettice.

'Where did you say it came from?'

'I'm not sure where its from,' admitted Lettice. She turned to her uncle. 'Where is the wine from?'

'What wine?'

'The wine you told me to offer Mr Brimstone when he asked for claret.'

'Oh don't give him that crap,' said Puffy. 'It's from Australia. Or South Africa. It's foreign anyway. But not the right sort of foreign.' He paused and addressed Biffo. 'You should never drink wine that comes from a country where they play cricket.' He sighed. 'Forget the wine.'

'Good advice,' agreed Biffo, with a nod. 'I'll have another beer, please,' he said to Lettice.

Lettice poured him a beer and then disappeared back into the kitchen to turn bread into toast and to heat up some tomatoes.

'Something I ought to tell you,' said Puffy. He took a deep breath. 'I told you a bit of a white lie about my wife Prudence.'

Biffo tried to make the sort of facial gesture which would indicate that he did not hold this against Puffy.

'My wife isn't up north on family business,' confessed Puffy. 'She ran off.'

'Oh,' said Biffo, feigning surprise. 'I'm sorry to hear that.'

'With a soft drink salesman,' said Puffy. He shook his head and closed his eyes at the shame of it.

They drank in silence for a while.

'Here's your tomatoes on toast,' said Lettice, suddenly appearing from the kitchen carrying a large plate of toast topped with a huge mound of tomatoes. 'Where's Cheesy going to in such a hurry?' she asked, nodding towards the door.

Puffy and Biffo both turned and watched Cheesy disappear.

'He's gone to see a man about a dog,' said Puffy.

'Oh,' said Lettice. She put the tomatoes on toast down in front of Biffo.

'Funny saying that,' said Biffo. 'I've often wondered where it came from and why people say it.'

Puffy, clearly puzzled, looked at Biffo and frowned but said nothing.

~ Chapter 18 ~

'AND THE SMALL CHAP WITH the thick spectacles?' said Biffo. 'Who's he?'

'Ah, that's Justin, our wicket keeper' said Puffy. 'You always know where you are with Justin. Of course, he'll always let you down but that's part of his charm.'

Biffo frowned. 'I'm a bit confused,' he admitted. 'If he always lets people down how on earth can you know where you are with him?'

'People expect him to let them down so they are never disappointed,' explained Puffy. 'It's a form of reliability.'

'Terrific carpenter and a very keen gardener,' said Puffy. 'He grows huge vegetables which win lots of prizes at all the local produce shows but they're so woody that they are totally inedible and so his wife buys all her vegetables from Miss Box's shop.'

'Blind as a bat but put a chisel in his hand and he's a bloomin' artist. He used to play professional football. But when his eyesight went he had to give it up. Even with his glasses on he couldn't see where the goal was. Still, he hasn't lost touch with the game,' Puffy continued. 'He's a referee now,' he said after a pause.

'Really?' said Biffo.

Puffy looked at him and raised an eyebrow a millimetre or so.

'Sorry,' said Biffo, feeling fairly stupid.

'He's so blind he doesn't even drive a car any more,' said Puffy. 'Just as well, really, considering the bridge.'

'What happened with the bridge?' asked Biffo, on cue.

'There's a small stone bridge over the river Ripple about fifteen miles away from here,' began Puffy. 'It's been there for centuries and because it was built before cars, or even horse drawn carriages, it's very narrow. These days it's part of a bridle path which is popular with walkers. People drive here from all over the place to walk along that path though I've never understood why they don't just stay at home if they want to go for a walk. Seems daft getting into the car and driving somewhere so that you can go for a walk doesn't it?' He stopped talking long enough to transfer a third of a pint of beer from his glass to his stomach. Biffo guessed that Puffy was probably used to living in a beautiful English village and therefore didn't realise just how joyful a walk in the country can be to someone who is usually surrounded by endless acres of tarmacadam and concrete.

'So, a few years ago,' continued Puffy, 'when he was coming home one night after a boozy dinner to celebrate the fact that the team he played for had been relegated Justin suddenly got it into his head that he was going to get stopped by the bluebottles and breathalysed.'

'Hang on a minute,' said Biffo, scratching his head. 'I don't understand something here. Why were they celebrating the fact that the team had been relegated?'

'Because the players all got a bonus every time they won a match,' explained Puffy. 'They all knew that if they went down into a lower league the competition wouldn't be as stiff and they would win more matches.'

Biffo, decided that there were probably some steep learning curves to be negotiated before he could count himself as being properly assimilated into village life in Fondling-Under-Water.

'There was no real reason for him to worry about being breathalysed because there hasn't been a police vehicle in these lanes for years – unless you count Constable Hobbling's moped which most people don't since a moped is not actually the sort of vehicle that would be top of your chosen list if you had to get involved in a car chase would it?'

'I suppose not,' agreed Biffo who hadn't actually seen Constable Hobbling's moped but assumed that in speed terms it probably held no great advantage over other mopeds.

'And anyway after six o'clock at night Constable Hobbling is either in here or tucked up in bed with Avril Showers, the insurance man's widow. Why would he want to be riding around the lanes on a draughty moped when he could be keeping himself occupied taking down Avril's particulars?'

Biffo decided that this question did not require an answer or even a nod. He just sipped his beer and listened.

'But Justin was convinced that the lanes were going to be crammed full of policemen waiting to leap out of hedgerows and arrest him,' continued Puffy. 'So, he turned off the main road just behind Myrtle Berry's cottage and headed off down the bridle path.'

'Unfortunately, he forgot that his car – a pale blue 1953 Morris Minor which was in such tip top condition that a car collector from the North of England was so keen to buy it that he asked Justin to name his own price – was just ever so very slightly wider than the bridge over the river.'

'So, there was Justin pootling down the bridle path in the pitch dark. There was a good moon and so to save electricity and avoid giving himself away to the non-existent police force hiding in the bushes Justin turned off his lights.'

'All went well until he reached the bridge. He didn't slow down because he knew that there was a steep hill on the other side and he wanted to give the Morris a good run at it.'

'The next thing he knew, he was stuck. His car had been travelling fast enough to get onto the bridge but once there it fit like a cork in a bottle.'

'What's more he couldn't even open the car doors, of course, and so there he stayed until Myrtle Berry took her dogs for a walk and found the bridge blocked.'

'It was four hours before we got there and another two hours before Albert Ross, who has the antique shop the other side of the church, pulled him off the bridge with his Volvo. Because no one had a camera to record the scene for posterity, we had to wait for someone to go back to the village and fetch Maude Lynn who had a box Brownie. Naturally, she didn't have any film for it so we all had to sit around and wait while Ivy Bridge pedalled over to Miss Box's shop to pick up a roll.'

'How terrible!' said Biffo. 'Especially since he loved the car so much.'

'Loved the car?' said Puffy, puzzled. 'What made you think he loved the car? His aunt left it to him when she died. He'd only had it a week.'

'You said that he turned down that car collector who asked him to name his price,' said Biffo.

'Don't be daft,' said Puffy.' I didn't say anything of the sort. When the car collector asked him to name his price Justin asked him for £200 which was just £10 more than he'd been offered by Mel Bourne at the garage. But it turned out that the car collector was all mouth and no wallet.'

'Oh,' said Biffo. 'Still, it must have been a nasty experience for him.'

'I wouldn't say that,' said Biffo. 'Justin sold his car as scrap to a gypsy for £20, reported it stolen, put in a claim and got £250 from his insurance company.'

~ Chapter 19 ~

'AND THE VERY SHORT, ROUNDISH sort of chap in the toupee and the oily jeans?' asked Biffo, now back on a stool at the bar. He had thoroughly enjoyed the plate of tomatoes on toast which he had eaten alone at a small table near to the empty fireplace. 'Roderick, didn't you say his name was?'

'That's Roderick Hedrubb,' said Puffy. 'We call him Itchy.'

'Does he play in the team?'

'He used to, but he won't touch a bat or a ball these days. He retired with a career batting average of 10.01 and a career bowling average of 39.87 runs per wicket. He's terrified that if he plays another match his batting average will go under 10 and his bowling average will go above 40. We've tried to persuade him to come out of retirement – he was one of the best players we've ever had – but he won't consider it. He's our groundsman now.' He frowned. 'How did you know he was wearing a toupee?'

'Because it looks as if it might be on back to front,' said Biffo.

'I don't think it is,' said Puffy, peering at Itchy's head. He gave up, leant a little closer to Biffo and spoke confidentially. 'Don't tell Roderick you could tell he was wearing a toupee,' he said. 'He's quite proud of it. He bought it at the White Elephant stall at last year's village fête. It used to belong to Ernie Showers.'

'Avril's former husband?' asked Biffo.

'That's the one,' replied Puffy. 'You're getting the hang of things.'

Just then Cheesy returned. He was holding a lead. On the end of the lead there was a dog.

'He really did go and see a man about a dog!' exclaimed Biffo, genuinely surprised.

'Of course,' said Puffy. 'Where else do you think he went?'

~ Chapter 20 ~

'And Helmut – the huge chap who looks a bit like a walrus with a hangover?' asked Biffo, nodding in the direction of a huge fellow who looked very much like a walrus might look if it had a hangover. The bear of a man who had brought in a bag full of second-hand trophies had returned. He had removed his tattered sheepskin coat and underneath it was wearing a tweed jacket, a pair of tweed plus two trousers and knee length socks.

'Ah, Helmut,' said Puffy. 'Helmut Walton. He was last year's Middle Order Batsman Of The Second Half Of The Season.'

Biffo thought about this for a moment. 'Does absolutely everyone in the team get some sort of award?' he asked.

'Of course,' said Puffy. 'I was Best Upper Middle Order Batsman Of The First Half Of The Season.'

Biffo thought again for a while. Eventually he spoke. 'I don't want to appear stupid,' he said at last. 'But I don't really understand.'

'We always have an annual dinner at the end of every season,' explained Puffy. 'For years we used to have a player of the year. The club members would vote for the player whom they felt had contributed most to the club. But in the end we had to give that up.'

'Why?' asked Biffo. 'It sounds like quite a good idea.'

Puffy seemed a little embarrassed. 'It was difficult to find a winner,' he admitted. 'When we added up the votes we found that there was never a clear winner.'

'The voting was always too close?'

'Sort of. Everyone used to vote for themselves so no one ever got more than one vote.'

'Oh,' said Biffo. 'I can see that that would make sorting out a winner a little tricky.'

'So, we did a bit of reorganising,' said Puffy. 'Now everyone in the club gets an award.'

'That sounds very fair,' agreed Biffo.

'It works quite well,' said Puffy. 'There aren't any complaints.'

'Why does that chap have the nickname Helmut?'

'Actually, I think that Helmut is his real name,' admitted Puffy. 'But his second name is totally unpronounceable so we call him Walton. Helmut Walton.'

'He's German, though you wouldn't believe it,' continued Puffy. 'He doesn't have the average German's highly developed sense of humour. He speaks English with a curious Welsh accent because at school his teacher was a Miss Jones who came from Cardiff. He's really very foreign.'

'Nothing wrong with being foreign,' said Lettice, anxious that her uncle would not appear to have politically incorrect views on such matters.

'No, I suppose not,' agreed Puffy, rather hesitantly. 'Although I wouldn't like to be foreign myself.'

'We're all foreign to someone,' said Biffo.

'Good heavens, I hope not!' said Puffy. He shuddered. 'What a terrible thought.' He shuddered again. 'How could you and I possibly be foreign? We're English!' He looked at Biffo. 'You are English?'

'Oh yes,' said Biffo. Puffy seemed reassured.

'Helmut runs a reclamation yard,' said Lettice. 'He sells old tiles and window frames to people trying to restore old houses. It's a good business. If you wanted to build an 18th century house from scratch today he could sell you everything you need.'

'He's as strong as an ox and probably the most intimidating player I've ever seen on a cricket pitch,' said Puffy. 'He's got enormous hands. He's the only person I know who can bowl overarm at skittles.'

'He never seems to remember any of the rules of cricket but he enjoys the game,' said Lettice. 'His only problem in life is that his wife doesn't like letting him out of her sight for very long.'

'Marriage and fatherhood have destroyed more good cricketers than beer, whisky, gambling and wild women put together,' said Puffy.

Lettice looked at her watch and moved a little closer to Biffo. She smelt of scented soap. 'He'll be leaving in just under five minutes,' she said softly.

Biffo, puzzled, looked at her. 'How do you know that?'

'Helga – that's his wife – allows him half an hour in the pub every evening,' explained Lettice. 'But out of that half hour he has to walk here and walk back home. He lives about five minutes away so he really only gets about twenty minutes drinking time. And he's already been here for a quarter of an hour.'

'I don't believe you!' said Biffo, starting to laugh.

'No, really. I'm serious,' said Lettice. 'It's true, isn't it Puffy?'

Puffy nodded his head. 'I'm afraid so,' he agreed. 'He used to be quite a tearaway. But not any more.' He turned to Lettice. 'Do you remember that cricket tour to Corfu he went on a few years ago?'

Lettice laughed. 'I'd forgotten all about that! Tell Biffo!'

'When Helmut was much younger he worked for a firm of accountants in the stockbroker belt in Surrey and played cricket for the firm's side. The firm's boss was a bloke called Douglas Kent and the firm was called Kent Accounting so the cricket club was called Kent Accounting Cricket Club.'

'Helmut was single in those days and the team he played for used to go away on a cricket tour every year. One year they would go touring in the West Country and another year they would go up into Yorkshire – that sort of thing.'

'One summer Helmut and his pals went off to Corfu. When they got there they were welcomed at the airport and given a pretty royal reception. They were interviewed for the local TV and radio, taken into town on an open bus, given rooms at the best hotel and invited to a special dinner by the local dignitaries.'

'The next morning they were asked if they would do a bit of coaching at a couple of local schools and then taken along to play their first match.'

'Now, you have to remember that Helmut and his chums usually played local club third teams. And by and large third teams at local clubs are made up of social cricketers – guys who enjoy a game of cricket but hardly ever practise and don't take the game too seriously. They go there for a bit of fun, a bit of mild exercise and an excuse to have a drink or three with some congenial chums. Most of them have kit which is falling apart and half of them don't even have bats of their own.'

'So Helmut and company should have been worried when they got to the club where they were playing and found that there were several hundred spectators sitting around waiting for the match to begin.'

'At home Helmut and his team would have thought themselves lucky if they had attracted an audience of two old men and a mangy dog. Here they were faced with tiered seating, a proper pavilion, a working scoreboard and a real crowd.'

'It wasn't until the television cameras turned up that they really got worried. And the worry turned to panic when they wandered round the back of the pavilion and watched the local team practising in the nets.'

'They finally twigged what had happened when a reporter started to interview the team captain.'

'When the team's visit had been booked it had all been done on the telephone and the person in Corfu who had taken the call had misheard. He'd thought it was Kent County Cricket Club that wanted to come and play a few games. Not surprisingly the locals had been thrilled to bits.'

'What on earth happened?' asked Biffo, laughing.

'Mr Kent the accountant, and his merry team of bean counters, decided that there was only one thing for it. They went into the bar and got absolutely plastered. The locals were a bit disappointed when the visitors were all out for under twenty – I think they were probably looking forward to watching Colin Cowdrey knock up a quick hundred – but they were absolutely thrilled to win by ten wickets and the visitors had a good excuse because most of them could hardly stand up without support.'

'Would you say that Cheesy, Itchy and Helmut are fairly typical members of the Fondling-Under-Water Cricket Club?' Biffo asked.

'Oh absolutely,' said Puffy. 'Pretty typical. Maybe a bit duller than average.' He thought for a moment. 'Yes, perhaps a bit duller than the average. Do you want to hear about Rupert Fitzwalter? That's the chap in the red shirt at the far end of the bar.' He sighed admiringly. 'Now Rupert is really quite a colourful character.'

'I'd love to hear about Rupert Fitzwalter,' said Biffo honestly. 'But if I don't go to bed pretty soon I'll drop off this bar stool. It's been a long day and I've got to get up early in the morning.'

'You get up whenever you feel like it,' said Puffy.

'I've got to start work at eight,' said Biffo.

'Start work?' said Puffy, surprised.

'I'm starting work in the transport business,' said Biffo, unsuccessfully stifling a yawn. He clambered off the bar stool, said goodnight to everyone within range and tottered up the stairs to bed.

~ Chapter 21 ~

PEOPLE WHO DON'T HAVE ANY MONEY, and who know that their own worries are often generated by a lack of ready funds, frequently imagine that the rich must live worry-free lives.

They are, of course, quite wrong in this for the rich worry constantly about losing the money they have and becoming poor again. Generally speaking, the rich worry just as much as the poor. Indeed, it is possible that they may worry more than the poor about money.

As Bill Stickers hurled his Rolls Royce Corniche through the gates of his elegant country seat he was as worried about money as he had ever been in his pre-lottery win days, when every penny of his mortgage, plus the grocery bills, the electricity and gas bills and the garage bills, had all had to be paid for out of the modest wage he earned through shaving, snipping and singeing.

Bill stopped the huge car far too quickly, skidding and sliding on the gravel and sending a spray of fine chippings into the rose bed outside the library windows. He leapt out of the Rolls Royce the moment it stopped, giving the heavy door a careless push so that it clunked back into place. His blood pressure had now risen to a point where the expensive Harley Street physician whom Bill routinely visited for check ups would have been doing a lot of lip pursing and brow furrowing.

'Pansy!' he called out, once he was inside the house. He repeated the cry half a dozen times before Pansy, who had been keeping herself busy watering the plants in the conservatory, heard him and came rushing into the hall. She was still wearing a pair of pink rubber gloves and carrying a little green plastic watering can.

Mrs Pansy Stickers was a small, slight woman who had never really come to terms with being rich. When her husband had cut hair for a living she had worked in a video shop (her official title had been 'Home Entertainment Consultant' but she had never felt truly comfortable with the word 'consultant' and had only worn her name badge when she knew that the shop's owner was likely to call).

When she had been married to a poor person she had worried because they didn't have much money. Now that she was married to a rich person she worried several times as much as she had before. She worried because she didn't really believe that they were rich. She worried that if they really were rich then people who had known them when they were poor wouldn't like them because they would feel jealous, while people who didn't know them before would now dislike them because their money had come from a lottery win. Pansy felt that money won in a lottery wasn't really very solid money. She felt that it had come so easily that people would one day be able to come and take it away from them. She envied those who had inherited their money. She felt that inherited money that had come down from generation to generation was the best sort of money. It had, by definition, been in the same family for years and therefore probably had better staying power.

Pansy's constant worry was that if they really were rich they might lose it all one day and become poor again. If it was possible to get Olympic medals for worrying Pansy would have had antique trophy cabinets filled with gold medals.

'What the hell has happened?' demanded Bill.

'Oh dearie me,' said Pansy, putting the watering can down on a small mahogany table so that she could wring her hands. 'Oh dearie me, it's such a worry.'

Bill snatched up the watering can and wiped his sleeve

over the top of the mahogany table so that there wouldn't be a water stain on the wood. 'Where is it?' He put the watering can down on the floor.

'Oh dear,' said Pansy, still wringing her hands but now looking at the table too. 'Has it left a mark?' The rubber gloves she was still wearing squeaked.

'Don't worry about the table,' said Bill, whose blood pressure was now in the opposite of freefall. 'It doesn't matter. Where's the fax? On the telephone you said there had been a fax from the bank.'

'Oh, I'm sorry. I've marked it haven't I?' Pansy bent down so that she could examine the table more closely.

'Forget the table,' said Bill, speaking through clenched teeth. 'Where is it?'

'Where's what?' asked Pansy.

'The fax!' said Bill, trying to stay calm but finding it extremely difficult. He spoke slowly and carefully so that each word in the sentence stood alone. 'The fax you said had come from the bank.'

'Oh, I put it somewhere safe so that I'd be able to find it when you came home,' said Pansy, looking around her in despair. The rubber gloves squeaked a good deal more before she finally found the fax (she had folded it twice and slipped it into the patch pocket on the front of her pinafore).

The fax had come from Bill Stickers' Personal Account Manager at the private bank in the Channel Islands to which he had entrusted the management of his lottery winnings.

Bill had chosen the offshore bank because it had a very important-sounding name and extremely expensive-looking cheque books. When his personal wealth had suddenly increased from £345.67 pence (all in a Building Society deposit account) to a considerably more impressive £7,460,345.67 he had taken great delight in closing his account with the local High Street bank (where the manager had once turned down his application for a £1,000 loan to buy a second-hand car) and moving to a bank where the staff welcomed rich customers with an obsequious smile and all the respect they wanted whether their money was inherited, earned or won.

Bill, enormously impressed by the folder (embossed in gold with the bank's substantial-looking crest and a motto in Latin) which he had been given in which to store his portfolio statements, had happily, indeed enthusiastically, handed over his entire fortune (including the £345.67) and signed documents which gave the management of his new bank *carte blanche* to do with his money as they saw fit.

Although he had once berated a stony-faced counter assistant at his local Building Society for not telling him that they had another account which offered an extra 0.15% interest, Bill had been enormously, even pitifully, grateful that the bank had accepted him as a customer.

The money had, in truth, frightened him. He didn't know what to do with it and he had been grateful to the bank for taking it off his hands.

Every quarter he received a statement which he had carefully filed in the expensive folder they had given him. He had never really understood the statements but in the beginning he hadn't liked to ask anyone about them because he didn't want them to think he was as ignorant as he was (he was frightened that they would laugh at him behind his back) and as the months went by it became impossible to ask questions because to ask questions would be to admit that he had been too embarrassed to ask the same questions before and then they would be able to laugh at him for being both ignorant and frightened of them.

He read the fax carefully. Like all faxes from the bank it was on plain paper (the bank regarded confidentiality as vital) though he recognised the signature at the bottom.

Dear Mr Stickers,
Due to a recent downturn in the markets in which you are currently invested we have to inform you that after liquidating your portfolio to pay our charges your balance with us is currently £0.13. Since this is a lower sum than our minimum balance requirement we look forward to receiving further funds from you at your earliest convenience.
Yours sincerely,

'Is it serious?' asked Pansy.

Bill read the fax again. It still said exactly the same as it had said the first time he had read it.

'The bastards have lost all our money,' said Bill.

'All of it?' said Pansy. She was still wringing her hands.

'All of it!' said Bill. 'How could they lose seven million quid?'

'Oh dear.' said Pansy. 'Oh dear.'

Actually, she wasn't shocked by the news because she had been expecting it to happen for a long time. Now that it had finally happened she actually felt very calm about it. Many of her biggest worries had now disappeared.

'Take those bloody gloves off!' said Bill.

'Yes, dear,' said Pansy. She took the gloves off. 'So we're poor again?'

'The bastards have stolen my money!' said Bill. He looked at his watch. 'And they'll be shut now. I can't ring them until the morning.'

'Never mind,' said Pansy. 'You can always go back to hairdressing.' She looked at him, desperately trying to think of something comforting to say. 'It's nice that you have a skill.'

Bill glared at her and opened his mouth.

'Shall I make some tea, dear?' asked Pansy.

Bill shut his mouth, sat down and put his head in his hands. It would be fair to say that he did not feel at his best.

~ Chapter 22 ~

THE BEDROOM WHICH BIFFO HAD shared with Edwina for so much of his adult life had been fitted with spacious, built-in wardrobes, and although rather more than three quarters of the available space had been filled with Edwina's fine collection of designer dresses and associated ancillaries there had, nevertheless, been a not inconsiderable amount of space available for her husband's clothes.

Biffo had, over his half a lifetime, accumulated a fairly impressive collection of suits, shirts, shoes, sweaters, socks and so on.

It was, therefore, something of a surprise and modest disappointment, to discover that he had, in his haste and confusion, brought with him two pairs of extra thick walking socks (originally bought especially to be worn exclusively with a pair of walking boots which he had not brought with him), half a dozen monogrammed handkerchiefs, a box containing a variety of collar studs, a cummerbund, (but, naturally, no dinner jacket with which to wear it), five pairs of brand new sock suspenders still in their original packaging (something he had never worn his life), two left hand gloves, a black bow tie, a brassiere (which, he assumed, must have got into one of his drawers by mistake) and two brand new dress shirts in their original and probably virtually impenetrable packaging (which he had received the previous Christmas as a gift from Edwina).

He had, in short, not brought with him any spare clothes that would be of any use at all. For an Englishman, the most alarming discovery was the fact that he had forgotten to bring any pyjamas. He liked the idea of starting his new life without too much baggage (either physical or emotional) but he would have liked a pair of pyjamas.

Standing in his shirt and socks Biffo tried to decide whether it would be more appropriate to remove his shirt (and, indeed, his socks) and go to bed naked (and thus reduce the amount of washing he would ultimately have to do) or to keep on his shirt (and, possibly, his socks as well) and therefore go to bed prepared for those awesome eventualities, such as fire, flood and middle of the night pestilence, which had always concerned Edwina so much.

As Biffo contemplated this dilemma, realising that whatever he decided to do the shirt he had on today would be the shirt he wore tomorrow, there was a timid knock on the door.

'Yes?' said Biffo, puzzled. 'Who's there?'

'May I come in for a moment?' asked a male voice.

Biffo, grateful that he had kept his shirt on, opened the door and found a tall, thin, wiry-looking fellow in a red shirt standing there. Biffo had seen him at the bar with the other cricket club members but didn't know his name.

'Hope you don't mind my troubling you so late,' said the

stranger. 'My name is Rupert. May I have a word with you?' He looked up and down the corridor before adding the final two words. 'In private?'

'Rupert Fitzwalter?' asked Biffo.

'That's right!' agreed the stranger, apparently not surprised that Biffo knew his name. He walked into Biffo's room, sat down on the bed and peered into Biffo's open suitcase.

'What on earth are these?' he asked, picking up a pair of sock suspenders.

'Sock suspenders,' explained Biffo.

'Oh,' said Rupert, putting the sock suspenders back into the suitcase. He picked up another, identical pair. 'And these?'

'Sock suspenders,' explained Biffo, again.

'Ah,' said Rupert, putting the sock suspenders back into the suitcase. 'I'll come straight to the point,' he said, leaning forwards and looking first towards the door and then towards the window, as though anxious to make sure that they were not being overheard. 'I want to help you earn a little extra beer money.'

'Really?' said Biffo. 'What can I do for you?'

'I run a book in the pub on how many people will hit their heads on the beam over the entrance to the public bar.'

Biffo nodded. 'I see.'

'If you're staying here for a while,' said Rupert, 'you're likely to be the most important contributor to the numbers.'

'You mean I'm likely to hit my head more than anyone else?'

'You'll probably be the only person hitting your head. But to soften the blow I'll be happy to pay you £5 every time you bang your head on that beam between today and Saturday. Up to, say, a dozen times in all.'

'You want to pay me to bang my head?'

'Up to £60 worth!' agreed Rupert.

'Do you get a kick out of seeing people in pain?' asked Biffo.

'Not a bit of it,' said Rupert. 'You don't have to hit it too hard. You could always pretend to given yourself a rather bigger bang than you really have,' he added.

'And if I bang my head often enough you don't have to pay out anyone?'

'That's about the size of it,' agreed Rupert.

'But isn't that crooked?' asked Biffo.

'Not really,' said Rupert. He looked at Biffo and thought carefully. 'I call it realigning the odds a little,' he said.

'Sorry, no,' said Biffo firmly.

'Oh,' said Rupert, disappointed. 'I hope you're not offended by my suggestion?'

'Not at all,' said Biffo. 'It's just that I've got an eggshell skull,' he lied. 'I could fracture my skull if I banged it against that beam too often.' He paused. 'I could die,' he added.

Rupert looked concerned. 'Gosh!' he said. 'I'm most terribly sorry. Will you please forget I ever spoke?' he asked. He leant forwards and tapped Biffo on the knee. 'Would you do that for me? Forget I ever spoke.'

'Of course,' said Biffo. He stared for a moment and then smiled. 'Forget what?'

'Thanks,' said Rupert. 'And, er, I'm sorry to hear about your skull...'

'Don't you worry about it,' said Biffo, by now almost believing the story himself.

Rupert stood up and headed for the door. Just before he left he turned back. 'Do you mind if I ask you something?' he asked.

'No,' said Biffo.

'Why are you so frightened of your socks falling down?'

Biffo, puzzled by the question, looked at Rupert.

'All the sock suspenders,' explained Rupert.

'Oh those!' said Biffo, understanding. 'I never wear them,' he said quite honestly. 'My wife's sister always used to give me a pair for Christmas.'

'And you are in love with your wife's sister and you don't like going anywhere with the presents she's bought you?'

'No. That's not it at all. The truth is that I can't stand her. I picked them up by mistake,' admitted Biffo. He stared into the suitcase sadly. 'In fact everything I brought was a mistake,' he added.

'Oh, I say, what rotten luck,' said Rupert. 'You must have been in a hurry. Bit of a tiff with the wife?'

'You could say that,' agreed Biffo.

'Sorry to hear it,' said Rupert. He paused and looked at the suitcase again. 'So, what are you going to do with all the stuff in the case?' He put a hand into the case and rummaged around a little. 'Do you mind?'

'Not at all,' said Biffo.

'I'm going to dump it all,' Biffo heard himself say. He realised that he quite liked the idea of starting again from scratch. With just the clothes he had come away in.

'I'll give you £20 for the lot,' said Rupert, holding up Edwina's brassiere and examining it carefully. He seemed impressed. 'Cash.' He reached into his trouser pocket and took out a roll of notes.

'What on earth do you want with this junk?'

'Dunno,' said Rupert. 'But it's what I do. I have a junk shop. Few antiques. Books. Bits and pieces people don't know what to do with.'

'OK,' said Biffo. 'It's a deal. He started to take stuff out of the suitcase.'

'In the case,' said Rupert.

'It's a Louis Vuitton,' protested Biffo. 'They're very expensive.'

'I'll need something to carry the stuff in,' said Rupert, handing over two ten pound notes.

'Yes. I suppose you will,' agreed Biffo, taking the notes. It was, he realised, the second time in a day that he had been out negotiated. He tried to put the notes into his trouser pocket but was interrupted in this endeavour by the fact that he wasn't wearing any trousers. 'Not those!' he said suddenly, as Rupert picked up his jacket and trousers from where they lay on top of the bed and started to stuff them into the suitcase. 'Those are the only clothes I've got left!'

Rupert examined the jacket professionally. 'Not worth much anyway,' he said, putting it back down on the bed. He closed the suitcase, picked it up and headed for the door.

'Nice to have met you,' he said. 'Sleep well. I hope you

wake up healthy, wealthy and wise.' And then he left.

Biffo, who thought this seemed rather a lot to expect from a night's sleep, removed his shirt and put it into a drawer. He closed that drawer and put his trousers into a second drawer. He then removed his jacket and carefully lay that down in a third drawer. Finally, he took off his socks. He put one sock in each of the smaller drawers at the top of the chest.

And thus, quite naked and unashamed, he climbed into bed for his first night at The Gravedigger's Rest and fell asleep the moment his head touched the pillow.

Moments later Tiger, who had been curled up at the foot of the bed, sat up, got up, stretched, padded silently up the bed, climbed onto Biffo's chest, lay down and purred contentedly.

~ Chapter 23 ~

PYJAMAS WERE NOT THE ONLY essential item Biffo had forgotten to pack when he had left home. He had also omitted to bring with him his alarm clock. And as a direct result of this omission when he woke the next morning and looked at his watch he was horrified to see that it was twenty past seven. He immediately felt almost overwhelmed by a powerful sense of guilt. For as long as he could remember he had woken every morning at 7.00 am sharp.

Biffo leapt out of the bed with the same sense of physical urgency he would have undoubtedly displayed if he had discovered that he was sharing the sheets with a frog. He immediately realised, with some considerable embarrassment (for although he would have described himself as a free thinking libertarian he had rather modest views about such issues) that he had slept in the nude.

Grabbing the shirt he had worn the previous day (he had to open three drawers to find it) and clutching it to those parts of his body most central to his personal sense of privacy he padded bare foot across the wooden floor to the bedroom window and looked out.

The scene he had watched the day before had not changed

and for a brief moment Biffo wondered if he had perhaps accidentally stepped into some sort of time machine. The large mowing machine was still there and the groundsman, Roderick Hedrubb, was still hitting it with what appeared to be a heavy blunt instrument. As he watched Mr Hedrubb abandoned his attack on the machine and marched purposefully off the field in the direction of The Gravedigger's Rest. Since he was still clutching the blunt instrument he looked a rather fearsome sight and even at that distance he made Biffo feel rather nervous.

Biffo turned away from the window, and, with some urgency, dressed himself and fed Tiger. He had two priorities. First, he needed some breakfast. And second, he had to get to Miss Box's shop by eight o'clock.

Downstairs the pub, which smelt of stale beer and old tobacco smoke, was silent and utterly deserted.

'Hello,' called Biffo, rather tentatively. There was no reply.

'Is there anyone there?' called Biffo again, this time rather more loudly but with an equally complete lack of response. The Gravedigger's Rest was beginning to make the Marie Celeste look overcrowded.

Biffo walked tentatively along a rather lengthy corridor, knocking on each door as he came to it. 'Hello! Is there anyone there?' he called out, each time he knocked, the volume of his cry rising as he grew in confidence and frustration.

Suddenly, one of the doors that Biffo had passed, and knocked on, was pulled open from the inside. 'What's the matter?' demanded a rather angry sounding voice. 'Are we on fire?'

Biffo turned and saw the landlord, Puffy Harbottle, sleepily rubbing at his eyes and yawning. The landlord of The Gravedigger's Rest was wearing a baggy and faded pair of blue and red striped pyjama trousers and a pale yellow pyjama jacket, which was unbuttoned. A snowy white paunch hung over the top of the pyjama trousers like frozen snow hanging over a roof edge. The landlord's feet were encased in a pair of tartan carpet slippers which had clearly done lengthy service in the foot warming department.

'Oh! I'm sorry!' said Biffo. 'Did I wake you?'

'What time is it?' asked Puffy, leaning forward and peering through half closed eyes in an attempt to locate and identify the source of the interruption. His pyjama trousers decided to obey the call of gravity and Puffy caught them in the nick of time.

'Nearly half past seven,' said Biffo, brightly.

'Morning or night?' asked Puffy, unfastening the cord around his trousers and then tying it a little tighter.

'Morning.'

Puffy, eyes closed, sleepily scratched his naked chest and yawned. 'Can't you sleep?'

'Yes, thank you, I slept very well,' said Biffo, mistaking the question for one which required an answer. 'Where can I get some breakfast?' asked Biffo.

Puffy frowned, squinted and licked his lips, though he did not perform all these tricky manoeuvres at the same time. 'Breakfast?' he asked.

'Am I too early?' asked Biffo rather tentatively. It seemed a pretty good bet that he wasn't too late.

'You want breakfast?' asked a squinting Puffy.

'I am rather peckish,' admitted Biffo.

'What time did you say it was?'

'Er, just after half past seven,' replied Biffo, taking another peek at his watch.

'Lettice is an early riser. She should be up and about at 9.30,' said Puffy firmly. 'If you speak to her nicely she'll make you a piece of toast.'

'Thank you,' said Biffo, but the door was already shutting.

'Puffy, can I borrow your lawnmower?' demanded a voice Biffo didn't recognise but which seemed to come from someone standing immediately behind him. Since Biffo had no idea that there was anyone standing behind him he turned sharply and then jumped several inches into the air when he saw Itchy. The goundsman was still clutching the menacing blunt instrument with which he had been offering encouragement to the large piece of machinery in the middle of the cricket pitch.

Unshaven, wild eyed and with his toupee balanced precariously on the back of his head Itchy looked as though he was made up to appear in a horror movie. He was covered in oil stains and grass cuttings and his clothing would have been regarded as quite unsuitable for resale by even the most desperate of jumble sale stall holders.

'What?' demanded Puffy, peering through a six inch gap.

'It's me, Itchy,' said Itchy. 'Can I borrow your lawnmower, Puffy? And your extension lead?'

Puffy growled something which Itchy obviously took to be a 'yes' for the wild eyed groundsman muttered a quick 'thank you' before scurrying off back down the corridor towards the back door and, presumably, the garden shed where Puffy kept his lawnmower.

Biffo, abandoning the idea of breakfast, headed for the exit. On his way out he banged his head on the top of the door frame. After rubbing it for a moment or two he tottered delicately over to the bar and hunted around underneath the counter. When he found the slate upon which Lettice had been keeping score he rubbed out the figure seven and replaced it with a figure eight. He then headed back to the door, ducked, carefully watched his feet to make sure that he didn't trip, and miraculously left The Gravedigger's Rest without more incident or injury. The front door, like the back door through which Itchy had entered and departed, was not locked.

~ Chapter 24 ~

WHEN A STILL HUNGRY BIFFO arrived at the village shop there was a new addition to the collection of ephemera lined up outside that emporium. Leaning against a tree was an extremely elderly black sit-up-and-beg bicycle which had obviously seen rather better days. A large metal pannier was attached to the front of the bicycle and this had been filled to the brim and way beyond with groceries, fruits, vegetables and other goods from the shop.

Biffo examined the unstable-looking delivery vehicle with some trepidation. He couldn't help wondering whether having such a large pannier attached to the front of the bicycle would affect its handling. He rather wished he had an opportunity to test drive the vehicle in its pre-loaded state. He took his trouser clips out of his pocket and put them into position. It was the first time he had had to wear special equipment for work and it made him feel very professional.

Abandoning his gloomy examination of the well-loaded bicycle he stepped gingerly between the two wicker baskets in the shop doorway and leant forwards slightly. 'Hello! I'm here!' he yelled into the darkness on the other side of the open door.

'I can see that,' said Miss Box, from no more than a couple of feet away. 'I'm not blind and I'm not deaf.'

A startled Biffo jumped backwards, stumbled against the wicker basket full of kindling, and fell over. 'I'm sorry,' he said, from his position on the ground. 'I couldn't see you.' He scrambled to his feet with as much agility as could be expected of a man of his age, brushed the dust from his trousers and started to pick up miscellaneous bits of kindling and put them back into the wicker basket.

'I've loaded up the bicycle,' said the shopkeeper, stepping out from the shadows. 'The first delivery is for Mrs Kennedy at Porterhouse Farm.'

'Right!' said Biffo, trying to sound more enthusiastic than he felt. He kept trying to forget that it had been a long time since he had ridden a bicycle. He wondered if the machine had gears. Looking at it he wondered if it had brakes. And he was hungry. 'Where is Porterhouse Farm?'

'Go down to the church, take the first left, ride for fifteen minutes or so, ignore the lane on the left and then turn right,' said Miss Box, snapping out the instructions without hesitation. 'If you see a whitewashed cottage with a thatched roof on your right you've gone too far. Go past the cottage where Cyril Player was born and about five minutes further on you'll see a small, bumpy farm track on your left. Take it. But watch out – it's easy to miss the turning. Porterhouse Farm is twenty minutes or so down that track. You'll have to take care down the track because of the potholes. I don't want those tomatoes getting bruised.'

'Do you mind if I write all that down?' asked Biffo, already not quite sure which turnings to take and which to avoid.

It occurred to him that in order to follow these instructions he would need to know how fast Miss Box would cycle.

The shopkeeper began impatiently to repeat what she had just said.

'Er, excuse me,' said Biffo, diffidently interrupting his new employer. 'Do you have a pencil I could use to make some notes?'

'With or without a rubber on the end?'

'I don't mind,' said Biffo.

'The ones without a rubber on the end are ten pence each. The ones with a rubber on the end are twelve pence.'

'Oh,' said Biffo. 'I don't suppose you've got a little stub of pencil I could borrow?' he asked.

Miss Box looked at him sharply.

'Of course not. I'm sorry.' Biffo apologised. 'I'll have one with a rubber on the end,' he said, recklessly.

'I can let you have a dozen for a guinea,' said Miss Box, already out of sight.

Biffo tried to remember what a guinea was and whether this was a good offer.

'Do you want a notebook?' called Miss Box, already somewhere deep inside the shop.

'Yes, please,' said Biffo. 'I suppose so.' He thought for a moment and was about to ask the shopkeeper if she had any old, unwanted, used envelopes he could use for scribbling maps and messages. But when he remembered the look he had received when he had enquired about pencil stubs he thought better about this and kept quiet. 'Just one pencil will do, thank you,' he said.

'Lined or unlined? Hard or soft cover? Small, medium or large?'

'Soft. Unlined,' said Biffo, reasoning that these choices would minimise his expenditure. He was beginning to worry that his expenses might exceed his profits.

'Good morning Miss Box!' cried a now familiar voice.

Biffo turned and saw Roderick Hedrubb standing outside the shop. Itchy was holding several electrical extension cables looped over his arm.

Mrs Box looked up and raised a solitary eyebrow. 'Good morning, Itchy!' she said. 'What do you want?'

'Do you have an electrical extension cable I could borrow?' asked Itchy.

Mrs Box sighed.

'I'll bring it back!' promised Itchy.

Muttering to herself Miss Box turned and disappeared back into the darkness inside the shop.

'Are you collecting them?' asked Biffo.

Itchy frowned. 'Collecting what?'

'Extension leads,' said Biffo, pointing to the leads looped over Itchy's arm. 'You seem to have quite a few already.'

'Here you are,' said Mrs Box, emerging from the darkness and holding out an extension lead which Itchy took from her. 'A shilling an hour.'

'It's for the cricket club,' protested Itchy.

Miss Box snorted. 'All right then,' she said. 'But mind you bring it back in good condition. I don't want you wearing it out by putting too much electricity through it.'

'I'll bring it back!' promised Itchy, trudging off down the lane.

'Before Christmas!' called Mrs Box after him.

Itchy half turned and waved his free hand.

'Hrmph,' said Mrs Box. 'Small, medium or large?'

Biffo was still wondering what Itchy was planning to do with so many extension leads.

'Small, medium or large?' repeated Mrs Box.

'I beg your pardon?' said Biffo. 'I'm sorry. I wasn't concentrating. Were you talking to me?'

Mrs Box looked around. 'There isn't anyone else here, is there?'

'Er, no.'

'So, do you want small, medium or large?'

Biffo had no idea what Miss Box was talking about. 'Er, small, medium or large what?'

Miss Box sighed. 'Notebook,' she said, impatiently.

'Small, please,' said Biffo. 'Something I can fit into my pocket.'

'That will be 30 pence,' said the shopkeeper. She disappeared into the shop. 'Do you want to pay cash?' she said when she reappeared. 'Or shall I put the 42 pence against your wages?' She handed a pencil and a notebook to Biffo.

'Put it against my wages, please,' said Biffo. 'But could I have a receipt for the pencil, the notebook and the trouser clips?'

Miss Box looked at him and raised an enquiring eyebrow.

'For my accountant,' explained Biffo. 'They're all deductible expenses.'

The shopkeeper snorted, ignored this and looked at her watch. 'I suggest you get on your bike,' she said. 'Your employment officially started two minutes ago and since I'm paying you by the hour I don't intend to stand around here paying you to chit chat.'

~ Chapter 25 ~

BIFFO CYCLED FOR HOURS AROUND the village of Fondling-Under-Water and its immediate environs.

He delivered a box of assorted groceries to a cheerful, bosomy farmer's wife with bright red hair and a snorty laugh that could be heard half a mile away; a monthly magazine and a pound of butter to a doctor's widow and a bottle of pickled gherkins and a packet of runner bean seeds to a stout, red-faced retired colonel who had gout, two large, dribbling bulldogs and a thin sister. He met Itchy, also travelling by bicycle, as he came away from the bosomy farmer's wife and the doctor's widow. He had, on both occasions, obviously added more extension leads to his growing collection.

He delivered two rolls of lavatory paper and a packet of prunes to the vicar and a freshly dry-cleaned winter coat to a retired schoolmistress with flirty eyes who invited him in for a glass of elderberry wine and seemed extremely disappointed when he politely declined on the grounds that the wine might affect his ability to handle the bicycle safely. He delivered a packet of pipe tobacco to a young mother-to-be who was expecting a box of disposable nappies and a box of disposable nappies to a retired bank manager who had nothing to put in his pipe and was not amused by the error.

Miss Box had an old-fashioned policy of doing anything to please her customers and so on one occasion Biffo cycled four miles to deliver a box of matches to a cottage in the middle of a forest. And after he had cycled two and a half miles to deliver a bag of flour to half of a pair of semi-detached cottages Miss Box sent him straight back to the owner of the adjoining property who had, in Biffo' absence, telephoned with an urgent order for a bag of sugar and a ball of string.

Biffo got chased by dogs on four separate occasions and completely lost six times. He fell off the bicycle twice. One of these incidents required a large sticking plaster (anticipating future disasters of a similar nature Biffo bought an economy-sized packet of sticking plasters from Miss Box for 98 pence).

At noon an extremely weary and ravenous Biffo purchased from Miss Box a small loaf of bread (70 pence), a large slice of cheddar cheese (£1.20), an apple (32 pence) and a bottle of beer (£1.50) and with the aid of his faithful old pocket knife he turned these simple ingredients into a picnic lunch which he ate, while sitting on a hand-carved, genuine rustic garden bench (£79.99 to buy but Biffo only sat on it) with much pleasure and four pickled onions (84 pence).

After he had finished one of the cheapest but tastiest and most satisfying meals he had ever eaten Biffo decided to take a short walk around the village to stretch his sore legs.

Attracted by the high, persistent whine of something that sounded like an strained electric motor Biffo walked around the side of The Gravedigger's Rest and leant over the gate. He then found out why Itchy had been so keen to corner the local market in electrical extension leads.

Itchy, who was using Puffy's tiny garden-sized lawnmower, to cut the several acres of grass on the Fondling-Under-Water cricket field, had connected dozens of electrical extension leads together so that he could plug the mowing machine into a socket in his own kitchen.

Biffo watched Itchy and the lawnmower for a few minutes. Even from beyond the boundary's edge Biffo could see small puffs of white smoke coming from the tiny engine. There was a distinct and pungent smell of burning in the air.

~ Chapter 26 ~

AT SEVEN FIFTEEN THAT EVENING an exhausted Biffo arrived back at the shop to discover, to his absolute relief, that the shopkeeper had already started moving her display of fruits and vegetables and other objects back into the safety of the shop for the night (not, she assured him, because of any fear of human burglars or vandals – for such monstrous behaviour was not known in the quiet village of Fondling-Under-Water – but to ensure that her goods were not drowned by a sudden burst of rain or eaten by foxes, mice, rabbits and other rural marauders).

Wearily, Biffo clambered off the bicycle and stood rubbing those delicate parts of his body which had suffered most. He watched as the shopkeeper wheeled the bicycle into an open shed at the side of the shop where, with some considerable difficulty, she eventually managed to lay it to rest for the night in a very narrow gap between an enormous pile of empty wooden apple boxes and an equally enormous pile of bags containing garden fertiliser and potting compost.

'Well at least you won't be wanting tomorrow afternoon off for the cricket,' said the shopkeeper as she turned from her labour and stood, breathing rather heavily, hands on hips, in front of the shed.

'Well actually,' began Biffo, 'I'm afraid I did say...'

'Oh, don't tell me they've roped you into their damned silly games already!' said the shopkeeper, rolling her eyes to the heavens.

'I'm afraid so,' admitted Biffo.

'Well just you make sure you're here bright and early in the morning,' said the shopkeeper. 'Six thirty,' she said, nodding to Biffo, picking up the wicker basket containing bundles of kindling, and disappearing into the dark interior of the village shop.

'Goodnight Miss Box!' called Biffo to the disappearing shopkeeper.

'Hrmph!' was all that came out of the shop.

It wasn't far from the village shop to the pub but it took Biffo all the effort he could muster to walk that short journey. After a day of unaccustomed exercise on an elderly bicycle his muscles seemed to have gone on strike. Biffo just hoped that all this pedalling would not stop him being able to perform satisfactorily at the cricket match the following day.

~ Chapter 27 ~

IT WAS ONLY WHEN HE had taken a bath that Biffo remembered (much to his annoyance) that he didn't have any clean clothes to wear.

The shirt, socks and underwear which he had worn that day he had washed with him as he had lain in the bath, and these were now draped over the window-sill drying very slowly in what remained of the day's sunshine.

Biffo began to think that perhaps his cavalier decision to start his life completely afresh might be just a tad foolish. After all he had plenty of clothes hanging in the wardrobe he had so recently agreed to hand over to his wife. He decided to swallow his pride and ring home.

Edwina answered the telephone with her usual polite formal greeting, giving the caller her name, followed by the telephone number in its entirety.

'Hello,' said Biffo, when Edwina had finished.

There was a moment's silence and then Biffo heard some muffled talking at the other end of the line. It sounded as though Edwina had put her hand over the telephone and was talking to someone.

'Well!' said Edwina eventually. 'And what do you want?'

'Are you all OK?' asked Biffo.

'We're all very well,' said Edwina. There was the sort of pause which could most accurately be described as pregnant. 'I was hoping you would ring,' she said.

'You were?' said Biffo, rather surprised and a little nonplussed. A frisson of alarm spread through his body.

'Damien wants to speak to you.'

'Damien?'

'Damien Washbrook. My lawyer.'

'Oh yes,' said Biffo, remembering. 'The suntanned blond.'

'He's my lawyer,' said Edwina sniffily.

There was a little fumbling and some whispering and then another voice came onto the line.

'Mr Brimstone?' said the new voice. It was a very plummy, public school voice.

Biffo confirmed his identity.

'My name is Damien Washbrook,' said the new voice. 'I am Mrs Brimstone's legal representative in this matter. Do you have legal representation of your own?' the voice asked.

'No,' said Biffo. 'I don't know any lawyers and to be frank with you I'd like to keep things that way for as long as possible.'

'I must recommend to you, entirely without prejudice of course, that you seek legal representation at the earliest available opportunity,' said the plummy voice.

'What do I need a lawyer for?' asked Biffo. 'I've already agreed to give my wife everything I've got. She can't have any more than everything.'

'If you were to have taken professional legal advice I am sure that your advisor would have warned you that the observation you have just made is not strictly accurate,' said the plummy voice. 'Mrs Brimstone is entitled to ask the court to give her a percentage of your future earnings.'

'I told my wife she could have everything I've got,' said Biffo, who was still trying to unravel the plummy voice's previous sentence which seemed far enough removed from the English language to be of legal significance. 'I didn't know she was going to want more than everything.'

'When your wife becomes your ex-wife she may be entitled to a portion of your earnings,' said the plummy voice. 'Am I correct in believing that your previous employment was terminated yesterday by yourself?'

'Spot on,' agreed Biffo.

'And have you obtained a fresh position since the cessation of your previous employment?'

'I have,' said Biffo, rather proudly.

'Aha!' said the plummy voice. There was a silence again while the plummy voice and Edwina discussed this unexpected, and to them potentially profitable, development.

'Er, in what capacity are you now employed?' asked the plummy voice.

'I'm in transport,' said Biffo, proudly.

'Ah. Transport?' said the plummy voice, clearly overcome with visions of large tankers, cargo aeroplanes and fleets of lorries.

'Deliveries, to be precise,' said Biffo.

'Ah. Deliveries. And that would be delivering what exactly?'

'All sorts of things,' said Biffo. 'Apples, carrots, toilet rolls, string, mousetraps.'

'A wide variety of goods are transported?'

'Oh yes.'

There was a pause while the brain connected to the plummy voice digested this information and instructed the hand to take notes. 'And are you employed in an executive capacity?'

'I don't think you could really describe it as being an executive position,' admitted Biffo. It was his turn to pause. 'I ride a delivery bicycle for the local village shop.'

'I'm sorry,' said the lawyer, pausing and laughing rather nervously. 'I thought I heard you say you ride a delivery bicycle?' He laughed again though it wasn't the sort of laugh that would have cheered a comedian.

'That's it. I ride a delivery bicycle.'

'You sit on an ordinary, old-fashioned bicycle with one of those little baskets at the front?' The lawyer was clearly still finding this concept difficult to understand.

'Yes. It's a very old-fashioned bicycle actually. I don't think the manufacturers of the bicycle had quite got the hang of what brakes are supposed to do when they made this model. Maybe they got on top of things with a later model. The front brake on the one I'm using seems to work quite well sometimes – though it is difficult to know in advance when it is going to be working well and when it is not going to be working at all – but the back brake doesn't ever work. I was riding back from a delivery late this morning and neither brake worked as I came down Primrose Hill. I don't suppose you know Primrose Hill, in fact I didn't know it myself until this morning, but its very steep and there's a really nasty left hander at the bottom...' Biffo was enjoying teasing Damien.

The solicitor didn't seem terribly keen on hearing any more about Biffo's brake problem. 'And you deliver groceries to customers?' he interrupted.

'That's right!" said Biffo.

'And this isn't part of, how shall I put it, a publicity stunt of some kind?'

'Oh no. Not at all.'

This was a cue for another silence and this time the muffled mumblings and mutterings went on for much longer and seemed much more desperate.

'I understand from Mrs Brimstone that you have agreed to an immediate separation, a divorce as soon as possible and a settlement of all chattels and effects exclusively in Mrs Brimstone's favour?' said the plummy voice.

'Yes!' said Biffo.

'We need to see you in order to get some documents signed and witnessed,' said the plummy voice. 'Where are you staying at the moment?'

'The Gravedigger's Rest,' replied Biffo.

'And what exactly is The Gravedigger's Rest?' demanded the plummy voice. 'Is it some sort of an hotel?' The voice was now thickly laced with undisguised contempt.

'It's a pub,' said Biffo.

'I see,' said the plummy voice. There was a pause. 'A public house?'

'That's right. But I've always thought that calling a place a pub makes it sound much friendlier and more fun than calling it a public house. Big cities have public houses on corners and people go there to get drunk and fight. Villages have pubs and people go there to....'

The plummy voice turned away from the telephone but this time the owner of the plummy voice forgot to put his hand over the telephone receiver. Although the voices coming through the earpiece were faint Biffo could just about hear them.

'He's staying in some sort of public house,' said the plummy voice.

'He's clearly gone potty,' said Edwina, sounding worried. Biffo was quite touched. 'I just hope no one I know finds out.' Biffo was strangely relieved to discover that Edwina hadn't changed.

'I really do think we should get down there as soon as we can,' said the plummy voice. 'We need to get him to sign these documents before he changes his mind and decides he wants a more equitable share of the community property.'

'Ask him where he is,' said Edwina. 'Better still get him to come back here and sign the forms.'

There was a scrambling noise as the telephone receiver was dragged across the surface upon which it had been lain.

'Whereabouts exactly are you?' demanded Damien, picking up the telephone again.

Biffo told him.

'It would obviously be in your best interests if you signed the separation agreement fairly quickly,' said Damien. 'I think I can persuade Mrs Brimstone to agree to that. I could draw up the appropriate documents on behalf of you both.'

'Gosh!' said Biffo. 'That's very good of you.'

'Let's fix up an appointment for tomorrow. Shall we say in my office?'

'I'm afraid that won't be possible,' said Biffo. 'Not tomorrow. I've agreed to play in a cricket match and I've got a lot of deliveries to make in the morning.'

'A cricket match?' said the plummy voice, as though Biffo had announced that he intended to take part in a shark wrestling contest.

'That's right.'

There was another pause. And then Edwina came on the telephone. 'You don't play cricket!' she said, rather indignantly.

'I do tomorrow,' said Biffo.

Edwina sucked in about forty litres of air and blew it out again very quickly. 'We're doing this for you,' she said. 'Damien is a very busy man.'

'I'm sorry,' said Biffo. 'But I really can't get up there tomorrow. I have to do the deliveries in the morning and then there's a cricket match in the afternoon.'

'Well, if you're going to be difficult then I suppose we'll have to come down there,' Edwina said. 'Where on earth are you anyway?'

Biffo started to explain but Edwina, bored by the instructions, had handed the telephone to her lawyer and paramour and so Biffo gave the plummy voice the name of the village and agreed to meet them at The Gravedigger's Rest at one o'clock.

'Will the chef do us a little luncheon there?' asked the plummy voice.

'I think they may be able to manage a snack,' said Biffo, cautiously. 'Tomatoes on toast is something of a local speciality. And you can always stay on and watch the cricket.'

There was a pause. 'I don't think we'll bother with luncheon,' said the plummy voice. 'Or the cricket. We'll see you tomorrow.'

'Oh, there is one thing,' said Biffo, before the plummy voice rang off. 'Do you think you could bring some of my clothes with you? I came away with hardly anything and having something of a cash flow problem I don't have the wherewithal to buy any spare stuff. That's what I called about actually.'

'I'll put you onto Edwina,' said the plummy voice.

Biffo repeated his request.

'Oh, I gave all your clothes to Oxfam,' said Edwina. 'Toby filled the car and took them down there yesterday afternoon.'

'But...yesterday afternoon?' said Biffo. He would have been shocked if he hadn't known Edwina better. 'I only left yesterday!' It seemed a lot longer than that.

'I didn't want the children to be disturbed by seeing your stuff about the place,' said Edwina. 'Besides you took a suitcase full of clothes with you.'

'There wasn't anything I could wear in there,' said Biffo. 'I wasn't thinking very clearly when I packed.'

'I'll have the suitcase back,' said Edwina. 'It was a Louis Vuitton.'

'Er, I'm afraid I sold the suitcase,' admitted Biffo. 'Together with everything that was in it.'

'You sold it?'

'Yes.'

'The suitcase?'

'Yes.'

'How much did you get for it?'

'Twenty pounds.'

'Twenty pounds! It cost more than twenty times that much!'

'I know,' admitted Biffo, guiltily. 'I don't seem to be as hot at negotiating as I thought I used to be.'

Edwina did the thing with forty litres of air again.

'Well, don't forget to give me the £20 tomorrow,' she said.

'You want the £20?'

'You did agree, did you not, that I would have all the property that we owned prior to your leaving me.'

Biffo sighed. 'Yes. I did.'

'That's what I thought.' said Edwina. 'We'll see you tomorrow and you can give me the £20. Oh, by the way, there's a letter for you. It looks boring so I haven't opened it. I'll bring it with me.'

~ Chapter 28 ~

AFTER HIS DISTURBING CONVERSATION WITH his wife and her plummy solicitor Biffo sat in his room and cuddled Tiger.

'There are some people it is very easy to loathe,' he said.

Tiger purred, as was her wont on these occasions and stretched out a leg.

After half an hour Biffo felt much better, as he always did. He had long been convinced that if more people lived with cats depression would be a much rarer disease. He always found it difficult to stay gloomy after chatting to Tiger about his problems. Tiger always seemed to understand.

When he had fed Tiger he clambered stiffly down the stairs to the bar. Puffy Harbottle and most of the village cricket team were gathered at one end of the bar having what looked like a serious discussion about something or other. Since it was serious it was probably about cricket. Biffo started to sit down on a stool at the empty end of the bar but changed his mind and, instead, just leant on the bar. He was wearing very damp clothes which felt rather uncomfortable even when he was standing. He thought they would feel even worse if he sat down. Besides, after a day on a bicycle the attractions of sitting down seemed slight.

'How do you like working for Miss Box?' asked Lettice, who was leisurely washing a glass in the small sink underneath the bar counter.

'It's pretty hard work!' said Biffo, rubbing his back and grimacing. 'The countryside round here looked pretty flat when I arrived on the bus. It seems to have suddenly got a lot hillier.' He paused. 'And I don't think I'll ever find my way around.'

'Oh you will,' said Lettice, reassuringly. 'When I first worked here a customer ordered a pint and a half of lager. I spent twenty minutes looking for a glass big enough to take a pint and a half.'

'You didn't!'

'I did. I notice you're not sitting down.'

'I prefer to stand,' said Biffo, wryly. 'Still, the job has its good points. I reckon I could win the Tour de France next year.'

Lettice laughed. 'Not really your cup of tea, then?'

'I'm not entirely sure that I'd choose to spend the rest of my life riding a delivery bicycle,' admitted Biffo ruefully. 'But for the time being it fills the bill very nicely. Fresh air, plenty of exercise, beautiful countryside and Miss Box doesn't make me read daily mottoes.'

'Daily mottoes?' smiled Lettice, puzzled.

'My last employer was a great believer in daily mottoes,' answered Biffo, very seriously. 'He apparently hired someone to write them.'

'Who was that?'

'The chap who wrote the mottoes?'

'No. Your last employer.' Lettice rinsed a glass under the cold tap.

'A television company,' replied Biffo. 'Better Television.'

'What did you do for them?'

'I was a producer.'

'Good heavens!' said Lettice. 'I am impressed!' She shook

the excess water from the glass and then picked up a tea towel from the radiator behind her. The radiator didn't work, and never had because Puffy had run out of money long before the planned central heating installation had been completed. But it made a convenient towel rail.

'You shouldn't be impressed,' said Biffo. 'It was a terrible company – well I suppose it still is, I don't expect it has miraculously improved just because I left. And working in television really isn't very glamorous, you know. Most of the time it's about as exciting as accountancy. Come to think of it most of the time there isn't a lot of difference between being a television producer and being an accountant.'

'Were the mottoes the last straw?' asked Lettice. 'There's usually a last straw, isn't there.' She had finished drying the glass and she paused and half turned to put it away on the shelf behind her. 'Or shouldn't I ask?'

Biffo thought for a moment. 'It wasn't the mottoes,' he said. He thought again. 'I didn't like my life very much. I had become everything I hated when I was 18. I'm still not sure how it happened but I know I'm lucky to have a second chance,' he said. 'If there was a last straw it was when they told me they wanted me to produce a quiz programme.'

Biffo thought again about the years he had spent at Better Television. 'Actually, I never really liked working in television very much,' he confessed. 'I only really got into it because they paid me obscenely well and my wife rather liked money. Well, still does to be accurate.'

'Where is your wife? Is she joining you here?'

'Good heavens, no!' said Biffo. He shuddered at the thought. 'Well, oddly enough, come to think of it she is,' he corrected himself. 'She'll be here tomorrow at lunchtime. She's coming down with her lawyer, though to be honest I have it on good authority that they are a little closer than is usually considered appropriate for lawyer and client. But I don't expect they'll be here for long. I'm afraid I don't think they like tinned tomatoes. They'd be a little more comfortable with something disgusting done with quails' eggs, frog's legs, Californian spinach and Peruvian sun-dried tomatoes. My wife is one of those people who doesn't value food for its nutritional qualities or its taste but for its appearance. Given the choice of eating healthy, cheap food that tasted good but looked horrible and expensive food that tasted horrible but looked good she would take the latter every time.'

'And what's wrong with my tinned tomatoes?' asked Lettice, feigning indignation. 'There's a lot of skill involved in plopping heated up tomatoes onto two pieces of toast.'

'There is absolutely nothing wrong with your tinned tomatoes,' replied Biffo. 'In fact, if they're still on the menu I'd like to put in an order for them for this evening.'

'We've got plenty of bread and tons of tomatoes,' said Lettice.

Biffo looked around the bar. 'I must say I do like it here,' he said. 'It seems like a good place to restart my life.'

'Is that what you want to do?'

'What?'

'Restart your life?'

'Yes,' said Biffo, without hesitation. 'I suppose it sounds a bit dramatic. But my last life was such a disaster that I really feel that starting again is the only option.'

'And what exactly do you want to do with your second life?' Lettice smiled.

Biffo looked at her quizzically. 'You seem to be assuming that I don't want to ride a delivery bicycle for Miss Box for the rest of my days?'

'I'm assuming that you don't want to ride a delivery bicycle for Miss Box for the rest of your days,' confirmed Lettice. 'Besides I suspect you might find that Franklin Minton will want his old job back when he recovers.'

Biffo picked up a beer-mat and played with it for a moment. 'You won't laugh?'

'Not if it's your dream I won't. I never laugh at people's dreams.'

Biffo carefully positioned the beer-mat on the bar counter so that a third of it was projecting out into the air. He then used his fingers to flick it up into the air so that it performed half a somersault. He caught the beer-mat in his hand before it fell. He then took a deep breath. 'I'd really like to find a cute little cottage in the middle of nowhere – thatched roof, roses and honeysuckle round the door, log fire in a stone hearth, you know the sort of thing. Somewhere cosy and comfortable where Tiger and I can settle down. The snag is I don't have any money so the idyllic little cottage is going to remain pretty much a dream.'

'I thought you said you worked in television because it paid well.'

'I did. But my wife was very good at spending money. She had several diplomas in shopping.'

'And she managed to spend everything you earned?'

'Not all of it, no. There's the house, of course. Furniture, cars and some money in the building society. But I've agreed to give her the house and everything we owned when I left.'

'That was very generous of you.'

Biffo shrugged. 'I didn't want a long drawn out argument. I just want to get on with my new life.'

'You could always rent a cottage,' said Lettice.

'I hadn't thought of renting. I was brought up to think that renting wasn't a good financial move.'

'If you can't afford to buy somewhere it's a pretty damned sensible financial move.'

'Yes. I suppose it is. Are there any cottages to rent around here?'

'Oh yes. In fact I can show you particulars for two or three if you're really interested. Rents aren't very high. Not many holiday-makers come here and it's always the holiday-makers who push up the rental prices. Even with what Miss Box pays you should be able to afford something.'

'You're the first barmaid I've ever come across who has a sideline in cottage rentals.'

'It's really the other way around,' said Lettice. 'My real job is as an estate agent. Or at least it was until I moved in here temporarily to help my uncle in the pub when my aunt left.'

'You're really an estate agent?'

'Sort of. I still do a little part-time work for one.'

'You don't look like an estate agent.'

'What do estate agents look like?'

'I suppose I mean you don't seem like an estate agent,' said Biffo, pedalling backwards.

'What do estate agents seem like?' asked Lettice, slightly raising one eyebrow.

'I don't know...' mumbled Biffo. He felt himself blushing. 'I suppose...because you're, well...you seem honest.' It wasn't what he wanted to say. But it was what came out.

'We're very good at pretending to be honest,' said Lettice, teasing him. 'We take courses in it.' She disappeared for a moment and returned clutching half a dozen brochures.

'Have a look at these, if you like,' she said, handing the brochures to Biffo. 'It will give you an idea of what's on the market.' She turned away again.

'Have you got to go?' asked Biffo, spreading the brochures out on the bar counter.

'I have to get to work in the kitchen,' called Lettice, who had disappeared and could be heard opening cupboards and drawers. 'I seem to remember being given an order for tomatoes on toast.'

~ Chapter 29 ~

BILL STICKERS HAD NOT HAD a good night. He had done a lot of tossing and quite a lot of turning but not a great deal of sleeping.

He had given up trying to sleep at six that morning and had got up and made himself a cup of tea. He had very much enjoyed being rich and he didn't think he was going to like being poor.

He didn't understand what had happened and how the bank had managed to lose all his money (his name had been on the lottery ticket and he always thought of it as 'his' money rather than 'their' money) but he also had a strong suspicion that there wasn't going to be anything he could do about it.

Bill sat, in his Jermyn Street pyjamas and his Jermyn Street dressing gown, and sipped at his Earl Grey tea and, through the double-glazed kitchen window, watched the sun come up over his neatly-manicured one acre of garden, well-kept five acres of mixed woodland and four and a half acres of paddock.

The house in which he and Pansy lived had, back in the days when vicars had been important and wealthy members of all rural communities, been the Fondling-Under-Water vicarage. The 'exquisite, beautifully proportioned Georgian building' had, according to the estate agents, been 'restored sympathetically and comprehensively equipped with an impressive range of modern facilities'.

Acting on his new bank's advice Bill had purchased the house with a loan. Although he had what he thought was quite a lot of money sitting in his account the bank had successfully managed to persuade him to borrow a lot more money. These additional funds naturally came from them but they had assured him that there were lots of mysterious tax advantages to be gained by borrowing money. The smart (in all senses of the word), exceptionally well-dressed men from the bank had used words like 'leverage' and 'gearing' and although Bill hadn't had the foggiest idea what they had been talking about he had nodded wisely because he had been far too embarrassed to admit just how ignorant he really was.

The early morning went slowly but, as mornings usually do if you leave them alone to get on with it, it eventually went. And at one minute past nine o'clock Bill made a telephone call to his bank.

'What's this fax all about?' he asked, when he finally got put through to an anonymous bank employee.

'Which fax is that?' asked the anonymous man in a suit.

Bill read out the contents of the communication he had received.

'Yes, that seems to be correct, Mr Stickers,' said the bank employee.

'You've lost my money?'

'Well, the bank hasn't lost your money, Mr Stickers,' said the man at the bank. 'There has, to put it quite simply, been a global down turn in the economy and your portfolio has consequently suffered a downward re-appreciation.'

'A downward re-appreciation?'

'Er, that means that financially speaking your portfolio is not worth as much as it was.'

'It isn't worth anything, is it?'

'Strictly speaking that is accurate, Mr Stickers.'

'You've lost all my money!'

'Oh no, Mr Stickers. We haven't lost your money. It is true that you gave the bank discretionary powers over your investments but we kept you fully informed of our plans. It is most unfortunate that the collapse in the Japanese electronics market, a deterioration in the value of the South African rand and an unforeseen alteration in the value of sterling all coincided with a rise in the value of the dollar.'

'Is there anything left?'

'I'm afraid not. That's why we sent you the fax.'

'What about my £300?'

'Which £300 would that be?'

'The £300 I started off with.'

'All your monies were incorporated in your portfolio.'

'You've lost that too?'

'The economic downturn seems to have affected your entire portfolio...'

'And my house? Do I still own that?'

There was a lengthy pause while the anonymous voice played with the keyboard in front of him.

'Your house is actually owned by one of your registered companies.'

'Oh, good!' said Bill, feeling a little brighter. For a moment or two he had feared that he had lost everything.

'But the company, which is registered in the Virgin Islands, is a wholly owned subsidiary of another company which you own and which is registered in Turks and Caicos.'

'Where?'

'Turks and Caicos. There are considerable tax advantages in having a company there, Mr Stickers.'

'And I have a company registered there?'

'Yes, Mr Stickers. You'll find all the details in your portfolio.'

'So I still own that company?'

'Oh, I'm afraid that's gone into liquidation, Mr Stickers.

It was unable to pay back the loan your associated company in Andorra had arranged with the Lithuanian branch of this bank.'

'So I don't own my own home?' The respite had been a short one. Bill wondered where he had put his hairdressing scissors.

'Indeed that is correct, Mr Stickers.'

'So we've lost our home?' said Bill, feeling extremely tired. 'Don't I own anything any more?' He wondered if the short back and sides was still a popular cut. The shaved head seemed to be popular in some quarters and he thought he could probably manage that fairly well.

There was another pause.

'Well there does seem to be one land transaction listed here,' said the anonymous banker. 'It's a very small value deal which you made shortly after joining us and which our investment people seem to have completely overlooked and failed to incorporate into your general portfolio.'

'Land?' said Bill. 'I don't remember any land. When did I buy land?'

'It's a modest plot of a few acres in a place called Fondling-Under Water,' said the banker. 'You seem to have made the purchase, much against the advice of our investment team I should point out, from someone called Lord Hepplewhite.'

'The cricket ground!' cried Bill. 'I still own the cricket ground.'

'It doesn't mention cricket here,' said the banker. He sighed. 'Anyway, that appears to be your only asset that the bank is aware of. Perhaps you can sell it and buy yourself a small property with the proceeds? According to our records the land has planning permission for residential building use.'

'Sell it?' said Bill, horrified. 'But that's the village cricket ground!'

'Well, it's your choice,' said the banker. 'But land which has planning permission always fetches a good price. Something of that sort of area should fetch...oh...£80,000. Perhaps more. I see there's a river nearby. Is it a pretty setting?'

'Yes, its very pretty.'

'Then you might be able to get £100,000 for it. If you

would like to invest that sum with us we would be happy to manage your investments.'

'No, thank you,' said Bill quickly. 'If I've got anything left I'll lose it myself. I can probably do it more slowly than you did.'

'I'll arrange for all your accounts with us to be closed,' said the banker. 'It's been a pleasure looking after you.' The telephone went dead and Bill automatically replaced the receiver. He felt as though he was in a dream.

'Is everything all right, dear?' asked Pansy, who had entered the room while Bill had been on the telephone.

'No,' said Bill.

'Oh dear. We've lost all our money haven't we?'

'Yes.'

Pansy felt strangely relieved by this piece of news. Now that they no longer had any money she no longer had to worry about becoming poor again.

'We've lost the house too,' said Bill. 'All we have left is the cricket field.'

'Well, that's nice, dear,' said Pansy, who knew how much Bill enjoyed being captain of the village cricket team.

'We'll have to sell it,' said Bill.

'Shall I get you some breakfast?' asked Pansy, beginning to bustle. She was at her happiest and best when preparing food. If she had been given a free choice about how to spend her life she would have chosen to spend it making sandwiches. She obtained enormous satisfaction out of turning loaves of bread, packs of butter, blocks of cheese and jars of pickle into sandwiches and was a vital member of the Fondling-Under-Water Cricket Club's tea making team. 'How many slices of toast would you like?' she asked when her husband failed to respond to her original question.

~ Chapter 30 ~

BILL STICKERS WASN'T THE ONLY person in the world whose day had started rather badly.

While Bill was nibbling his toast and trying (not very successfully) to persuade himself that he was hungry (and still wondering how his highly paid financial advisers had managed to lose over seven million pounds without any help from him) Damien Washbrook was convinced that he was having a heart attack.

Damien and Edwina were driving along in Damien's late model Mercedes when his mobile telephone rang. He answered it and immediately wished he hadn't. It was his brother George and he knew instantly that something had gone wrong.

'What's the matter?' Damien demanded. 'What's gone wrong?'

'How do you know something has gone wrong?' asked George.

'Because everything was going well. Things couldn't get any better could they?'

'No. I suppose not.'

'So if they couldn't get any better they could only get worse.'

'I suppose so,' said George. 'I must say that's pretty damned smart for a lawyer.'

'I wish you wouldn't do that!'

'Do what?'

'Keep on putting me down.'

'Only a joke Damien.'

'Yes, I know. But you do it when there are other people around. It makes me feel like a fool. People laugh at me.' He glanced at Edwina, sitting impassively in the passenger seat. She raised an eyebrow an eighth of an inch, but said nothing.

'Well you're a lawyer,' said George. 'You have a choice. You can either have people despise you or have them laugh at you. Personally I'd rather have people laugh at me.'

'Why can't I have people just plain like me?' demanded Damien.

'Because you're a lawyer,' said George. 'No one will ever like you.'

Damien sighed. He could never win with his brother. 'So, what has gone wrong?'

'Summerton has pulled out.'

'Pulled out?'
'Pulled out.'
'Just like that?'
'Just like that.'
'He can't.'
'He has.'
'But it's not fair!'
'No one ever said life was going to be fair,' said George. 'You should know that. You're a lawyer.'
'But it's so desperately, desperately unfair!' whined Damien. 'What are we going to do?' He sounded like a small and timid boy who has just hit a cricket ball through next door's greenhouse and who now needs his older brother to take charge. There was no cricket ball or greenhouse involved, and no glass had been broken, but George, Damien's older brother, was a property developer who always had deals bubbling in Europe, America and Asia. If all of his deals had been pies he would not have had enough fingers to keep one in each.
'We have to find another site,' said George. 'And we have to find it by next Monday.'
'Or what happens?'
'Unless you can find space for 87 prefabricated buildings in your back garden we've got just the teeniest weeniest bit of a problem,' said George. 'Basically, the whole deal goes sour and we're out a good deal of money.'
'Can't we get them to delay the delivery date?'
'No.'
'But if we explain to them what has happened...'
'...it won't make any difference at all.'
'I've put every penny I can raise into this deal,' said Damien, who had for years struggled with unrealistic delusions of adequacy. 'I know it doesn't matter much to you but to me this is a matter of life and death.'
'Don't exaggerate Damien.'
'I'm not exaggerating!'
'Yes, you are! You might lose all your money but you're not going to die.'
'I will probably have a heart attack!'

'Of course you won't. I'll sue you if you do,' said George. 'We'll be fine if we can just find another site. So look around. Talk to a few people.'

'Don't you know anyone who can help?'

'No,' said George. 'I've got to fly to New York. I'll be back on Sunday. Just make sure that you've found us a new site by then. Remember, the deal is that the buildings are erected on Monday'

'New York! You can't!'

'I have to,' said George. 'I'll be back on Sunday. Just make sure that you've found another site by then and everything will be absolutely fine.' Click.

'George?' cried Damien. But George had gone.

'What was all that about Damien?' asked Edwina. 'What's the matter?'

'How do you know something is the matter?'

'Because I heard your end of the conversation and half of your brother's end. And because you are bright red and dripping with sweat. And because you are panicking.'

'No I'm not.'

'Yes you are.'

'I don't panic.'

'Yes you do. You're doing it now.'

'I'm not! I'm not! It's just that there's a crisis.'

'What's happened?'

'It's...it's a business thing...'

'Well, are you going to tell me about it?

Damien didn't answer for a moment.

'Damien!' said Edwina sharply. 'What have you done?'

'I got involved in a deal with my brother...'

'Your brother is a crook!'

'He's not. He's very successful. He makes a lot of money.'

'So what's the problem then?'

'George bought some prefabs from a man he knows.'

'Prefabricated buildings? Are they still making those?'

'These are modern prefabs. Beautifully equipped. They make them for the army but they would make splendid holiday homes.'

'And you bought them with him?'

'Yes. Equal partners. He let me in as a favour.'

'Oh Damien! You are stupid sometimes. From what I've heard of him your brother doesn't do favours.'

'No, no! It's a great project.'

'How many prefabs did you buy?'

'Eighty seven.'

'Eighty seven! What are you doing? Starting your own city?'

'George got them for a very good price. The man we bought them from is going to erect them and everything.'

'Who is this man?'

'Some sort of middle man. I think he bought them from the government. It's all very honest and above board.' Damien paused to gesture at a cyclist who had dared to stray out of the gutter for a moment. 'George then did another deal with a man called Summerton.'

'This isn't the man who sold you the prefabs?'

'No.'

'And what is Summerton going to do?'

'He isn't going to do anything any more. He was going to sell us a piece of land on the coast.'

'And Summerton has changed his mind.'

'Yes.'

'Why?'

'I don't know.' Damien peered at a road sign.

'So what happens if you can't find anywhere? Can't you pull out of the deal to buy the prefabs? Just pay a forfeit or something?'

'This isn't a party game,' snapped Damien. 'We had to pay the money in advance to get the buildings at such a good price,' said Damien. 'It didn't seem a risk at the time,' he added lamely.

'I see,' said Edwina. 'So, to sum up, on Monday you take delivery of 87 prefabricated buildings but you don't have anywhere to put them.'

'That's about the size of it,' admitted Damien.

~ Chapter 31 ~

WHILE DAMIEN AND EDWINA WERE driving gloomily down to Fondling-Under-Water Biffo was riding Miss Box's bicycle around the narrow, twisting lanes of their destination. The sun was shining, the sky was blue and decorated with a few small, harmless fluffy white clouds, the birds were twittering their little hearts out as though auditioning for chorus parts in the latest West End musical, and as far as Biffo was concerned all was pretty much well with the world.

It is true that he was not looking forward to the arrival of his wife and her legally-qualified paramour but his feelings about this were more than counterbalanced by his excitement at the prospect of playing in his first cricket match for the best part of half a century.

It was shortly after delivering a new broom handle (Biffo quickly found that this was not the easiest item to carry on a bicycle), six red clay flower pots and a pair of pillow cases to a neat, semi-detached cottage occupied by a retired civil servant and his wife that Biffo jammed on his brakes, put both his feet on the ground and skidded, unsteadily, to a halt.

When Lettice had given him a fistful of house brochures the previous evening Biffo had flicked through the first half a dozen brochures without much interest or enthusiasm. None of them made his heart go zing. But the seventh and final brochure, for a property known as Buttercup Cottage, had captured both his interest and his enthusiasm and had set his heart zinging like a fire alarm.

Buttercup Cottage had been built in the late nineteenth century by a builder who knew exactly what a country cottage should look like. Unencumbered by fancy architects or petty-minded members of the local planning department, he had built a small, solid, simple stone cottage with leaded windows and a solid oak front door and had topped the whole thing off with a stone chimney and a red-tiled roof. He had painted the walls white. The front door was protected from the elements by a stone porch which contained two windows and two very solid slate seats. A crazy paving path connected the front porch to a white wooden gate positioned in the middle of a white wooden fence. A small, fast flowing stream separated the fence from the lane and a small slate bridge connected the lane to the crazy paving path. Behind the cottage there was a thirty acre wood, largely comprised of oak and chestnut trees and according to the agent's details a natural spring in the wood provided the cottage with a plentiful supply of fresh, pure, cold drinking water. The front windows of the cottage looked over fields, and since the cottage had been built on a slight rise, looked down upon The Gravedigger's Rest, the cricket field and the rest of the village of Fondling-Under-Water.

Biffo stared at Buttercup Cottage and, despite the peeling paint, the overgrown garden and the unhappy-looking roof (the loft had been used by squirrels as a playground for some years) it was, for him, undisputed love at first sight. It was the country cottage of his dreams. He leant his bicycle against the hedge on the other side of the road and stood, with his hands before him resting on the top of the creaky gate, and drooled.

After a while Biffo let out a huge sad sigh, turned, walked back over the bridge and climbed back onto his bicycle to continue his deliveries. There was, he knew, absolutely no way in which he could convert his dream into reality.

The asking price was by no means unreasonable. The former owner's beneficiaries, and the estate agents selling the cottage, were very much aware that the dilapidated appearance put it firmly into the 'cottage with potential for renovation' category rather than the considerably higher priced 'suitable for immediate occupation' category.

The monthly rental fee mentioned was not high. But Biffo was relying on his wages from Miss Box to pay his bill at The Gravedigger's Rest and he didn't think he would get a very positive response if he asked a bank manager to lend him money to buy a cottage on the basis of his job as delivery boy.

He could just imagine the conversation.
'And what is your annual income, Mr Brimstone?'
'I'm not sure.'
'You're not sure?'
'Miss Box hasn't told me yet.'

'I see. Well, the bank normally lends three times a home owner's annual salary. So, that would mean that we would be happy to lend you three times 'not sure'. Would that be all right?'

Biffo winced at the thought, climbed back onto his bicycle and pedalled off to deliver a brace of pheasant, a slice of Stilton cheese, a reel of pale blue cotton and a socket wrench to Major Gregory at the rather grandly named 'Windsor House'.

Thirty five minutes later, having returned his bicycle, complete with its now empty basket, to Miss Box's shop, Biffo strolled round to The Gravedigger's Rest. He strolled because it was the way of the village to stroll. No one hurried. But he also strolled because he didn't have much option. Biffo was becoming seriously concerned that he might have to spend the rest of his life sitting on a bicycle. After a morning spent delivering an enormous variety of items to an only slightly less extensive variety of homes within the apparently unending Fondling-Under-Water catchment area, Biffo had discovered that he could hardly walk. The muscles which enabled him to ride a bicycle were simply tired. The muscles which should have enabled him to walk seemed to have shrivelled up and died.

For his lunch he had purchased, and consumed, two bread rolls (46 pence), a large chunk of cheese (74 pence), an apple (32 pence) and a small bottle (99 pence) of lemonade. All these sums were to be taken from his end of the week wages and Biffo had a sneaking suspicion that at the rate he was going he could well end up owing Miss Box money. He wished he could summon up the courage to ask her what she was going to pay him.

As he approached The Gravedigger's Rest Biffo could see that a large, silver Mercedes was selfishly parked across the centre of the forecourt, blocking the whole area.

Biffo assumed, quite accurately, that Edwina and Damien had arrived.

~ Chapter 32 ~

'AH, BERNARD!' SAID EDWINA, CLIMBING out of Mercedes as she saw Biffo approaching. She was wearing a navy blue suit and a white blouse and carrying blue leather gloves and a capacious blue leather handbag. She wore navy blue shoes. 'We were rather expecting to see you arrive on your little bicycle. '

'I've returned it to the shop,' said Biffo. 'Have you been here long?'

'We've just arrived,' said Edwina. 'Is it black with one of those nice little baskets on the front?'

'What?'

'The bicycle?'

'It is black,' said Biffo. 'But the basket is quite a big one.'

'I have to confess that I didn't even know you could ride a bicycle,' said Edwina. 'How very clever of you. And I certainly never imagined that for all those years you had been harbouring a secret desire to ride a delivery bicycle.'

'It wasn't an ambition,' said Biffo. 'It was just the only job available.' He instantly felt cross with himself for explaining. He didn't owe this woman any explanations any more.

A tall, thin, suntanned, arrogant-looking man with a sneer fixed onto that part of his face where most people smile climbed out of the driver's side of the Mercedes. He opened the rear passenger door on his side and took a jacket from a wooden hanger. He put the jacket on and then reached into the car and removed an extremely expensive-looking brown leather briefcase. In recognition of the fact that he was coming to the country he was wearing a green and brown three piece tweed suit with a matching houndstooth cotton shirt and a green, knitted tie. His feet were shod in highly-polished brown brogues.

'Do you know Damien?' Edwina asked Biffo, regally waving half a set of immaculately-manicured fingernails in Damien's general direction.

'I think we may have met,' Biffo replied.

'Damien is my lawyer,' said Edwina.

'And slightly more than that I understand,' Biffo thought it appropriate to remind her.

'Perhaps,' agreed Edwina. She tried to smile but it didn't quite come out as a smile. Smiling wasn't Edwina's strong point. She hadn't had a lot of practice. Biffo felt the muscles around his head begin to tighten. He hoped he wasn't going to get one of his tension headaches. Not with the big match coming up.

'I want you two to be friends,' said Edwina. 'Shake hands,' she ordered them.

Damien walked around the car and walked across to where Biffo was standing. He held out a damp, limp hand which, to avoid any unpleasantness, Biffo took. He was instantly and unpleasantly reminded of the time when he had gone fishing with a friend and had held a rainbow trout while the friend disengaged the hook from the unfortunate fish's mouth. He shuddered and hoped the involuntary movement had not been noticeable.

'I have brought with me some documents which require your signature,' said Edwina's lawyer. He looked around and allowed his lip to curl a little further into a fully fledged sneer. 'Can we go somewhere a little more private?'

'I'm sure we will be able to find a corner in the bar,' said Biffo, heading towards the front door to The Gravedigger's Rest. 'Do you want something to eat?' he asked over his shoulder

'Here?' said Damien, so horrified that he actually stopped for a moment.

'No thank you, Bernard,' said Edwina, with studied politeness. 'I really don't think so.' She put on her gloves to protect her hands from any parts of the building with which she might be unable to avoid physical contact.

Biffo led the way into the public house. He remembered to duck and therefore avoided the beam and he remembered the step down just in time to correct his trip into the bar. Sadly, he forgot to warn the two who were following him of these twin unnatural hazards.

Edwina, was short enough to miss the beam but her lack of stature provided no protection against the step down into the bar. She tripped, half fell, almost recovered her balance and then crashed into one of the tables. Behind her there was a loud crack, followed by an equally loud curse, as Damien's skull and the entrance door beam fought for supremacy. Biffo was surprised and quite impressed by the extent of Damien's vocabulary but less surprised to see that the beam had come off best.

Holding his head, knees bent with the shock, Damien

had no chance with the step. He fell forward and crashed into Edwina. The two of them ended up stacked horizontally on the bar floor. Edwina flat on her face and Damien stretched out on top of her. Damien's partial denture (a souvenir of an unhappy incident involving a plumber and a disputed bill), being lighter but subjected to the same degree of force as had the mouth in which they normally resided, had accelerated faster than Damien, and lay on the floor several feet in front of them both.

'What on earth...?' demanded Lettice, rushing into the bar and looking alarmed.

'One more for the beam,' said Biffo. He pointed to the two figures on the floor. 'The woman in the blue suit is my wife,' he said. 'The man lying on top of her, in what could only be described as an entirely inappropriate position, is her solicitor.'

'Are you both all right?' asked Lettice. As she spoke she reached under the bar for the slate and chalk.

'We're hine, hank you!' said Damien, using his arms to lever himself up onto his knees. As soon as he heard himself speak he was well aware that he had been separated from his denture. Being well aware that an absence of teeth did nothing to enhance his appearance Damien immediately clasped a hand across the lower part of his face.

'I'm not!' snarled Edwina. Scrabbling around on the floor she pushed her bottom up into the air with such ferocity that Damien received a powerful blow in what can perhaps most appropriately be described an exceptionally delicate area. Groaning in agony he collapsed on top of her again, flattening her once more on the floor and squeezing all the air out of her lungs.

Biffo, trying hard to maintain a straight face, looked across at Lettice who was leaning forward over the bar and staring at the two people on the lounge floor in some astonishment.

'What the hell is going on?' demanded Puffy Harbottle, suddenly appearing as from nowhere. He looked over Lettice's shoulder and raised both eyebrows. 'Better throw a bucket of water over them,' he said to Lettice, before disappearing again.

'Get off me you stupid oaf!' said Edwina in a voice Biffo recognised very well.

'I was hying to het hoff you!' protested Damien, rolling

sideways off his client and mistress. He lay on his back, eyes closed, and breathing heavily. His lower face had a sort of, well, empty look.

'Damien?' said Lettice. 'Is that you Damien? What the hell are you doing here?'

The lawyer opened his eyes instantly and looked across to where the sound had come from.

'What on earth are you doing here?' Lettice repeated.

'Hettice!' said Damien, scrabbling to his feet, tidying his hair and straightening his tie.

'Damien, I want you to sue these people!' insisted Edwina, who, now that she was liberated, was struggling to her feet. 'My suit is ruined!' she cried.

'There's no point in suing Puffy,' said Lettice. 'He hasn't got any money.'

'Who the hell are you?' demanded Edwina, rudely.

'Lettice,' said Lettice. 'I'm the landlord's niece. And you'd be wasting your time if you sued him because he hasn't got any money.'

'He must have insurance,' said Edwina.

'I wouldn't bank on it,' said Lettice.

'Not having proper insurance is probably against the law!' said Edwina. 'I could sue him for that!'

'Is this your wife?' Lettice asked Biffo.

'Yes.'

'Golly,' said Lettice. 'You poor thing.'

'Do you hear, Damien?' demanded Edwina. 'I want them sued. This place is a death trap. I could have broken my neck.'

'And what is he doing here?' Lettice demanded, ignoring Edwina and pointing at Damien.

'I understand that he is here in something of a joint role,' explained Biffo. 'On the one hand he is acting as my wife's solicitor. On the other he is also her bit on the side.'

Lettice laughed out loud. 'He and your wife? An item?'

'Yes. What's so funny?' asked Biffo.

'That's my ex-husband!' said Lettice, pointing to Damien.

'Him?' said Biffo.

'Yes.'

'Damien!' said Edwina, looking around. 'Who is this...' she paused, as though searching for a more appropriate label, but eventually settled for the most obvious word '...woman?'

Damien opened and closed his mouth several times without anything at all coming out.

'I gather that Lettice is Damien's former wife,' said Biffo, trying to be helpful.

Edwina glared at Lettice. 'Is that really your name?'

Lettice smiled. 'Yes.'

Edwina glowered at Damien. 'You were married to a damned salad?'

Damien opened his mouth again. Once again the energy was wasted for no words escaped.

'I should pick those up before someone treads on them,' Biffo said to Damien, nodding towards the lonely looking dentures on the carpet.

'Aaarrrghh!' said Edwina, seeing Damien's denture for the first time and staring at it as though it had been a King Cobra about to strike.

Damien, awakened from his panic induced inability to speak or move, leapt across the room, grabbed his denture and thrust it into his mouth in one fluid movement.

'Damien!' said Edwina, pulling a face. 'Take those teeth out this minute. You didn't wash them!'

Obediently, Damien removed his teeth. He clearly didn't know what to do with them and so he pushed them into his jacket pocket.

'Not in your pocket, you fool!' said Edwina.

Damien took his teeth out of his pocket again.

'Is that woman your former wife?' demanded Edwina.

'Yeth.'

'Why wasn't I told about this woman?'

'I hold you I had been harried!' protested Damien.

'But you didn't tell me you had been married to this woman!' said Edwina, triumphantly.

'I hidn't hnow she wath here!' said Damien, desperately. He turned to Lettice. 'Ith there somewhere I han wash my heeth?' he asked.

161

'There's a wash-basin in the gents,' said Lettice. 'It's out in the passage.'

Damien didn't need telling twice. He made a beeline for the door, the passage, the wash-basin and safety.

'Mind the step...,' Lettice reminded him.

She was too late. Damien, hurrying, tripped.

'...and mind the beam!' added Lettice.

A moment later she reached under the counter for the slate. Outside in the corridor Damien seemed to be whimpering.

~ Chapter 33 ~

THREE QUARTERS OF AN HOUR later the documents Damien had brought with him had all been initialled, signed, countersigned and duly notarised.

Keen to start his new life unencumbered by memories of his old life Biffo had happily agreed to give Edwina everything the two of them had once owned together.

He signed documents giving her sole ownership of their house, their cars, their furniture and their savings accounts. In return Edwina signed documents to confirm that she would be responsible for all the bills relating to house, cars and so on and that she would have no claim over any of Biffo's income, earnings, winnings or acquisitions from the day when he left the marital home. With considerable glee she also signed a paper giving Biffo sole custody of Tiger the cat.

At the end of all the signing Biffo shook hands with Edwina and with Damien and Damien and Edwina kissed each other on the cheeks. Lettice served them all glasses of tonic water which was, she apologised rather ruefully, the nearest thing they had got to champagne.

'Miss Box has a very good selection of champagnes,' she told them. 'I'd have asked her to send a bottle round if I'd known.' She smiled. 'Miss Box has an excellent home delivery service.'

'I'm afraid we must be getting back,' said Edwina. 'Lots to do.' She put down her almost untouched glass of tonic water and stood up.

Damien responded immediately, emptying his glass and standing up.

'Before we go,' he said to Biffo. 'I wonder if I could just ask you a question?'

'You can ask. I may not be able to find an answer.'

'While I was in your lavatory I couldn't help noticing a large flat area of land just behind the public house,' said Damien. 'Pretty little spot. Seems to be right next to the river. Do you happen to know who owns it?'

'That's easy,' said Biffo. 'That's the cricket ground and the owner is a chap called Bill. Bill Stickers.'

'Bill Stickers? Odd name.'

'Well, his real name is Cedric. But everyone calls him Bill.'

'Don't suppose you happen to know if its for sale, do you?'

'What? The cricket ground? For sale?'

'Yes.'

'Good heavens, no!' laughed Biffo. He looked at his watch. 'I'm glad you reminded me. I must get a move on. The match is due to start in a few minutes.'

'Oh, yes, of course. Your cricket match. Right ho,' said Damien. 'Thanks anyway.' He and Edwina started to head towards the door. They both paused in front of the step. Damien ducked and stepped up cautiously. Edwina followed him. 'Oh, I've just remembered,' she said, pausing on the step and rummaging in her handbag. 'A letter came for you this morning.' She pulled out a long, thick white envelope and handed it to Biffo. 'And you owe me £20.'

Biffo took the envelope, glanced at it, and stuffed it without thinking into his trouser pocket. He took £20 out of his pocket and handed it to Edwina. He didn't have much left but he didn't care. 'Are you coming to watch?' he asked Lettice.

'When I've tidied up a bit,' she said.

Biffo, leaving the bar, turned to wave goodbye.

'Careful!' cried Lettice.

But it was too late. She winced and then, once again, she reached under the counter for her slate and chalk.

~ Chapter 34 ~

HAVING SPENT THE LAST DAY and a half cycling around and around the village Biffo could at least console himself with the thought that he now knew his way around Fondling-Under-Water almost as well as some of the locals. Despite the discomfort he felt, as a result of his efforts he had acquired a genuine and steadily growing affection for the village.

The natural beauty of the place was unquestionable. Instead of the endless acres of hedgeless prairies so favoured by huge commercial farms, the countryside in and around Fondling-Under-Water still consisted of gently rolling hills, divided by thick, tree-studded hedgerows into small, green fields. The local river, the river Ripple, which snaked through the village from East to West, had neither been sucked dry by a water company hungry for water nor polluted by farmers or a chemical company using the river as a dumping ground for their waste.

The local woodlands were comprised of oak, beech, sycamore, horse chestnut, hazel, rowan and other indigenous, deciduous species. An occasional fir tree acted as a reminder of what might well have been if the commercial foresters had taken over.

The architectural beauty of the village was unquestionable too. Fondling-Under-Water remained unspoiled by concrete and breeze block and there were no fake wooden beams because those properties which required beams had real ones. The absence of any architectural horrors, dreamt up by BMW driving whizz kids with a penchant for silk suits, French ties and copper roofs, was a tribute not to the strength of purpose and good sense of the local planning department but to the fact that its geographical position meant that Fondling-Under-Water was neither suitable for turning into a dormitory town nor convenient for siting a weekend cottage.

The cricket field in Fondling-Under-Water had originally been created by one of the present Lord Hepplewhite's ancestors, a man for whom cricket had been both an addiction and a constant joy. He had had the field rolled as flat as a convex billiard table and had built a pavilion, which, although it was considerably smaller, was modelled on the pavilion at the famous cricket ground in north London named after Thomas Lord.

The closer Biffo got to the Fondling-Under-Water cricket field the greater his apprehension grew. He hadn't played cricket since he had left school and even then he hadn't played very often.

He could remember standing, with the rest of his form at school, in a long line while the two best players in the class chose their sides. Biffo remembered this as an extremely humbling and humiliating experience. He, and a boy who wore spectacles and suffered badly from asthma, had remained together in the line at the very end; unwanted by either captain. At the time he had regarded this as exceedingly unjust. Because he collected stamps and read books he had acquired a reputation amongst his school fellows as being bookish, scholarly and no sportsman. The result of this prejudice was that he had never had much of an opportunity to exhibit his talent at cricket – or, indeed, any other sport.

He remembered that on one occasion an epidemic of mumps within the school had removed the ability of the two captains to be quite so choosy. His delight and pride at being picked for one of the teams had been tempered by the knowledge that with only sixteen fit pupils to choose from the two captains had not had a great deal of choice. He remembered the occasion being spoilt by the pity and shame he felt when he joined the team for which had so belatedly been selected, turned and saw that the asthmatic boy in spectacles, still standing alone and now an automatic and unavoidable choice for the other team, was crying. He remembered thinking how terrible life must be if, as he had so often been told by his father, his school days were to turn out to be the happiest days of his life.

It was at this point that Biffo stopped walking and stood still for a moment or two.

Part of him wanted very much to play in the village cricket match. He had always wanted to feel someone slap him on the back and say 'Well done!'. He had always wanted to hear people shout out to him 'Catch it!' 'Good shot!' or 'Well bowled!'. Even a 'Hard luck!' or a 'Well tried!' would have done.

But part of him, a bigger, stronger part, was terrified and full of self doubt. He was frightened that he would let down the side, drop a vital catch, be given out first ball ('bowled first ball by a full toss' seemed to be a phrase which he remembered as meriting large amounts of personal shame) or bowl an over in which every ball was hit for six.

The prize (sporting success and companionship) was great. But the prospect of failure seemed just too great.

Suddenly, Biffo heard a cheery shout from a familiar voice.

'Hello, Biffo!' cried Puffy Harbottle, The Gravedigger's Rest landlord. 'Ready for the match?' He approached Biffo with a wave and a big smile.

Biffo, who most certainly was not ready for the match, either physically or mentally, smiled faintly and shook Puffy's hand.

'You look a bit off colour,' said Puffy, concerned. 'Are you sure you're feeling OK?'

'Rather exhausted, actually,' admitted Biffo. 'Cycling is much harder work than sitting behind a desk. And to tell you the truth I'm also feeling just a trifle nervous,' he added. He lowered his voice. 'To be honest with you I can't remember when I last even saw a cricket match!'

'Don't you worry about a thing!' said Puffy cheerily. 'I'll give you ten to one you'll be absolutely fine. Nothing to worry about at all. We all take our cricket pretty seriously but try to put that out of your mind.'

'Thanks,' said Biffo, making a brave attempt to smile. 'Thank you very much.'

~ Chapter 35 ~

ALTHOUGH THE CRICKET PAVILION IN Fondling-Under-Water had been designed along the same general lines as the pavilion at Lord's cricket ground in London it was rather noticeably smaller.

There was a small white picket fence in front of the pavilion and in the middle of this fence, reached from the pavilion by a row of slate steps, a small wooden gate through which cricketers and umpires walked on their way to the wicket.

Between the fence and the front of the pavilion, and on both sides of the slate steps, there were six rows of wooden benches, all painted white, upon which vice presidents of the cricket club, and their guests, could sit in well-wrapped attention.

The pavilion was divided into three main rooms. On the right was the dressing room used by the Fondling-Under-Water cricket team and on the left was the dressing room used by the visiting team. In between these two rooms was the largest and main room in the building – known as the Short Room in homage to the Long Room at Lord's – where the older, more fragile members could sit on stools and high, long-legged chairs to watch the match.

Just as cricketers at Lord's can only reach the playing area by walking through the Long Room so players at Fondling-Under-Water could only reach the front door of the pavilion, and thereby the gate, by passing through the Short Room.

When the pavilion had been built, the club's original owner and benefactor had arranged for a large glass-fronted cupboard to be erected against the back wall of the Short Room. It had been his intention that the cupboard should be used to store the club's trophies but, sadly, the club's achievements had been slight or, to be more accurate, non-existent in this area.

And so the cupboard was used instead to store and display such club memorabilia as the bat used by Bert Jenkins to score an undefeated 45 runs during a league match in 1953 (the highest score by any Fondling-Under-Water player) and the ball used by Nigel Tiverton to dismiss four opposition batsmen with his medium pace off breaks (described as such because no one, least of all Nigel, was quite certain how to define his bowling style).

Behind the Short Room there was a small but well-planned kitchen, and behind each of the two dressing rooms there were small communal bathrooms – each one being equipped with a single, large, rectangular bath in which eleven grown men could share soapy water and bathe and scrub together. For nearly a decade there had been a campaign to have the baths replaced by showers. It was argued that this would be more hygienic. This proposal, regularly put forward at the club's

Annual General Meeting, was always defeated by a hefty majority since there were many in the club who felt that the sense of camaraderie produced by communal bathing far outweighed such petty considerations as the possible spread of infection. Those who favoured the status quo were strongly supported by evidence, submitted annually, which indicated that when Gilbert Runcorn picked up an unfortunate and uncomfortable infection while on a trip to Amsterdam in 1969 not one other member of the team had acquired the same infection.

'Most of you have already met Biffo, haven't you?' said Puffy, as the two of them entered the pavilion.

There were six people, already changed into their cricket whites, sitting or standing in the Short Room and five of them nodded, smiled and said 'Hello!'. Biffo recognised them as having been in the pub on Monday evening.

'Welcome to Fondling-Under-Water cricket club,' said the sixth, whom Biffo had certainly not yet met, a tall, bearded fellow whose cricket trousers, shirt and jumper were so white that they almost sparkled. He carefully leant an expensive-looking, bat against a nearby stool and held out a beautifully manicured hand. 'Paddy Fields,' he said, introducing himself. 'I'm the vice captain. Sorry we haven't met before. I understand that you're staying at the pub for a few days?'

'That's right,' agreed Biffo, accepting the outstretched hand, but having the presence of mind to wipe his own rather clammy palm on his trousers first. 'I'm afraid I haven't got any cricket gear with me,' he apologised.

'Don't you worry about that, old fellow,' said Paddy, cheerily. 'We'll fix you up with everything you need.'

'And I have to confess that it's been quite a while since I actually played a game of cricket,' continued Biffo.

Paddy airily waved a hand to indicate that this was of absolutely no consequence. 'You'll soon get the hang of things,' he said. He leant forwards a few degrees. 'One small thing,' he said, putting a hand on Biffo's shoulder. 'If there is ever any doubt, I would like you to remember that you're on our side.'

Biffo, who was puzzled by this, stared at him for a moment or two. 'Of course,' he said at last.

'Speaking for myself I'd much prefer a totally objective approach,' he said. 'But one has to be practical and in my experience that's the way the opposition tend to deal with these things.'

'Er, yes,' said Biffo who had no idea what Paddy was talking about.

'And this is, after all, our quarter final match in the Worthiness Best Bitter Nationwide Cup competition' explained Paddy. 'In thirty two years of trying we've never reached the quarter finals before. We've been pretty lucky so far this year. We beat Caverdale in the first round – mind you they could only find nine fit men and two of them were over 80 – and we had a walk over in the second round when our opponents never got here. It turned out that the driver of the coach they'd hired was absolutely plastered and when he suggested that they stop off in a gateway for a rest the team agreed, thinking it was an opportunity to get a bit of shut eye themselves. They all fell fast asleep and didn't wake up until six the following morning when a farmer banged on the coach door because he wanted to get his tractor into the field.'

'Ah,' said Biffo.

'The Wanderers – our opponents today – come from near Bristol or Northampton, or somewhere like that. They spend a fortnight touring around. They've been coming here for seventy four years.'

'Are they good?' asked Biffo.

'Not really,' replied Paddy. He smiled. 'They usually beat us, of course.' He thought about this for a moment. 'But never by very much,' he added. 'So we think we could be in with a chance. It's been pretty close a few times. In 1922 they won by just six wickets and 1937 the margin was just 98 runs. We even played them right through both World Wars,' said Puffy proudly. 'In 1940 our side consisted of three men over 60, two over 70, three women, three boys under 16 and a sheep dog. The sheep dog fielded – one of the best fielders we've ever had they say, he took two stunning catches in the deep – but didn't bat, of course. Their side contained a chap with a wooden leg, a chap who was registered as blind and a woman who was eight months pregnant and who kept wicket because she didn't think she ought to run about too much.'

There was a sudden clatter of metal on wood as the remains of the Fondling-Under-Water team left the dressing room and marched into the Short Room. It occurred to Biffo that the players he had met in the pub now all seemed to be considerably taller than they had been two days earlier. This puzzled him. He couldn't understand whether this was because he had shrunk or because they had suddenly grown.

Biffo turned to Puffy Harbottle, who was standing next to him. 'I know this seems a bit silly,' he said, 'But everyone seems, I don't know, well, sort of, taller.'

Puffy leant a little closer to Biffo. 'It's the extra long spikes.' he explained. He turned his head and looked in the direction of the visitors' dressing room, checked to make sure that the door was still closed, and then leant closer still. 'We generally wear very long spikes when we play at home,' he whispered. He paused. 'The ground is always a little damp down near the river,' he said. He then winked. 'The local blacksmith makes the spikes for us. They're twice the normal length.'

'Ah. I see,' nodded Biffo, who didn't see at all. He was secretly already beginning to think that he might have been wiser to spend the afternoon cycling around Fondling-Under-Water delivering groceries for Miss Box.

'Tell me about the vice captain,' Biffo said, nodding in Paddy's direction.

'Ah that's Paddy Fields, the local carpenter,' said Puffy. 'Has his clothes specially built in Savile Row. He's the only Russian aristocrat who's ever played for us.'

'He doesn't sound very Russian,' said Biffo. 'And to be honest I've never thought of Paddy as being a Russian name.' He thought a bit more. 'How does he come to be working as a carpenter in Fondling-Under-Water?'

'His great great grandfather – I may not have the right number of greats in there – was apparently pretty bright. He insisted that everyone in the family had a trade so that when the revolution came they could all earn a living and wouldn't starve. They all learned something different. Paddy's grandfather was the carpenter. After the revolution he came over here and started a business. Paddy is a third generation carpenter.'

Just then the door to the visitor's dressing room burst open and a small round fellow with a very pink face and half a dozen strands of ginger hair combed across a very pink scalp strode out as though looking for a fight. He was wearing a cream shirt and a pair of slightly off white and rather rumpled trousers. He had used a multi-coloured tie instead of a belt to hold up his trousers though the trousers looked so tight that it seemed unlikely that gravity would have been able to work its wonders even without the belt.

'Right!' he said, clapping his hands together and giving them a hard rub. 'Let's get the show on the road!'

'Good afternoon,' said Paddy, who had raised both eyebrows at his opponent's choice of phrase. He introduced himself. 'And this is our captain,' he said, introducing Bill Stickers.

'Daniel Potterton,' said the small, round fellow. 'Captain of the Wanderers Touring Team.'

The two captains shook hands with one another. And Paddy shook hands with Daniel.

'Shall we go out and toss?' asked Daniel.

'After you!' said Bill, opening one of the twin doors at the front of the pavilion and ushering his opponent out with a genteel wave of his hand.

'I'm beginning to feel a little guilty about being here,' said Biffo to Puffy, trying to prepare the ground for an early departure.

Puffy looked at him and raised an eyebrow. 'What do you mean, 'guilty'?'

'I feel bad about leaving Miss Box,' explained Biffo, wishing he was a better liar. 'It's only my second day on the job and she does seem to have an awful lot of deliveries to get through. Maybe I should go back and give her a hand.'

'Oh, don't you worry about her,' said Puffy, reassuringly. 'She'll manage. If there's anything urgent she'll just pop it into her car and drive round when she closes this evening.'

'She's got a car?' said Biffo, greatly surprised.

'Of course!' said Puffy, clearly surprised that Biffo was surprised.

'Then why does she have everything delivered by bicycle?' asked Biffo, puzzled.

'Because that's the way her father did things and the way she's always done things, I suppose,' said Puffy. 'She's very keen on tradition. Wonderful woman. Build and delicacy of a rhinoceros, jaw carved out of solid granite, and a moustache any adolescent would be proud of. She regards being irritable and rude to the customers as an essential part of her job.'

'Has she ever been married?' Biffo asked.

'Miss Box?'

'Yes.'

'No!' laughed Puffy. 'Cheesy reckons she did have a fling about thirty years ago with a touring fast bowler. His yorker broke her delivery boy's shin bone and he felt so bad about it that he stayed on to help while the delivery boy's leg mended. There was a rumour that the shop bicycle wasn't the only thing he had his leg over. Tough old bird, though.'

'All the same,' said Biffo. 'I do feel as though I'm letting her down...'

'Don't be silly,' said Puffy. 'With our big match coming up it's vital that you get your eye in today.'

'OK,' sighed Biffo. He paused, not entirely sure that he wanted to know the answer to the question he was about to ask. 'What is the big match – and why is so important? I thought today's match was important.'

'Many, many years ago,' began Puffy, putting an arm around Biffo's shoulder, 'a young lad called Cyril Player strode out onto the cricket pitch as a keen young member of the Fondling-Under-Water cricket team. He was the youngest player to get into the team, the youngest player to score 20 and the first to take 50 wickets in a season. He was, in short, a boy wonder.'

'I rather vaguely think I may have heard of him,' said Biffo, thinking hard. 'Didn't he become a professional?'

'He did indeed,' said Puffy. 'He became – and still is – an extremely successful professional. He's even played for England.'

'I see,' said Biffo. 'Or at least I think I do.' He frowned. 'Actually,' he admitted. 'I don't. Is he playing for our opponents today?'

'Good heavens, no!' replied Puffy. 'Mr Player and a team of selected professionals will be here on Saturday. It's a big match for us. The biggest most of us have ever played in. For one thing it's the only chance most of us will ever get to play against professionals. It is also a chance for us to give Mr Player a poke in the eye. He's not terribly popular around here. The general view is that he's become rather too big for his size elevens in recent years.'

'I see,' said Biffo. 'It's a sort of grudge match.'

'In a way it is,' said Puffy. 'But there is even more to it than that. In the sort of cricket we play each team only ever has one innings. We only ever play one day matches you see. They bat, we bat and that's it. But this match is different.'

'It's going to last more than one day?'

'Oh no! These guys are professionals. They're only giving up a day of their time as a favour to Mr Player. It's his benefit year and they're all scratching his back so that in due course he'll scratch their backs.'

'You mean they are playing in his team – to help him raise money – so that he will play in their teams to help them raise money?'

'You've got it.' said Puffy. 'So the match will all be over in the day. In the afternoon, actually. But – and this is the crucial factor – the Fondling-Under-Water team gets to bat twice!'

'And the opposition doesn't?'

'Certainly not,' said Puffy. 'This was all agreed months ago. Since they're professionals and we're decidedly not it was thought necessary to give us some sort of advantage. To even up the odds a little.'

'So you all bat twice and they just bat once?'

'That's it. For most of us it's the first – and probably only – time we'll get a second chance.'

Biffo looked around to check that no one was within earshot. 'I wanted to ask you about Paddy,' he said. 'He sort of behaves a bit as though he's the club captain doesn't he?'

'Ah well,' said Puffy. 'Interesting that you've noticed. That's because he would be captain if it wasn't for the fact that Bill wants to be captain and owns the cricket field. Bill is really much more interested in being called captain than in having to worry about field placings, batting orders and deciding who is going to bowl next. So it works out quite well. Bill gets to be captain and Paddy gets to boss everyone around.'

Just then the two captains, who had been attended and surrounded by several members of their respective teams while they tossed to see who would bat first, reappeared at the front of the pavilion. The visiting captain, Daniel Potterton, had a broad smile on his pink face. Puffy, followed by Biffo, stepped out through the pavilion door and stood on the step outside.

'I take it you lost the toss again?' said Puffy to Bill.

Bill nodded. 'We lost,' he agreed.

Puffy turned to Biffo. 'When he wins the toss it's always "I won",' he said, in a stage whisper. 'But when he loses it's always "We lost".'

Paddy, the vice captain, allowed the corners of his mouth to twitch a little. Biffo felt it likely that this was as much of a smile as the vice captain could manage.

'They've decided to bat,' said Paddy.

'Ah, good,' said Puffy.

'Why is that good?' asked Biffo, in a whisper.

'Because if they bat first then, with any luck, it will be some time before they remember about the damp patch down by the river,' replied Puffy, after looking round to make sure that none of the opposing team were listening to him. 'It's much worse this year than it was last time they were here.'

'Is that important?' asked Biffo.

'Crucial,' said Puffy. 'There isn't any point in hitting a ball along the ground down that part of the field. It'll just get stuck. But you can safely hit the ball in the air down there because any fielder who tries to catch it will probably get bogged down and be unable to run properly.'

'Ah, right,' said Biffo, nodding as though he understood the significance of all this, which to be perfectly honest he didn't.

Around and behind them there was much clattering from the Fondling-Under-Water side, and much shuffling from the Wanderers cricketers (who were all wearing pumps or cricket shoes with studs rather than boots with long spikes) as the cricketers prepared themselves for battle.

One or two of the Fondling-Under-Water team, who were due to field, started to wander out onto the cricket field, throwing a cricket ball to one another in a desultory attempt at practice. Biffo was secretly rather relieved to notice that most of the players flinched and jumped out of the way when the ball travelled in their direction. The Fondling-Under-Water players did not take kindly to opponents who did a lot of practising before a match; it simply wasn't regarded as cricket. Indeed, it was generally considered that there was a very narrow line between practising and cheating.

Most of the Wanderers team settled themselves down onto the benches at the front of the pavilion while their opening batsmen walked through the Short Room and into their dressing room to put on their batting pads in preparation for the first overs of the match.

'Shouldn't I be getting ready,' said Biffo to Puffy, as a very short, gnarled fellow walked past them wearing a rather battered straw panama hat and a white coat which reached down to his ankles. 'Who's that?' Biffo asked, allowing this to supersede his previous question.

'Who?' asked Puffy, looking around.

'The chap in the white coat,' said Biffo, nodding to the gnarled fellow, who was now chatting to the visitors' captain. 'He looks like an ice cream salesmen.'

'Oh him!' said Puffy. 'That's Hamish Jones, the 'Wanderers' umpire.'

'They brought their own umpire?'

'Oh yes,' said Puffy. 'Each team supplies its own umpire.'

'Really?' said Biffo, genuinely surprised. 'I never knew that.' He looked down and pointed at his faded green corduroy trousers and his brown brogues. 'You said you had some kit I could borrow,' he said. 'I can't really go out there like this...'

'Oh yes, of course,' said Puffy. 'I'm sorry. I'll have a word with Paddy. He'll know where it is.'

He disappeared down the steps to speak to the vice captain. Moments later he returned. 'Follow me,' he said. 'It's in the dressing room.'

Puffy led and Biffo followed.

In the dressing room, which smelt of a strange mixture of oil of wintergreen, cheap aftershave, carbolic soap, disinfectant and a wide variety of less chemical and more personal odours, Puffy rummaged around among a collection of clothes hanging on a large peg on the back of the door. Within seconds there was a pile of trousers, jackets, shirts and other items, several feet thick on the floor.

'Ah! Here it is!' said Puffy, at last. He pulled a fairly short and grubby white coat off the peg and handed it to Biffo.

'What's this?' asked Biffo, automatically accepting the coat.

'Your coat!' said Puffy.

'My coat,' said Biffo. 'What do I want a white coat for?'

Puffy looked puzzled. 'All umpires wear white coats,' he said. He looked at the coat he had handed to Biffo. 'Well some umpires wear slightly off white coats,' he said, correcting himself. 'I could get it washed for the next match if you like.'

'Umpires?' exclaimed Biffo in horror. 'You want me to umpire?'

At first glance umpiring might seem to be a rather less demanding occupation than batting, bowling or fielding. But Biffo had immediately realised that umpiring a cricket match was likely to be fraught with danger — and opportunities to annoy and upset all sorts of people.

'Yes, of course,' said Puffy. He paused, clearly a little puzzled by Biffo's reaction. 'What else did you think we wanted you to do?'

Biffo opened and shut his mouth several times. 'I don't know,' he said at last. 'Well, what I mean is that I thought...,' he swallowed. 'I didn't realise you wanted me to umpire.'

Puffy stared at Biffo for a moment. 'You didn't think we wanted you to play, did you?'

'Oh no, oh no, of course not!' said Biffo.

'Didn't think you would,' said Puffy, nodding sagely. 'Why would we invite a complete stranger to play in the team, eh? Even for a relatively friendly match? Be pretty silly, wouldn't it?'

'Oh absolutely,' agreed Biffo, nodding furiously. 'Very silly.'

'Do you want a hat?' asked Puffy. 'Franklin always wears

a battered old panama.' He rummaged around among the pile of clothes on the floor. 'It must be here somewhere,' he said.

'Franklin?' said Biffo.

'Franklin is our regular umpire,' Puffy reminded him.

'Is this what you're looking for?' asked Biffo, removing an extremely tatty hat from one of the white coat pockets.

'That's it!' said Puffy. 'Put it on and let's get out there. The rest of the blokes will be wondering where we've got to.'

Biffo put on Franklin Minton's hat, which was at least two sizes too small, and followed Puffy out towards the centre of the cricket pitch. He couldn't remember ever being so frightened in his whole life. He could not have been more nervous if there had been a scaffold awaiting him.

~ Chapter 36 ~

'IT'S ABSOLUTELY PERFECT!' WHISPERED DAMIEN, even though there was no one within a hundred yards of where they were standing. 'Nice piece of flat ground with a river running alongside. Just what we're looking for. Plenty of space for our buildings.' He pointed to the far corner of the field. 'And we can knock down that little white shed and put up a Family Leisure Centre.'

'Are you sure you'll be able to buy the land?' asked Edwina. She moved a little closer and put her arm around him. She wasn't normally a person who liked emotional or physical displays of affection (particularly in public) but she was, at that moment, very proud of Damien.

Damien turned and looked at her. 'I know how to deal with these yokels!' he sneered. His lip curled and if he had had a moustache he would have undoubtedly given it a twirl.

'Oh, Damien!' said Edwina, giving his arm a squeeze. 'You are wonderful.'

In the distance a group of men clad in white trooped out of the pavilion.

'Which one do you think is Stickers?' asked Damien.

'We'll ask,' said Edwina.

'Good idea!' said Damien.

~ Chapter 37 ~

Biffo afterwards swore that he could not remember how he got from the pavilion to the cricket square in the middle of the Fondling-Under-Water cricket ground. To say that he felt dazed and confused at the discovery that he was to act as an umpire would be as much of an understatement as saying that Napoleon didn't feel full of the joys of spring after his bad day at Waterloo.

Biffo's memory of that afternoon's events restarted when he was met in the middle by the other umpire – the small, gnarled fellow with the ankle-length white coat who had arrived with the touring team.

'Mr Jones,' said the small gnarled fellow. 'Mr Hamish Jones.' He looked up at Biffo as though expecting him to make some comment and winked.

'Pleased to meet you,' said Biffo, holding out his right hand. He wasn't sure whether or not he should wink back.

The small gnarled fellow kept both his hands in his pockets and stuck out a bony chin. 'My father was Welsh and my mother was Scottish,' he said defiantly. He winked again.

'I see,' said Biffo. He wondered if winking was perhaps a sort of umpire's secret code – like a Freemason's handshake. And so he winked too. It was a rather half-hearted wink, it is true. But it was undeniably a wink.

'Which end do you want?' the gnarled fellow asked. He seemed somehow disappointed, as though he had expected Biffo to make more of a comment about his mixed ancestry. 'I'll take this end.' he added without waiting for Biffo to reply. He winked again.

'Er, well, I'll take the other end,' said Biffo, winking.

'Right,' said Mr Jones. Biffo had thought he might be pleased that they had been able to come to an amicable agreement but instead he seemed a little irritated. He winked again.

'Right,' said Biffo, winking goodbye and starting to walk down the pitch and smiling and waving nervously to Puffy.

'OK?' asked Puffy, walking towards the new Fondling-Under-Water umpire. 'Is everything all right?'

'Not really,' admitted Biffo, quietly. He looked around to make sure that no one was close enough to overhear. 'What, exactly, am I supposed to do?'

'Simple. If any of our bowlers appeals you give the batsman out,' explained Puffy. 'If any of their bowlers appeals you give the batsman not out – unless the stumps are down and it's too late to call 'no ball'. Try to remember to call 'no ball' at least once an over when they're bowling.'

Biffo frowned. 'Is that entirely fair?' he asked.

'No, but it's what their umpire will do,' replied Puffy. 'That's why each side has its own umpire.'

'Oh,' said Biffo. 'And why does their umpire keep winking at me? Is it some sort of secret code?'

'Don't worry about him!' said Puffy. 'It's just a twitch. He winks at everybody. When he first came down here a few years ago Itchy winked back at him every time he winked. Itchy thought he was just being friendly but it made Mr Jones quite furious. He thought Itchy was taking the mickey.'

Biffo swallowed hard and hoped that he hadn't annoyed Mr Jones too much. He thought a subtle change of subject might be sensible. 'It's a long time since I played cricket,' he whispered, without exaggeration. 'I'm worried that I may be a little rusty about one or two things.'

'Like what?' asked Puffy.

'Well, for a start, exactly how many balls are there in an over?' asked Biffo, teasing him.

Puffy, clearly rather startled by this confession of ignorance, looked around to make sure that no one was listening to this heresy. 'There are six balls in an over,' he whispered. 'And you do this,' he held up a finger in front of his nose, 'when you want to give a batsman out.'

Meanwhile, the Fondling-Under-Water cricketers were arguing over the positions they had been allocated by the vice captain.

'Why can't I go in the slips?' demanded a sensitive looking fellow with collar length hair and a hooked nose.

'Because the captain wants you at third man,' replied Paddy, in his very best 'I-don't-even-want-to-talk-about-this' voice. 'Since you're our most junior player you get to field in the wet patch.'

'But it's muddy down there,' protested the sensitive looking fellow who, despite his apparent youth, was none other than the local vicar, the Reverend Hubert Counter. 'My wife will complain if I go home with dirty trousers.'

'Can't I be in the gully today?' asked Cheesy. 'I'm fed up of fielding at long off.'

'But you always field at long off,' said the vicar.

'That's why I want to be at gully,' replied Cheesy, not unreasonably. 'I never asked to field at long off.'

'But you're a specialist in that position,' protested Paddy.

'A long off specialist?' said Cheesy. 'Whoever heard of anyone being a specialist long off fielder?'

'I'm going home if I have to field at third man again,' announced the vicar firmly. He had folded his arms across his chest and was holding his head back, making it perfectly clear to all and sundry that he had no intention of moving. Since his bowling was generally considered vital to the team's hopes of success his threat could not be ignored.

Biffo, who had now arrived at the other end of the pitch, put the panama hat he was carrying onto his head and thrust his hands into the pockets of his white coat; a creased and grubby garment which, Biffo surmised quite accurately, had not been washed or pressed for several seasons. He found half a dozen small, round pebbles in one of the coat pockets and, puzzled, started to flick them into the air to get rid of them.

~ Chapter 38 ~

'SO, YOU'RE THE NEW UMPIRE!' said a voice Biffo did not recognise. He looked round and down at a small, wizened individual wearing a massive pair of yellow pads and a huge pair of ageing, red-leather wicket-keeping gloves.

Biffo agreed that he was the new umpire. 'You must be the Fondling-Under-Water wicket keeper!' he said. Justin had been pointed out to him in the bar at The Gravedigger's Rest.

'You're bright, I'll give you that,' said the wizened wicket keeper. He held out a gloved hand. 'Justin Wilson,' he said. Biffo shook hands with the glove. The leather was cracked in several places.

'I've been keeping wicket for sixty six years,' said the wizened wicket keeper. 'I've got arthritis, diabetes and epilepsy and I've had two heart attacks. I've got cataracts in both my eyes, a spot on my lung and I'm allergic to seven different antibiotics.'

'Ah!' said Biffo. 'Aha.'

'But the doctor says I've got athlete's feet,' said the wicket keeper proudly. 'I've always looked after them you see.' He stopped and thought for a moment. 'Though maybe I was born with them. What do you think? Do you think you're either born with athlete's feet or you're not?'

'I see you've met Justin,' interrupted Puffy. 'Quite a character isn't he?'

Biffo nodded in agreement.

'He's really three fielders in one,' continued Puffy. 'Two short legs and he keeps wicket too!'

Justin pulled a face.

'His heart condition means that we have to appeal very quietly,' said Puffy. 'He can't cope with too much excitement. When Len appeals he has to put cotton wool in his ears.'

Biffo fastened the white coat. It was difficult to persuade the buttons to connect with their respective button holes. He had to breathe in to bring the two sides of the coat together. Fastening the buttons was such a struggle that in the end he only managed to fasten three of them. It was clear to Biffo that he was considerably larger than Franklin Minton. The hat, now sitting crumpled in his pocket, had sat balanced on the top of his head like a thimble on an apple. And the white coat felt uncomfortably tight.

'Justin was offered your job when Franklin had his accident,' said Puffy.

'Really?' said Biffo. He turned to Justin. 'Why did you turn it down?'

'I wanted something with better promotion prospects,' said Justin. He drew himself up to his full height. 'I want a career not a job,' he said indignantly.

'Justin hasn't actually started work yet,' said Puffy. 'He's still hunting for the right position.'

There was a loud and weary-sounding sigh from a fielder somewhere nearby. 'I'll field at third man,' said Len, the source of the sigh. Len, a nineteen stone tractor driver, was a big man in every direction. 'But only if I can move up a place in the batting order. I don't see why I should always bat at number eleven.'

'Thanks Len,' said Paddy, rather wearily. 'You can bat at number ten. Vicar you field at third slip. Happy?'

'Yes,' said the vicar, who had brightened up considerably. 'I suppose so.'

'What do you mean 'I suppose so'?' demanded Paddy. 'I thought you wanted to field at slip.'

'I do,' said the vicar. 'But why do I have to be third slip. Why can't I be first slip or even second slip.'

'What difference does it make?' asked Paddy.

'It makes a lot of difference,' said the vicar. 'First slip sounds a lot more important than third slip. It's like in an orchestra. First violin is much more important than third violin.'

'It's nothing like it is in an orchestra!' insisted Paddy.

'But my wife will want to know why I was third slip and not first slip,' said the vicar.

Paddy sighed. 'OK vicar,' he said. 'You field at first slip.'

'Thank you, skipper,' said the vicar, raising his right index finger and touching his forehead.

'If you're letting the vicar field at first slip then it's only fair that you let me field at gully,' said Cheesy.

'Don't you think you are a bit, well, sort of slow to field at gully?' asked Paddy.

'Who says I'm slow!' demanded Cheesy. 'What about that catch I took when we played Little Chigford?'

'That was in 1956,' Paddy pointed out, rather bluntly. He seemed to be running out of patience.

'I had to run twenty yards round the boundary,' said Cheesy. 'It was a magnificent catch. Everyone said so. And it wasn't 1956.'

'You were a lot younger then,' said Paddy. 'When was it if it wasn't 1956?'

'It was 1954,' said Cheesy.

'There you are,' said Paddy. 'It was a long time ago. You were a lot younger and faster then.'

'Exactly!' said Cheesy, wagging a finger at Paddy. 'It's about time one of the younger blokes fielded at long off. You need someone agile and fast at long off. What you need at gully is someone with a safe pair of hands.'

Paddy, who had seemed to be coping remarkably well, put his head in his hands and groaned. After a moment or two he removed his hands and looked around. 'Who'll field at long off?' he shouted.

There was no reply.

Paddy sighed. 'OK,' he said, wearily. 'We won't have a long off.'

'But we always have a long off,' protested Cheesy.

'Well we won't have a long off this time,' said Paddy.

'But long off is a very important position,' said Cheesy.

'I know it is,' said Paddy.

'Someone ought to field there,' said Cheesy.

'But no one wants to field there,' protested Paddy.

'You're the captain,' said Cheesy. 'Why don't you just tell someone to field there.'

Paddy said nothing but just stared at Cheesy.

Cheesy sighed. 'If no one else will field there then I'll field there,' he said. 'Someone's got to field at long off,' he muttered as he walked away. 'The trouble with this team is that no one realises just how important a position long off really is.'

~ Chapter 39 ~

WHILE THE MEMBERS OF THE Fondling-Under-Water fielding side were arguing about who was going to field exactly where, a far more significant drama was taking place near to the boundary.

Edwina Brimstone and Damien Washbrook, standing in the narrow strip of land between the boundary rope and the boundary hedge, had identified the owner of the Fondling-Under-Water cricket pitch and had called him over to where they were standing. Edwina had wanted to totter onto the pitch to talk to him but had been dissuaded from this course of action by Damien who remembered enough from his cricket playing days at school to know that women wearing high heeled shoes are not, generally speaking, welcomed onto the pitch. (If he had spoken to the Fondling-Under-Water groundsman he would have discovered, possibly to his surprise, that Edwina – and, indeed, any other woman – would have been welcomed onto certain parts of the outfield since her high-heeled shoes would have helped to provide much needed drainage holes.)

'Lovely day,' said Damien, smiling. He knew that people who lived in the country always loved talking about their weather. Just as some men like to think of themselves as racing drivers or professional golfers so Damien liked to think of himself as a wheeler dealer. He had read synopses of several American bestselling textbooks on sales techniques and knew that building a relationship with the customer was a significant first step in the selling process. Damien wasn't actually selling anything, of course, but he felt that trying to buy a cricket field from a man who doesn't necessarily want to sell it might require some of the skills of a salesman.

'It will be if it doesn't rain,' said Bill, who had spent several years of his life talking about the weather when working as a hairdresser. It was no longer one of his favourite topics of conversation. He had learned that whatever you said about it, and whatever you wanted it to do, weather would come and go as it pleased.

'What's it going to do, then?' asked Damien, looking up at the sky, quizzically.

'Dunno,' said Bill, who didn't much care and wondered why these two over-dressed strangers had been so keen to call him over.

'I'm told that you're the owner of this piece of land,' said Damien.

'The cricket ground?'

'That's right.'

'It's a very nice field,' said Edwina, conscious of the fact that her lover was having a little trouble getting the negotiations under way. 'Close to the river.'

Damien tried out several possible opening gambits in his mind.

'Oh it is that,' said Bill. 'A very nice field.' He paused. 'Close to the river,' he agreed.

'Do you think the authorities would ever allow building on it?' asked Edwina 'It would make a lovely spot for a few houses don't you think?'

'It already has planning permission,' said Bill. 'It had planning permission when I bought it.'

Damien felt his heart beating faster. 'I don't suppose you've thought about selling it?' he said, rather tentatively.

'How much do you want to pay for it?' demanded Bill.

This rather surprised Damien who was mentally still quite a long way from this crucial point in the negotiations. He had expected a good deal more tiptoeing around before they got down to the nitty gritty.

'Er...,' he said. 'Well, er...,'

'Might sell it for the right price,' said Bill who had suddenly realised that he might have suddenly found a way to solve his cash flow problem.

'Well, I might buy it at the right price,' said Damien. He felt rather pleased with this retort which, it seemed to him, kept the negotiations moving along at quite a pace. 'It's a nice field,' he added. 'A very nice field.' He smiled and showed a lot of teeth in the way that he'd seen politicians smile when trying to win votes. 'I want to start a holiday theme park,' he said. 'It'll be a real asset to the village.' He warmed to his theme. 'It'll bring in lots of visitors.' He paused. 'All very classy,' he added, reassuringly. 'Nothing tacky, you understand.'

'Ah!' said Bill, nodding. He didn't want to hear any more of this. He loved the village of Fondling-Under-Water and he couldn't bear to think of this terrible couple spoiling it with regiments of holidaymakers. But, on the other hand, he and his dear lady wife were penniless and facing an extremely uncertain future. All in all it was, he felt, a tricky situation.

'We'll sell holiday rights in our accommodation so that the people who come here will have a vested interest in maintaining the quality of their environment,' said Damien.

'Holiday rights?' said Bill. 'What's that?'

'Er, its well, er a sort of timeshare arrangement,' said Damien, rather guiltily.

'Ah!' said Bill. 'Timeshare.'

'Timeshare has had a bad press in recent years,' said Damien defensively. 'And it is true that there have been some unreliable operators. But we're right at the top end of the market.'

'Of course,' agreed Bill.

'So, what do you think?' asked Damien.

'I think it depends on what sort of money you're offering,' said Bill.

Damien rubbed his hands down the side of his trousers. He suddenly felt very nervous. 'Can I think about that?' he asked. He desperately wanted to speak to his brother.

'Look,' said Bill, 'the match is about to start. Why don't you have a think about it and then we'll have a word during the tea interval.'

'Fine!' agreed Damien. 'Splendid idea.'

'But let's just keep this between the three of us,' said Bill, looking around belatedly to make sure that there was no one close enough to hear.

'Of course!' nodded Damien. 'Absolutely!'

'You be here during the tea interval,' said Bill. 'I'll potter over and we'll have a chat.'

'Right!' agreed Damien. 'Er, when is the tea interval?'

'Couple of hours or so,' said Bill. 'You'll know it's the tea interval because everyone will disappear for an hour or so.'

'An hour?' said Damien. He tried to remember back to his school days. He didn't remember tea intervals taking up so much time.

'We take our teas seriously round here,' said Bill, hurrying back towards the centre of the cricket field where he was both relieved and surprised to see that play had still not begun.

~ Chapter 40 ~

'CRICKET,' THOUGHT BIFFO, LOOKING AROUND the Fondling-Under-Water cricket ground from his unique vantage point behind the stumps at the bowler's end of the wicket, 'is a very peaceful game. I think I could get to like this.'

On his right Biffo could see the back of The Gravedigger's Rest. Straight ahead, was the Fondling-Under-Water parish church, a magnificent piece of ancient English architecture.

On Biffo's left there was nothing much to see but the fields, hedgerows and rolling hills of the local countryside, studded with occasional farms and cottages and criss-crossed with a network of tiny lanes. And behind him, temporarily out of view, somewhere beyond a pasture, a small wood and half dozen cottages lay Miss Box's village shop.

Biffo stood drinking in the view; feeling more rested and relaxed than he could remember feeling for years. And then he felt someone tugging on his sleeve. He turned his head and saw Cheesy Stilton standing beside him. He looked like a boy waiting to ask the teacher if he can be excused to go the lavatory.

'Can we get on with the game?' asked Cheesy

'Pardon?' said Biffo, frowning.

'I don't like to be any trouble,' said Cheesy apologetically. 'But do you think I could start now?'

Biffo stared at him. 'I beg your pardon?'

'Can I begin bowling now?' asked Cheesy nervously. He didn't want to annoy an umpire; especially an umpire he didn't know very well; particularly the umpire whom he had reason to believe might treat his more marginal appeals rather favourably.

'Of course you can,' said Biffo. He looked around and seemed surprised to see that half a dozen of the Fondling-Under-Water players had gathered round.

'You're supposed to say 'play',' Cheesy explained.

'Am I?'

'Yes. It means the over can start.'

'Ah,' said Biffo. 'OK. Play.'

~ Chapter 41 ~

'So, how much do you think we should offer?' asked Damien.

'I thought Biffo was supposed to be playing cricket!' said Edwina. 'What's he doing standing there in that grubby white coat?'

'He seems to be one of the umpires,' said Damien. 'Maybe he'll play later on.'

'Isn't an umpire like a referee?' asked Edwina.

'Sort of.'

'How can he be an umpire and a player? He could end up giving himself out offside or having to disallow a goal he'd just scored.'

'They don't have goals in cricket, dear.'

'Don't nit-pick. Whatever. You know what I mean. And don't be patronising.'

'I wasn't being patronising!'

'Yes you were. You called me 'dear'.'

'I was just being affectionate.'

'Well, I don't like it.'

'Sorry.'

For a few minutes the two of them stood just beyond the boundary's edge watching the cricket match. Since neither of them knew any of the players, one of them knew absolutely nothing about the game and the other had absolutely no interest in any sort of sport they didn't have a great deal of fun. It wasn't one of those little moments in life that captures the heart and hangs around to warm the spirit in later years.

'There isn't even anywhere to sit,' complained Edwina.

'There are some seats over there,' said Damien.

'Where?'

'By the pavilion.'

'I'm not going over there.'

'Why not?'

'We might have to talk to those people. Some of them look very common.'

'Oh,' said Damien. 'Well, there is a gate just over there. We could sit on that.'

'A gate? You expect me to sit on a gate?'
'You could sort of lean against it...'
'I'm not sitting or leaning on or against a gate.'
'No,' said Damien. 'Of course not.'

There was another long silence during which quite a lot of exciting things happened on the pitch.

'So, how much do you think we should offer?'
'For the land?'
'How many acres are there?'

Damien looked around the field. 'Five or six I would guess.'

'How much does land around here fetch these days?'
'I don't know.' Damien looked around and thought for a moment. 'I think farm land usually goes for around two thousand pounds an acre at the moment.'

'So offer him ten thousand. He'll probably fall at your feet drooling but it'll be quick and painless.'

'I don't think he will,' said Damien. 'The land already has planning permission. And I think I might have made a bit of a mistake when we talked to him earlier on.'

Edwina looked at him sharply. 'Why? What sort of mistake?'
'I told him what I was planning to do with the land.'
'So?'
'So, he knows I'm going to take advantage of the planning permission and to build on the land. That changes the value.'
'So you'll have to offer him a bit more.'
'That's the problem. How much more.'
'How much can you afford?'
'I'm not sure. We've got a lot of money tied up in those prefabricated buildings.'

Edwina looked at Damien for a long moment. 'Are you sure you know what you're doing?'

'Maybe we can fix up some sort of contract that gives us the right to pay him in instalments. That way we won't have to find the money in advance.'

'Can you do that? Will he agree to it?'
'I'll put a delayed payment clause into the contract as an option and hide it on page 17,' said Damien with a snigger. 'He

won't even know it's there until he's signed and we own the land.'

'What sort of delay?'

'Ten. Maybe twenty years.'

Edwina laughed and reached out and held Damien's arm. 'You're a tricky devil, aren't you?'

Damien looked down at her uplifted face and smiled, rather pleased with himself.

'If you do that then it doesn't really matter what you offer him, does it?'

Damien thought about this for a moment. 'No,' he agreed. 'It doesn't really, does it?' He bent his head to kiss her but she turned her head so that his lips brushed her cheek.

'Not on the lips,' she said, sharply. 'You'll mess up my lipstick.'

~ Chapter 42 ~

'WE PLAYED BADLY,' MUTTERED PUFFY, as he and Biffo walked side by side off the pitch.

'But they were all out for 95 runs!' Biffo pointed out. 'That's not bad, surely?'

'They played pretty badly too,' admitted Puffy.

When the fielding side, the last two batsmen and the two umpires reached the pavilion they found that Fondling-Under-Water's loyal band of tea makers had been hard at work.

The sandwiches, half of which were made with white bread and half with brown bread, were filled with slices of cheddar cheese and home-made chutney, sliced tomatoes and salad, egg and cress or sliced ham. Two large pork pies had been laid out on mismatched dinner plates (each pie neatly chopped into a dozen equally sized pieces) and four dozen well-filled sausage rolls lay neatly in lines on two large baking trays.

For those with a sweet tooth there was a large chocolate cake, two sponge cakes (one filled with strawberry jam and the other filled with plum jam and cream), a couple of dozen chocolate éclairs, four dozen jam tarts and a large mound of scones, filled with jam and clotted cream. Everything on the table was home-made and packed with calories and looked quite delicious. Mrs Betty Cleavidge, a gloriously buxom woman who had been guardian of the cricket club teas for several decades, was always careful to make sure that her team's teas were unbeatable.

'Streuth!' said Biffo, impressed and amazed by the mountain of food that had been prepared. 'Is all this for us?'

'Making the teas for a local cricket club is a big responsibility,' said Puffy.

~ Chapter 43 ~

BILL STICKERS NORMALLY ENJOYED A cricket tea just as much as any other player. He was particularly partial to Mrs Betty Cleavidge's chutney and was so keen on cream horns that he had once eaten five during a single tea interval. (He had, not surprisingly, been unable to take the field after tea on that occasion.)

But, on this occasion, while the rest of the players were in the pavilion doing damage to the pile of sandwiches and cakes that had been prepared for them, Bill walked briskly across the cricket field to where Edwina and Damien were standing. Not normally a man for whom 'brisk' could safely be used to describe anything he did, Bill was in a hurry because he wanted to get back to the pavilion before all the food disappeared.

'Enjoying the match?' he asked, as he approached Edwina and Damien. He couldn't remember their names and wasn't even sure he had ever known them. He didn't know a great deal about business negotiations (not ever having taken part in any it would perhaps be more accurate to say that he knew absolutely nothing about business negotiations) but he seemed to remember having read somewhere that good negotiators always try to make the opposition feel comfortable and relaxed before getting down to the nitty gritty.

'It's wonderful!' said Edwina, smiling sweetly.

'Terrific stuff,' agreed Damien. 'Riveting.'

'Well, do you want to make an offer?' asked Bill. Having

made the opposition feel as comfortable and as relaxed as he intended to make them feel, and having got the niceties out of the way, he wanted to get down to business as quickly as possible. He had spotted some chocolate éclairs among the food that had been prepared and he liked chocolate éclairs almost as much as he liked cream horns.

'I think so,' drawled Damien, slowly. 'Without prejudice, of course. And notwithstanding any clauses which may be aforementioned or discussed hereinafter.' He stretched each word almost to breaking point and managed to inject a considerable amount of doubt into these words. He had decided to play 'Mr Cool' in order to try and get the land as cheaply as possible.

'Jolly good,' said Bill. He stood and waited.

'You have to understand that I would be taking a considerable risk,' said Damien.

'How much?' asked Bill.

'Ten thousand,' said Damien. 'For the whole field, of course.'

'Bye!' said Bill, turning round and heading back towards the pavilion. He may have been inexperienced but he wasn't stupid. 'He's going!' hissed Edwina, as Bill marched back towards the pavilion. 'You'll lose it.'

'That's just my opening offer, of course,' Damien called after the disappearing land owner.

Bill looked behind him but didn't stop walking. 'What's your best offer?' he called.

'Twenty five!' called Damien.

Bill just kept walking. The cricket field was the only thing he had left. He didn't really want to sell it. If he sold it then he would undoubtedly lose the post of club cricket captain. And he liked being captain. He knew that he wasn't any good as a captain and he was under no illusions about his organisational skills (he had once overheard Cheesy say: 'our captain couldn't organise a prayer meeting in a nunnery') but none of that mattered because he had Paddy to deal with the complicated stuff like field placings. Bill had practised coin tossing for hours and that was an aspect of the captaincy which he believed he could master. He liked being president and chairman too. If he sold the ground he wanted every penny he could get for it.

'Fifty!' called Damien, now walking swiftly after Bill. 'I'll pay fifty.'

Still Bill kept walking.

Damien broke into a jog. Although he looked fit he wasn't a man who was accustomed to real physical exercise. 'What do you want?' he asked when he caught up with Bill.

'A hundred,' said Bill, without hesitation. 'A hundred thousand.'

'What!' said Damien. 'That's absurd.'

'It's a fair price,' said Bill, remembering what the banker had told him.

'Ninety?' offered Damien, unable to conceal the desperation in his voice.

'A hundred,' said Bill, who hadn't stopped walking, or even slowed down.

'OK!' said Damien. 'OK! I'll pay you a hundred thousand.'

'Great!' said Bill, stopping walking for a moment and finding himself unable to prevent a big smile spreading across his face. He held out his hand.

Eventually Damien realised that Bill wanted to shake his hand. Assuming either that this was some strange rural ritual or that Bill wanted to find out if he was a Freemason, he put out his hand (giving the sign) and the two men shook. Bill didn't do anything funny with his fingers and so Damien rightly assumed that he wasn't a Freemason.

'I'll bring down some papers for you to sign in the next day or so,' said Damien. 'Where can I find you?'

Bill gave his address and telephone number and Damien wrote the information down in a small pocket diary.

'Splendid!' said Bill, who wanted to jump and down but felt that it was probably not the thing to do. He hurried back to the pavilion with three chocolate éclairs and two glasses of orange squash where he celebrated (very privately).

Damien, hurried back in the opposite direction where he was quickly reunited with Biffo's wife and his client.

'What happened?' demanded Edwina.

'I got it!' said Damien, as excited as a schoolboy with a new bicycle. 'I did the deal!'

'Fantastic! said Edwina, who immediately had visions of their having to move to Monaco to minimise their tax problems. 'Congratulations!'

They embraced, but did this cautiously so that Edwina's make-up would not be disturbed.

'What did you get it for?' asked Edwina.

'I beg your pardon?' said Damien, who as a young lawyer had been taught to pretend he hadn't heard the question if he wanted time to think before giving an answer.

'How much do you have to pay for the land?'

'Oh, I got it for a hundred!' said Damien brightly, who, being a lawyer, was devious. He wanted to give the impression that he was delighted with the price he'd agreed to pay.

'Oh.' said Edwina, rather disappointed. She had had higher hopes for Damien's negotiating skills.

'But don't worry,' added Damien quickly. 'Just because I've said I'll pay that much it doesn't mean that I'll actually have to hand over the money.'

Edwina was greatly reassured by this.

~ Chapter 44 ~

'READY THEN?'

Biffo turned round and saw the other umpire standing behind him.

'Time to get back out there,' said the visiting umpire. He had cake crumbs around his mouth and several stains down the front of his white coat. He lifted his left arm and made a great show of displaying his watch. 'Tea interval's over!' he explained. He rubbed his hands together, though Biffo wasn't sure whether this was because he was looking forward to the second half of the match or because his hands were cold.

'Right!' agreed Biffo, looking around for somewhere to put his plate. He balanced it, rather precariously, on top of a pile of crockery sitting right on the very edge of the large table which dominated the centre of the Short Room.

'Ready?' enquired the visiting umpire.

'Ready!' agreed Biffo. He automatically tried to button his white coat but discovered that most of the buttons had disappeared.

The two men left the pavilion and headed for the wicket.

They were half way there when there was a loud crash. The pile of crockery to which Biffo's plate had been the ceramic equivalent of the final straw had finally decided that it had no choice but to obey the law of gravity. Several dozen cups, plates and saucers had shattered on the Short Room floor.

For a moment or two there was silence in the pavilion. Those who were standing closest to the table shuffled cautiously away from the wreckage and universally adopted looks of surprise and horror.

'Who did that?' demanded Mrs Betty Cleavidge, emerging from the kitchen. She took two steps forward and then stood, her hands on her hips, and a scowl on her face, staring at the wreckage around her feet.

'It wasn't me!' said Len, quickly.

'Nor me!' said Cheesy.

These were followed by many other protestations of innocence.

'Never mind,' said a brave but foolish member of the visiting side. The speaker was an innocent youth who did not know Mrs Cleavidge and was not aware of the danger of antagonising such a formidable woman. 'It'll save you a lot of washing up.'

Upon hearing this bold attempt at what the visiting cricketer would have probably described as a 'joke' the Fondling-Under-Water cricketers swarmed towards the door, left the pavilion *en-masse* and were well on the way to the pitch before they realised that it was the visitors' turn to field and their turn to bat.

They turned round and retreated to the pavilion just in time to see the foolish visitor disappearing into the distance with an unhappy Mrs Cleavidge, dish mop aloft, in hot pursuit.

For Bill Stickers, club captain and property dealer *manqué*, the attraction of chocolate éclairs trumped the threat posed by

Mrs Betty Cleavidge. He had not budged and welcomed his team back into the pavilion by holding out a large plate of cream-filled scones.

Mrs Cleavidge chased the visiting jester for a hundred yards and returned to the pavilion wheezing and looking pale. She immediately had one of her funny turns and had to rest in a deck chair behind the pavilion. She sat warming her hands (always cold because she had terrible circulation, and usually red and chapped because they spent more time in washing up water than out of it) around a nice cup of tea. This was for her a strange treat for although she made gallons of tea every weekend she rarely ever had time to drink any of the stuff.

Meanwhile, the visiting side had distributed themselves around the ground in what they felt could appropriately be described as fielding positions.

Daniel Potterton was an enthusiastic captain, whose eagerness could never be faulted but, like Bill Stickers, he would have never claimed that he was a master tactician.

He had no difficulty in working out where fielders should stand when he was watching other people play cricket. When seated high in the stands at a Test Match ground he never felt shy about offering his advice to the England captain. But somehow everything seemed different when he was standing on the mown grass of a cricket ground. He never seemed to have enough fielders to fill all the positions which he felt needed filling.

He had discovered, through bitter experience, that although his bowlers always wanted four slips, two gulleys, a leg slip, a forward short leg and a silly mid on they were not always able to bowl in such a way as to take full advantage of such an aggressive field setting. It was, therefore, his custom, based on a good deal of experience, to allow the fielders to position themselves around the bat in a fairly large and well spread out circle.

On this occasion, however, there was such a large and noticeable gap in the field that even Daniel could see that the Fondling-Under-Water batsmen might notice and take advantage of the space.

Daniel knew, of course, that very few batsmen in village

cricket are good enough to deliberately place the ball into gaps between the fielders but his mathematical skills were well enough developed for him to realise that when a quarter of the ground is unpatrolled there is a reasonable chance that one shot in four will lead to an increase in the batting side's total.

'There's a big gap down there!' shouted Daniel, who was standing in what could perhaps best be described as a mid-wicket position. He waved and pointed to the gap.

The rest of his side pretended not to hear him. The secret of the Fondling-Under-Water damp patch was not, it appeared, quite such a secret as the Fondling-Under-Water players believed. Three of the visiting players examined the sky above as though looking for enemy aircraft, three scrutinised their fingernails as though they had never noticed them before and five aspiring botanists bent down and carefully studied the grass at their feet.

'There's a big gap!' Daniel shouted again.

The wicket keeper, who since he was wearing a pair of thick wicket keeping gloves had been denied the opportunity to examine his fingernails and had chosen the looking down at the grass option rather than the looking up into the sky option because looking upwards always made him feel dizzy, raised his eyes, looked across at his captain and then looked around, as though searching for this alleged gap.

'Where?' he demanded, at last.

'Over there!' said Daniel, pointing to the gap.

'Oh yes!' said the wicket keeper, apparently seeing the gap for the first time.

'Someone should fill it!' shouted Daniel.

The other nine members of his team continued to study sky, grass or fingernails, depending upon whim and personal preference.

'I think you'll have to go down there yourself, skipper,' said the wicket keeper.

'Why won't anyone field there?' demanded Daniel.

Jack Hobbs, one of the Fondling-Under-Water opening batsmen, turned to Biffo. 'It's going to get dark soon,' he muttered.

Jack was standing at the non-striker's end, next to Biffo,

since it was his partner's turn to take the first ball. His real name was Cedric and he worked as a farm labourer. For twenty seven years he had opened the Fondling-Under-Water batting together with a retired blacksmith called Herbert Sutcliffe. Herbert, whose real Christian name was Simon, and whose surname was Wrigglesworth had been given his nickname and his position in the Fondling-Under-Water side by Donald Box, founder and proprietor of the village shop and father of Delphinium Box. Mr Box, who had captained the side for twenty years, had been tickled pink by the prospect of captaining a batting side opened by Hobbs and Sutcliffe, in his view probably the best known and most successful opening partnership the England cricket team had ever had.

'Mr Ruggles!' called Daniel, addressing the nearest fielder.

Newton Ruggles abandoned his careful study of his fingernails and looked up.

'Would you be kind enough to field in that gap over there, please?'

'Which gap?'

Daniel pointed to the gap. 'That gap!'

'Oh that gap,' said Mr Ruggles, as though he had not noticed the gap before. 'That's what we call 'third man' skipper.'

'Well, whatever it's called there isn't anyone there.'

'It's too muddy.' said Mr Ruggles, shaking his head. 'I'm not fielding down there. My wife will only wash my cricket trousers every four games.'

Daniel looked around the rest of the field, desperately trying to catch someone's eye. But looking round doesn't help much when eyes don't want to be caught.

Daniel sighed. It was a very loud and very tired sigh. 'I suppose I'll have to go down there myself,' he said, standing with hands on hips and looking around and waiting for someone to contradict him. But no one contradicted him.

'It looks like you'll have to go down there yourself,' said Hamish Jones, the Wanderers' umpire.

Grunting, scowling, shaking his head and generally looking very unhappy Daniel headed off for the damp patch.

'He looks a bit disgruntled,' said Biffo to Jack Hobbs.

'Funny word that,' said Jack.

Biffo looked at him, puzzled. 'Why? What's funny about it?'

'Disgruntled,' said Jack.

'Why?' asked Biffo, frowning. 'Why is it funny?'

'Disgruntled,' said Jack. 'Take the dis off it and you're left with gruntled. Normally when you take the dis off a word the word you're left with means roughly the opposite. Take dis off disclaimed and you get claimed. Remove dis from disappointed and you get appointed.'

Biffo thought about this for a moment. 'Yes,' he said, not quite understanding what Jack was getting at.

'But what does gruntled mean?' asked Jack.

'I don't know,' said Biffo. 'I suppose it ought to mean happy.'

'Funny that,' said Jack, thoughtfully. He sighed, toyed with his bat for a moment and then nodded towards Daniel who was now picking his way through the damp patch and discovering why none of his team wanted to field down there. 'He seems to have discovered the secret of the damp patch,' he said.

'It's all soggy down here!' Daniel shouted, lifting a leg and pointing to the splashes of mud which had reached almost to his knee. He had discovered why none of his team wanted to field at third man.

No one took any notice of him.

'Shall I start?' asked Hugo Wimpole-Bassett, the Wanderers opening bowler.

'I think so,' said Biffo. 'Go!' he said, loudly.

The opening bowler looked at him. 'What do you mean?' he asked.

'Go!' said Biffo. 'You can start.'

'But what does 'Go!' mean?' asked the bowler.

'It means you can start bowling,' explained Biffo. He looked across at Jack Hobbs and lowered his voice. 'Isn't that what I'm supposed to say?'

'I think you're supposed to say 'Play!',' said Jack. 'But if you want to say 'Go!' that's absolutely fine by me.'

'Oh yes,' agreed Biffo, though he really couldn't see that there was a great deal of difference between 'Go!' and 'Play!'.

He cleared his throat and called out: 'Play!'

Hugo Wimpole-Bassett had bowled the first four balls of his over when the sea mist started to roll in.

~ Chapter 45 ~

BIFFO'S EXPERIENCE OF SEA MISTS was limited. Apart from spending two weeks of most summers sheltering behind canvas wind breaks on Cornish beaches he had never spent much time at the seaside and sea mists, being predictable creatures of habit, are most often to be found in the vicinity of the sea.

Biffo was more accustomed to land mists. These tended, in his experience, to be fairly slow moving; steady and reliable diminishers of visibility. A land mist is polite and always gives a little notice of its arrival. It sort of trickles into place; and could perhaps be most accurately described as the dripping tap of mists.

A sea mist, on the other hand, is no trickler and is unconcerned with polite niceties; it is the burst pipe of mists. One minute it is somewhere else entirely, unseen and quite unsuspected, and the next minute it is there.

One minute the sun was shining on Fondling-Under-Water and the next minute the cricketers were all enveloped in a vast, wet blanket of impenetrable dampness.

'I say,' cried Daniel, the first member of the visiting side to be overwhelmed by the sea mist and to realise that he could no longer see. 'I can't see a thing!' There was a pause and then a panicky shout. 'It's either gone very foggy or else I've suddenly developed cataracts.' The voice came out of the mist clearly enough but the owner of the voice was already quite invisible.

Within minutes the mist was so thick that the cricketers in the middle could not see the pavilion, and the spectators (and more importantly the scorers) in the pavilion could not see what was happening on the pitch.

'What shall we do?' asked a voice which Biffo vaguely recognised. He peered through the mist and just managed to identify Hugo Wimpole-Bassett who was standing about three feet away from him.

'I don't know,' said Biffo. 'It seems to be a bit misty.' He turned around through what he thought was three and sixty degrees, looking for Jack or Herbert. He couldn't see anyone at all.

'Maybe we should get some torches,' said Hugo. 'Or get people to turn their car headlights on.'

'I don't think that will help much,' said Biffo. 'Jack?' he called. 'Herbert?'

'Who's that?' came back a wheezy voice.

'It's Biffo' said Biffo. 'Who's that?'

'Herbert,' said Herbert, who was clearly short of breath.

'Are you at this end?' asked Biffo.

'Yes,' said Herbert. 'We ran three.' He wheezed a bit more. 'It's a long time since we ran a three,' he said.

'How long is this mist likely to last?' asked Biffo.

'It could be over in a few minutes,' said Herbert. There was a long pause while he did some more wheezing. 'Or it might last for the rest of the day,' he added. He felt very miserable. He had scored a total of 48 runs in his last eight innings and until the mist had come down he had felt confident that he would be able to reach his fifty in this match. (Fondling-Under-Water players did not limit themselves to a single match when it came to reaching batting milestones. Herbert Sutcliffe's first hundred had taken him eight years and 96 innings.)

'Shall I finish the over?' asked Hugo Wimpole-Bassett.

'What do you think, Herbert?' Biffo asked.

'Oh, let's carry on,' said Herbert. The pause was noticeably shorter this time. 'We don't usually let the weather interfere with play.' He sighed dreamily. 'We could do with Wally Sticklepath today.'

'Who was Wally Sticklepath?' asked Daniel.

'We never lost a match when it was misty and we had Wally Sticklepath playing,' said Herbert, nostalgically. 'He was a great mimic and he could throw his voice. When it was misty he would have the opposition batsmen running all over the place. He would stand at third man, pretend he was one of the batsmen and yell out 'Run Two'. We ran out both batsmen at once thanks to him. One had gone to square leg and the other one was last seen getting off a bus in Middlesbrough.'

Biffo cleared his throat. 'Carry on,' he said. 'Play!' he added quickly.

There was a long silence and then Biffo heard a voice. It was coming from a body he couldn't see.

'Er, do you know which direction the stumps are in?' asked the bowler, rather diffidently.

Biffo, who now had no idea which way he was facing or where anything was did not need to think before replying. 'No,' he said. 'But maybe we ought to find out. Let's find the stumps at this end first.'

He bent down and waved an arm around. 'Use your bat,' he said to Herbert. 'See if you can find the stumps.'

'I won't be out if I hit the wicket will I?' asked Herbert.

'No,' Biffo assured him. 'We need to find the wicket so that we can work out where the other end is.'

'I've got them!' called Hugo, a moment or two later.

'Keep talking,' said Biffo. 'So that we can find you.'

'What shall I say?' asked Hugo.

'It doesn't matter,' said Biffo. 'Just keep talking.'

'Do you like semolina?' asked Hugo.

'Pardon?' said Biffo.

'Do you like semolina?' asked Hugo.

'Not particularly,' said Biffo. 'What on earth do you want to know that for?'

'I don't really want to know,' said Hugo.

'Then why did you ask?'

'You said to keep talking,' said Hugo. 'I couldn't think of anything else to say.' He paused. 'People tell me I'm not terribly bright,' he said, rather sadly.

'Oh I'm sure you are,' said Biffo.

'No, really, I'm not,' said Hugo. 'I'm actually most terribly thick. But it's OK because my dad is stinking rich and I work for him so it doesn't really matter.'

'Oh, good,' said Biffo.

'I can see you!' said Herbert.

'Who? Me?' said Biffo.

'No. The bowler,' said Herbert. 'And the stumps.'

'I can see you,' said Hugo, sounding quite excited.

'Me?' said Herbert.

'No, I can see the umpire,' said Hugo. 'Oh, I can see you too, Herbert.'

'I can see both of you too!' said Biffo, feeling relieved. 'Right!' he said, standing behind the stumps and peering into the distance. 'Jack?'

'Yes!' said a voice, which seemed to come from behind him.

'Is that you Jack?'

'Yes.' replied a voice which now clearly belonged to Jack but which still seemed to be coming from behind them.

Biffo and Herbert peered through the mist at one another. 'Where did that come from?' asked Biffo.

'Behind us,' said Herbert.

They walked around the stumps and faced the opposite direction. 'Are you still there?' called Biffo.

'Where would I be going?' called Jack. 'I'm staying with the stumps.'

'Hugo is going to bowl in a minute,' shouted Biffo. 'I'll tell him to call out when he delivers the ball. Try not to hit a six because if you do we'll never find the ball.'

'Right!' replied Jack, optimistically.

'Call out when you deliver the ball,' Biffo said to Hugo.

'OK,' said Hugo. He walked away from the stumps and then walked back again.

'What shall I call out?' he asked.

'Anything you like,' said Biffo. 'Anything. It's just so that Jack knows the ball is coming.'

'Right,' said Hugo.

'But not that question about the semolina,' said Biffo. 'It will confuse him. He'll probably try and answer.'

Hugo walked away again and disappeared for a few moments. And then he came back.

'I'm not taking a full run,' he said.

'Very sensible,' said Biffo.

'I might get lost,' said Hugo.

'Right,' said Biffo. 'Play!' he shouted. He peered into the mist ahead of him.

'I haven't seen it yet!' called Jack.
'It hasn't been bowled yet,' said Biffo.
'I heard someone call out,' said Jack.
'That was me,' said Biffo. 'I just said 'Play!'. Hugo will call out when he bowls.'
'OK,' said Jack.
'I like semolina!' called Hugo, as he delivered the fifth ball of his over.
Jack, who was not surprisingly, rather puzzled by this unexpected statement did not see the ball. And nor did any of the fielders.
'Who's got the ball?' called Biffo.
No one answered.
'Has anyone seen the ball?' shouted Biffo.
There was a general murmuring of 'No's from around the field.
'Oh,' said Biffo. He sighed. 'We seem to have lost the ball.'
'Use the spare!' suggested Herbert. 'Franklin always carries a spare.'
Biffo pulled the spare ball from his coat pocket and handed it to Hugo.
'Another ball is coming!' shouted Biffo.
'Did you find that one then?' called Jack.
'No,' said Biffo. 'It's another ball.'
'Tell me when it's coming,' said Jack.
'Listen out for Hugo,' said Biffo.
'Do you like semolina?' called Hugo, delivering the sixth and final ball of his over.
'I told you not to say that!' said Biffo.
'Ouch!' came a fierce yell from twenty two yards away.
'What happened?' called Biffo.
'It hit me!' replied Jack, rather put out.
'The ball?'
'What the hell else do you think hit me?'
'Owzat?' cried Hugo.
'Are you all right?' called Herbert.
'Am I still alive?' asked Jack.
'Can you see the ball?' called Biffo.

'No,' said Jack. 'It bounced away somewhere. I don't know where it's gone.'

'Owzat?' asked Hugo.

'What do you keep shouting that for?' asked Biffo.

'I was appealing,' said Hugo. 'He might be out. The ball hit him. Maybe it hit his pads.'

'Don't be silly,' said Biffo, who was running out of patience. 'How can I give him out? I can't even see him.'

'We can't find the ball!' Biffo heard someone shout.

Since they had now lost the only two balls they had there was little choice but to abandon the match.

'We'll have to go off,' said Biffo.

'What for?' asked Herbert.

'I don't know,' said Biffo. 'Bad light?' he suggested.

'The light is fine,' said Herbert. 'It's just that we can't see anything.'

'Lost balls,' said Biffo. 'Play abandoned due to loss of balls.'

'I doubt if they are really lost,' said Herbert, pedantically. 'They're bound to be around somewhere. We'll find them when the mist lifts.'

'OK,' sighed Biffo. 'Play abandoned for mislaid balls.' He raised his voice. 'Does anyone know where the pavilion is?'

~ Chapter 46 ~

BY THE TIME DANIEL POTTERTON, Herbert Sutcliffe and Biffo arrived at The Gravedigger's Rest they were all soaked to the skin. The mist had turned to rain and the rain had turned quickly and apparently effortlessly into a fully blown storm.

'Well, look who's here!' said Len, as they trooped in through the door to the public bar. Herbert, being local, ducked and didn't bang his head on the lintel. Nor did he trip down the step into the bar. Biffo, remembered the step but forgot just how low the door was and banged his head. Daniel Potterton, never having entered The Gravedigger's Rest before banged his head and fell down the step.

Rupert smiled contentedly.

'Is it raining?' demanded Itchy, anxiously.

Shaking the water from his head, like a dog just out of a bath, Biffo confirmed that it was.

Itchy swore quietly. 'I'm going to get soaked.'

'Do you have to go out somewhere?' asked Biffo.

'I need to water the pitch later,' explained Itchy.

'Your lot have gone,' said Len, helping Daniel to his feet. Daniel, dripping water onto the carpet, held his head with one hand and rubbed his left knee with the other. He looked around. 'Gone?'

'They wanted to get to wherever it is that you're supposed to be playing tomorrow,' said Len.

'They left a message for you,' said Itchy. 'I wrote it down so that I wouldn't forget it.' He picked up a soggy beer-mat, eased himself off his bar stool, and took the beer-mat over to Daniel.

Daniel took the beer-mat in the hand he had been using to rub his knee and read out the message it contained. 'Riddles Best Bitter – For The Discerning Drinker.' He looked puzzled.

'Try the other side,' suggested Itchy.

'The biggest iceberg ever seen was larger than Belgium,' read Daniel. 'No 37 in a series of 101 Amazing True Facts Brought To You By Riddles Best Bitter'. He paused for a moment, clearly puzzled. 'Is it in code?' he asked, looking around the bar, as though asking for help.

'Maybe that was the wrong beer-mat,' said Itchy. He turned back to the bar and started to examine the other beer-mats. 'Ah!' he said, gleefully, after picking up and examining both sides of half a dozen beer-mats. He handed Daniel the newly discovered beer-mat upon which a single word had quite clearly been written in blue ink.

Daniel accepted the beer-mat gratefully and read out loud the word which had been scrawled upon it. 'Gone.'

'Well, that's a help,' he said.

'I wanted them to stay,' said Rupert.

'You wanted them all to come into the pub so that they'd all bang their heads,' said Puffy, standing behind the bar and drying glasses with a grey tea towel.

'You wanted them to come in so that they'd buy your beer,' was the retort from the bookie.

'You lot drink all the beer I can keep in stock,' said Puffy. 'If I could get you to pay for it I'd be a happy man.'

'Is that it?' asked Daniel. 'Is that the message?' Having absorbed, assessed and memorised the message he had put the beer-mat back down on the bar and was now rubbing his knee again.

'They said you'd know where they'd gone,' said Puffy.

'I had a copy of the itinerary,' agreed Daniel. 'But it was in my bag.'

'So, where is your bag?'

'In Mr Ruggles' car.'

'Ruggles?'

'Newton Ruggles. The bank manager. I came in his car. 'They took my licence off me last year.'

'Who did?' asked Itchy, looking puzzled.

'The police,' replied Daniel. 'Well, to be accurate the magistrate actually took my licence from me. But I don't entirely absolve the police from blame.'

'They really did that?' said Itchy.

'They said I had too much alcohol in my blood,' said Daniel.

'Crumbs!' said Itchy, who led a sheltered life and knew surprisingly little about the ways of the world. He was genuinely shocked. 'Can they really do that? Where do you live?'

'Birmingham,' said Daniel. 'But it was a magistrate in Middlesex who took away my licence,' he went on. 'That's sort of Londonish,' he explained.

'Middlesex has always had quite a good cricket team,' said Itchy, genuinely surprised. 'I'm surprised a county like that would take your licence away, just for having alcohol in your blood.'

'So I sold my car,' Daniel went on. 'My wife doesn't drive so there didn't seem much point in keeping the damned thing in the garage.'

'Let me get this straight,' said Len, who was obviously having some trouble understanding what had happened. 'The police took away your driving licence because you had blood in your alcohol?'

'Alcohol in my blood,' said Daniel. 'They took away my licence because they said I had too much alcohol in my blood.'

'How can you have too much alcohol in your blood?' asked Len, who seemed to find this whole concept genuinely puzzling. When an inhumane barmaid in Wednesbury had once told him that he had had enough to drink Len had logically and indignantly explained to the barmaid that if he had had enough to drink he wouldn't have wanted any more. 'Who said you had too much?' he demanded, without waiting for an answer to his previous question.

'It's the law,' said Daniel.

'Have you heard of them doing that?' Len asked Constable Hobbling.

'Heard of them doing what?' asked Constable Hobbling, when he had finished emptying his fourth pint of best bitter.

'Taking away a bloke's driving licence because he had too much blood in his alcohol.'

'Alcohol in his blood,' said Daniel.

'Constable Hobbling is a policeman,' Len explained to Daniel, 'He's bound to know about stuff like this.'

'Oh yes, they can,' agreed Constable Hobbling, nodding wisely.

'Phew!' said Herbert Sutcliffe. 'That's terrible.'

'Blood in the alcohol,' said Len to himself.

'Alcohol in the blood,' said Daniel.

'Alcohol in the blood,' said Herbert, clearly thinking hard. He looked around. 'So, that would be a driving offence?'

'Yes,' said Len. 'Daniel says he lost his driving licence because the police said he had too much blood in his alcohol.'

This time Daniel, feeling slightly confused himself, did not bother to correct Len.

'Oh yes,' said Constable Hobbling, nodding wisely. 'They do it in the towns.' He put down his empty glass, put his hands behind his back, rocked backwards and forwards on his feet and closed his eyes.

'They do it everywhere these days,' said Daniel.

'They do,' confirmed Biffo.

'I think it's the Road Traffic Act,' said Constable Hobbling, opening his eyes and looking pleased with himself at this piece of legislative knowledge. He frowned and thought for a moment. 'Either that or something else.'

'They don't do it here,' said Len, pulling a face and shaking his head vigorously. 'It doesn't happen here,' he said firmly and with some considerable pride.

'We don't have any trouble like that round here,' added Herbert, earnestly shaking his head.

'What do you mean?' asked Biffo, confused. 'Do you mean that people don't drink and drive?'

'Well I've never heard of anyone in the village losing their licence for having too much blood in their alcohol,' said Len firmly. 'Have you?' he said to Puffy.

Puffy shook his head.

'Are you the village policeman?' Daniel asked Constable Hobbling.

'Community constable,' replied Constable Hobbling. 'Lived here all my life. Community constable for twenty seven years.'

'And you have never had to arrest anyone for drunken driving?'

'Certainly not,' said Constable Hobbling, indignantly. 'It's my job to keep the peace not to start a war.' He took a large sip from his glass and leant forward as though to share some confidential item of gossip. 'Besides,' he said softly. 'I only have a moped so I couldn't really chase anyone.' He thought for a moment. 'I certainly couldn't chase them if they went up a hill.'

Hardly had these sensible words left Constable Hobbling's mouth when there was a loud cry of something that sounded like 'Drip!' from the far end of the bar.

Daniel and Biffo, both being new to Fondling-Under-Water were surprised by this shout. They both assumed it to be the result of some sort of argument between two of the drinkers at that end of the bar. Daniel, coming from a part of the world where an insult would invariably soon be followed by the throwing of glasses and punches, instinctively ducked and tried to look as small as possible while Biffo, who was surprised at the modest and non-profane nature of the insult, merely peered through the smoky gloom to try and identify the originator.

But, with these two exceptions, everyone else in the bar seemed to know exactly what the cry meant.

Behind the bar Puffy, who was busy filling a beer glass with beer, stopped what he was doing, bent down out of sight for a moment and reappeared clutching four old saucepans which he proceeded to position on the bar counter. He seemed to know exactly where the saucepans should be. Meanwhile, Lettice, a couple of yards away from him, was handing empty beer glasses out to the customers who were rushing about placing the empty glasses on the floor and on the small tables which were scattered around the public bar. Everyone seemed to know what they were doing and everyone, apart from Biffo and Daniel, seemed to know what was going on.

'What's going on?' Biffo asked Len, when everyone seemed satisfied that they had placed empty vessels in all the appropriate places.

'One by the door, please, gentlemen!' called Puffy, holding out an empty beer glass.

Itchy took the glass from him and carefully placed it on the floor near to the door. He stood back, examined the position where he had placed the glass for a moment and then leant forward and moved it two inches to the left.

'What's going on?' Biffo asked again.

'Sssshhhhh!' said Len, holding a finger to his lips.

'Sorry!' whispered Biffo, automatically. He looked across at Daniel, who shrugged. He looked equally confused. The bar was now quite silent.

And then Biffo heard it. 'Drip. Plunk. Drip. Plunk. Drip. Drip. Drip. Plunk. Plunk. Drip.' It was, he thought at first, rather like one of the absurdly unmusical symphonies which modern composers insist on writing and which his television programme, 'The Arts This Week', had, for reasons which he would now readily admit he did not understand, promoted, publicised and fêted. After listening to the 'Drip. Plunk. Drip' for a minute or so more he came to the conclusion that he was quite wrong. The sound of all those drips landing in all those empty beer glasses and saucepans was far more musical, far more imaginative and far more appealing to the ear than the cacophony produced by the over-hyped and arrogant composers whose work had appeared on his television programme.

Biffo watched, fascinated, as Puffy, Lettice and the drinkers in the bar, carefully examined each receptacle to make sure that it was correctly positioned. One or two needed moving a fraction of an inch or so but the majority seemed to be positioned perfectly to catch the water which was now falling through the ceiling in a couple of dozen places.

'Thank you gentlemen,' said Puffy, loudly, a moment or two later. 'And lady!' he added, nodding towards Lettice who smiled at him and made as much of a curtsey as you can make when wearing a tight skirt and standing in the narrow space behind a bar.

'What on earth is happening?' asked Biffo.

'Leaky roof,' answered Len.

'Yes, I rather thought it might be,' admitted Biffo. 'But how come you all know where to catch the leaks?'

'Because when it rains hard enough and long enough the water always comes in through the same places,' replied Len, as though explaining something very simple to someone very stupid.

'So wouldn't it be better just to have the roof repaired?' asked Biffo

'It doesn't cost anything to catch the water in glasses and saucepans,' replied Len.

'I suppose not,' agreed Biffo. 'But the water up in the loft must be doing quite a lot of damage.'

'I don't expect it does the upstairs rooms much good either,' said Len.

Biffo looked up.

'It doesn't usually start coming through down here until it's been raining for an hour or two,' explained Len.

'So why not get the roof repaired?' asked Biffo, redirecting the question to the landlord of The Gravedigger's Rest.

The 'Drip. Plunk. Drip. Drip. Plunk.' had now started to become a much softer 'Splish. Splash. Splosh' as the receptacles had started to fill.

'No money,' said Puffy with a shrug.

'Can't you claim on your insurance?'

'No insurance.'

'I'd better go and check my bedroom,' said Biffo, emptying the glass from which he had been drinking, standing up ready to head for the passageway which led to the stairs which led to his bedroom.

'Do you want an umbrella?' asked Puffy.

Biffo thought that this was a joke until Puffy produced an umbrella and offered it to him.

'No, thanks,' said Biffo. 'I'll just dodge the drips.'

Puffy looked at him and frowned. He started to say something but Biffo had gone. The drips in the passageway and on the staircase, none of which were being collected by beer glasses or saucepans, had already collected together on the floor and on the stairs and had created noticeable puddles.

It was, however, when Biffo reached the upstairs corridor which led to his bedroom that he realised why Puffy had offered to lend him an umbrella. In several places there was enough water coming through the ceiling to create a very respectable shower.

When he opened the door to his room Biffo realised why the bed had been placed in such an eccentric, diagonal position. He was very pleased that he had never found the time or the energy to move it. Although water was dripping steadily through the bedroom ceiling, the bed was positioned in such a spot that it had remained perfectly dry. Splashing around on the floor Biffo picked up his briefcase and tossed it into a drawer so that it would have some protection from the rain. As he looked around he wondered what Edwina would have to say if she saw a bedroom turned into a furnished paddling pool. He felt a migraine headache starting as he toyed with the horror of having to explain to her what had happened. And then he remembered that Edwina wouldn't be around to see what had happened and the blossoming migraine headache disappeared as quickly as it had arrived.

It wasn't until he was about to go back downstairs again that he realised that Tiger had disappeared.

~ Chapter 47 ~

'TIGER HAS GONE!' SHOUTED BIFFO, running into the bar in a considerable state of distress. When he had left the bar to check on his room his clothes and hair had already shown some signs of having started to dry out but his short trip up the stairs and back down again had left Biffo, once more, soaked to the skin. He could almost feel a sneeze coming on.

The panic which followed this simple and heartfelt announcement can, in hindsight, be both excused and explained by the simple fact that most of his listeners mistakenly assumed that the three word sentence which Biffo had uttered had been a four word sentence and that the three words which he really had spoken had been preceded by the definite article.

There is, of course, a considerable amount of difference between the simple sentence 'Tiger has gone!', uttered by an unhappy cat owner who is worried that he may have suddenly and tragically become a former cat owner, and the far more doom laden, and entirely different, sentence 'The tiger has gone!' which seems to suggest that a man-eating beast may have escaped from its place of confinement and be about to help itself to a tasty human snack or two.

Instead of offering help, sympathy and comfort (as they might reasonably have been expected to do) approximately half of Biffo's audience climbed onto tables while the remaining number picked up chairs and brandished them in the manner normally favoured by circus lion tamers.

'What's the matter?' demanded Biffo, taken aback by this unexpected response.

'People around here tend to be a bit nervous about tigers,' said Len, who had managed to climb onto the bar counter and was now clearly trying to pluck up the courage to leap several feet into the air and wrap his arms around an ancient and rather moth-eaten stag's head which was hanging on the wall.

'Tigers?' said Biffo, puzzled. 'Who said anything about tigers?'.

'Where did it escape from?', 'How many are there?', 'What was it doing here?', 'Has anyone got a gun?', 'Are they man eating tigers?' and 'Get your foot off my neck!' were just some of the most popular questions and exclamations that Biffo heard during the next fifteen seconds or so. No one seemed to be listening to anyone else and no one seemed in the slightest bit interested in finding or offering answers to any of these questions. 'Isn't your cat called Tiger?' Lettice asked Biffo. She was the one small oasis of calm in the emotional maelstrom which had now taken over the public bar of The Gravedigger's Rest.

'Yes,' said Biffo, failing in his struggle to stop a sneeze. 'She's disappeared.'

'Did you search your room?'

'There isn't a lot to search!' said Biffo. 'But I looked everywhere,' he added.

'Did you look under the bed? Maybe she crawled under there to find somewhere dry.'

Len had finally found the courage to make the leap up to the moth eaten stag's head. Sadly, the mounting which had for so long managed to restrain the stag's head from obeying the dictates of gravity was nowhere near sound enough or strong enough to hold Len's weight as well. A loud, rumbling and tearing sound was quickly followed by a cloud of plaster dust and a number of expletives as Len and the stag's head made gravity happy by falling to the ground together.

'There's a puddle an inch deep on my floor,' replied Biffo, ignoring Len and the falling stag's head and answering Lettice's question. 'Cats hate water. But, yes, I did look under the bed. And she's not there.'

'What the hell is going on?' demanded Puffy.

'Biffo's cat is missing,' explained Lettice.

'Probably eaten by the damned tiger,' said Puffy. 'I'm no veterinarian but it seems to me that if you keep a cat and a tiger in one room you're asking for trouble. Is there a lot of mess? Blood everywhere? Maybe we can follow the bloody footprints?'

'I think I've done my back an injury,' said Len.

'There are no bloody footprints. There wasn't a tiger,' insisted Lettice. 'Just a cat.'

'So, what the hell makes him think the cat's been eaten by a tiger?' asked Puffy, now thoroughly confused.

'He doesn't think the cat has been eaten by a tiger,' explained Lettice. 'There never was a tiger!'

'Then why the hell frighten the life out of everyone by saying there was?' said Puffy, irritability replacing confusion.

'I didn't say that a tiger had escaped!' insisted Biffo. 'My cat is missing.'

'I heard you say it!' screamed Puffy.

'You misheard!' said Lettice.

'And I suppose everyone else misheard too!' shouted Puffy.

'Yes!' shouted Lettice.

'What?'

'Yes.'

'Yes what?'

'And my arm hurts,' said Len.

'Yes, everyone else misheard too,' said Lettice.

'There isn't a tiger?'

'No.'

'There never was a tiger?'

'My arm hurts worst,' said Len.

'No.'

'Oh,' said Puffy, now much quieter. 'You should be more careful about starting scares like that,' he added a moment or two later. 'Crying wolf they call it,' he muttered. 'Someone might have had a heart attack.'

'The beer glasses are full,' said Itchy, who, reassured by the fact that Biffo, Lettice and Puffy hadn't climbed up on the bar or picked up chairs with which to defend themselves, had walked over to the bar to share this item of news with the landlord.

'You should put a small billiard table in here,' said Cheesy.

'Why?' said Puffy.

'You could call it the pool room.'

Puffy ignored him.

'A pool room because it's full of water,' explained Cheesy. 'It's a sort of joke.'

'I think I've broken something,' said Len, who was still lying flat on the floor.

'Er, thanks Itchy,' said Puffy, ignoring Cheesy. 'Would you mind asking the lads to empty them?'

'What about the tiger?' asked Itchy, looking around rather nervously.

'There is no tiger,' said Puffy, speaking very slowly and clearly, as though trying to make a deaf person, a child or a foreigner understand.

'Oh,' said Itchy. And then he laughed and punched Biffo on the arm. 'You little tinker!' he said. 'You had us all going for a minute there.' He turned to face the rest of the bar. 'No tiger,' he called. 'Blame the practical joker here!' He laughed and playfully punched Biffo on the arm again.

There was some muttering but by and large most people climbed down off their tables and put down their chairs with smiles of relief on their faces.

Biffo rubbed his arm which hurt quite a lot. Itchy's idea of a playful punch was Biffo's idea of a knockout blow.

'Let's empty the glasses and saucepans,' said Itchy, setting a good example by picking up two beer glasses and carefully pouring the contents onto the floor.

'My cat is missing,' said Biffo very quietly. He had not realised until this moment just how much Tiger meant to him. Tiger was Biffo realised, his only true friend.

'We'll help you find her,' said Lettice, kindly. 'She'll be all right just you wait and see.'

'I'm going to faint,' said Len. 'I'm fainting...I'm faint...I'm...'

'She may have slipped out when I opened the door,' said Biffo, fighting hard to keep his voice steady. 'I'm going to look for her,' he added, turning and heading back down the corridor away from the bar.

'Wait!' called Lettice.

Biffo stopped, turned and waited.

'We'll help you,' she said. 'You don't know your way around. We'll organise a search.'

'Get up, Len!' said Puffy, kicking one of the unconscious man's feet.

Lettice clapped her hands to attract the attention of the customers, most of whom were now busily engaged trotting backwards and forwards to the gents' lavatory emptying saucepans and beer glasses. (They could have saved themselves a lot of time by using the ladies' lavatory which was far more conveniently situated but prejudices and old habits die hard and although Lettice was the only woman in the bar no one had the courage to break with years of tradition and stout taboos and push open the door with the figure of the little lady glued on it.)

'Len?' said Puffy. He bent down and realised for the first time that Len really was unconscious. 'I say,' he said, raising both his head and his voice. 'Len seems to be unconscious!'

'He probably thinks he's fainted,' said Itchy, who had returned from his trip to the gents' lavatory. It was well known that Len was an experienced hypochondriac who constantly enjoyed imagining that he was enduring poor health.

'No, seriously,' said Puffy. 'I think he may be injured!'

'Don't move him!' said Cheesy. 'More serious injuries are caused by bystanders moving accident victims than are caused by accidents.' He had read this somewhere and learnt it by heart.

'I wasn't going to move him!' said Puffy.

'So what do we do?' asked Jack Hobbs. 'We clearly can't leave him there. Puffy won't be able to move about behind the bar with him lying where he is.'

'Maybe you should ring for an ambulance,' suggested Daniel Potterton.

'The nearest ambulance station is an hour away,' said Puffy. He sighed. 'I suppose we'll have to get the doctor to take a look at him.'

'I clearly can't do anything to help here,' Biffo whispered to Lettice, during the silence. 'Do you think anyone would mind if I went and started looking for Tiger.'

'Wait just another minute,' whispered Lettice back. 'As soon as they've sorted out what to do with Len I'll organise a search party to help you.' She reached out, took his hand and squeezed it.

'So, where do we find your local doctor?' asked Daniel.

'Oh finding him isn't going to be any problem,' said Puffy. He stood up. 'Doc!' he called.

'You mean he's already in here?' said Daniel.

'Oh yes,' said Puffy. He peered around the bar. 'But I can't see him? Has anyone seen the doc?'

Biffo, who had been listening to this conversation, was as surprised as Daniel clearly was to discover that the local doctor was in the bar. He looked around trying to identify the physician. Cheesy? Unlikely, surely. Itchy? Impossible. Rupert? Surely not. Jack? Herbert? It couldn't possibly be.

'Here he is!' called Herbert, as a figure emerged from the gents' lavatory clutching two empty beer glasses.

'Doc!' called Puffy. 'We've got a patient for you!'

~ Chapter 48 ~

'TEN TO ONE HE'S GOT a broken humerus,' said Dr Rupert Fitzwalter, kneeling beside the now conscious but moaning Len. He had prodded and probed with surprisingly delicate and gentle fingers. 'Broken the neck of the bone, right up near the shoulder.' He looked round. 'Any takers?'

'Put me down for a quid, doc,' said Herbert.

'Fifty pence for me, doc,' said Jack.

'I'll have a quid too, doc,' whispered Len; the brave patient hedging his bets by taking a wager against his own doctor's diagnostic skills.

'Is he really the village doctor?' Biffo whispered to Lettice.

Lettice looked at him, smiled and nodded.

'He doesn't seem very much like any doctor I've ever known,' whispered Biffo.

'He likes to gamble,' admitted Lettice. 'But he's a good doctor although he does always enjoy having a bet with his patients when he makes a diagnosis.' She shrugged. 'The last doctor we had was always as drunk as a skunk so as far as the villagers are concerned Rupert is a great improvement. With Rupert they at least have the consolation of knowing that if he makes the wrong diagnosis they get to take some money off him.'

'What does it mean?' asked Len, who was considerably whiter than the sheets between which Biffo had spent the previous night. He moved slightly and winced as he did so.

Rupert, bit his lower lip and didn't speak for a moment.

'You can tell me, doc,' said Len hoarsely. 'I can take it,' he added bravely. He was now taking great care not to move at all.

Rupert looked down, paused, and gave Len the bad news. 'You're going to miss the next six matches at least,' he said.

It was then poor Len's turn to stay silent for a moment. 'I thought as much,' he said. He looked quite utterly wretched. He angrily brushed away a tear which had appeared in the corner of his right eye.

Rupert looked down at Len. 'I'm going to drive you over to the hospital,' he said. 'Before we go do you want something for the pain?'

'Oh yes, please,' said Len with pitiful eagerness.

'Give him a double whisky, Puffy,' said Rupert, heading for the door.

While Puffy poured Len a double whisky ('Are you sure that's a double?' asked Len, when handed a large tumbler two thirds full of whisky. 'It's at least four doubles!' replied Puffy. 'Maybe you should just fill it up to the top,' suggested Len.) Lettice began to recruit villagers for a search party to help Biffo look for Tiger. 'We don't want too many people,' she said to Biffo. 'Six should be plenty. If we have too many people wandering around the poor little thing will probably be terrified. Besides, we need to leave a few people behind to help Puffy look after Len. He'll probably be unconscious in a few minutes and then he'll need carrying out to Rupert's car.'

'What are we looking for?' asked Itchy, who had been the first to volunteer.

'A cat,' said Lettice.

'I realise that,' said Itchy. 'But what sort of cat? I don't want to totter around in the rain pouncing on just any old cat I see and dragging it back here for inspection.'

'It's a sort of...' began Lettice, rather uncertain as how to describe Biffo's feline friend.

'Tiger is a mackerel tabby,' interrupted Biffo. 'Quite small and skinny though you'd wonder why if you saw how much she eats.'

'Tiger?' said Herbert. 'That's the cat's name?'

'That's the cat's name,' agreed Biffo.

'Ah,' said Herbert, who wasn't the fastest thinker in the village, 'Now I'm beginning to understand.'

'And she'll come if we call her by name?' asked Daniel.

'I'm not exactly sure about that,' admitted Biffo. 'Cats are pretty independent creatures. She usually comes when I call her – especially if she's hungry.'

'Why don't we just go and look for her?' said Lettice. 'If anyone spots a mackerel tabby they can call out for Biffo so that he can hurry over and investigate.'

And so the great cat hunt began. It was, as Itchy pointed out later, the first Tiger hunt Fondling-Under-Water had ever seen.

~ Chapter 49 ~

BIFFO, DANIEL AND CHEESY STOOD just outside the back door of The Gravedigger's Rest public house and tried to take some modest shelter from the rear of the building. These three had volunteered to begin the search for Tiger outside in the rain. Lettice, Itchy and Herbert were searching for Tiger inside the pub.

The storm was increasing in ferocity and the rain, driven by the fierce wind, was travelling almost horizontally. The white metal garden furniture and the large sunshade umbrellas in the small back garden had been blown over and were now piled in an untidy and tangled heap against a tattered wooden fence. The fence was leaning at a distinct angle to the usually favoured vertical.

'This sea mist is getting a bit serious,' shouted Daniel.

'Well, at least it's not windy,' shouted Cheesy, stepping out from the shelter of the pub's back wall, and leaning forward at an angle of forty five degrees to stop himself being blown backwards. With his eyes half closed and his hair streaming behind him he rather looked as though he was riding a motorcycle.

'This isn't windy?' shouted a disbelieving Daniel, holding onto a rusty metal downpipe with one hand and clutching his shirt collar tighter about his throat with the other.

'Oh no,' shouted Cheesy, as calmly as a man can be when he is shouting to make himself heard against what would, if it was swirling around London, probably be classified as a hurricane. 'Sometimes it's really blowy,' he shouted.

There was a great crash a yard or two in front of them and a sheet of rusty corrugated iron, blown by the wind, landed just a few feet away from where Cheesy was standing.

'Where the hell did that come from?' demanded Daniel, letting go of the down pipe and using his hand to shield his face as he peered up into the utterly impenetrable black sky. The down pipe, which had been loose for months, and which had been dislodged slightly more by Daniel holding onto it, responded to being deprived of Daniel's supporting hand by sliding slowly and very noisily to the ground.

'Strewth!' cried Daniel. 'The whole place is falling down!'

'Just a drain pipe,' shouted Cheesy, calmly. 'Nothing to worry about.' The piece of guttering which had been supported by the downpipe fell down next, narrowly missing Daniel's head.

Daniel looked up into the blackness in a pointless attempt to see if anything else was about to fall down. 'I need a batting helmet. And where did that piece of corrugated iron come from?' he demanded.

Cheesy peered through the blackness at the rusty and now badly bent piece of metal as though making a genuine attempt to guess at its provenance. 'Difficult to tell,' he replied, at last. But having covered himself, in that way that experts do, he proceeded to offer his opinion. 'I think it's probably come from the shed at the bottom of Herbert's garden.' He paused. 'But before that it probably came from the roof of the big barn behind Scattermouth Farm. Or it may have been from somebody's boundary fence.'

'You make it sound as though the air is thick with flying sheets of corrugated iron whenever there is a bit of wind,' shouted Daniel, peering up at the sky rather nervously.

'Oh yes,' shouted Cheesy, calmly. 'People don't bother too much about losing the odd sheet of corrugated iron. You usually get back pretty much what you've lost. Herbert will probably end up with another sheet of iron from Scattermouth Farm.'

'And Scattermouth Farm?' shouted Daniel. 'Do they just supply the whole neighbourhood with sheets of corrugated iron?'

'Oh no,' shouted Cheesy, 'they always get stuff blown from farms at the South Western edge of the village.'

'Why do people in the country always fill in hedges with bits of corrugated iron?' asked Biffo.

'Boundaries are very important to us,' shouted Cheesy, very seriously.

'Is that just to keep the animals in the fields?' asked Biffo.

'No,' said Cheesy. 'It's just that boundaries are very important to us. In the country it's much safer to mess with a bloke's car or his wife than with his boundary. When there are gaps in hedges or fences we fill 'em in with whatever is handy.' Exhibiting all the caution of a man who was once bitten on the nose by a rat he peered into a dustbin which had long since lost its lid. 'Tiddles?' he called.

'It's Tiger,' shouted Daniel.

'Yes, I know,' yelled Cheesy. 'But I feel silly shouting Tiger.'

Daniel opened the door to a small shed and peered inside. 'Tiger?' he called. 'Tiger?' Empty tins which had been piled up precariously close to the doorway fell over with a great crash. 'We really need torches,' he shouted. 'I thought I saw something move in here but it's so damned dark I don't have the foggiest idea what it was.'

'Do you really think Tiger would be out in this?' Daniel shouted to Biffo, who was now just a dimly visible figure at the far end of the garden.

Somewhere, high in the sky and far away from the storm, a sliver of moon was providing mellow background lighting, and although Daniel was reluctant to offer any criticism of the great lighting man in the sky he did feel that the light provided was woefully inadequate for a night time search for a dark coloured cat.

'I don't know,' shouted Biffo back. He shrugged but no one saw the shrug. 'But if she's frightened – which she will be – she could have run anywhere.' Like the other two he was now soaked to the skin. The whole thing seemed hopeless. He was desolate. He could not rid himself of the awful feeling that he would never see Tiger again.

~ Chapter 50 ~

MEANWHILE, INSIDE THE GRAVEDIGGER'S REST, Lettice, Itchy and Herbert may not have been quite so wet but they were no happier, or indeed much more comfortable, and they certainly weren't having any more luck in their search for Biffo's missing cat.

The Gravedigger's Rest had originally been built as a rather compact inn. But generations of landlords, builders and designers (some professional, some amateur and some not having the foggiest notion what they were doing) had added bits here, raised ceilings there, taken out walls here, put in doors there, removed panelling here, added partitions there, installed plumbing here, added electrical wiring there and generally, through a mass of miscellaneous repairs altered the structure and the internal geography of the building so much that if the original builder had been blindfolded and placed in the middle of it he would neither have recognised his own structure nor had the foggiest chance of being able to find his way around it.

There were, as there are in most buildings of a certain age, a seemingly infinite number of hiding places for a cat.

There is great hiding potential in cupboards which are not quite properly closed, spaces between the floorboards of upper floors and the ceilings of lower floors, and the readily reachable gaps which always exist between and behind walls.

To make the search even more frustrating the inn was, like all old buildings, positively awash with a vast quantity of resident fauna.

The result was that every ten or twelve seconds or so Itchy or Herbert or Lettice would hold up a hand, go 'Ssshhh!' and cup a hand around one ear in order to make it clear to the others that they were listening very carefully to something.

'Tiger! Tiger!' they would call, in that slightly obsequious way that people use when trying to persuade a cat to respond to them.

'What's in there?' asked a thoroughly soaked Itchy, wearily pointing to a door which was open just wide enough to let a cat through.

'I haven't the foggiest notion,' admitted an equally soaked, equally weary Herbert. He was so utterly lost that he wasn't even entirely sure that he could find his way back to the bar.

Itchy entered first and went through the rotten floorboards with his first stride into the room. A split second later his feet and legs crashed through the water-weakened plaster ceiling of the bar below.

'Who the hell is that?' demanded Puffy, in the bar below. He brushed pieces of soggy plaster out of his hair and examined the wriggling feet and legs which were dangling just inches away from his head. He seemed surprisingly calm about the fact that the ceiling to his public bar now contained a large hole.

'It's Itchy,' replied Jack, looking up.

'How can you tell?' asked Puffy, curious.

'I'd recognise those soles anywhere,' replied Jack, who supplemented his modest income with a little semi-professional cobbling.

'Silly bugger,' said Puffy. 'Come down the stairs like everyone else,' he shouted up to the dangling and wriggling lower portion of the Fondling-Under-Water groundsman.

Itchy, who had heard this comment, muttered something back but his words of protest and self-defence were lost in the plasterwork.

'Why on earth did you do that?' demanded Herbert.

There is one school of thought that Itchy, already deeply embarrassed and annoyed by the predicament in which he now found himself (not to mention the fact that he was in some considerable physical discomfort since his two legs had managed to slide either side of a rather stout beam) may not have been thinking clearly when he asked Herbert to help pull him out. There is, however, another school of thought, which puts forward the theory that Itchy knew exactly what he was doing. Both schools of thought are united in the belief that Herbert's rash and, indeed, reckless behaviour did not reveal anything new about his intellectual capacity.

The result was that when Biffo, Daniel and Cheesy, as sad and soggy a trio as has been seen since the three man tea room orchestra went down with the Titanic, tottered back indoors to take a break from their fruitless outdoor search for Tiger, and to check on how the indoor search was going, they found that one third of the indoor search party, Lettice, was standing in the bar with Puffy, staring up at the combined legs of the other two thirds of the indoor search party.

'No luck?' Biffo asked Lettice.

'None, I'm afraid,' said Lettice.

A cloud of plaster dust showered the bar as Itchy, dangling above, struggled to free himself from his predicament.

'I think we'd perhaps better give up for tonight and try again in the morning,' said Biffo, dolefully.

'Maybe she will have come back by then,' suggested Lettice hopefully.

'I doubt it,' said Biffo, woefully.

'You two might just as well come down this way,' Puffy shouted up at the pair above. 'The ceiling is a complete disaster anyway. You can't do any more harm.'

He was wrong about that. The two of them managed to do a good deal more damage, and make a great deal more mess.

'Thanks everyone,' said Biffo, shaking hands with Daniel, Cheesy, Lettice and the plaster-covered Itchy and Herbert. 'I think I'll go up to bed.'

'Have you got a spare bed I could use?' Daniel asked Puffy.

'Help yourself to whatever you can find,' said Puffy. 'There are plenty of spare rooms.'

'Check the floor first,' said Itchy.

'How do I do that?' asked Daniel.

'Stand on it,' said Itchy. 'If you go through then you'll know that the floor is rotten and you shouldn't have gone in there.'

'Thanks,' said Daniel, drily.

'Have a drink to help you sleep,' said Puffy. 'On the house.'

'The usual,' cried the regulars, in chorus.

'I was talking to our visitor,' said Puffy.

Daniel thought for a moment. 'I'll have a port, please.'

'What sort would you like?' asked the landlord. He looked around. 'I've got Taylors, Cockburns...'

'Oh, any port will do in a storm,' interrupted Daniel.

Puffy took down a bottle, poured out a large port and

handed the glass to Daniel. He then poured drinks for Biffo and the others.

'Goodnight, Daniel,' said Biffo, a few moments later as Daniel tiptoed timidly into the room next to his.

'Goodnight, Biffo,' said Daniel. 'Sleep well.'

'Thanks,' sighed Biffo. 'I'll try.'

Wearily and miserably Biffo, removed his sodden white coat and the rest of his soaking clothes and let them lie on the floor where they fell. More out of habit than anything else he gave his hands and face a perfunctory wash and cleaned his teeth. His towel, when he took it off the towel rail, turned out to be soaking wet. Water was still trickling through the ceiling but surprisingly, and thankfully, his bed still seemed to be dry. Biffo pulled back the covers, ready to collapse into bed.

'Miaow!' said a familiar and comfortable looking (dry) face, looking up at him.

'Tiger!' said Biffo gleefully.

And suddenly the world seemed an infinitely brighter and better place. After giving Tiger a cuddle he rushed next door and then downstairs to tell his new chums the good news. Everyone was genuinely pleased. No one complained or said 'You mean that we got soaked for nothing?'

It was, thought Biffo, as he climbed back up the stairs again, the first time in his life that he had had real friends – people who would help him simply because they liked him and with no thought of gain for themselves – and the first time he had felt part of a real community. It felt good.

~ Chapter 51 ~

WHEN BIFFO WOKE THE NEXT morning the rain had stopped, the sky was blue, the sun was shining brightly and the birds outside were singing gaily, puffing out their little chests and letting rip with all their favourite melodies.

But the night's heavy storm had created havoc within The Gravedigger's Rest public house. The carpets were sodden, the wallpaper was clinging to the walls with about as much enthusiasm as a politician clinging to a pre-election promise and water was still dripping through the ceilings.

Biffo said good morning to Tiger, who politely miaowed back from her temporary perch on the windowsill, squeezed and shivered into damp clothes and sensibly emptied half an inch of water from his shoes before putting them on.

Walking gingerly, in case he followed the example set by Itchy and Herbert, Biffo left his room, tiptoed along the corridor and slowly and cautiously made his way downstairs. Puffy was sitting in the public bar. He looked miserable.

'Glum, isn't it?' said Puffy. He was unshaven and bedraggled. He was sitting on a bar stool and had a glass in front of him and an almost empty bottle of whisky at his elbow. 'You should see the kitchen,' he said. 'The whole ceiling has come down.'

On the tables and floor around the bar the glasses and saucepans which had been put in position to catch the worst of the drips were all full and overflowing. Although the rain had stopped, the water which had filtered through the rooms upstairs was still leaking through the ceiling in a dozen or more places.

'You're up early,' said Biffo, doing his English best to ignore the obvious crisis and concentrate on the niceties of life. 'It's a lovely day outside.'

'Haven't been to bed,' replied Puffy, who didn't look as though he had. A loose piece of plaster fell from the ceiling and crashed onto a table behind him. The weight of the plaster tilted the table so much that it fell over. Two beer glasses full of rain water crashed to the ground. With some surprise Biffo noticed that the glasses did not break. Puffy didn't even turn round.

'What now?' asked Biffo.

'Oh, the usual!' sighed Puffy. 'The big tidy up.'

Biffo wished he could think of some way to help his new friend mend his roof. But he couldn't. He could however help in a more immediate and more practical way. 'I've got to do the deliveries for Miss Box,' he said. 'But would you like some breakfast first? I could easily pick up some bread, some marmalade and some tea and milk before I go. If you light the fire we can use one of those saucepans to boil water and make a cup of tea.'

'A cup of tea would be rather welcome,' agreed Puffy.

'And if you can find a fork or just a stick we can toast bread on the fire too,' added Biffo, heading for the door. He looked back. 'Toast and marmalade and a nice cup of tea. What more could you possibly want?'

'Sounds pretty good to me,' said Puffy. With a considerable effort he levered himself off his chair. 'I'll light a fire.'

~ Chapter 52 ~

'Did you manage to finish your cricket match before the rain started?' asked Miss Box, who was busy carrying trays of fruit and vegetables out to the front of her shop when Biffo arrived.

'I'm afraid not,' admitted Biffo. 'I'm not really sure what happened in the end. The match was more or less abandoned.'

'Because of a little rain?' said Miss Box, stopping what she was doing and looking up. She was clearly surprised.

'It was very misty,' said Biffo. 'The bowler couldn't see the batsman, the batsman couldn't see the bowler and no one could see the ball.'

'Sounds exactly like my sort of cricket match,' said Miss Box, laying out cucumbers neatly in a row. 'I'm glad you're here early I've got a lot of deliveries for you today.'

'Er, actually, I came to pick up a few things for breakfast,' said Biffo, feeling himself flushing slightly. 'Quite a few ceilings collapsed in the pub during the storm last night so things are in rather a state.' He wondered why on earth he was going red and feeling guilty.

'Franklin never thinks of excuses as good as that,' said Miss Box. 'Just you remember that I start paying you when you start working.' She picked up a brown paper bag and started filling it with plums. When the bag was nearly full she placed it on a set of old-fashioned weighing scales.

'That's fine,' said Biffo.

'That's just as well,' said Miss Box. She didn't have any weights for the scales but instead used items which she had once had weighed at the butcher's shop in Lesser Wheeping. She put a can of peaches and a small tin of sardines on the other side of the scales and then, one at a time, added half a dozen boxes of matches. For heavier items she used large tins of dog food and a salt lick. 'So, what do you want?' She added two more plums to the paper bag and then removed it from the scales and screwed up the top.

'Bread, margarine, marmalade, tea and, er, sugar,' said Biffo.

'Sliced bread or unsliced?' asked Miss Box.

'We're going to toast it, so I guess sliced would be easier,' said Biffo.

'No milk?' asked Miss Box, collecting together the items Biffo had ordered.

'Oh, yes, and a bottle of milk, please,' said Biffo. Miss Box put a pint of milk with the other things on the counter in front of her.

'On your account as usual?'

'Yes please,' said Biffo, as Miss Box popped the items he had bought into a large brown paper sack.

'And when will I see you ready for work?' asked Miss Box, handing him the paper sack containing the items he had ordered.

'Less than an hour,' shouted Biffo, already hurrying back to pub with his arms full of breakfast ingredients.

~ Chapter 53 ~

WHEN BIFFO GOT BACK TO the pub Puffy already had a magnificent looking fire going in the fireplace. He had also emptied the dirty rain water from a saucepan and refilled the pan with fresh water from the tap. And, from somewhere in the pub, he had unearthed a long-handled brass toasting fork. A teapot, a tea strainer, two mugs, two plates, two spoons and two knives were laid out on a small table.

'Is Tiger OK?' asked Puffy, sticking a slice of bread onto the toasting fork while Biffo struggled to balance the saucepan on the blazing fire.

'She's fine,' said Biffo. 'I feel really guilty about all that fuss last night.'

'Don't be,' said Puffy. 'The important thing is that she's

OK. Some people don't like cats. I do.'

'How's Len?'

'Oh, he's not too bad,' Puffy replied. 'Rupert was right. He's got a broken arm.' He withdrew the slice of bread he was toasting from the flames so that he could examine it. It hadn't even started to go brown.

'Poor old Len!' said Biffo.

'Oh, he'll be OK. He'll enjoy all the attention.'

'I was really surprised to discover that Rupert was the local doctor,' said Biffo. 'He doesn't, well, seem like a doctor. I thought he told me that he ran an antique shop.'

'He does run an antique shop. It doubles as his waiting room.' He examined the piece of bread again and then put it back in front of the fire.' And what should a doctor be like?'

Biffo laughed. 'I'm not sure,' he admitted. 'Maybe it would be more accurate to say that Rupert is the most unusual doctor I've ever met.'

Puffy looked across at him and smiled. 'Rupert is OK,' he said. 'He's a good doctor. The villagers like him.' He examined the piece of bread yet again. This time it was beginning to go brown. The water in the saucepan began to bubble.

'Wrap something round the handle before you try and lift that saucepan off the fire,' warned Puffy. 'There are some small towels behind the bar.'

Biffo did as Puffy suggested. 'Is that piece of bread supposed to be on fire?' he asked.

'Damn.' said Puffy. He shook the burnt bread off the toasting fork into the fire and then put another slice of bread onto the fork. He thought for a moment. 'Actually,' he said, 'it's a good thing to have a doctor who has another interest. He understands life a bit more than some doctors I've known.'

Biffo made the tea, Puffy finished making the toast and then they sat in silence for a while and ate.

'There must be some way to get the roof repaired,' said Biffo. He felt better with some toast and tea inside him.

'Let me know if you think of it,' said Puffy.

~ Chapter 54 ~

'You're steaming!' said Miss Box.

'I beg your pardon?' said Biffo.

'You're steaming,' repeated Miss Box in her very matter of fact voice. 'Look at yourself.'

Biffo looked down. It was absolutely true. Standing there in the morning sunshine he actually was steaming.

'Are those clothes damp?' demanded Miss Box.

'I'm afraid so,' admitted Biffo. 'We lost my cat last night.' He meant this to be an explanation but realised as he said it that as explanations go it lacked a little certain something.

'And you were out in that storm looking for her?' said Miss Box perceptively.

'Yes,' said Biffo. 'Although to be honest it was probably as wet inside the pub as it was outside.' He pulled at his trouser legs to separate the material from his skin. 'The roof of The Gravedigger's Rest isn't terribly waterproof.'

'Did you find her?'

'Yes. She wasn't really lost at all.'

'Cats never are.'

Biffo, puzzled, looked at her.

'They may not be in the place you want them to be,' said Miss Box. 'But that doesn't mean that they are lost.' She reached across, took a corner of Biffo's jacket in her hand and squeezed. Drops of water fell onto the ground. 'These clothes are soaking wet. Get back to the pub and take them all off. Put on something dry before you get rheumatics.'

'Er, well, there's a bit of a problem there,' said Biffo. 'I'm afraid I haven't got anything dry to change into.' But he knew Miss Box was absolutely right and that even if he did his rounds dressed in a towel he had to get out of his wet clothes. His shirt was sticking to his back as eagerly as his trousers were sticking to his legs and he felt extremely uncomfortable. 'I don't suppose you have anything suitable I could buy?'

Miss Box scratched her head. 'I don't carry a full range of men's clothing,' she said, rather apologetically. 'When my father was alive we used to carry a large range of sports jackets and flannel trousers.' She thought for a moment, keen to help and unwilling to lose a sale. 'But I expect I can find you something dry to put on.'

~ Chapter 55 ~

THE HEAVY-DUTY NAVY BLUE BOILER suit Miss Box had unearthed from a large cardboard box at the back of the shop had been made for a very short man and there were four inches of bare white leg visible in between the bottom of the trousers and the top of the very short thick green woollen socks that encased Biffo's feet.

'Don't worry about the gap,' she said. 'The wellington boots will cover that.' She bent down and tugged at the material in an attempt to pull the trouser legs down a little further.

'There's a lifetime guarantee with this!' said Biffo, when he had finished wincing and had regained his balance. He was reading the label attached to the boiler suit. 'What exactly does that mean? Does it mean that it's guaranteed for my lifetime?'

'It means the suit is guaranteed until it wears out,' said Miss Box.

Biffo, who had picked up the green, rubber wellington boots which Miss Box had brought him, thought carefully about this. 'So, if it wears out tomorrow that's the end of the lifetime guarantee?'

He stood on one leg and attempted to pull on one of the wellington boots. The boots seemed a little tight.

'That's what a lifetime guarantee means,' said Miss Box, rather testily. 'You don't expect it to be guaranteed after it's worn out, do you?' Somehow what she said sounded sensible. Even if Biffo had had the courage to argue with her he wouldn't have been able to think of anything constructive to say.

Biffo, encased beneath the boiler suit in a pair of ex-officers' top quality underpants and a green and brown check woollen shirt, was too grateful to be dry to question the fundamental principle of the guarantee at any length.

'Do you have a bigger size in the boots?' he asked, almost

overbalancing. 'These are a little tight.'

'One size fits all,' said Miss Box. 'They don't come in different sizes.'

'One size fits all?' protested Biffo. 'But these are boots. Boots always come in different sizes.'

'Not these boots,' said Miss Box, making it quite clear that this was not a topic for further discussion.

Biffo tried again and by alternately jumping up and down and pulling as hard as he could he eventually managed to get his feet into the boots. He had to scrunch his toes together to do it.

'There you are!' said Miss Box, with her hands on her hips. 'What did I tell you?'

'One size fits all,' said Biffo, defeated.

'Exactly!' said Miss Box, gleaming.

'You're absolutely right!' said Biffo, wincing as he tried to walk. He abandoned the effort after a couple of paces and gave silent thanks for the fact that he had a bicycle to ride and would not have to travel around the village on foot.

'Let me see, now,' said Miss Box, taking a slip of paper and a stub of pencil out of her trouser pocket. 'That will be £27.50 for the boiler suit, £15.95 for the shirt, £2.50 for the officer's shorts, £3.00 for the socks and £18.45 for the boots.'

'Do you want me to charge it to your account?'

'Yes, please,' sighed Biffo, 'I'm afraid so.' He wondered how long he would have to work before he started to make a profit from his career as a delivery boy.

'I'll put these in the sun to dry,' said Miss Box, hanging Biffo's damp clothes over a low branch on a nearby tree. 'Is there anything in the pockets that you want? Room key? Stuff like that.' She marched off towards the shop. 'Captain Trilby telephoned and ordered two large marrows and some mushrooms just before you came,' she said. 'I'll start packing your bicycle.'

'I don't have a key,' said Biffo, to the disappearing Miss Box. 'There aren't any keys at The Gravedigger's Rest.' He stopped and thought for a moment. 'But I'd better get my notepad and pencil,' he added, more to himself than to Miss Box.

He rummaged around in his jacket and trouser pockets until he found his notepad and pencil. The notepad was slightly damp but still useable. He also pulled out a folded and crumpled long white envelope. He stared at the envelope for a moment trying to remember where it had come from. Eventually he remembered. Edwina had given it to him the day before.

He examined it carefully. There was no return address on the back and no clue as to the sender on the front of the envelope. His name and old address were typed neatly on the front of the envelope. Eventually, with a shrug he stuck a thumb under the flap, tore open the envelope and pulled out the contents.

The envelope contained two things: a letter and a cheque.

The letter was from the chief accountant at Better Television and this is what it said:

'Dear Mr Brimstone,
The chairman of Better Television has instructed me that he has terminated your employment with this company forthwith. As per clause 15 B of your contract under which this company has to give two years notice if terminating your employment I am therefore enclosing a cheque in lieu of our salary obligations to you. The appropriate tax and national insurance contributions have been deducted from this payment. Acceptance of this cheque in full and final payment of our obligations to you will be taken as your agreement that your employment is terminated and that you have no further claim on the company.
Yours sincerely

*James Tennyson
Chief Accountant*

Biffo read the letter through twice before he examined the cheque. He couldn't understand why Better Television had sent him a cheque until he remembered the chairman refusing to accept his resignation and telling him that he was fired. He felt extremely grateful for the chairman's vanity.

He also remembered, with some relief, that the agreement he and Edwina had signed meant that every penny he now received was his to keep.

Slowly, he turned the cheque over and examined it carefully.

It was the largest single cheque he had ever handled. It was for £93,456.78.

He was still staring at the cheque two minutes later when Miss Box emerged from her shop clutching several of her large, stout brown paper bags (all packed right to the top) and two huge marrows.

'Come on!' she said, sharply. 'I'm not paying you to stand around all day.' She nodded to where the delivery cycle was leaning against a fence post. 'Bring the bicycle over here so that I can pack your basket.'

Biffo stuffed the cheque into a pocket of his boiler suit and got to work.

~ Chapter 56 ~

'OH I SAY! I DO like the new look,' said Lettice, when Biffo walked into the bar that evening. He remembered both the low beam and the step and felt quite proud of himself. The buckets and beer glasses had all been emptied and put away and someone had swept up most of the debris. The bar looked tidy and almost clean.

Biffo looked at her and raised an eyebrow.

'It's very, er...' began Lettice.

'I think that says it all,' agreed Biffo mournfully. 'It's very, er...' He climbed onto a stool and ordered a pint of beer. He was thirsty and hungry.

Biffo had had a busy day. He had spent the morning cycling round and round the village, constantly surprised at the appetite of the villagers for Miss Box's stock. The bicycle delivery service which Miss Box offered made it easy for villagers to buy from her. To visit the local supermarket they had to drive or catch a bus into the nearest town. To buy from Miss Box they had only to lift up the telephone.

Twice Biffo cycled past 'Buttercup Cottage'. And each time he paused for a few moments.

He remembered the old lady he had met on the bus which had brought him to Fondling-Under-Water. 'If you don't know what you want you'll never find it,' she had said. Biffo didn't know whether it was luck or fate that had guided him but he now knew what he wanted. He wanted to live in Fondling-Under-Water and he wanted to live in Buttercup Cottage. He wanted to write books and become a well-established member of the cricket club and deliver groceries for Miss Box whenever Franklin Minton fell off his bicycle and injured himself.

At lunchtime he took several bread rolls, a hunk of cheese and an apple with him and travelled by bus to Widdlecome-Over-The-Moor where there was a small branch of one of the big banks. He opened an account, paid in the cheque from Better Television and slept most of the way back to Fondling-Under-Water.

He spent the afternoon repeating his tour of the village, and delivering a wide range of goods to a relatively small range of villagers. After several hours of hard pedalling he returned to The Gravedigger's Rest, fed Tiger, thought about having a bath and decided instead to go down to the bar.

'It's quiet tonight,' said Biffo, looking around. This was something of an understatement since the bar was empty.

'It'll get busy later on,' said Lettice. 'The village cricket club is holding its Annual General Meeting here tonight.'

'What time?'

'It's due to start at nine,' said Lettice. 'Can I get you anything to eat?'

'I take it the duck à l'orange is still off?'

'I'm afraid so.'

'Tomatoes on toast?'

'I can do tomatoes on toast.'

~ Chapter 57 ~

'So, WHAT SORT OF DAY did you have?' asked Lettice, an hour or so later. The tomatoes on toast had been cooked, eaten, enjoyed and digested. The cook had been duly and appropriately complimented and had acknowledged the compliment with a glorious smile.

'Pretty good,' replied Biffo. 'You know that cottage I liked?'

'Buttercup Cottage?'

'That's the one. Is it still for sale?'

'Yes, of course,' said Lettice with a surprised laugh. 'Property around here doesn't sell that quickly.'

'I pedalled past it today. Twice. I really do like it. Do you think I might be able to have a look inside?'

'Of course! We can go round tomorrow if you like. The Trubshaws who own it have the keys. I'll give them a ring.'

'Thanks. That would be wonderful.'

'It would be lovely if you could buy it,' said Lettice. 'I can just see you living there.'

'I was rather thinking that I might, well, you know, make a sort of offer,' said Biffo

'Really!' said Lettice, genuinely excited. 'That's terrific!' She picked up the telephone and began to dial. 'I'll ring the Trubshaws and see if they're in.' She paused. 'So you're going to stay in the village, then?'

'Yes,' said Biffo.

'I don't mean to be rude,' said Lettice. 'But how, er, can you raise the money? I only ask because the other day you said you were completely broke. Did your wife agree to let you have half the house? Oh, hello Aunt Moira! It's Lettice. I'm ringing with my estate agent's hat on. I've got someone who wants to look around Buttercup Cottage. Yes, he's a serious buyer. His name is Mr...er...' Lettice put a hand across the telephone mouthpiece and looked across at Biffo. 'Sorry,' she whispered, 'I've forgotten your second name.'

'Brimstone,' said Biffo.

Lettice lifted her hand from the telephone mouthpiece. 'Mr Brimstone,' she said to the person at the other end of the telephone. 'Now? I don't see why not. I'll have a word with him.' She put her hand across the telephone mouthpiece again. 'Moira Trubshaw – she and her husband own the cottage – says if you want to go round now you can pick up the keys this evening. Is that OK?'

'That's great!' said Biffo. 'Is it far?'

'Just a few yards down the lane,' Lettice said to Biffo. 'I'll tell you how to get there. I'd really love to come with you but Puffy has disappeared and I can't leave the bar.'

'I'll go and get the keys and then perhaps we can go and see it tomorrow?' suggested Biffo.

'Wonderful!' said Lettice. She took her hand away from the mouthpiece. 'Mr Brimstone will be right round for the keys,' she said. She gossiped a little, mentioned the fact that she had seen her ex-husband the day before, agreed that the weather was very changeable, asked Moira to pass on her best wishes to her husband, said goodbye at least three times and eventually put the telephone down. 'Right!' she said. 'You can't miss their cottage. You turn left out of the pub, take the first right...'

'...down towards two large wholemeal loaves, three pints of milk and a copy of the Daily Telegraph?'

Lettice laughed. 'I beg your pardon?'

'You probably know it as White Gables Farm,' said Biffo.

'That's right.' said Lettice. 'What was all that other stuff about...?'

'That's their daily order from Miss Box's shop.'

'Oh? Really? Well, go down there for a quarter of a mile and then take the second on the left...'

'The lane that goes down to one small Hovis loaf, a copy of The Times and a pint of milk?'

Lettice just looked at him.

'Major Cranberry.'

'Absolutely right!' laughed Lettice. 'I'm very impressed.'

'I've been learning while I ride,' explained Biffo. 'Did you know that Major Cranberry sends all his clothes to the laundry? Even his socks and ties?'

'No,' said Lettice. 'I confess I didn't know that. I've never known anyone who sent ties to a laundry.'

'I probably shouldn't have told you that,' said Biffo, leaning across the bar and lowering his voice. 'It's probably highly confidential. Do you think there is a confidentiality oath for bicycle delivery boys? Do you think I could be removed from the saddle for revealing trade secrets?'

'I don't expect so,' giggled Lettice. 'But if there is Major Cranberry's little peccadillo is safe with me.'

'So how far past Major Cranberry's place is the Trubshaw's cottage?'

'Oh, about two hundred yards. On the left.'

'Is it a pink cottage? With a tumbledown lean-to with a corrugated iron roof hanging onto one side of it?'

'That's the one!'

'You've only been down that lane in a car, haven't you?'

'Yes.'

'That pink cottage is more like a quarter of a mile past Major Cranberry's,' said Biffo, sternly. He got up from the bar stool upon which he had been sitting and looked at his watch. 'I'll be back in four or five hours,' he said. 'If I'm not back in a week send out a search party.'

Lettice said she would.

'Oh, by the way,' said Biffo, heading for the door, 'in answer to your question, my wife didn't give me half the house – in fact, she didn't she give me anything. I've got some money to buy the cottage because I found a cheque for £93,000 this morning.'

'What do you mean?' asked Lettice, puzzled.

'What do you mean, what do I mean?'

'How did you just happen to find a cheque for £93,000?'

'It was in my trouser pocket.'

'How did it get there?'

'I put it there.'

'You put a cheque for £93,000 into your trouser pocket and forgot about it?'

'I put the envelope into my pocket. I didn't know it contained a cheque for £93,000.'

'Oh,' said Lettice. 'I know what you mean. You'd be surprised at how often that happens to me. I'm always putting envelopes into my bag and finding out afterwards that they contain cheques for £93,000.'

'It was an unexpected redundancy cheque,' explained Biffo.

'That was pretty decent of your former employers! But why was the cheque unexpected? Surely they didn't just send you a cheque for £93,000 without telling you about it?'

'I walked out and so they really didn't have to pay me anything,' said Biffo.

Lettice was clearly puzzled. 'Why did they pay you if they didn't have to?'

'Because the boss wanted to be able to say that he sacked me,' explained Biffo.

'What odd people there must be working in television!'

'There certainly are.'

Lettice blushed. 'Oh, I say, I didn't intend that to be rude.'

'I know,' laughed Biffo. 'It's OK.'

'Do you mind that he can say he sacked you?'

'Not in the slightest,' said Biffo. 'Especially since he bought the privilege with a rather generous cheque.' He pointed to a stock of chocolate bars and small packets of biscuits which Puffy kept behind the bar. 'Would you give me one of those small packets of biscuits, please? I still feel a bit peckish.' Lettice handed over the biscuits which Biffo stuffed into one of his pockets.

'Don't forget the cricket club Annual General Meeting,' said Lettice as Biffo left. 'It's due to start at nine.'

Biffo, just about to leave the bar, turned to acknowledge Lettice's reminder. As he did so he remembered the step but forgot the beam. He stopped, cursed quietly, rubbed his aching head, turned and watched while Lettice took out the slate from underneath the bar-counter.

'Does that count?' he asked. 'You distracted me.'

'It counts,' said Lettice.

'Bye, Lettice,' Biffo said.

'Bye, Biffo,' Lettice replied. 'Mind how you go.'

~ Chapter 58 ~

OUTSIDE, IT WAS A BEAUTIFUL evening. The sun was deep orange and low in the sky. Biffo's legs were stiff after a full day in the saddle and he was looking forward to a walk through the village. Overhead the birds were settling down in the trees for the night. In the fields around him rabbits were racing about innocently, playing games and having fun.

The lanes of Fondling-Under-Water were deserted and Biffo strolled in peace and safety towards the Trubshaw's cottage. As he walked Biffo took out the small packet of biscuits he had stuffed in his pocket. With some considerable difficulty he eventually managed to open the cellophane packet.

He was chewing a rather tasty ginger biscuit and reflecting on the thought that, all things considered, life really wasn't all that bad after all when he heard a noise behind him. He turned and was surprised to see a sheep trotting along the middle of the lane, just a few yards behind him.

'Get back to your field!' he said sternly to the ewe. 'You'll get run over.'

As he said it he realised that this was, in many ways, a pretty empty threat. The ewe faced a far more certain death if she went back to her field than if she continued to trot along the road. On an impulse he took a biscuit out of the packet he was holding, stopped, turned, and offered the biscuit to the ewe. She too stopped and stood a yard or two away from him, staring at him rather nervously.

'It's OK,' said Biffo. 'It's a biscuit. You can eat it.'

The ewe, curious but still nervous, edged forward a few inches. Biffo shuffled back in the ewe's direction and held his arm out a little straighter. The ewe moved forward another six inches.

They continued this peculiar food-based courtship for a couple of minutes and then, at last, the ewe managed to overcome her fear and took the biscuit from Biffo's hand.

'Now, you'd better go back,' said Biffo firmly, when the biscuit had disappeared and the ewe had eventually stopped munching.

The ewe, who had huge mournful eyes, just stared at him.

Biffo turned and continued the remainder of his walk to the Trubshaw's cottage. Every few yards he turned round to see if the sheep was still there. She was.

The ewe was still there, just a few yards behind him, when he approached the Trubshaw's tiny cottage. And, despite his appeals she was still there when, in the absence of bell or knocker, he used his knuckles on the Trubshaw's door to announce his arrival.

A rustic name plate, hand-made out of a slice of tree trunk, informed callers that the name of the cottage was 'Dunbattin'. It seemed a fair guess that Mr Trubshaw had, in his youth, played for the Fondling-Under-Water cricket team.

'Come in!' said the tiny woman who answered the door. She was dressed in a smart tweed skirt and a pale pink blouse and Biffo guessed that she was probably in her eighties (give or take a decade). Biffo was rather surprised to see that despite the fact that it was a warm evening she wore three cardigans. The outer one was beige and had large patch pockets on the front. This one was unbuttoned. The middle cardigan was brown and one of the buttons was fastened. The inner cardigan was pale blue and all the buttons were fastened. On her feet she wore huge sheepskin slippers.

'My name is Brimstone,' said Biffo. 'I've come for the key for Buttercup Cottage.'

'You're Mr Brimstone,' shouted Mrs Trubshaw. 'You've come for the key for Buttercup Cottage. Come in and have some cake and a cup of tea.' She peered around Biffo at the ewe which was standing in the lane outside. 'Come on sheepie,' she added. 'It'll be cold out there.' When she spoke to the sheep she lowered her voice to a normal talking level. Biffo decided that the sheep must belong to her and Mr Trubshaw. He knew that some people living in the country did keep sheep as pets.

Biffo walked into the cottage and into a small room that was clearly used as a living room. To his surprise the lonely sheep followed him. She seemed to know where she was going. The room was crammed with furniture and with a fire blazing in the hearth it was as hot as a sauna.

Biffo, wondered if the sheep was allowed into the living room. He tried to turn the sheep round. But the ewe was heavy and determined and behind him Mrs Trubshaw had already shut the front door.

'You aren't cold, dear, are you?' shouted Mrs Trubshaw, closing the door to the living room.

'No, no,' said Biffo, unzipping the front of his boiler suit and wiping sweat from his brow. 'I'm, er, fine thanks.' He wanted to say something about the sheep but couldn't think of anything appropriate. Mrs Trubshaw seemed quite unperturbed by the sheep's presence and Biffo was relieved by this. The sheep seemed to feel at home.

'This is Mr Trubshaw,' shouted Mrs Trubshaw, waving an arm in the direction of a large, red-faced man of eighty something who sat or, more accurately, lay in an easy chair beside the fire. He was wearing a thick, three piece woollen suit, a shirt and a tie, highly-polished, black lace up shoes and a green flat cap with a finger-stained peak. His left knee was about a foot away from the blaze. He was watching a quiz programme on an old-fashioned television set which was equipped with a twelve inch screen. The programme appeared to be set in a community hall. The sound was switched off.

'Mr Brimstone, dear,' shouted Mrs Trubshaw.

The sheep was eating a hand-embroidered tablecloth which was hanging enticingly at mouth level.

'I'm not deaf,' shouted the old man.

'What?'

'I'm not deaf.' shouted the old man, so loudly that Biffo had to shake his head to get rid of the noise.

'Of course you are!' insisted Mrs Trubshaw, loudly. She shuffled away into a small kitchen at the back of the cottage.

The old man turned towards Biffo. 'She's as deaf as a post so she thinks everyone else is deaf,' he said. He frowned. 'Who are you?' he demanded.

'Brimstone,' said Biffo. 'I just came for the key to Buttercup Cottage.' He couldn't help staring at the television screen. A young woman in a very short dress was talking to the camera. She seemed rather nervous. Two groups of four people stood behind them both. One group of four consisted of celebrities whom Biffo vaguely recognised. The other four people were very clearly ordinary members of the public. The young woman bore an uncanny resemblance to someone he knew but he couldn't quite remember who it was.

'Ah,' said the old man. He pointed to a chair the other side of the fireplace. 'Sit down.'

Biffo sat down and tried to keep his knees as far away from the fire as possible. He peered at the television set again.

The old woman returned from the kitchen carrying a large, empty metal tray. She put the empty tray down on a low table directly in front of the fire.

'The fire is going out!' yelled Mr Trubshaw, pointing to the fire which was blazing strongly and seemed to Biffo to have several hours' life left in it. He grabbed his wife's arm and, thereby, her attention. 'It needs more wood!' he said, pointing to the fire.

'Are you cold?' Mrs Trubshaw asked Biffo.

'No, no!' cried Biffo. The sweat was now dripping off his forehead into his eyes and off his chin down onto his new boiler suit.

'He always wants more wood on the fire,' shouted Mrs Trubshaw, nodding towards her husband. She shuffled off towards the kitchen again. 'He thinks it grows on trees,' she muttered to herself. She turned, just before she disappeared. 'You think wood grows on trees!' she shouted. Mr Trubshaw, vaguely aware that his wife had spoken, nodded and smiled at her.

The sheep, having destroyed the hand-embroidered tablecloth, had now turned its attention to an antimacassar on the arm of Biffo's chair. Biffo tried to pull the antimacassar out of range but the sheep already had a firm hold on the material and the more Biffo pulled the more determined the sheep became. Eventually, Biffo decided that he was doing more harm than good and he let go. The sheep, still pulling, shot off backwards into a glass fronted china cabinet, causing a considerable amount of damage and embarrassing Biffo greatly.

'Where's the key then?' asked Mr Trubshaw.

Biffo was puzzled. 'Er, I'm sorry,' he said. 'Which key is that?'

'The key to Buttercup Cottage,' said Mr Trubshaw. 'My wife said you've brought it back.'

'No,' said Biffo. 'I've come to collect it.'

'Ah,' nodded Mr Trubshaw, sagely. 'You're locked out again.'

Biffo glanced at the television set. He suddenly remembered the identity of the woman on the screen. It was Voluptua Bradshaw, the secretary he had shared with his friend 'Streaky' Bacon. She was waving and blowing kisses at the camera. She seemed relieved that the programme was over.

Mrs Trubshaw emerged from the kitchen carrying one cup and a saucer. She placed the cup and the saucer on the tray.

Biffo, now standing, pointed to the shattered china cabinet. 'I'm terribly sorry,' he said. 'The sheep...'

'Oh dear!' shouted Mrs Trubshaw. 'Is the poor thing all right?'

'Did you try a ladder?' asked Mr Trubshaw. 'I once climbed in through a bathroom window when I had locked myself out.' He thought about this for a while. 'Mind you, I was younger then,' he confessed.

'Yes, dear,' shouted Mrs Trubshaw, smiling at him, and patting his arm. 'It's a very nice sheep,' she said to Biffo. 'Sit down I'll bring you some cake.' She disappeared.

'And thinner I expect,' said Mr Trubshaw.

Biffo gave up and sat down. The credits for the quiz programme were finishing. He watched the screen. The final credit was one he recognised. 'Directed and Produced by Frank Bacon'.

'Are you warm enough?' Mr Trubshaw asked him.

Mrs Trubshaw reappeared from the kitchen, carrying a large plate upon which there stood half of a very large fruit cake. The cake was covered in a thick layer of what looked at first glance like blue icing but which, Biffo could see, was actually mould.

Mrs Trubshaw carefully put the cake down on the metal tray. She then returned to the kitchen.

'I feel the cold,' said Mr Trubshaw.

'Yes.' agreed Biffo, who had worked this out for himself.

The sheep was now chewing one of the curtains. Biffo tried not to look.

Mrs Trubshaw reappeared from the kitchen carrying a teapot. She poured tea from the pot into the cup and handed the cup to Biffo.

'Thank you,' said Biffo, taking the cup. Something seemed odd but he couldn't quite put his finger on it. When he lifted the cup to his mouth he realised what it was. Mrs Trubshaw had forgotten to heat the water and the tea was stone cold.

Mrs Trubshaw disappeared.

'Aren't you having a cup of tea?' Biffo asked Mr Trubshaw.

'Oh no,' said Mr Trubshaw. 'She always forgets to boil the water.'

'Ah,' said Biffo, nodding.

The sheep, still chewing the curtain, paused for a moment to do what sheep do but usually in fields.

'Having a sheep in the house must cause quite a lot of damage,' said Biffo.

'Yes,' agreed Mr Trubshaw. 'I would think so.'

Mrs Trubshaw reappeared carrying a small plate and a large knife. She cut a large slice of cake and placed it on the small plate. 'Have some cake,' she shouted.

'Oh, that's very kind of you but I don't think I could,' said Biffo. 'I ate at the pub just before I came out.'

'How's your tea?' asked Mrs Trubshaw, smiling at him.

'Very nice, thank you,' said Biffo. He took a sip and smiled back at her. 'Lettice said you would let me have the key to Buttercup Cottage,' he reminded her.

'Oh, the key!' she shouted. 'Why didn't you remind me you silly thing. I nearly forgot the key.' She looked around. 'Now where did I put it?' She picked up the small plate, together with its cargo of mould encrusted cake, and handed it to Biffo. 'Eat your cake,' she shouted, before shuffling off to the far side of the room and starting to rummage in the top drawer of an old bureau.

Biffo looked around, trying to think of a way to dispose of the cake. He looked across at Mr Trubshaw who had fallen asleep and was now snoring quietly. Without hesitating Biffo tossed the whole piece of cake onto the fire. The reaction was instantaneous. It was as though he had thrown a cup full of petrol onto the flames.

'Here you are, dear!' shouted Mrs Trubshaw, holding out two keys dangling on a piece of string. 'Oh, you've finished your cake. Would you like some more?'

Biffo beamed broadly, stood up and took the proffered

keys. 'Oh, no thank you!' he said. 'I really couldn't. But thank you.' He paused, thought for a moment and hesitated. He didn't like telling fibs. 'It was delicious,' he lied.

Mrs Trubshaw smiled.

Biffo felt instantly relieved of guilt. He headed for the door, stepping over the debris which lay in front of the shattered china cabinet.

'Let me pay you for the damage,' he said. 'It was partly my fault that the sheep backed into the cabinet.'

'Pardon?' shouted Mrs Trubshaw.

'I want to pay you for the damage,' shouted Biffo.

'What damage?' asked Mrs Trubshaw, frowning.

'Goodbye,' sighed Biffo, holding out a hand. 'And thank you.'

'Our pleasure, dear,' said Mrs Trubshaw. 'It was lovely to see you. Give our love to Lettice.' She smiled at him again. 'Don't forget your sheep,' she said.

Biffo went quite cold and stared at her. 'I beg your pardon?' he said.

'Your sheep,' said Mrs Trubshaw. 'Don't forget your sheep.'

'It's not my sheep,' said Biffo, trying not to sound as hysterical as he felt. 'It's your sheep.'

'Oh we couldn't,' said Mrs Trubshaw. 'It's very nice of you, dear, but we couldn't. You must keep it.'

Biffo stood outside in the lane while Mrs Trubshaw skilfully shooed the sheep out of the living room and out of the cottage.

'Bye!' she shouted, standing on the doorstep and waving to him.

'I thought...,' began Biffo. 'The sheep...' he said. 'I'm sorry...' he apologised. 'The damage...he said. 'Let me pay for everything...' he pleaded. The sheep stood beside him in the lane, chewing on an antimacassar she had brought with her as she had been ejected.

'It was lovely to meet you both!' shouted Mrs Trubshaw. She lowered her voice, clearly now talking to herself. 'Such a lovely couple,' she muttered.

As Biffo walked back to the pub he had an idea for a way to help get the roof of The Gravedigger's Rest mended.

~ Chapter 59 ~

When Biffo walked back into the bar at The Gravedigger's Rest the Fondling-Under-Water cricket club Annual General Meeting was just about to start. The great Don Bradman would have been impressed by his perfect timing. Biffo had walked back briskly, pausing only to slip into the village telephone box and telephone his friend and former colleague Streaky Bacon at home.

Biffo's new friend, the antimacassar-loving ewe, had followed him all the way back to the pub but Biffo had managed to slip through the front door, leaving the ewe outside. The ewe had, for the first time since their meeting, made a few loud noises of protest. However, finding herself on a stretch of lush grass on the infrequently cut verge outside the pub she had settled down for a spot of grazing. Sheep, whatever their breed, have two strong qualities: an ability to turn long grass into short grass and endless supplies of patience.

Bill Stickers, Paddy Fields and an elderly, tall, extremely slender man who had a pince-nez balanced precariously on the end of a generously proportioned nose were sitting on three chairs at the far end of the bar.

The tall, slender man with the generously proportioned nose, who was sitting in the middle of the trio, was wearing a dark green tweed jacket together with a matching pair of plus twos, a checked shirt, a large floppy green bow tie that looked such a mess that it had obviously been hand tied, a pair of knee length green socks and (evidence that his memory was not quite as good as it had once been) a pair of red velvet slippers. He had a large, red and white spotted handkerchief tucked into the breast pocket of his jacket and from time to time he provided loud practical evidence that this handkerchief had a functional as well as a decorative value.

In honour of the importance of the occasion Bill and Paddy were both wearing a suits. Most of the rest of the village (and all of the cricket team) were sitting, standing, lounging or leaning around the rest of the bar. No one else wore a suit or a tie.

'I know Paddy and Bill,' whispered Biffo to Lettice, who

was standing, arms folded, at the end of the bar furthest away from the trio. 'But who is the odd looking chap in the middle?'

'He isn't odd,' whispered Lettice. 'He's a Lord so he's eccentric.' She paused to give Biffo a chance to understand this social nuance. 'That's Lord Hepplewhite,' she explained. 'He's the club patron.'

When he saw Biffo enter Paddy immediately stood up and walked across towards him. 'Just the fellow I wanted to see,' said the club vice captain, approaching Biffo with what Biffo immediately recognised as the smile of a man who wants something but doesn't have terribly much to offer in return. Biffo instinctively recoiled, rather hoping that Paddy's remark had been aimed at someone else. It hadn't of course.

'Are you free on Saturday?' Paddy asked, when he finally had Biffo pinned up against the dartboard.

'Saturday?'

'Saturday,' agreed Paddy, widening his smile and putting a hand on Biffo's shoulder in a friendly, 'Let's be the very best of chums' sort of gesture. 'We have a match that day and the captain and I wondered if you might be free?'

'Ah,' said Biffo, hesitantly. He wasn't at all sure that he wanted to be an umpire again.

'I'm not entirely sure that I'm cut out for umpiring,' he said at last. He decided to try and take the seriousness out of the moment with a little humour. 'I'm not sure that I have the finger for it,' he added, diffidently holding up the index finger of his right hand and examining it critically. 'I think a successful umpire needs a finger with rather more bite to it, don't you?'

'Oh you misunderstand,' said Paddy quickly. 'We don't want you to umpire. We want you to play!'

This was unexpected and for the 23,458th time in his life Biffo didn't really know what to say. It sometimes seemed to him that he spent most of his life not knowing what to say. It was a constant disappointment to him that a *bon mot* was invariably an afterthought. He would usually think of a sharp retort a week, or more often two weeks, too late.

'We're playing a charity match on Saturday and now that Len's injured we're short of a player,' said Paddy.

'And if you're half as bad a cricketer as you are an umpire,' said Len who had wandered over with Paddy, 'I won't have to worry about getting my place back when this damned bone has mended.' Len had his arm in a plaster cast and a sling.

'Ah,' said Biffo, conscious of the fact that he was beginning to sound rather simple minded.

'Would you say you're primarily a batsman or a bowler?' asked Paddy. 'Wicket keeper?' he added, hopefully.

'I'm not really much of a batsman or a bowler,' admitted Biffo, with rare honesty. 'To be honest it's been a while since I...'

'All rounder then!' said Paddy, beaming.

'I would have thought so,' said Biffo, cautiously. 'Perhaps,' he added.

'What sort of stuff do you think you might bowl?'

'Well, er, probably not too fast, and not spinning very much,' said Biffo. He held an imaginary ball in his hand and brought his arm over as though about to bowl a ball. 'Sort of like that, I guess,' he said. He tried to smile but it didn't feel quite right and he suspected that what he had produced was probably closer to a grimace.

'Bat?'

'Oh I would imagine so,' nodded Biffo. 'Although I have to confess that it's been quite a time since I, er, batted,' he warned.

'We'll perhaps give you a net,' said Paddy. 'See how you get on. Help you with a few bits of advice if necessary.'

'I rather think he'd be better off if you gave him one of those wooden things,' said Rupert who was standing nearby.

Everyone looked at him but no one laughed or spoke.

'A bat,' explained Rupert. 'He'd be better off with a bat.'

Still no one laughed or spoke.

'Better off with a bat than with a net,' said Rupert.

The silence continued.

'It was a joke,' said Rupert.

'Thank you, Rupert,' said Paddy.

Rupert sighed. 'Bloody philistines around here have got no sense of humour at all.'

'I think I'd probably rather just get thrown in at the deep end,' said Biffo who suspected that if lots of people gave him advice he would simply end up feeling extremely confused. 'But who will umpire?' he asked, suddenly feeling an entirely mistaken sense of loyalty towards his former post.

'Oh don't you worry about that!' said Paddy. 'We can get anyone to umpire.' As soon as he had spoken he obviously realised that he had not been entirely tactful. 'Not that it isn't a skilled position, of course,' he added. 'I meant to have a word with you after the last match and congratulate you on the way you handled a very difficult set of circumstances.'

'Oh, I don't know,' said Biffo, diffidently. He felt himself blushing like a small schoolboy being praised by a master.

'Shall I put you down for six?' asked Paddy. 'Perhaps seven?'

Biffo, who wasn't sure whether this was a time or a donation failed to hide his confusion. 'Er, six...er...seven, er...?'

'Batting order,' explained Paddy. He thought for a moment or two. 'Perhaps you'd be happier at seven? Give you a chance to get a good look at the opposition bowling!'

'Good idea!' agreed Biffo, nodding his agreement. 'Very good idea.'

'Splendid,' said Paddy. 'Splendid!' He took a small notebook from his jacket pocket, opened it, carefully made a note in it and then closed it and put it away again. He did everything slowly and meticulously. He nodded at Biffo and then walked back to the table where he resumed his position alongside Cedric 'Bill' Stickers and Lord Hepplewhite.

As soon as the vice captain had sat down Bill, who had clearly been waiting for him, stood up and cleared his throat noisily. He did not look well. He had had a drink or two to settle his nerves but he hadn't had quite enough to drink to soothe away the guilt he felt. His face was pale and he did not look as confident as he normally did. The cough was clearly an attempt to show that the meeting was about to start. Unfortunately, no one took any notice of him. He took the teaspoon from the saucer of the cup of coffee in front of him and attempted to bang it on the table. Unfortunately, although the table was large and the spoon was small, he completely missed the former with the latter.

'Isn't Bill the club patron?' whispered Biffo, resuming his conversation with Lettice.

Lord Hepplewhite raised one hand in a diffident but nevertheless imperious gesture, as though summoning a waiter in his club. The response was instantaneous. Everyone fell silent.

'No.' whispered Lettice. 'Bill is everything else but he isn't the club patron. They made Lord Hepplewhite the club patron when Bill bought the cricket field and took over as president.'

Bill cleared his throat again. 'The first item on this evening's agenda is the club's intended purchase of a lawnmower,' he announced.

Puffy, who was standing next to Lettice, spoke. 'Where does Bill get his suits?' he whispered. Neither he nor Lettice were busy, despite the fact that the bar was crowded. Everyone present had stocked up with drinks, crisps, pork scratchings, peanuts and all the other essentials before the meeting had started. ('I don't want any of those new-fangled natural foods,' said Jack Hobbs when examining the ingredients list on a packet of crisps. 'At my age I need all the preservatives I can get.')

'As some of you will know our present lawn mowing machine has for some time been prone to reliability problems,' said Bill. 'Our groundsman, Mr... er...Itchy...Mr...Hedrubb, has done magnificent work in keeping the mower in active service for as long as he has.'

This remark was greeted with a modest amount of applause and several members of the Fondling-Under-Water cricket club made pertinent observations of their own.

'I don't think that shade of brown poplin has ever been particularly fashionable,' whispered Puffy.

Lettice, responding to Puffy's remark, giggled. She was a nice giggler. Some grown women giggle like little girls, which can be slightly disturbing. Some women snort when they giggle, and that can be even more disturbing. But to Biffo Lettice's giggle seemed natural and cute. Biffo loved it when she giggled. 'Don't be bitchy!' she whispered, admonishing her uncle. 'Bill doesn't need to look rich because he is rich.'

'I now call upon the Fondling-Under-Water cricket club ground committee chairman and senior groundsman, Itchy, to say a few impromptu remarks on the subject of the lawnmower,' said Bill. He sat back down on his chair. He really did not look well. He looked as though he was burdened by a huge secret, which, of course, he was but since it was a secret no one knew this.

'What can I get you to drink?' Puffy whispered to Biffo.

'I'll have a whisky, please,' replied Biffo, equally quietly. 'I've just had a rather nerve-wracking experience. In fact,' he added, 'I think I've had several nerve-wracking experiences. A Macallan. A double, please.'

Itchy, who had been leaning against the wall next to the fireplace, pushed himself upright and coughed rather nervously. He was not a man who would describe himself as an accomplished public speaker and in his right hand he held a thick sheaf of paper which he held up. It was clear that these were his notes for his impromptu remarks. He cleared his throat several times and asked to be given a glass of water. Naturally, no one in the pub had a glass containing water. Someone called across to Puffy to fill a glass with water and send it across.

'How did you get on with the Trubshaws?' whispered Lettice as Puffy stopped work on Biffo's malt whisky and busied himself with the water tap and a glass.

'Mrs Trubshaw sent you her love,' whispered Biffo. 'Is she really your aunt?'

'Oh no, not really. I just call her auntie. Aren't they both sweet?'

'Er...yes, I suppose so,' agreed Biffo, although he wasn't entirely sure that this was the most suitable adjective he could think of.

'Some people think she's a bit dotty,' said Lettice. 'But she's lovely and really quite quick-witted in her own way. A couple of years ago a locum GP who visited her was so worried about her that he sent her to see a psychiatrist. I can't imagine why but the psychiatrist asked her for the name of the Prime Minister. 'Does it matter?' Aunt Moira asked. 'They're all the same, aren't they?' The psychiatrist didn't know what to say to that. He wrote and told the GP that he wasn't sure whether Mrs Trubshaw was completely batty or the sanest person he'd ever met.' A sudden thought occurred to Lettice. 'You didn't eat any of Aunt Moira's cake, did you?'

'No,' said Biffo.

'That's good,' said Lettice, clearly relieved. 'Did you get the keys?'

Biffo took the keys out of his pocket and held them up.

Puffy had now filled the glass with water and it was making its way across the room to where Itchy was waiting for it.

'What keys are those?' asked Puffy.

Lettice explained.

'Lovely place,' whispered Puffy, putting Biffo's double malt whisky down on the counter. 'Needs a little restoration work, of course.'

'Are you sure you want me to come with you tomorrow?' asked Lettice. 'I'll be happy to show you round and answer any questions you have but if you'd rather go by yourself that's fine.'

'I'd love it if you showed me round!' said Biffo. 'Thanks!'

The glass of water had now reached Itchy who took a sip and put the glass down on a nearby window sill. 'Thank you, Mr President,' Itchy yelled. He spoke very loudly, as though addressing a large open air audience. He bowed slightly in the direction of Lord Hepplewhite. 'And your Lordship.' He stopped for a moment and took another sip from the glass of water. 'I would like to begin by saying what an honour and...', he paused and looked hard at the piece of paper he was holding. 'I would like to begin by saying what an honour and a...', he paused again and carefully studied the piece of paper he was holding.

'What's the matter?' asked Rupert Fitzwalter.

'I can't read this word,' said Itchy. He brought his voice down from a yell to a shout and showed the doctor the piece of paper he was holding. 'There's an oil stain on it.'

Rupert studied the paper for a moment. 'It's a surprise,' he said.

Itchy stared at him, puzzled.

'The words are 'a surprise'.'

Itchy looked at the piece of paper again. 'Are they?'

'Yes.'

'Are you sure?'

'Yes.'

'OK,' sighed Itchy. He cleared his throat, took another sip of water and began again. 'I would like to begin by saying what an honour and a surprise it was when the club president unexpectedly invited me to speak at this meeting,' he yelled. 'As chairman of the ground committee I have to report that the Fondling-Under-Water cricket club lawn mowing machine has suffered a total of 78 separate instances of total mechanical or electrical malfunction during the twelve months of the year which have passed since our last Annual General Meeting which was held, er...,'

At this point Itchy paused and turned over the piece of paper from which he was reading.

'...a year ago.'

Itchy looked around the room to make sure that this information had been absorbed by his audience. There was a good deal of thoughtful nodding and some tutting and many lips were pursed. Itchy seemed satisfied by this response. 'Malfunction means it broke down,' he said, feeling confident enough to ad lib a little. This much needed translation was well received.

'As chairman of the ground committee of the Fondling-Under-Water cricket club I authorised myself, in my position as head groundsman of the Fondling-Under-Water cricket club, to commission and authorise an outside examination and appraisal of the machine's condition and capabilities,' yelled Itchy. He paused, took a deep breath and lost his place in his notes. 'As chairman of the ground committee,' he began again, 'I authorised myself, in my position as head groundsman, to commission and authorise...' at this point Itchy realised that he was reading something he had already read. He stopped, frowned and read on silently for a few moments.

'Give us a song and dance, Itchy!' shouted some would-be wag from a dark corner of the room. The would be wag was shushed by Itchy's friends and many sympathisers.

Itchy ignored this inappropriate request and continued to read his notes. He concentrated so hard on doing this that when he got to the bit he hadn't read out he forgot to stop reading in silence and start reading out loud. After two or three minutes of total silence the audience became a little restless and the would be wag who had invited Itchy to perform a song and dance gained fresh courage and repeated his request. This time the request received more support from other members of the audience. Someone standing next to Itchy nudged him and whispered something in his ear.

Itchy blushed, coughed, took another sip of water and began again to share his notes with his audience.

'The outside experts commissioned by myself in my capacity as chairman of the ground committee of the Fondling-Under-Water cricket club duly and subsequently subjected the said machine to an exhaustive mechanical and electrical overhaul and eventually, after some considerable consideration, came to the regrettable conclusion that the machine was, and is, in an irrep...' Itchy stumbled over this bit and tried again, 'in an irrepeparepara...' he tried again, 'in an irreparabab...' he stopped, licked his lips, shrugged his shoulders, paused, sighed, looked around and then carried on. 'The fact is,' he said, lowering his voice by fifty or sixty decibels, 'that it's a twenty five year old pile of crap that ain't worth the mending of'. He looked around and shrugged. 'In non technical language it's buggered.'

At this point Lord Hepplewhite, who had developed cramp in his right leg, suddenly decided to stand up to exercise his muscles and try to get rid of the cramp. There was much scraping of chairs and stools as the rest of the audience stood up out of politeness. The Fondling-Under-Water Cricket Club was no republican hot bed. The members had never been visited by the Queen but they had Lord Hepplewhite and in Her Britannic Majesty's absence they were more than happy to treat him with the respect they would have shown to her.

Itchy, who thought he was getting the beginnings of a standing ovation, paused, blushed a little and tried not to look embarrassed.

'You used to work in London, didn't you?' whispered Puffy to Biffo.

Biffo agreed that this was true.

'Do you know how a chap would set about getting an export licence for flies?'

Lord Hepplewhite managed to get rid of his cramp. He sat down again. Everyone who had stood up out of respect for him also sat down again.

Biffo, who wasn't entirely sure that he had heard correctly, looked at Puffy and then asked him to repeat the question. Biffo thought about the question again, trying to decide whether or not he had missed a few essential chapters in the plot. Meanwhile, Itchy, flushed with pride, was continuing his report.

'That's it! Give it to us straight, Itchy!' called someone.

'We can take it,' added someone else, bravely.

But Itchy was unwilling to abandon his carefully prepared report. After the slight deviation from the script he continued reading from his notes.

'Despite this report which had, I might say confirmed my own personal observations as to the value of the said piece of equipment, and, at the same time, in view of an unofficial conversation with, from and to the club president and chairman in which I had it confirmed to me personally and verbally and in speaking that there was an absence of any available monetary funds with which to purchase a replacement machine with which to cut the grass of the aforesaid club, as chairman of the ground committee of the Fondling-Under-Water cricket club I instructed myself, in my capacity as head groundsman of the Fondling-Under-Water cricket club, to continue to use the aforesaid piece of equipment until such time as the previously aforesaid piece of equipment could not be used any more for that purpose for which it had been used in the past.'

Itchy, exhausted by his hard work, and leaking liberally from every pore, took a large yellow handkerchief from his trouser pocket and mopped his face several times. He still had several pages of his impromptu speech to read.

The handkerchief, like most of his clothing, was heavily oil-stained and left smears of oil across his forehead, cheeks and chin. He ended up looking like a soldier camouflaged for jungle warfare.

'Let the man have a drink!' said Puffy, filling a pint glass with best bitter and handed the glass across the bar. The glass was then passed from hand to hand until it reached the intended recipient who grasped it gratefully.

'This speech is going to be longer than the Gettysburg address,' murmured Puffy to Biffo. He paused and thought for a moment. 'Although probably slightly less significant in historical terms,' he added.

'You did say flies?' replied Biffo.

'That's right.'

'I'm probably going to regret asking this question,' whispered Biffo. 'But why would anyone want to export flies?'

'Herbert Sutcliffe asked me to ask you,' whispered Puffy. 'He didn't like to ask you himself.'

'I can understand that,' whispered Biffo.

'He's got a lot of flies on his manure,' said Puffy. 'He thought that if he put them into milk churns he could probably sell them to the French.'

Biffo thought about this for a while but eventually had to give up and ask the obvious question. 'Why would the French want to buy British flies?'

'He was thinking of the frog farmers.'

'The farmers? Why would French farmers want to buy flies?'

'Not just any old farmers. The frog farmers.'

'Yes, I understand that. The farmers in France. The frog farmers.'

'No the frog farmers in France.'

'Frog farmers?'

'Yes, the French farmers in France who breed frogs.'

'Do farmers in France breed frogs?'

'Of course they do. Where do you think they get all those frogs' legs? They can't go hunting them down one by one in people's back garden ponds can they? Never get the throughput. A leg here, a leg there. There wouldn't be any continuity in supply, would there?'

'I hadn't thought about it much,' confessed Biffo. 'But I suppose not.'

'Well frogs eat flies,' explained Puffy. 'So Herbert thought that if he collected all his flies together he could sell them to the French frog farmers.'

'I see,' agreed Biffo, who did.

'But the chap at the local business advice centre didn't know anything about exporting flies.'

'I'm not surprised,' mumbled Biffo.

'So you can't help then?'

'Afraid not.'

'Thanks. I'll tell him. Worth a try. Hope you didn't mind my asking.'

'Not at all.'

'He thought you might know since you're from London,' said Puffy.

'In my capacity as head groundsman I therefore continued to use the aforesaid piece of equipment,' continued Itchy. 'Unfortunately, I have to report that,' at this point he reached the end of the piece of paper from which he was reading. He shuffled the papers in his hand and then continued reading, 'Our young Jerry has been walking out with a dental hygienist from Warrington. They met while she was on a touring holiday with her parents. They had a little blue caravan which they parked in the field across the lane from us. She has a strong body with a good bosom and a nice smile and Jerry is very smitten. She is due to go back on Saturday but Jerry has invited her to come back down for a weekend shortly. His mother and I have told him that she can have the spare room and no hanky-panky.'

Itchy had been concentrating so hard on reading from his script that he was not, until this point, aware that something had gone wrong. The words had been going in through his eyes and out through his mouth without any noticeable contact with his brain.

His attention was brought to the fact that all was not well by the laughter that this last sentence brought from his audience. Blushing an even deeper red he moved the errant page (part of a letter he had been writing that afternoon to his brother in East Anglia) to his trouser pocket and shuffled through his papers to find the correct continuation sheet.

'Unfortunately, I have to report that,' he began again, 'a day or two ago, as I was preparing the wicket for the club's last match, the Fondling-Under-Water grass cutting equipment finally became what I can only describe as functioning only in an entirely non-operational state.'

This statement was received in silence while the members of the cricket club tried to work out exactly what it meant. Itchy, who hadn't understood what he had read any more than the listeners had understood what they heard, stopped for a moment and scratched his head.

'Don't scratch too hard,' yelled the wag who had wanted the song and dance routine. 'You'll get splinters.'

'Would I be right in thinking that you are telling us that the lawnmower finally gave up the ghost?' asked Paddy, the club vice captain.

'That's it,' said Itchy, nodding furiously. 'The bloody thing she just stopped and wouldn't go no matter how hard I hit her.'

'Er, do you mean that when the machine wouldn't go you, er, well, hit it?' asked Bill, who was apparently surprised by this revelation.

Itchy nodded again. 'I hit her with a spanner first of all and then when that didn't do no good at all I gave her a really good thwack with a wrench. Then when even that did no good I gave her a damned good bashing and thrashing with the scaffolding pole what I keep for serious breakdowns.' He paused, satisfied that he had given a fair and full account of what he regarded as sophisticated attempts to repair and restore the errant machinery. Bill and Biffo, neither of them having had much experience of dealing with mechanical equipment, were the only ones in the room who were surprised by the relative simplicity of Itchy's maintenance programme. Every other citizen of Fondling-Under-Water, including the club patron Lord Hepplewhite, recognised that when mechanical equipment falters it is necessary to treat it sternly.

'And the machine failed to respond?' asked Lord Hepplewhite, in what he thought was a kindly and sympathetic way. Lord Hepplewhite, being a perceptive man, had noticed that Bill, the club president, seemed dangerously close to failing to grasp the fact that the head groundsman had dealt with the lawnmower in a positive and practical way. Lord Hepplewhite was deaf and did not like hearing aids which he regarded as new-fangled nonsenses. He found that if people spoke up he could hear them perfectly well some of the time. In order to ensure that he could hear himself talking, and to help any other deaf people whose paths crossed his, he himself spoke extremely loudly. Those who were not particularly tactful called it shouting.

'That's right, your Lordness,' agreed Itchy, flustered at being addressed directly by a peer of the realm and particularly flustered at being shouted at by a peer of the realm.

'Machines do that,' agreed Lord Hepplewhite, nodding wisely. 'I remember a machine, er, doing that to me once. It...er...it was a sort of machine...it, er...it was a moment I'll, er, never forget.' He paused and stared in the distance. Lord Hepplewhite was a sympathetic and perceptive man but he was also sometimes rather forgetful. He sometimes lost his train of thought and forgot what was he was trying to say, he sometimes forgot what someone else had said and he sometimes forgot to whom he was talking and why.

Itchy, puzzled, and slightly worried that he had missed something significant, looked across at Lord Hepplewhite. 'What was that, your Lordship?' he asked.

'What was what?' demanded Lord Hepplewhite.

'The, er, the...er, the something you said you'd never forget...' said Itchy.

'I know it was something I'll never forget but it's...er...escaped me for the moment,' replied Lord Hepplewhite, without embarrassment. He beamed at Itchy. 'It will come back in due course I expect.'

'Ah,' said Itchy, sweating profusely at having been engaged in such a lengthy conversation with a peer of the realm. He was totally confused and didn't have the foggiest idea what Lord Hepplewhite was talking about.

'And so what happened then?' boomed Lord Hepplewhite, adjusting his pince-nez so that he could look over the top of them at Itchy.

Itchy stared at him.

'When the club machine failed to respond to your encouragement,' Lord Hepplewhite reminded him.

'I borrowed a lawnmower from Mr Harbottle,' said Itchy.

'Was this arrangement satisfactory?' Lord Hepplewhite asked.

'Not really,' admitted Itchy. 'Mr Harbottle's lawnmower was an electrical model intended for domestic use. I had to borrow every electrical extension cord in the village in order to reach the far side of the field.'

'Most inconvenient, I would imagine,' said Lord Hepplewhite.

'It was,' said Itchy. 'Besides,' he added, with something of a shrug, 'I can't use Mr Harbottle's lawnmower again.'

'Oh,' said Lord Hepplewhite, surprised. 'And why is that?'

Several heads turned in Puffy's direction. Puffy shrugged his shoulders to make it clear that he didn't know the answer to the question.

Itchy, who suddenly seemed rather embarrassed, certainly knew the answer to the question. 'It sort of...' he began, diffidently. 'It sort of, well, it sort of blew up,' he replied. Those parts of his face which were not covered in oil blushed. (The parts which were covered with oil probably blushed too).

'Eh?' said Puffy, who had not heard about this before. 'What do you mean: 'It sort of blew up'?'

Itchy thought about this for a while, and scratched his head. 'I'm not sure how else to put it, Puffy,' he said at last. He spoke sadly, and with regret. 'There was a lot of smoke and a few flames and a big sort of phut sound and it sort of, well, sort of blew up...sort of thing.'

'Thanks, Itchy!' said Puffy, who really wasn't feeling grateful at all. 'You might have let me know.'

'I cleaned all the soot off it and put it back in your shed!' protested Itchy, in self defence. 'It won't cut grass but it looks smarter than it did when I borrowed it.' He frowned, clearly thinking hard. 'You could sell it!' he said brightly.

Several dozen people in the room made a mental note not to buy a lawnmower off Puffy Harbottle in the near future. Puffy, realising that Itchy's suggestion was a sensible one, but also realising that he would never now be able to sell the mower in the village, made a mental note to take the mower into the next town in order to sell it.

Itchy looked around. 'I had to cut the last bit of grass with a pair of shears I borrowed from Mr Harbottle's shed.'

'And so what is your conclusion and your recommendation to the club?' asked Lord Hepplewhite.

Itchy opened his mouth, closed his eyes, opened his eyes, raised his head and looked at the ceiling, rubbed his chin and waved a hand around as though he had been asked to explain Einstein's theory of relativity to a deaf and dumb Chinaman. He liked being the cricket club groundsman because he liked cutting grass. But public meetings and public speaking would always come pretty low down on his list of his favourite activities.

'Using the shears gave me blisters,' said Itchy. 'It took me three hours to cut just a few square yards. It would take me months to cut the whole field with shears.' He paused and thought hard for a few moments, although thinking was clearly not his favourite activity. 'The grass would grow faster than I could cut it,' he added.

This last remark, though not intended to be humorous, caused amusement and produced some giggling and a little light laughter.

'Use your notes!' hissed Cheesy as Itchy floundered in silence.

Itchy, who had clearly forgotten that he was holding a sheaf of carefully prepared notes (these notes were written it has to be said with a great deal of help from his daughter who was studying social sciences through the Open University) brightened up considerably. He rummaged around among his notes looking for the appropriate page.

'There's something I wanted to ask you,' whispered Biffo to Puffy, taking advantage of this new opportunity. 'Would you consider having a television programme broadcast from The Gravedigger's Rest?'

Puffy frowned, clearly puzzled. 'What sort of television programme?'

'A quiz programme.'

'Why would anyone want to broadcast a television programme from here?' asked Puffy, clearly puzzled. He looked around the pub. Even though Puffy, with the help of Lettice and some of the regulars, had cleared away most of the debris the pub still had what could perhaps most politely be described as a slightly used appearance.

'The television company I used to work for makes a quiz programme,' explained Biffo. 'Every week it's transmitted from a different venue – a village hall, a hotel or a pub.'

'But not this sort of place,' said Puffy, looking around at his water stained bar and at the holes in his ceiling.

'The producer is a friend of mine,' said Biffo. 'I spoke to him a few minutes ago and he's agreed to make a programme here if you'd like him to.'

Puffy shrugged. 'Why not?' he said. 'I suppose it could be fun. And I'd probably sell some beer to the television people.'

'Ah,' said Biffo. 'The deal is a bit better than that.'

'They'll pay a fee?' asked Puffy.

'No, they won't pay a fee,' said Biffo. 'But I think I can probably persuade them to repair the roof, put in a new ceiling and cover up the worst of the water damage.'

Puffy looked at Biffo. 'Is this for real?'

'Absolutely.'

'I could kiss you!'

'You lay one lip on me and the whole deal is off.'

'When can they come?'

'As soon as you like. My pal was due to travel up to a working men's club in the North of England tomorrow. But he'll postpone that trip and come here instead if you like.'

'The sooner the better!' said Puffy.

'Can I borrow the phone?' asked Biffo.

'As chairman of the ground committee it is, therefore, my recommendation that the club authorise forthwith the purchase of a new grass cutting machine,' said Itchy.

'What does forthwith mean?' asked Cheesy.

Itchy frowned. 'What?'

'What does forthwith mean?'

'I don't know.'

'You said it.'

'It's written down here,' explained Itchy.

'Oh,' said Cheesy.

'As chairman of the Ground committee it is, therefore, my recommendation that the club authorise forthwith the purchase of a new grass cutting machine,' said Itchy. 'As head groundsman of the Fondling-Under-Water cricket club I have, on the club's behalf, conducted research among a number of local retailers,' he continued. 'I have discovered that we can expect to purchase a decent second-hand machine for between £1,800 and £1,900. It is, therefore, my recommendation as chairman of the ground committee of the Fondling-Under-Water cricket club that we allocate this amount of money for such a purchase, er, forthwith.' Itchy, his ordeal over, folded up his notes and stuffed them into his trouser pocket. He then tried to make himself look as small and as inconspicuous as possible.

Around the room a lot of air was sucked in very sharply.

'Wow!' said Puffy quietly to Lettice. 'That's a hell of a lot of money!' He thought about it. 'Just for cutting grass.'

'Has the club got that much money?' asked Lettice.

Puffy looked at her. The look made it clear that there was little doubt about the answer.

'Where's Biffo?' asked Lettice, suddenly realising that he was missing.

'He's on the phone,' said Puffy.

Bill stood up. 'I would like to propose a vote of thanks to the chairman of the ground committee and to the head groundsman of the Fondling-Under-Water cricket club,' he said.

'I'll explain in a minute,' Puffy whispered to Lettice. He winked.

'Go on then!' shouted the wag who had previously made attempts to contribute to the evening's entertainment.

'Er, I would like to propose a vote of thanks to the, er, chairman of the ground committee,' said Bill.

'I second that!' said Paddy quickly.

Bill then asked the members to vote.

'Motion passed anonymously,' he announced a few seconds later, after looking around the room.

'Unanimously,' whispered Paddy.

'And unanimously,' added Bill.

'I would like to propose an, er, vote of thanks to the, er, head groundsman,' said Bill.

'I second that!' said Paddy, automatically.

Bill then asked the members to vote.

'Motion passed anonymously,' he announced.

'Unanimously,' whispered Paddy.

'And unanimously,' added Bill.

'I propose that the club spends the appropriate sum, subject to the availability of the necessary funds, on the purchase of a new lawnmower,' said Cheesy.

'Seconded,' said Itchy quickly.

'I don't think you can second the motion,' said Paddy.

Itchy looked hurt.

'Not quite cricket, old chap,' said Paddy.

'Seconded,' said Constable Hobbling.

Bill then asked the members to vote. About half of those present put up a hand. The rest were too exhausted by the previous votes to raise their hands.

Bill did not allow this to worry him or to delay matters. 'Motion passed anonymously,' he announced, without hesitation. He looked as if he really wanted to be somewhere else, doing something else. Paddy didn't bother to correct him this time.

'How much do we have in the kitty?' asked Puffy. He looked around the room. 'Have we even got enough money for a down payment on a new lawnmower?'

These two questions seemed to throw everybody into a good deal of confusion. They had not been expected.

Meanwhile, Bill decided that he really had to get away. Very quietly, he leant towards Paddy and whispered in his ear and asked him to take over.

'What's the matter with the captain?' enquired Lord Hepplewhite, as Bill wriggled his way to the door and disappeared.

'Says he's not feeling well,' replied Paddy.

'I thought he looked a bit off colour,' said Lord Hepplewhite. 'Got something on his mind no doubt. These millionaire chappies have always got deals going on somewhere in the world.' The peer chuckled loudly. 'He's probably selling a couple of oil wells in Texas so that he can buy a yacht and another island in the Caribbean.'

A moment later Biffo reappeared.

'How did you get on?' demanded Puffy, anxiously.

'It's all set!' said a grinning Biffo. 'My chum will be here tomorrow. He's looking forward to meeting you.'

'Who will?' demanded a curious Lettice. 'Will someone please tell me what is going on?'

~ Chapter 60 ~

'DOES ANYONE HAVE THE ACCOUNTS?' asked Paddy, looking around the public bar in The Gravedigger's Rest.

No one would admit to this. There was a good deal of muttering and many heads were shaken.

'Who exactly is the club treasurer this year?' demanded Lord Hepplewhite, loudly.

No one seemed anxious to acknowledge this responsibility.

'Do we actually have a treasurer?' asked Paddy.

'Oh, we must have a treasurer!' said Puffy.

'Perhaps it'll be in the minutes of last year's annual general meeting,' suggested Lord Hepplewhite.

Paddy picked up several pieces of paper from the table in front of him and looked at each of them in turn without finding the name of the club treasurer.

Lord Hepplewhite stood up and cleared his throat. The room fell silent. 'Ladies, gentlemen, I suggest we have a short recess while we endeavour to identify the identity of the club treasurer. Shall we say twenty minutes?'

There was a short polite pause and then everyone stood up, elbows out, and attempted to break the world sprint record for ten yards in a race for the bar.

Puffy and Lettice started serving drinks as though they were on the Titanic and someone had just announced: 'We've hit an iceberg, there aren't enough lifeboats and most of you are going to die!'

'Do you want a hand?' Biffo asked, having to shout to be heard about the clamour of: 'Four pints of the usual, two gins and a couple of packets of pork scratchings.'

'You could wash some of those if you like,' said Lettice, nodding towards along line of dirty glasses which had been deposited on the counter. Both her hands were busy pulling down pint glasses from the rack behind her, filling them and handing them over to eager drinkers the other side of the bar.

Biffo, not waiting to be told twice, slipped under the bar hatch, put a squirt of washing-up liquid into the metal sink beneath the bar and then added hot water. Bubbles developed and steam rose. The former television producer, now grocery delivery cyclist, had drifted down the social scale and become a glass-washer. But if anyone had been interested enough to take time to ask him how he felt he would have had to admit that he hadn't felt as happy for years. Washing up can be a curiously satisfying experience.

'I've been sort of...well...invited to play in Saturday's match,' said Biffo to Puffy, when the rush on the bar had subsided a little.

'Great!' said Puffy, genuinely pleased. 'That's terrific!'

'It's the match against the professionals, isn't it?' said Biffo.

'That's the one,' said Puffy.

'Mr Player has played for England, hasn't he?'

'He certainly has,' said Puffy. 'He was working as a coach for a local club when England went on a tour to Pakistan. Just about everyone in the touring party went down with food poisoning and he was the only player they could find still capable of wearing white trousers with any confidence. He was lucky to get an England cap. The rumour was that two television commentators and a journalist from one of the tabloid newspapers nearly got England caps on that tour.'

'Still,' said Biffo, with an envious sigh. 'He played for England!'

'He certainly did!' agreed Puffy. 'Twice. And he never lets anyone forget it either. It's his benefit this year and he's bringing a bunch of his team mates down here to play a friendly match against the village team. He may well bring a couple of England players. He's just written his autobiography. Can't remember the title though...'

'Do you mean we're going to be playing a bunch of internationals?' asked Biffo, going rather cold.

Puffy nodded. 'There's no need to worry too much,' he said. 'They'll probably be gentle with us.'

'Still,' said Biffo. 'It's quite a thing to be playing against men who've played for England.' He paused. 'Do you think they'll slow down their bowling?' he added, rather nervously.

'I would think so, as long as we let them win,' said Puffy.

'Well that shouldn't be too difficult,' said Biffo, smiling with relief.

'Absolutely,' agreed Puffy. 'Running for Cover!'

'I beg your pardon?'

'Running for Cover!' repeated Puffy. 'That's the title of Player's autobiography.'

~ Chapter 61 ~

AFTER ALMOST EXACTLY TWENTY MINUTES the twenty minute 'identify the treasurer' interval was over. And a small piece of paper which had been unearthed from the pile on the table, and which contained the tell tale words 'Treasurer: Helmut Walton' had enabled Paddy and Lord Hepplewhite to identify the treasurer as Helmut Walton. Constable Hobbling, loyal and sober representative of the forces of law and order, had been dispatched to fetch the club accountant from his home on the other side of the village green and a few minutes later the village bobby duly returned with his mission accomplished.

'Sorry I couldn't be here earlier!' apologised Helmut, when he appeared, slightly out of breath and a trifle tousled. 'I had a bit of an emergency to deal with.'

'Nothing serious, I hope?' said Lord Hepplewhite, anxiously.

'Oh no,' said Helmut. 'My wife had her potato peeler lost. So I had to through the compost heap go in case she had it thrown away.'

'All sorted satisfactorily, I trust?' said Lord Hepplewhite.

'Really not, I am afraid,' admitted Helmut. 'I could not it find.' He seemed downcast.

'We're sorry to drag you over here,' said Paddy. 'But the chairman of the ground committee...'

Helmut looked puzzled.

'Itchy,' explained Paddy.

'Ah,' said Helmut, nodding wisely.

Paddy cleared his throat and began. 'The chairman of the ground committee,' he continued, 'has reported that the club's grass-cutting equipment has cut its last blade of grass. That's the rather sad news. I'm sure we were all rather attached to the old mower. Been with us a long time. The bad news is that he has told us that we need to buy a new machine at an estimated cost of between £1,800 and £1,900. What we need you to do is to tell us that we have enough money in the bank.'

'Ah,' said Helmut, his voice full of regret. 'I could tell you that if that is really what you want me to be telling you...' He looked around and paused for a few seconds, then shook his head sadly '...but I fear I would be lying'. He had brought with him a thick file of bank statements, invoices and other assorted bits of paper. He rummaged around for a minute or two and then produced a slip of paper which he seemed to regard as relevant.

'According to Snoring and Dribbling we seem to have a balance of £2,584,' he said, his brow furrowed. He shook his head. 'But I do not think that we can regard with confidence that figure as entirely one hundred per cent reliable.'

'Snoring and who?' said Lord Hepplewhite, frowning.

'Dribbling,' replied Helmut. 'Snoring and Dribbling. The club's accountants.'

'Ah,' said Lord Hepplewhite.

'But that sounds a very good figure,' protested Paddy. 'I rather like that figure. In fact I very much like that figure. Why isn't it reliable? Isn't that what we've got in the bank?'

'Exactly not,' said Helmut, the man with his finger pressed firmly on the pulse of the club's financial matters. He rummaged around amidst his papers again and this time produced a bank statement. 'Ah, no, I thought as much,' he said. There was now a good deal of regret in his voice.

'What is it?' demanded Paddy.

'Well, we seem to be in what I believe financiers like to call a negative flow cash situation,' said the treasurer.

'Snoring and Dribbling?' said Lord Hepplewhite again. He looked very confused. 'I don't think I know them. Are they local?'

'I call them Snoring and Dribbling,' said Helmut, mildly apologetically. 'But it is not their real name. It is a sort of joke.'

'How negative?' asked Paddy, frowning.

'Well, I rather seemed to have inadvertently overlooked a cheque I wrote to cover the council rates and according to the bank's figures we are now £117.65 in the red,' said the treasurer. 'And, much as the general dislike of banks I share, I'm afraid that in this case I am with reluctance rather inclined to believe that the bank's figures are to be pretty well adjacent to accurate likely.' He paused. 'Of course,' he added brightly, 'quite a few members have not yet their annual subscription fees paid so that might a little difference make.'

This remark was greeted in total silence not least since it was pretty well understood that a not insignificant number of members regarded the paying of annual subscription fees as optional rather than compulsory.

One or two members had slight coughing fits. Several members found something on the floor that required their undivided attention and other club members found that their watches needed winding, their pens suddenly needed cleaning or their noses urgently needed blowing. One or two members suddenly took a serious, almost obsessive interest in their fingernails.

'I have just come into a little money,' whispered Biffo to Puffy. 'Do you think it would be appropriate if I offered to pay for a new mower? I could afford it.'

Puffy looked at him and put a hand on his shoulder. 'That's very kind of you,' he said quietly. 'But, you should keep your money in your wallet. This is a community problem and we'll all be much better off it we solve it as a community.' He paused.

'Look at Bill,' he said, disregarding the fact that this was an impossibility since Bill had disappeared. 'He thought he could buy respect by buying the cricket field for the village. It was a wonderful gesture and we're all grateful but gratefulness gets in the way of mutual respect.' He looked at Biffo and raised an eyebrow.

'Thanks,' said Biffo, quietly.

'How much would we have in the bank if all the members paid their membership fees?' asked Lord Hepplewhite, who as well as being patron was also the club's only honorary life member and therefore one of the few people in the room who didn't owe the club money.

'Well, we would if every member paid up, have a credit balance of very nearly £3,145.00. But the chances...'

'Thank you, Mr Treasurer,' said Paddy. He looked at Itchy who looked as miserable and disappointed as a boy who has been told that instead of a brand new bike with gears and a bell he'll be getting a pair of indestructible woollen socks for Christmas. 'Don't you worry Itchy,' he promised. 'We'll get you that mower.' He looked around. 'I think it's pretty clear that we need to find some way of raising the money we need to buy a new mower,' said Paddy. He looked around the bar. 'Does anyone have any suggestions?'

'So what are they really called?' Lord Hepplewhite asked Helmut.

'Who?'

'Snoring and Dribbling. If they're not really Snoring and Dribbling.'

'Oh but they are,' said Helmut, nodding with some enthusiasm. 'They're snoring and dribbling. They absolutely are!'

Lord Hepplewhite frowned and thought for a moment. He had lost the plot. 'Are what?' he asked eventually.

'Snoring and dribbling,' replied Helmut. 'That's why I call them Snoring and Dribbling!'

The private confusion of Lord Hepplewhite had not disturbed the intense cerebral activity in the rest of the room. The members of the Fondling-Under-Water cricket club were not a mean or unusually tight-fisted lot but when they realised that they had a choice of either digging into their own pockets to pay for the new mower or thinking of other ways to raise the money they invariably came up with a host of splendid ideas. As far as money was concerned their speciality, if they could be said to have one, was finding ways to extract money from other people.

'Let's have a fund-raising fête and sports day!' suggested Cheesy.

It was immediately agreed that Cheesy's suggestion would be a painless and sure-fire way to raise the necessary funds.

It was, furthermore, agreed that since the grass was growing longer every day they should hold the fund-raising event as quickly as possible.

'We could combine next Saturday's match against Cyril's Eleven with a fund-raising day for the club!' suggested Puffy.

A unanimous vote was held, in the best democratic manner, and it was decided that the match against Cyril Player's Celebrity County Eleven should be the centre piece for a day designed to raise money to buy a new lawnmower.

This decision was greeted with considerable enthusiasm and the assembled throng was about to celebrate the moment by retiring to the bar and obtaining additional sustenance of the appropriate variety when, above the hubbub, a lone voice could be heard at the back of the room.

'Excuse me!' said a tall, unusually elegant and well-dressed figure at the back of the room. He had collar-length hair and a hooked nose. He seemed nervous and was so flushed that he was either exceptionally warm or he was feeling extremely nervous about something. He spoke diffidently but loudly enough to attract everyone's attention. It was the vicar, the Reverend Hubert Counter.

'I'm sorry to bother you all,' he said. 'But before the meeting draws to a close I would just like to say something of a rather personal nature.'

Everyone waited. Cricket club members are as partial to gossip as anyone else and what can be described today as information of a 'personal nature' can almost certainly be described as 'gossip' by the time tomorrow comes.

The vicar cleared his throat and continued. 'After a good deal of soul-searching, and a great many private discussions with

God, who has, I may say, been an extremely sympathetic and supportive listener, I have decided that I wish to reassign my gender disposition.'

He then paused, clearly expecting the assembled members of the Fondling-Under-Water Cricket Club to greet this news with some sort of response. But since no one had the faintest idea what he had said no one responded.

'I, er, think that perhaps I should be a little more blunt,' said the Reverend Counter, accurately diagnosing the reason for the lack of response. He thought for a moment, cleared his throat, and tried again. 'After a good deal of thought I have decided that my outward physical appearance, from a gender point of view, has for many years been inappropriate to the needs and feelings of my inner, emotional self. For some time I have attempted to deal with this dilemma by living two lives: a private life in which I have expressed my gender preference to my own personal satisfaction and a public life, in which I have maintained an established gender image with which my emotional self no longer feels entirely comfortable.'

'However, I no longer feel that this social dichotomy is appropriate. Indeed, I feel that in order to regain my feeling of self respect, my honesty and my integrity I should and must be honest with you all. I have, therefore, decided to depose my established persona and to replace it, on a full-time basis, with the alternative persona with which I can honestly say I feel more comfortable.'

'I have spoken to my dear lady wife at considerable length about my intentions and she has asked me to assure you that she stands right behind me. She would, indeed, be here today to share this moment with me. However, her latest batch of elderberry wine has to be bottled and she has asked me to ask you to excuse her absence while regarding her as being here in spirit if not in body. I have no plans to undergo surgery and Primrose and I, and our children Tarquin, Fiona and Tamarisk will continue to live together as a family. I have also spoken to the Bishop. Initially he had some reservations and felt that it might be better for the church – both locally and nationally – if I were to resign my living and seek an alternative calling. However, after lengthy discussions with my legal adviser, the Bishop eventually, and I may say generously, agreed that I should be allowed to stay here in Fondling-Under-Water and to continue to be your spiritual shepherd.'

The vicar stopped. And waited.

Again, nothing happened except that most people looked at someone else and everyone looked puzzled. There was some whispering.

'What did he say?' Biffo whispered to Puffy.

Puffy shrugged. 'No one ever really understands much he says,' he admitted. 'But this time I don't think I understand anything.'

The vicar, who seemed aware of the yawning gap which existed between what had been delivered and what had been received, swallowed and spoke again.

'Naturally,' he said, 'it would not be appropriate for me to continue to be known by the name of Hubert. In future, therefore, I would like to be known as Hermione.'

This time the assembled congregation did understand what he had said. Every lower jaw in the bar headed south as though wire operated and if there had been a dentist present he would have been able to perform check ups without more ado.

'Did he say what I thought he said?' Puffy asked Biffo and several dozen other people asked several dozen other people.

'If I heard what I think I heard then I think he probably did say what you thought he said,' said Biffo. He thought about it some more. 'But I'm not sure,' he added a moment later.

'What's the big deal?' asked Lettice, who was standing on Biffo's left polishing glasses. 'He's going to wear a frock all the time and wants to be called Hermione. He's a vicar and he always has worn a sort of frock anyway.'

'How do you know he's going to wear a frock?' asked Puffy.

'Because that's what he just said,' said Lettice. 'Anyway I thought everyone in the village knew he was a transvestite.'

'He's a transvestite?' said Puffy.

'Yes,' said Lettice.

'The vicar is a transvestite?'

'Yes.'

'You knew that?'

'Yes. Of course.'

'You never said anything.'

'I thought you knew. I thought everyone knew. Besides what would I say?'

'Well,' said Puffy, 'you could have told me. You could have said 'Hey, the vicar is a transvestite'.'

'Why?'

Puffy thought about this for a moment. 'I don't know,' he admitted. 'No reason apart from the fact that it's damned good gossip. But you could have told me. Anyway, how did you know?'

'The washing,' said Lettice.

'The washing?'

'Like every other woman in this village the vicar's wife hangs her washing out on Monday mornings. You can see the vicarage garden from the road. She's a flat-chested size eight with three small children. She hangs out bras and knickers and slips and dresses that fit her and she hangs out bras and knickers and slips and dresses that would fit a 38C size eighteen. Who else is there in the vicarage that would fit a 38C size eighteen?'

Puffy stared at her. 'You look at other people's washing?'

'Of course I do,' said Lettice. 'Don't you?'

'Of course I don't!' said Puffy, indignantly. 'And you can tell a woman's bust size just by looking at her empty bra?'

'More or less. I know that some of the bras the vicar's wife hangs on her line don't fit her.' Lettice paused. 'Besides,' she added. 'He sometimes doesn't get all his nail varnish off properly.'

'Under the circumstances,' said the vicar, 'I think it only fair to announce my resignation from the Fondling-Under-Water cricket team. However, my playing days have given me many happy memories and I would very much like to retain an interest in the club. I will be having a word with Mrs Cleavidge tomorrow to ask if I might help with the teas.'

If the vicar had announced that he intended to become a Satanist, use the knave for the celebration of black masses, and invite parishioners to strip naked, sacrifice one of the church wardens, and then drink the blood of a young virgin, the response might, just might, have been something close to the response this announcement produced.

'You can't do that!' cried three quarters of the people in the room. They spoke simultaneously, as though rehearsed, which they were not. The remaining one quarter of the people in the room, all of whom had been concentrating on ordering drinks, paying for drinks or drinking drinks, looked up in alarm to find out what it was that could not be done, and who it was that was not to be allowed to do it.

'What about Saturday's match?' cried Paddy, above the general despair.

'Well I don't think I can possibly play,' said the vicar with unaccustomed firmness. 'I will feel much more comfortable helping with the teas.' He daintily used his right hand to spread a little imaginary butter in the air and smiled sweetly.

'Can we talk about this?' asked Paddy. The vice captain had gone quite pale. He did not look well.

Reluctantly, the vicar agreed to talk privately with the club vice captain. The other members headed for the bar and ordered much larger, much stronger drinks than they had planned to order. Puffy would have benefited greatly from this unexpected side effect of the vicar's announcement if it had not been for the fact that most of the cricket club members asked Puffy to add the cost of their drinks to what they already owed. The cricket club members were not keen bill payers.

'What did you say these people did?' asked Lord Hepplewhite, joining the crowd at the bar and grabbing Helmut by the sleeve before he could disappear.

'Which people?'

'The Snoring and Dribbling people.'

'They're our accountants,' Helmut explained again.

The good Lord's confusion was clear. He scratched his head vigorously. 'Are you sure?'

'Absolutely.'

'They're called Snoring and Dribbling?'

'Well, not exactly,' admitted Helmut. 'But that's what I call them.'

Lord Hepplewhite paused for a moment. 'So what do other people call them then?'

'Winchester and Merriweather,' replied Helmut, rather agitated at being kept from the bar. 'They have offices in the old building at the fire station end of Victoria Terrace. Their place you cannot miss – it is just between the bespoke truss maker – what's his name..?'

'Clive Periwinkle,' said Lord Hepplewhite instantly regretting the speed with which he had expressed his familiarity with the region's premier truss maker.

'That's the one,' said Helmut. 'Surgical Supplies to the Landed Gentry. There is a pet food shop on the other side and a fish and chip shop run by two Chinamen across the road directly almost. Their cod is fine but I would not the battered sausages touch if I you were I.' Helmut, who had managed to extricate himself from the good Lord's grip, moved away and joined the queue for the bar. He looked at his watch. He had six minutes to drink his beer and get back home.

'Oh I know Winchester and Merriweather!' said Lord Hepplewhite, no less confused than he had been a little earlier. 'But why do you call them Snoring and...' He stopped himself in mid question and chuckled. 'Oh, I say, that's very appropriate,' he admitted. 'Very appropriate.' He chuckled again. 'Snoring and Dribbling,' he said to himself. 'Very good. Very apt. Very droll.' He nodded appreciatively. 'Snoring and Dribbling,' he repeated.

Among the other cricket club members the vicar's revelation that he intended to exchange his bat for a butter knife, and his role as a key bowler for a new position with a pot of shrimp paste and a sandwich loaf, was the favourite topic of conversation.

'Of course,' said Cheesy, 'if he does play we know where he'll be fielding.'

'Where?' asked Jack Hobbs.

'In the slips, of course,' answered Cheesy.

This inevitably led to a good many jokes about maiden overs and fine legs.

~ Chapter 62 ~

'Biffo!'

'Streaky!'

The two friends beamed at one another, shook hands and then hugged. It hadn't been long since they had seen one another but a great deal had happened to them both.

'You look fantastic!' said Streaky, when the two chums finally disentangled themselves from one another.

'I feel good,' agreed Biffo, grinning.

Streaky looked around, held out a hand and beckoned a long-legged redhead in an extremely tight white T-shirt and very short white skirt to climb out of his Porsche. Judging by the unfettered bulges underneath the T-shirt the redhead was waging a private war against the underwear industry.

'We're engaged!' Streaky said, with a sweet and rather charming mixture of modesty, pride and embarrassment.

Biffo looked at the redhead in amazement. On television she had looked completely different. And now she looked different again.

'I didn't have red hair the last time you saw me,' said the girl.

'No,' agreed Biffo.

'It's dyed,' the redhead explained.

'It's Voluptua!' said Streaky.

'I used to be blonde,' said the redhead.

'I know,' said Biffo, trying hard to disguise the fact that he could have hardly been more surprised if Streaky had announced that he had become engaged to Queen Victoria.

'Voluptua Bradshaw!' said Streaky. 'The future Voluptua Bacon. Our former secretary is a big star. Voluptua is the presenter for my new quiz programme.'

'I've always wanted to be an actress,' said Voluptua. She seemed very happy.

Biffo was having difficulty taking all this in. 'And you two are engaged?' he said.

Streaky nodded, grinned and kept on nodding.

'Congratulations to both of you!' said Biffo.

Streaky stopped grinning and stopped nodding. 'I was sorry to hear about you and Edwina,' he said, reluctant to spoil the moment but conscious that he should say something about Biffo's little personal problem.

'Don't be,' said Biffo, reassuringly. He sighed. 'It was all a bit of a relief, to be honest. And Edwina had got another bloke anyway.'

'Yes, I did hear something along those lines,' said Streaky. Embarrassed, he turned slightly and pointed at the village pub. 'So this is The Gravedigger's Rest, eh?'

Biffo and Voluptua turned and looked at the pub.

'Who was he?' asked Streaky.

Biffo frowned. 'Who?'

'The tired gravedigger?'

'I'm not sure,' admitted Biffo.

'Doesn't matter,' said Streaky. 'I can get the scriptwriters to make something up.' He looked admiringly at the pub. 'Beautiful building,' he said appreciatively.

'Of course it needs a bit of loving restoration here and there,' said Biffo.

'All these old places need a lot of tender, loving care,' agreed Streaky. He looked at Biffo. 'What does it need?'

'New roof, a few new ceilings and about fifty gallons of white paint,' said Biffo, quickly.

'That's all?'

'That's all.'

'I need to make the programme on Saturday.'

'I'm sure that will be OK,' said Biffo.

Streaky looked at the calendar on his watch and sighed.

'The blokes in the village will do most of the work,' said Biffo. 'Better Television has only got to pay for the materials.' He shrugged as though this were such a trifling sum that it would be hardly worth putting the claim form in to the accountant.

'Oh good,' said Streaky, with a sideways look at Biffo. 'As long as that's all.'

'That's settled then,' replied Biffo. 'Let's go inside and you can meet the landlord. I might even buy you both a beer.'

'Best offer I've had since I got here,' said Streaky.

'Mind your heads,' said Biffo. 'And watch your step.'

The warning was of limited value. Streaky banged his head. Voluptua tripped and landed flat on her face, showing that her dislike of underwear was complete.

~ Chapter 63 ~

'PERFECT!' SAID STREAKY, LOOKING AROUND the bar for the umpteenth time. He sipped at his beer and nodded approvingly. 'Good beer,' he said. He was drinking his fourth, or perhaps his fifth, pint of beer.

Voluptua, who was sitting next to him and who didn't like beer very much was still drinking her first pint. When she was sixteen someone had bought her a beer on her first visit to a pub. She hadn't liked it but hadn't liked to say so because she thought drinking beer was a terribly grown up thing to do. Because she had never said she didn't like beer people always bought her beer. And so, seven years later, she was known by everyone who was acquainted with her to be a regular beer drinker. A year or two ago she had, once or twice, tried to order something different but the die was cast. If she wanted to change her drink she would have to change her friends, her relatives and her job.

'I'd love to make one of our new quiz programmes in your pub,' Streaky said to Puffy. 'Can you provide me with an audience?'

'Oh I think we can manage that,' said Puffy, eagerly

'And a team to represent the pub?'

'Er...what sort of team were you thinking of?' asked Puffy, cautiously.

'A quiz team. You know the sort of thing: 'Which team won the Cup Final in 1952?' 'What year did Elvis Presley record Blue Suede Shoes?' That sort of thing. I'll bring down a bunch of celebrities to take on your team.'

'I should think we can put a team together.'

Streaky looked around. 'I have a small budget to pay for alterations which might be necessary and to cover the cost of damage and inconvenience,' he said. 'Of course I can't give you money for structural repairs – roof, ceilings, stuff like that.' He scratched his chin. 'But I'd like the inside of the pub to look truly traditional. Could you find some really old-looking chairs and tables? I'd like them to look battered and well-used.'

Puffy looked around. It would have been difficult to find chairs and tables which looked older, better used or more battered.

'And a fireplace,' said Streaky, with a big wink aimed at Puffy. 'I don't care what the weather is like – I'd like to have a log fire roaring.'

'We have a fireplace,' said Puffy. 'It works very well...'

Streaky held up a hand. 'You'd better get it checked. Swept. Cleaned. Hire some small boys and have them climb up and down inside it to get rid of the birds' nests.'

'Fine,' said Puffy, catching on at last. 'I can arrange that.'

'And see if you can lay your hands on a really old piece of carpet,' said Streaky.

'Would something moth-eaten and beer-stained do?'

'That would be perfect. Just the sort of thing an old-fashioned pub should have. I'm sure you'll be able to find something suitable.'

'I know exactly where I can get what we need,' said Puffy. He exchanged glances with Biffo and then looked down at the carpet on the floor. It was, of course, extremely moth-eaten and many of the stains with which it was decorated were undoubtedly caused by beer.

'And I need it all done by Saturday,' said Streaky.

'No problem,' said Puffy confidently.

'Fine,' said Streaky. 'Terrific.' He put his hand into his jacket pocket and took out a cheque book and pen. 'Do you think £10,000 would cover all that?'

Puffy swallowed hard. 'I should think so,' he said.

'That's a good job,' said Streaky. 'Because I can't give you any more than that.' He looked at his watch, sighed, stood up and looked down at the beautiful Voluptua. 'I suppose we'd better get back to London,' he said, rather glumly. He looked around and then looked at Biffo. 'How the hell did you find this place?' he asked.

Biffo shrugged. 'The bus stopped here,' he replied.

Streaky thought about this for a moment, nodded and headed for the door.

'Watch the step!' called Puffy.

'And mind your head,' added Biffo.

Streaky turned to thank them, tripped over the step and banged his head. Voluptua was more fortunate. She tripped over the step but her head missed the beam by an inch or so.

~ Chapter 64 ~

'THANKS,' SAID BIFFO, AS HE, Streaky and Voluptua walked towards Streaky's car. 'That was very generous of you. I didn't realise you'd got such a big budget.'

'I haven't got a big budget,' said Streaky. He handed the car keys to Voluptua. 'You'd better drive.'

'But you just gave Puffy a cheque for £10,000 to repair his pub!'

'My pleasure,' said Streaky. 'Nice pub. Nice bloke. And you're my pal.'

'Which key is it?' asked Voluptua, examining the key ring that Streaky had given her.

'The big one,' said Streaky. 'The little one is for the petrol cap. But you don't have to use the key. If you press that little button all the doors will open as if by magic.'

'How many weeks is the programme scheduled to run for?' asked Biffo.

Voluptua pressed the little button.

'Twenty.'

There was a squeal of delight as Voluptua discovered that the remote control device had opened the car doors.

'And what's your budget?'

'Ten thousand.'

'For each programme?'

Voluptua slid into the driver's seat, adjusted the driver's mirror and checked her hair and lipstick.

Streaky looked genuinely surprised. 'No! For the series.'

Biffo stared at Streaky. 'You've just spent your entire budget for the series?'

'Golly,' sighed Streaky, deliberately mistaking the question for a statement and accepting the news as though it was something he had not realised before. He tossed aside the information with a slight and careless shoulder shrug and then climbed into the passenger seat with the practised ease of someone who is accustomed to getting into a car which is much too small for him. He lowered the window. 'I'm terrible with money,' he said, partly as explanation, partly as apology. He waved a hand and grinned. 'I'll see you at the end of the week. Make sure the landlord spends the company's money wisely.'

~ Chapter 65 ~

LIVING IN A SMALL, CLOSELY-KNIT village is, in many ways, like being a member of a large family.

Between the inhabitants of the village there are, inevitably, many minor disputes and disagreements. Sometimes there are petty feuds which may last for decades – long after the cause of the original discontent has been forgotten.

It is written somewhere that where two or three are gathered together there will be misunderstandings and Fondling-Under-Water was no exception to this simple rule.

But that is the downside of village life and there is no need to dwell on such unpleasantnesses.

The upside of life in a village is that when one member of the extended village family needs help he can ask for it in the confident expectation that his need will be met without question or rancour. Indeed, the concept of privacy is such an alien one within a village community that in many cases the help that is required will be forthcoming before the person wanting that help has thought to ask for it. (There are even those who believe that on some occasions help is forthcoming some time before the person being helped is aware that he or she needs help.)

When it is the village publican who is in trouble and he

needs help to restore, repair and save the village pub the saviours are out in force.

And so it was that long before Streaky Bacon and the delectable Voluptua Bradshaw had arrived back in London the villagers of Fondling-Under-Water had begun to redistribute the manna which had fallen in such abundance from Better Television heaven.

Within an hour and fifteen minutes several thousand second-hand slates had been ordered and were on their way to Fondling-Under-Water from a demolition site in Cornwall.

Within an hour and forty minutes a complex gridwork of rusty scaffolding had been erected on the outside of The Gravedigger's Rest and a team of eager labourers had steadily begun to remove the fractured and patchwork collection of old slates which had contributed so much to the unwanted permeability of the village pub's aged roof.

Long before Voluptua (never a confident driver) had found somewhere to park Streaky's Porsche, and the two lovers had dragged themselves indoors and made a refreshing pot of Darjeeling tea, a brace of plasterers and a trio of carpenters (the best in the village) had been pulled off a job in Widdlecome-Over-The-Moor and were hurrying back to The Gravedigger's Rest in order to revise and reconstitute the weather-battered ceilings of that highly valued establishment.

Biffo, whose experience of building workers was confined to his previous life in the suburbs, had been startled when he had heard Puffy assure Streaky that he could restore The Gravedigger's Rest in the sort of time usually needed for a building estimator to draw a few deep breaths and find a piece of paper large enough to contain an estimate full of noughts.

But as Biffo cycled to and fro past The Gravedigger's Rest he gradually realised that living in a village has virtues and advantages which cannot be classified under such headings as 'lovely views', 'melodious bird song' or 'clean air'.

The village was rallying round in the way that the closest of families do and it was clear to Biffo that Better Television's money would be spent (the vast majority of it on materials for the villagers were happily giving their time for free) and The

Gravedigger's Rest would be restored to watertight but still unspoilt beauty well in time for Streaky, Voluptua and the television crew to excite the nation with yet another quiz programme.

~ Chapter 66 ~

'I'VE GOT SOMETHING TO TELL you all,' said Bill Stickers. He had gone such an unhealthy looking shade of white that he looked like a 'before' picture for an advertisement promoting some iron-rich health remedy. He paused, studied his fingernails for a while and then cleared his throat. 'It's not terribly good news,' he warned his audience. He looked miserable, desolate and terribly alone.

Cheesy, who was leaning against the bar, half turned. 'What the hell is this all about?' he asked Puffy. Members of the cricket club had been called in to The Gravedigger's Rest for a special meeting. They had been told that the captain, chairman and president had an important announcement to make.

Puffy shrugged. 'I haven't the foggiest,' he admitted

Bill blew his nose and started again. 'I discovered the other day that the bank which has been looking after my money had, er, apparently made some injudicious investments.' He spoke in a whisper but everyone could hear him. Somehow those listening knew that what he had to say was important. There was something at once both exquisitely embarrassing and irresistible about someone they all knew discussing his financial problems in public. This, they suspected, could be even more enthralling than the vicar's revelation.

'To cut a long story short,' said Bill, clearing his throat again. 'I found that I am not the wealthy man I thought I was when I had the money I, er, no longer have.'

Bill paused to mop his brow. 'I found that I was, er, slightly, not to put too fine a point on it, pretty well broke,' admitted Bill. He seemed ashamed of this admission. To most of the villagers his shame seemed odd since poverty was a condition with which most of them were well acquainted.

'In view of all this, and of subsequent occurrences,' said

Bill. 'I would like to offer my immediate resignation from the chairmanship, presidency and captaincy of the cricket club.' He paused and wiped his mouth. 'To take effect immediately,' he said.

'Nonsense!' cried Puffy. 'You don't have to resign just because you've lost your money.'

A strong murmur of support for this view ran swiftly around the room. It was commonly accepted that Bill Stickers had been appointed chairman, president and captain of the Fondling-Under-Water Cricket Club partly because of his wealth (and partly because he owned the ground upon which the club played its matches) but no one felt it right that Bill should be stripped of his titles simply because he had lost the wealth which had gained him the titles in the first place.

The people of Fondling-Under-Water were a kind-hearted bunch; unlike some of those working for banks and building societies they didn't like to see a man being kicked when he was down.

'I'm afraid you haven't heard the half of it yet,' admitted Bill quietly. He pushed his fingers through what was left of his hair and, at the end of the gesture, scratched the back of his neck. He rubbed his nose, tapped his front teeth with his thumb nail and pulled rather ferociously at an unfortunate ear lobe. 'It's taken me a long time to pluck up the courage to tell you this,' he said. He took a deep breath and then let it out in a rush. 'I've sold the cricket ground.'

These final few words (the most significant and only truly crucial part of the whole speech) were tossed out so rapidly that most of those present did not hear them properly. Those who were standing close enough to hear did not seem to register them as being of significance.

'I thought he said he'd sold the cricket ground,' whispered Cheesy to Puffy. He tried a small, nervous laugh but it came out sounding more like the desperate gargle of someone being strangled.

'So did I!' replied Puffy.

They didn't believe what they had heard but at the same time they weren't entirely sure that they hadn't heard it.

'Sorry, Bill,' said Paddy Fields, speaking for everyone

present. He paused and then spoke slowly and very clearly. 'Could you say that again?'

There was a long, long pause.

'I've sold the cricket ground,' said Bill. This time he spoke clearly and there was no mistaking his words. He looked more miserable and more desolate than he had when he had begun.

The dreadful news was greeted with total silence.

'And there's something else,' Bill went on.

No one spoke. They could not imagine what else there could possibly be. It was as though King Edward VIII had finished his abdication speech and then added...'and there's something else.'

Biffo could feel his own heart beating. He felt sure that everyone else present must be able to hear it. But they couldn't. They were all deafened by the cacophony their own hearts were making.

~ Chapter 67 ~

'THE CRICKET GROUND WAS THE only asset I had left,' said Bill rather weakly.

In the end he had been the only one able to break the forbidding, solid wall of silence he had created.

'I really didn't mean to sell it. But then a bloke came up to me out of the blue and offered me money for it.' He paused and then blew his nose noisily. 'Quite a lot of money,' he admitted.

'What's he going to do with the ground?' asked Paddy. It was the obvious question. The question they all wanted to ask. The question everyone present wanted answering. 'That's the something else you were going to tell us isn't? You know what he's got planned for the ground, don't you?'

'I don't think he's going to leave it as a cricket club,' said Bill weakly. He looked around. Everyone was looking at him. He sighed. This was the bit he was really dreading. 'He's going to build some sort of holiday camp there.'

'Oh well that's no problem,' said Paddy, trying hard to laugh and look unconcerned. 'He'll never get planning permission. My cousin is chairman of the local planning committee. He's dead keen on cricket.'

'The land's already got planning permission,' said Bill quietly.

Everyone stared at him.

'A few years ago Lord Hepplewhite was trying to raise money from his bank,' explained Bill. 'His solicitor told him that if he got planning permission for the cricket pitch the land would be worth more and the bank would lend him money against it.' Bill hesitated and shrugged. 'Lord Hepplewhite knows a lot of people. Getting planning permission probably wasn't difficult.'

There was a long, long silence during which those present attempted to digest this devastating news.

'Do you know the name of this fellow – the chap who has bought the cricket ground?'

'Washbrook,' said Bill without hesitation. 'Damien Washbrook. He's a solicitor.'

Biffo went quite cold. He asked Bill to repeat the name.

Paddy turned towards Biffo. 'Do you know him?' he asked.

'I think so,' said Biffo. 'If he's the bloke I think he is then he's my ex-wife's boyfriend.'

'Do you have any idea why he's bought the ground?'

Biffo shook his head slowly. 'Not really,' he confessed. He shrugged. 'I think he's a bit of a property dealer.'

'Do you think that his buying the land has anything to do with your being here?' asked Cheesy. There was a certain coolness in his voice.

Biffo looked at him. 'No!' he said. 'Of course not! How could it?'

'It seems a bit of a coincidence,' said Paddy sternly.

Biffo looked around the bar. Everyone was looking at him.

'I can understand how you all feel but you wouldn't have known I knew him if I hadn't told you!' protested Biffo.

'That's true,' said Paddy immediately. He took a deep breath. 'Sorry, Biffo.' he apologised. 'I think we're probably all a bit shocked.'

'Sorry!' said Cheesy. He looked embarrassed.

'That's OK,' said Biffo. 'I can understand why you were suspicious. In your place I would have probably felt the same.'

'Have you signed the contract handing over the land to this Washbrook fellow?' Paddy asked Bill.

Bill's lowered gaze answered the question.

'Maybe if we can raise the money we can buy the ground off this Washbrook chap,' suggested Itchy hopefully.

'How much did he pay?' Paddy asked Bill.

'£100,000,' Bill answered without hesitation.

Paddy whistled.

'He tried to get me to take it in instalments,' said Bill. 'But I didn't trust him so I made him pay me in cash. He complained a lot but agreed in the end. I've got the cash stashed in my greenhouse.' He paused. 'I'm sorry,' he said at last. Head down he darted for the door and disappeared out into the night. No one said goodbye.

Paddy was the first to speak. 'So,' he said at last. 'What are we going to do?'

'I suppose we'll have to find somewhere else to play,' said the vicar with a sigh.

Everyone looked at him as though he had suggested a summer tour of Mars.

'But we've always played on that ground!' said Cheesy.

'My dad played cricket on that ground,' said Itchy defiantly. 'I don't see why we should stop now...'

'...just because someone is going to build on it,' added Paddy drily.

~ Chapter 68 ~

'YOU LOOK AS IF YOU'VE just taken a wicket and found out that the umpire had called a no ball,' said Biffo to Puffy.

The landlord of The Gravedigger's Rest was sitting on a stool behind his bar, with his head in his hands. There was chaos all around him as carpenters and plasterers repaired the pub ceilings. No one had bothered to lift up the carpet which was now tattier and more badly stained than ever. At this rate, thought Biffo, the carpet would soon become a real collector's item.

'Have a drink,' said Puffy, pouring a large whisky for Biffo and taking a sip from his own. 'And thanks again for arranging all this.' He waved a hand around to indicate the work that was going on. 'I don't think we'd have got through another winter with the roof in the state it was in.'

'Pleasure,' said Biffo. A small chunk of plaster fell from the ceiling and fell into the glass. Drops of whisky splashed out of the glass and onto the back of Biffo's hand. 'But you're looking even more miserable than you were when I saw you last. What's up?' He licked the drops of whisky from his hand and carefully removed the chunk of plaster from his glass.

'I've just been talking to Paddy,' said Puffy.

Biffo looked around for somewhere to put the small piece of plaster.

'Just toss it on the floor,' said Puffy. 'We're going to have a clean up later.'

Biffo did as he was told and tossed the small piece of plaster onto the floor.

'Paddy rang his cousin,' explained Puffy. 'The one who is chairman of the local planning committee.'

'I remember,' said Biffo. 'But they've already given permission for the cricket ground, haven't they?' He took a swig from his glass. 'Cheers,' he said. 'And thanks.'

'Apparently it all happened some time ago,' said Puffy. 'Bill was absolutely right. Lord Hepplewhite explained to Paddy's cousin and a couple of other people on the committee that he needed planning permission on the land in order to get a loan from his bank. Under normal circumstances they wouldn't have dreamt of giving him planning permission to build on the cricket ground. But because everyone likes him, and they felt sorry for him, and he promised never really to build on the land, and no one likes banks and everyone likes the idea of pulling a fast one over a bank, they gave him the permission.'

Puffy sighed. 'It was just a ploy to help him get a loan from his bank.' He finished his drink and poured himself another. 'A refill?' he asked Biffo.

Biffo, understanding why his friend felt so depressed, followed the landlord's example and emptied his glass. Puffy immediately filled it for him.

Somewhere above them there was a yelp and a loud crash. They both ignored it.

~ Chapter 69 ~

MISS BOX'S BICYCLE WAS STURDY but it was built for strength and reliability rather than for speed. It had but three gears (one for whizzing downhill, one for pedalling on the flat and one for struggling uphill) and all the aerodynamic qualities of a small garden shed. It had been black when it had been delivered from the factory but it had, over the years, slowly turned brown with rust. When Miss Box had spotted Biffo rubbing off some of the rust she had told him off. 'Leave the rust where it is,' she had said. 'It protects the metal.' Biffo had looked at her as if she was potty. 'Remove the rust and the metal underneath will go rusty,' she had explained. 'Keep removing the rust and eventually there won't be any metal left.'

The brakes, as Biffo had discovered on several hair raising occasions, were more for show than for action and slowing down put a heavy burden on the toes and soles of the rider's shoes or boots.

There was a large metal basket at the front of the bicycle, in front of the handlebars, and another, very slightly smaller metal basket at the back. There was a bell but it had long since lost its ring.

Biffo had arranged to meet Lettice at Buttercup Cottage at 1 o'clock but an emergency delivery of pork sausages and a bag of potting compost had delayed him and it was ten past the hour when he finally skidded to a halt outside the cottage gate.

He leant the bicycle against the hedge on the opposite side of the road and rushed into the garden alternately shouting out apologies and calling Lettice's name.

'I was sitting in the summerhouse in the back garden,' said Lettice, calm and unperturbed, appearing from between an overgrown rhododendron bush and the corner of the cottage. She was wearing a light blue cotton dress with white lace-edging around the short sleeves and the scoop neckline. 'The grass needs cutting but the back garden is beautiful.'

'I gather Puffy's got a mower for sale,' said Biffo with a grin. He realised once again just how beautiful Lettice was.

'Have you got the key?'

Biffo rummaged around in his pockets. 'I'm sorry I'm late,' he said again. 'Miss Box sent me off with an emergency delivery. I didn't like to ask whether it was the sausages or the potting compost which was the emergency. One tries to please.'

'Please don't worry about it!' said Lettice. 'I could have happily sat all day in that summerhouse. It really is a beautiful spot.' She peered behind him. 'Is that yours?'

Biffo turned around. The ewe, recognising that she had become the centre of attention, baaed loudly.

'Well, in a sort of way I suppose she is,' he admitted.

The ewe had been waiting for him outside The Gravedigger's Rest and she had followed him around all morning. Whenever he had cycled too fast for her she had merely waited and nibbled at a verge until he came cycling back. She was now standing outside the gate, staring at him with huge doleful eyes. 'We met yesterday evening,' he said. 'It's a long story.'

'Do you know who she belongs to?'

'Haven't the foggiest.'

Lettice walked up the path, opened the gate and examined the sheep. 'She isn't marked.'

'What does that mean?' asked Biffo, whose areas of expertise did not include sheep markings.

'Farmers usually mark their sheep in case they get out and get lost. This one hasn't been marked since she was shorn last year so the chances are that she's probably been living wild for quite a while.'

'Ah.'

'Shall I let her in?'

'In where?'

'Into the garden? She can eat some of the lawn. If we leave

her out in the road she may get run over or cause an accident.'

'I suppose you'd better,' agreed Biffo.

The ewe did not need asking twice. The moment Lettice opened the gate she shot through the opening and into the garden. She baaed loudly at Biffo and then happily turned herself into a lawn eating machine.

Biffo pulled out the two keys which Mrs Trubshaw had given him. 'Do you know which key fits which door?' he asked.

Lettice took the two keys from him, selected the appropriate key for the front door and let them into the cottage. 'It'll be a little damp,' she warned Biffo. 'It's been empty all through the winter. I think Mrs Trubshaw did come up a couple of times and light a fire but it really needed a little more attention than that. These old cottages do need quite a bit of looking after.'

'It does smell a bit musty,' agreed Biffo. He stepped gingerly onto the bare floorboards in the hall. 'Is the floor safe?' he asked, recklessly bouncing up and down a little on his toes. He looked up at the walls. There were several large damp patches showing where rain had come in during the winter. None of these worried Biffo. He had always dreamt of living in the country. Damp stains seemed a small price to pay.

'Oh, I think so,' said Lettice. 'It's the roof which really needs some work doing on it. There were a couple of storms last winter and quite a few tiles were blown off. I'm afraid I don't think Mrs Trubshaw ever got around to having them replaced.'

'Who was the last owner?'

'Mr Rose. He was Mrs Trubshaw's brother.'

'And she inherited the cottage when he died?'

'That's right.'

Biffo wandered from the hall into a large, airy room which overlooked the back garden. Like the hallway it was quite bare.

'It's wonderful!' said Biffo. Some people would have seen it as lonely and out of the way. He saw it as quiet and secluded.

Lettice smiled at him. 'It needs quite a lot doing to it,' she warned him. 'But I think that is probably reflected in the asking price.' She hesitated. 'You could always make an offer,' she said. 'I think the asking price is pretty much just a sort of starting point.' She blushed. She suddenly realised that she very much wanted Biffo to buy the cottage and stay in the village.

'What happened to all the furniture and the carpets?' asked Biffo.

'There was a house auction. It's a pity in a way because quite a lot of the furniture really went well with the cottage. But with no one living in the cottage it was the wisest thing really.'

'I like the hearth!' said Biffo, indicating a huge, old-fashioned fireplace. It was big enough to walk into. There were two huge stone seats built into it. 'Do you know if the chimney works?'

'Of course it works!' said Lettice. 'You can burn logs cut from your own trees. There are working fireplaces in all the rooms.'

'Wonderful!' said Biffo, who meant it.

'Puffy always says that chopping up your own wood warms you up twice,' said Lettice. 'Once when you chop the wood and once when you burn the logs.'

Biffo unlocked a pair of French windows which opened out onto a small patio. The windows had swollen with the damp and were stiff and difficult to open. But with a little pushing and a little wriggling they opened eventually. A sliver of wood broke off the bottom of the door and stayed behind.

'The wood is a little rotten, I'm afraid,' said Lettice. 'And everything needs painting.'

'I haven't seen anything that a bit of loving care and attention couldn't put right,' said Biffo. He pulled the French windows shut and, with a little difficulty, eventually succeeded re-locking them.

'What are you going to do here?' asked Lettice.

Biffo looked at her. 'What do you mean?' he asked.

'I'm sorry,' apologised Lettice. 'That was very rude of me.' She had gone red.

'I'm going to tidy things up a bit,' said Biffo. 'Well, to be honest I'll try and find some people to help me tidy things up. I'm not very handy.' He paused. 'That isn't what you meant, is it?'

'No,' said Lettice. 'I was being nosy, I'm afraid.'

'That's OK,' said Biffo. 'Go on.'

'I think I've probably been living in this village too long. No one has any secrets round here. I meant to ask what you're going to do for a living. I'm assuming that you're not hoping to keep Franklin's job when his ankle gets better. And I'm afraid there isn't much of a demand for television producers in the village.'

Biffo laughed. 'I really don't know what I'm going to do,' he confessed. He paused and thought for a while. 'That's not entirely true,' he admitted. 'When I left home I told my ex-wife – actually she's still my wife I suppose but I already think of her as my ex-wife – that I was going to write a book.'

'How exciting!' said Lettice. 'A novel?'

'Yes,' said Biffo, feeling rather embarrassed. 'Or maybe I'll write a play.' He thought for a moment before continuing. 'Maybe I'll write a novel about a man who runs away from home and moves into a cottage in the country. I could call it 'The Escape Artist'.' He smiled. 'Meanwhile,' he said, 'I've got a little time to get myself sorted out thanks to the cheque Better Television sent me, so Tiger and I can settle here, write a novel and catch mice.'

'Really?' And which are you going to do?'

'Pardon?'

'Are you going to write the novel or catch the mice?'

'I thought I might leave the mice to Tiger,' Biffo replied.

'Sounds like a good idea!' agreed Lettice. 'Shall we go and see the kitchen?' suggested Lettice, heading back across the hall.

'Please!' said Biffo enthusiastically, following her.

'I'm afraid that Mr Rose never had it modernised,' said Lettice.

The kitchen, which was much larger than Biffo had expected, was dominated by three huge items of furniture: a massive and extremely dirty Aga cooker; a huge, old-fashioned white sink with two large wooden draining boards and a single cold tap, and a Welsh dresser that stretched from floor to ceiling. The floor, which was slightly uneven, was made of flagstones.

'The auctioneer didn't sell everything then!' said Biffo.

'He would have done if he could have,' said Lettice. 'But the Aga was far too big and heavy to move and the dresser has obviously been built where it is. It would be impossible to get it out of the room without chopping it up.'

'I'm glad they didn't,' said Biffo.

'A London dealer wanted to,' said Lettice. 'He was going to have it cut into three parts, take it up to London, sell it and have it put back together in someone's else house.'

'Why didn't he?'

'Mrs Trubshaw wouldn't let him,' said Lettice. 'The same dealer also wanted to dig up the flagstones.'

'But Mrs Trubshaw wouldn't let him?'

'Mrs Trubshaw wouldn't let him,' confirmed Lettice.

'Good old Mrs Trubshaw!' said Biffo, with enthusiasm. 'I like her more by the minute.'

'She also saved the huge cast iron bath upstairs,' said Lettice. 'And a huge wardrobe and four poster bed that have both obviously been in the house since it was built. Mrs Trubshaw says she thinks that the Welsh dresser, the wardrobe and the four poster bed were all built by the carpenter who helped build the cottage.'

'Let's go upstairs and have a look!' said Biffo, who had already decided that the cottage was exactly what he wanted.

Lettice led the way and he followed her up a narrow, extremely steep staircase which looked to Biffo as if it had been created by the same builder who had built the staircase at The Gravedigger's Rest.

'Mind your head at the top of the stairs,' said Lettice. 'And you'll have to be careful going into the bedrooms.'

'Oh don't worry about me,' said Biffo, 'I'm an old hand at dealing with low beams.' He had just finished the sentence when he cracked his head as he reached the top of the stairs.

'Are you all right?' asked Lettice, as Biffo rubbed the top of his head with his right hand.

'My skull must be getting harder,' replied Biffo, blinking, and stepping forwards gingerly. 'I'm not seeing as many stars these days.'

'You'll have to start wearing a motorcycle helmet,' suggested Lettice.

Biffo grunted something inaudible in reply.

'This is what we estate agents like to describe as the master bedroom,' said Lettice, leading the way into a spacious bedroom which had diamond-paned windows looking onto the back garden, the side garden and the front garden. The bedroom was furnished with a magnificent four poster oak bed and a matching oak wardrobe. 'Mind your head as you come in because although the ceiling is fairly high the door is a little low.'

'I wonder why they always used to build doorways for midgets,' asked Biffo, ducking so low that there was a full foot between the top of his head and the bottom of the door jamb.

'People were shorter when they built this house,' explained Lettice. 'If you visit a house built in the middle ages you'll find that their ceilings and doors were even lower then.'

'It's all that free school milk we used to have to drink when I was a kid,' said Biffo. 'It's turned us into a race of giants.' He walked over to one of the windows and looked out. The view was spectacular. The carpenter who had built the bed and the wardrobe had also built a window seat underneath each of the three windows. 'I think this is probably the most beautiful bedroom I've ever been in,' said Biffo.

'Me too, Lettice replied. 'It's wonderful, isn't it?'

Biffo tried to open the window overlooking the garden but the catch came away in his hand. 'Whoops!' he said, looking at Lettice. 'Sorry about that.'

'That's OK,' said Lettice. She wondered why it was that all the men she knew managed to look like guilty little boys whenever they had done something wrong. 'Don't worry about it.'

'What shall I do with this?' asked Biffo, holding up the broken catch.

'Oh, just leave it on the window seat,' said Lettice.

Biffo put the catch down on the window seat and then suddenly and utterly unexpectedly cried out in alarm as his right foot and lower leg disappeared, quite without warning, through the floorboards near to the window. He kept perfectly still (it would perhaps be more accurate to say that he froze) and for a moment or two neither he nor Lettice spoke.

'Are you all right?' asked Lettice. Gingerly, she walked

across to where he was standing.

'I'm fine, thanks,' said Biffo, who had gone a little pale. 'But part of me seems to have popped downstairs. I seem to have done an Itchy!'

'Can you pull your foot back up?'

'I think I'll lie down,' said Biffo, lowering himself to the floor. 'If I spread my weight around I'll perhaps be less likely to go through. I'm worried that if I push down with one foot while trying to pull the other foot up I'll probably end up with both feet downstairs.'

He lay down, wriggled about for a bit and eventually managed to free his foot and leg. His right shoe had disappeared.

'I'm terribly sorry,' said Lettice, as she backed away rather gingerly.

'Not your fault,' said Biffo, as he crawled towards the door.

'I suppose the rain must have got in and made the floorboards a bit rotten,' said Lettice.

'Let's have a look at the rest of the bedrooms,' said Biffo, gingerly standing upright again.

'Oh, are you sure?' asked Lettice, as Biffo edged past her. 'Do be careful!'

There were quite a few damp patches in the other rooms, and in several places it was possible to see the sky through the roof. But Biffo managed to wander around without making any more holes in the floor and the downstairs ceiling.

'It does need a bit more work on it than I had thought,' admitted Lettice, as they made their way back downstairs.

'I want to buy it,' said Biffo firmly.

Lettice looked at him. 'Are you sure?'

Biffo looked back at her and smiled. 'I thought estate agents were supposed to sell properties!'

'Well, I don't want you to get involved with something that is going to cause you too much trouble, heartache and expense...'

'I love the cottage!' said Biffo, with genuine enthusiasm. 'And I feel we've got a lot in common. We're both a bit worn out, we both need some loving care and attention and we're both about to start a new part of our lives.' He stopped on the stairs. 'What is the asking price?'

'£75,000,' replied Lettice. 'But in view of the condition I think we would be happy to recommend to Mr and Mrs Trubshaw that they accept considerably less than that.'

'Would £65,000 be fair?'

'I think that would be very fair. Do you want me to have a word with Mrs Trubshaw later on this afternoon?'

'Yes, please,' said Biffo, eagerly.

'Would you like to see the garden?' asked Lettice, heading for the back door. The door had stuck slightly. She kicked it gently with her foot. It opened. 'And the summerhouse?' she added, stepping out into the garden. The ewe, who was still munching away at the grass, looked up as the back door opened, baaed twice, and then put her head back down and got back to work. She seemed very happy.

'I certainly do,' said Biffo, hesitating for a moment. 'Tiger will love the garden. But before we go outside do you mind if I try to find my shoe?'

~ Chapter 70 ~

BIFFO HEARD THE NEWS THAT his offer for Buttercup Cottage had been accepted when he walked into the bar at The Gravedigger's Rest that evening.

'Congratulations!' said Lettice, smiling broadly.

'They accepted the offer?'

Lettice nodded. 'So now you've got somewhere to keep your sheep.' They had left the ewe happily quartered in the garden when they had left Buttercup Cottage.

'Thanks!' said Biffo. 'Drinks all round!' he added, overcome with generosity.

'Thank you,' said Itchy, the only person in the bar apart from Lettice. 'I'll have the usual!' He had not finished the pint in front of him but firmly believed in the philosophy that a pint in the glass is worth two in the cask.

'What's the usual?' Biffo asked, out of idle curiosity.

'A pint of Old Glorious,' replied Lettice, identifying Itchy's tipple of choice. She had already taken down a fresh pint glass from the shelf behind her.

'I'll have the same,' said Biffo. 'What are you having?'

'I'll have a bitter lemon, thanks,' said Lettice

'And a double whisky for me,' said Puffy, suddenly appearing as though by magic. 'I heard that someone was buying free drinks,' he explained to Biffo.

'What are we celebrating?' asked Itchy.

'I'm buying a cottage!' replied Biffo.

'Congratulations!' said Itchy. 'You're staying in the village, then?' He looked genuinely pleased.

'I certainly am!' agreed Biffo.

'Which cottage are you buying?'

'Buttercup Cottage.'

'Aha!' said Itchy, knowingly.

'You know it?'

'Oh yes.' said Itchy, nodding his head. 'I know Buttercup Cottage.'

'What do you think of it?' asked Biffo.

'Very pretty,' said Itchy enthusiastically. He scratched his head as he watched Lettice pour his pint of Old Glorious and put it down on the bar in front of him. 'It'll need a bit of work doing to it,' he warned.

'Oh yes,' agreed Biffo. 'I realise that.'

Itchy beamed. 'I'll have a look at it for you,' he offered. 'Tell you what you need to have done.'

'That's very kind of you,' said Biffo.

'You have to watch out with these old properties,' said Itchy. 'There's some folk who'll take advantage of you. You'll need someone you can trust.'

Itchy had started to tell Biffo how a firm of cowboy builders in another village had taken advantage of a couple who had bought a weekend cottage when Paddy staggered into the bar.

'Give me a drink, Lettice,' he said, clambering weakly onto a stool. The movement seemed to take every bit of energy he possessed.

'What would you like?' Lettice asked him.

'Whatever comes out of the bottle the quickest,' Paddy

replied. 'This is an emergency.' He cupped his head in his hands and stared at a beer-mat on the counter.

'Tough day?' asked Puffy, when Lettice had poured the vice captain a large brandy and the vice captain had put the brandy where it could do some good.

'I've just been to see the vicar,' explained Paddy, handing his empty glass back to Lettice. He held the glass in such a way that it was obvious that he wanted a refill.

Everyone moved a little closer and waited. The silence fell like snow. Even the clock behind the bar seemed to have stopped ticking.

Paddy leant across the bar and spoke directly to Lettice. 'Have you got a white skirt?' he asked her.

Lettice looked rather taken aback, and not a little puzzled; it was not a question she had expected. She put a fresh glass of brandy in front of the vice captain. 'I'm not sure,' she replied.

'Think hard,' pleaded Paddy. 'It's important.'

Lettice thought carefully. 'I've got a tennis skirt,' she said eventually. 'I haven't worn it since I was at school.'

'Do you think it would fit the vicar?'

Lettice stared at him, took a sip from the glass of brandy she had put in front of Paddy, swallowed, and thought about this for a few moments. 'I would think so,' she said at last. 'It wouldn't be difficult to let out the waist a bit if necessary.'

'Thank heavens,' said Paddy, clearly pleased. 'Can the vicar borrow it?' He drank half the brandy in a single gulp.

'Of course,' said Lettice. 'He can have it. I never wear it.'

Paddy reached across the bar, took Lettice's hand, raised it to his lips and kissed her fingers. 'Thank you,' he said quietly. 'You will be blessed for this.' He picked up his glass, finished the brandy, and put the empty glass down on the bar.

'I'll have another pint, please, Lettice,' said Itchy, holding an empty glass out in front of him. He looked pale.

'Me too,' said Biffo, finishing his pint of Old Glorious and placing the empty glass alongside Itchy's. He did not look quite as pale as Itchy but he had worked in television and was not such a stranger to the unusual.

Lettice refilled Paddy's brandy glass, filled Biffo's glass

and then poured herself a large whisky. Puffy filled Itchy's glass and poured himself a larger whisky. One of the advantages of owning a pub is that you can pour yourself big drinks.

'The vicar has agreed to play for us tomorrow,' Paddy explained. 'And he says he'll consider carrying on playing for the rest of the season.' He took a gulp from the brandy glass. 'But he'll only play,' he paused and took another gulp. 'He'll, er, he, er, says that he will only, er, play if he can, er, wear a skirt.'

'And he hasn't got a white skirt,' said Lettice.

'He's got a white blouse,' said Paddy. 'But apparently he hasn't got a white skirt.'

'He has now,' said Lettice, flatly.

'I think I'll ring him and let him know,' said Paddy. 'He'll be pleased.' He looked at Lettice. 'Are you sure he can keep it?'

'I'm sure,' said Lettice.

'You'd better ring him now,' said Puffy, handing the telephone across the bar. 'You may not be sober enough to dial if you keep downing the brandies.'

'Just tell him that if he wears high heels he has to wear those very thin ones!' said a worried sounding Itchy. 'Those thin ones aerate the grass nicely but I'm not having people in thick high heels running about on my wicket.' He finished his beer and handed the empty glass across the bar. Lettice took the glass and started to refill it for him. A moment or two later Biffo did the same; though, since Lettice was still busy, he handed his glass to Puffy.

They all sat quietly while Paddy telephoned the vicar with the good news.

'What do you think the vicar puts in his bra?' Itchy asked Biffo in a whisper. 'I mean, he hasn't got, you know, the sort of stuff that normally fills a bra, has he?'

'I've no idea,' Biffo whispered back. He thought about it for a moment or two. 'Old cricket balls?'

'Phew!' said Paddy, letting the telephone receiver fall back onto the handset. 'I could have done without that!'

Just then the door opened and Constable Hobbling came in, walked to the bar and removed his helmet. He placed his helmet on the bar and sat down on a stool. Puffy immediately reached for a glass and began to fill it with a pint of Old Favourite – known to him, and, indeed, to all the regulars, to be the constable's preferred beverage.

Constable Hobbling's arrival was greeted with numerous ribald remarks.

'Are you going to be playing in a frock too?' asked Itchy. 'Solidarity with the vicar and all that.'

'If you are wearing a frock, you'd better have a word with the vicar,' advised Puffy. 'Make sure your outfits don't clash.'

'It's OK,' Itchy pointed out. 'They'll both be in white.'

But Constable Hobbling wasn't listening. No one noticed the glum look on his face until he spoke. But when he had spoken he was not the only one with a glum look.

'I can't play,' the village policeman said, unhappily.

There was a long, long silence, broken only by the sound of Itchy emptying his glass in a single lift.

'Tell me he didn't say that,' said Paddy at last. He spoke quietly and his request seemed a genuine one. Sadly, all those present had heard what the policeman had said and none of them was prepared to lie.

'I'd love to play,' said Constable Hobbling. He sounded genuinely heartbroken. Biffo thought that the policeman might burst into tears at any moment. 'But I can't.'

'There was another long, long silence. This time the silence was broken only by the sound of Itchy placing his empty glass on the bar counter and pushing it across towards Puffy.

'I had a telephone call today from Police Headquarters,' explained the village policeman. 'They're unhappy with my arrest record.'

'Why?' asked Itchy, incredulously. 'What on earth is wrong with your arrest record?'

'I haven't arrested anyone for seven years,' said Constable Hobbling.

'Shows you're keeping law and order,' said Puffy. 'You haven't needed to arrest anyone because no one has done anything wrong. Everyone respects you and is too frightened of you to break the law. Simple.'

'It's not that simple,' said Constable Hobbling. 'A new

management team has taken over and they've set arrest targets.'

'What does that mean?' asked Lettice.

'It means that if I don't arrest someone within 24 hours they'll move me into the city and make me work in an office,' said Constable Hobbling. He sounded thoroughly miserable.

'Arrest someone?' said Puffy, horrified.

'In the village?' said Itchy, terrified.

'That's what they said!' said Constable Hobbling.

There was another long, long silence while everyone in the bar thought about this a little and drank quite a lot.

'How, er, exactly, er, how does, er, exactly, this prevent you from playing in the match?' asked Paddy tentatively.

'The Inspector says my weekend leave is cancelled,' explained Constable Hobbling. 'He says the Superintendent has given orders that I'm to be on duty until I make an arrest.' He lowered his voice and looked over his shoulder as though frightened that someone might hear him. 'He threatened to come up here and check up on me. If I'm not wearing my uniform at all times I could get into big trouble.' He thought for a moment. 'They could...,' he frowned. 'I don't know what they could do,' he admitted. 'But I'd be in big trouble.'

'Desertion?' suggested Itchy.

Constable Hobbling looked at him. 'Probably,' he agreed.

'Let me get this straight,' said Paddy, addressing the village policeman directly. 'The important thing is that you have to be on duty this weekend.'

'Yes.'

'And you have to wear your uniform?'

'Yes.'

'But virtually the whole of the village will be at the cricket ground won't they?'

'I suppose they will,' agreed Constable Hobbling.

'So it would obviously be important for you to be at the cricket ground too?'

Constable Hobbling thought about this for a moment. 'It would,' he agreed. He looked much brighter.

'In your uniform.'

'In my uniform.'

'But is there anything in the regulations which says that while you are on duty, wearing your uniform, you cannot play a little cricket?'

Constable Hobbling thought about this for some time. He was not quite as well acquainted with police regulations as he perhaps ought to have been and so this took some little time. But at long last, having trawled his memory for whatever he could remember of police regulations, he spoke. 'Not that I know of,' he admitted.

'So, there you are!' said Paddy, delightedly.

Constable Hobbling looked confused. 'Where am I?' he asked.

'At the cricket ground,' said Paddy. 'Playing cricket in your uniform!'

Constable Hobbling thought about this for a long time. He was not a man to whom thought came easily, and he was not a man who liked to leap recklessly to conclusions. He much preferred to take his time. He liked to allow thoughts, ideas and notions to seep deep into his brain before making any decisions. Over the years this habit had at the same time frustrated and annoyed his superiors, and endeared him to the citizens he was hired to protect.

'Playing cricket in my uniform?'

'Playing cricket in your uniform,' said Paddy. 'And if your Inspector turns up you can, if necessary, just totter over to the boundary, put your hands behind your back, do those knee bends that policemen do and say 'Evenin' all!' to everyone.'

'So I can play in the big match after all?' asked Constable Hobbling.

'Absolutely!' agreed Paddy. He looked around. 'I think we all agree on that, don't we?'

There was a ragged chorus of 'Oh yes.' and 'Absolutely!' from around the bar.

Suddenly Constable Hobbling frowned as he remembered something. 'There is one thing that's bothering me,' he said.

'What's that?' asked Paddy, hardly daring to breathe lest Constable Hobbling had found some fatal flaw in his fragile logic.

'Why did Itchy ask me if I was wearing a frock?' asked the

policeman. He turned and looked directly at Itchy.

'Ah,' said Paddy. 'Well, you know that our vicar has, er become, well a sort of vicaresse?'

'A what?'

'A lady vicar.'

'Ah, yes.' Constable Hobbling nodded wisely. There had been a circular from the Chief Constable about the hazards of racism and other -isms in the police force and he rather suspected that men who wanted to dress up in frocks might well be members of an -ism who were, therefore, entitled to extra respect.

'Well, he has agreed to play in the big match,' said Paddy. 'But he will be playing in a frock.'

'A skirt,' said Lettice. 'A white skirt. And a blouse. A white blouse. A white skirt and a white blouse.'

Paddy waved a hand as though to dismiss this correction as a piece of unnecessary semantics. 'Skirt, frock, whatever,' he said.

'There's quite a difference,' said Lettice. 'On the whole skirts tend to be cheaper than frocks,' she added, knowing that Paddy would find this difference memorable.

'Really?' said Paddy, tucking this apparently useless but quite possibly money-saving piece of information away in a convenient cortical crevice. Maybe next time he needed to buy his way out of a sticky situation at home he could do so by offering to buy a new skirt instead of a new frock.

Suddenly something occurred to Lettice. 'Will he be wearing a bra for the match?' she asked Paddy.

'A bra?'

'Yes, you know...,' said Lettice. She began to explain.

'I know what a bra is,' said Paddy. 'I'm a married man.'

'Yes. Well, do you know if he will be wearing one?' asked Lettice.

'Why?' asked Paddy.

'Well, he should remember to wear a white bra,' said Lettice. 'A black bra under a white blouse will look simply awful when he's playing cricket.'

'I don't think that's the sort of thing a captain can interfere with,' said Paddy hastily.

Puffy, who felt that discussions regarding feminine underwear were not wholly appropriate for a public bar, and deciding consequently that the conversation needed to change direction slightly, spoke to Constable Hobbling. 'Naturally, we will try not to say or do anything which suggests that we notice anything odd or unusual about the vicar's appearance.'

Itchy, who thought it exceedingly unlikely that twenty one players and two umpires could fail to come up with a constant stream of comments drawing attention to the vicar's unusual choice of apparel (regardless of the colour of his bra) spluttered and very nearly drowned in his beer.

'Naturally,' said the policeman, very sternly. He finished his pint of beer, put the correct amount of money down on the counter to pay for it and headed for the door. With his fingers on the door handle he turned.

'I've just remembered,' he said. 'I've still got to find someone to arrest.'

'Don't worry about that for the moment,' said Paddy, his voice full of gentle reassurance. 'You'll find someone to arrest.'

'Do you think so?' said Constable Hobbling. He seemed cheered by Paddy's confidence.

'No problem,' Paddy promised.

'That's a great relief,' said Constable Hobbling.

'You just concentrate on your bowling,' said Paddy.

~ Chapter 71 ~

THERE WAS A LONG SILENCE after Constable Hobbling's disappearance. The silence was broken only by the sounds of drinking.

'Who is he going to arrest?' asked Itchy at last. Itchy, having had several brushes with the law, was clearly a little sensitive on this issue.

'Whom,' said Puffy. 'I think you'll find it's whom.'

'What?' said Itchy. 'Who's he?'

'Whom' said Puffy.

'What's whom?' asked Itchy.

'Who's whom?' said Puffy, now thoroughly confused and bewildered, and wishing he hadn't bothered.

This might have gone on for some time if Biffo had not interfered and explained.

'OK,' said Itchy. 'Whom is he going to arrest?' He frowned and looked at Puffy. 'It doesn't sound right,' he said. 'It sounds funny.'

'It's right,' said Puffy. 'Isn't it?' he asked, addressing the question to Biffo.

'It's right,' said Biffo. 'If the person doing the arresting is the subject of the sentence.'

'Why should I believe him?' Itchy asked Puffy.

'I've got a degree in English,' said Biffo.

'I thought you said you worked in television,' said Itchy.

'I did,' said Biffo.

'There you are then,' said Itchy. 'Why should we believe you?' He thought for a while longer. 'And since when has the person doing the arresting done the sentence?'

Biffo thought about this moment. 'Pass,' he said. He sighed. 'I think you were probably right the first time.'

'Thank you,' said Itchy, feeling strengthened by what appeared to be a small victory. 'Who is he going to arrest?'

'Who?' asked Paddy.

'Don't let's start all that again,' said Lettice.

'No, I mean who *is* he going to arrest?' asked Paddy. 'It's a good question.'

'Thank you,' said Itchy. 'And I'd like a good answer. Preferably an answer that doesn't include my name.'

They thought about this for quite a while.

And then they all ordered another round of drinks.

~ Chapter 72 ~

IT WAS SATURDAY AND THE players and supporters of the Fondling-Under-Water cricket club were holding their hastily planned fund-raising event.

'Don't these things generally have to be organised a long

time in advance?' a puzzled Biffo had asked Lettice the day before.

Back in the place which he had once called home, in what now seemed a previous existence lived by someone else, his ambitious and social climbing wife Edwina had been chairman of the committee which had organised their annual local fête. He remembered that her committee (which consisted exclusively of ambitious, social climbing people) always started planning next year's fête on the day after a fête had finished. For the twelve months which followed they would meet twice a month. Everything had to be discussed in minute detail.

'Not here,' Lettice had replied. 'Only villagers who live in and around Fondling-Under-Water are going to come so there isn't much planning to do.'

'But what about hiring tents and organising the catering and so on?'

'We don't waste money on hiring tents,' Lettice had explained. 'And the cricket club tea ladies will do the catering.'

'Don't you have to find someone to open it?'

'Open what?'

'The 'do', the fund-raising event or whatever you call it.'

'Oh, you mean get someone like a vicar or a pop star to come along, make a boring speech and tell people when they can start enjoying themselves?'

'That sort of thing,' Biffo admitted, remembering that Edwina and her fellow committee members had once spent many hours trying to decide whether to invite their local MP or a television quiz show host to open their fête. He seemed to remember that status had won out over rank commercialism and the MP, a political nonentity who had about as much charisma as a bag of turnips, had been invited.

'Oh no,' said Lettice. 'It will just sort of start when people get there.'

'And you don't take out insurance for bad weather?'

Lettice had looked at him as though not quite sure whether he was teasing her. She eventually decided that he was serious. 'Do you really know people who do that?'

'Oh yes,' Biffo had assured her. 'Back in my previous existence the organisers of our local fête used to spend £1,500 every year on an insurance premium. If the event got completely washed out by bad weather they could make a claim.' He thought for a moment. 'I think it had to rain for five hours continuously before they could make a claim.'

Lettice had gaped at him open mouthed. 'We're only hoping to raise enough money to buy a lawnmower!' she had said. 'We have the cricket pavilion for shelter and if it rains too heavily we'll adjourn to the pub.'

'I do see your point,' Biffo had said. 'I must say it's rather nice to be able to organise a fund-raising event in less time than it takes the grass on a cricket pitch to grow.'

~ Chapter 73 ~

WHEN BIFFO AWOKE THAT SATURDAY morning he gently moved the sleeping Tiger off his chest and onto the bed covers a foot or so away (Tiger miaowed, stretched, looked around and immediately went back to sleep) and tiptoed across the cold (and still slightly damp) floor to the window. He could already see some action on the cricket field. Three men were carrying a large fence post across the outfield and just in front of the pavilion a small group of women in short white skirts, white T-shirts, white pumps and white socks seemed to be holding an early morning gym class. Someone, presumably Itchy, had driven eight metal stakes into the ground around the cricket square in the middle of the field in order to protect the turf there from children and women in the wrong sort of high-heeled shoes. In the absence of a long enough piece of string or tape Itchy had used the collection of borrowed electrical power leads to mark off the exclusion zone.

After shaving, dressing and putting down food for a still sleepy Tiger, Biffo made himself some toast and a pot of coffee and enjoyed a leisurely start to the morning for the first time since his arrival in Fondling-Under-Water. Except for a few weeks before Christmas Miss Box didn't offer her customers a Saturday morning delivery service. She would have liked to have offered a seven day a week service but Franklin Minton, her regular delivery cyclist, had always made it quite clear that if she wanted her customers serviced on a Saturday or a Sunday she could find someone else to do the servicing.

The consultant orthopaedic surgeon at the local hospital had, after another look at the X-rays, told Franklin Minton that he would not be fit to ride a bicycle for eight weeks and although (thanks to the cheque from Better Television) Biffo no longer really needed the money to pay for his board and keep at The Gravedigger's Rest he had happily promised Miss Box that he would continue with his job as locum cyclist for as long as she wanted him.

Franklin himself had been told by Paddy that his services as umpire would be required for the forthcoming big match after all. When he had pointed out that an inability to stand up would in most circles be considered something of a handicap for an umpire Paddy had suggested that he umpire in a chair.

'And how am I going to move a chair from one end of the pitch to the other?' Franklin had demanded. 'No one is going to want to start moving furniture after every over.'

'Get a wheelchair!' Paddy had suggested.

'Where am I going to find a wheelchair?' Franklin had demanded. 'The local hospital has a nine month waiting list for wheelchair loans. By the time I get one I'll be walking again.'

'Miss Box is bound to have one,' Paddy had assured him.

Technically, the vice captain was wrong about that. Miss Box didn't have one wheelchair. When Franklin told her what he needed she had asked him whether he wanted a metal one or a wooden one, a wheelchair which had to be pushed or a wheelchair which could be propelled by the occupier. In a wooden shed behind the shop she had, it seemed, a bigger collection of wheelchairs than most general hospitals can boast.

'Why didn't you tell me that you'd got all these wheelchairs?' said Franklin, indignantly, when Miss Box showed him her store.

'You didn't ask!' Miss Box replied, equally indignantly. 'Besides I didn't think you could afford to hire one.'

'You're going to charge me?' asked Franklin, incredulously.

Miss Box said nothing but just stared at him.

'Sorry,' said Franklin. 'Forget I said that.'

In the end Miss Box agreed to lend Franklin a wheelchair for the duration of the match without charge. 'But I want it back straight afterwards!' she had insisted.

Daniel Potterton, who had been staying with one of Mrs Cleavidge's tea ladies (there was, naturally, much talk about the precise nature of the relationship) called in at The Gravedigger's Rest before catching the bus back to the nearest railway station.

'If I don't go now I'll never go,' he told Biffo. 'I can catch up with the rest of the team by tonight and play with them for the rest of the tour.' He looked around the now repaired but still battered-looking public house and, through the window, across at the cricket field with its absurdly over decorative cricket pavilion and shook his head. 'I don't know what it is about this place,' he said with a sigh. 'But I know one thing – if I ever run away from home this is where I'll come.'

'Are you busy?' asked Puffy, wandering in just as Biffo was finishing his second cup of coffee. He had eaten, and thoroughly enjoyed three slices of buttered toast and a large quantity of Thicke Cutte Olde Englishe marmalade. The label was unbearably pretentious but the marmalade was excellent.

'Not at all,' said Biffo, putting down his cup.

'Do you think Miss Box would lend you her bicycle? We've got a bit of an emergency.'

'I would think so,' replied Biffo.

'Paddy has just been on the telephone,' said Puffy. 'We need dear old Percy to help with the public address system but he isn't on the telephone and his cottage is at the end of a very narrow track. You can't drive down there. Paddy wondered if you'd cycle over and ask him to be at the cricket field at lunchtime. Tell him there will be a couple of pints of beer in it for him – and as many sandwiches as he can eat.'

Biffo said he would be delighted to help. Pausing only to get instructions on how to find Percy's cottage he tottered around to Miss Box's shop and asked if he might borrow the bicycle for an hour or so.

'Of course you can,' said Miss Box magnanimously. She

disappeared into the shop for a few minutes and came out wheeling the bicycle. The front basket was full. 'Just drop these few things off at Mrs Kendall's for me. I wouldn't ask but she needs them all terribly urgently.' The urgent delivery consisted of a plastic dustpan and brush, a large courgette, two small plastic rubbish bins, an alarm clock, a large quantity of wire wool, two wooden coat hangers and a small gas cylinder.

'Ah. Emergency coat hangers!' said Biffo, drily.

Miss Box paused on the very threshold of prudence. She did not like talking about her customers. 'Mrs Kendall has her in-laws coming,' she explained, looking around to make sure that no one was listening. 'She discovered last night that she's only got those cheap wire coat hangers that dry cleaners use.'

Biffo realised that by sharing this confidential information with him Miss Box was paying him quite a compliment. He felt a lump in his throat. It was not a large lump but it was a lump. 'Where does Mrs Kendall live?' he asked, before he was overtaken by emotion.

Miss Box explained. Biffo was not surprised when he learned that Mrs Kendall lived in precisely the opposite direction to Percy's cottage.

'She'll give you a bale of hay and a sack of Brussels sprouts,' said Miss Box, as Biffo threw his leg over his bicycle saddle and prepared to pedal off. The gas cylinder, although small, weighed a lot and made it difficult to get up any speed.

Biffo paused, wobbled, stopped and looked back.

'We occasionally do a little bit of bartering in the village,' explained Miss Box. 'It's our way of helping to save the trees.'

'The trees?' said Biffo, puzzled. He was also slightly worried about how he was supposed to carry a bale of hay and a sack of Brussels sprouts on a bicycle. But he didn't like to say anything about this. Miss Box clearly had no doubts about the viability of the exercise and Biffo was beginning to take a pride in his work.

'It cuts down on the paperwork,' said Miss Box. 'No invoices. No bills. Nothing on paper.'

'Ah,' said Biffo, understanding. He was to learn in due course that the economy of the village depended almost totally upon fiddling insurance companies and avoiding tax.

'But don't bring the hay back here,' said Miss Box. 'That goes to Captain Giles. It's for his daughter's horse.'

Biffo did not succeed in hiding his sense of confusion.

'Captain Giles always cleans and services my Aga,' explained Miss Box. 'I send him an occasional bale of hay.'

'And does he get the Brussels sprouts too?'

'No, of course not!' said Miss Box, as though surprised that anyone could possibly be quite so stupid. 'The sprouts are for Miss Daventry. She makes jam which I sell in the shop.'

'Sprout jam?' said Biffo. He had long suspected that people living in the country did things with food which might not have been regarded as usual in London. They certainly grew foods which never seemed even to reach the big city. He had, for example, never knowingly seen a turnip or a swede on the menu in any smart London restaurant but large areas of the countryside seemed to be dedicated to growing these two crops. Somebody, he reasoned, must be doing something with all the swedes and turnips that were being grown. He liked to think of himself as broadminded, and if people living in the country liked to eat jam made out of sprouts then that was fine by him.

Miss Box sighed. 'Miss Daventry gives the sprouts to Mrs Peabody,' she explained, her patience clearly running out. 'Mrs Peabody grows strawberries and always has a few punnets more than she and her family can eat. So she gives the leftovers to Miss Daventry to turn into jam.'

'Why doesn't Miss Daventry simply give Mrs Peabody a few pots of strawberry jam?' asked Biffo.

'Because Mrs Peabody doesn't like strawberry jam,' said Miss Box.

Biffo, who was beginning to realise that there was far, far more to Fondling-Under-Water than he had previously realised, decided that if he was going to get to Percy's cottage before the match began he would have to call a temporary halt to his tutorial in bartering.

He called a cheery goodbye to Miss Box, bravely waved one hand, and wobbled off down the road to deliver the plastic dustpan and brush, the large courgette, the two small plastic rubbish bins, the alarm clock, the large quantity of wire wool, the two wooden coat hangers and the gas cylinder.

~ Chapter 74 ~

IT WAS AN HOUR AND a quarter later when an extremely leg-weary and saddle-sore Biffo finally pedalled and free-wheeled down the path to Percy's cottage.

When Biffo had arrived at Mrs Kendall's cottage he had unloaded his bicycle quickly in the hope that he could make a speedy get away. But Mrs Kendall's existing gas cylinder wasn't quite empty and she refused to let Biffo connect up the new one until the old one was empty. And so, in order to burn up the remaining gas they had turned the gas fire up as high as it would go and had sat in front of it sweltering, waiting for it to go out.

'Would you like a nice cup of tea?' Mrs Kendall had asked. Biffo didn't really want one but knowing that Mrs Kendall cooked by gas he reckoned that if he said 'yes' it would use up a bit more gas. He had drunk three cups of tea in all. Despite this it had taken twenty minutes to use up the remaining gas. And having to deliver the hay and the bag of sprouts, and to return the empty gas cylinder to Miss Box's shop, had taken another forty minutes.

As he waited for someone to appear he looked around. Percy's cottage appeared to have no more than one room downstairs and another upstairs. Heavy, wooden shutters covered all the windows. A metal windmill, twenty or thirty feet high, stood at the rear of the cottage. A pile of neatly-chopped logs were stacked up against the wall. A massive bow saw and a variety of tools hung on nails on the outside wall of the cottage. The air was thick with the smell of wood smoke.

'Who are you and what do you want?' demanded an angry voice from somewhere up above. The voice was rich, deep and vaguely familiar. Its owner spoke slowly and with quiet dignity, announcing each word with care and deliberation.

Biffo looked up and could see that one of the upstairs

shutters and an upstairs window had been opened a couple of inches. He could not see the owner of the voice.

'My name is Brimstone,' explained Biffo. 'I'm a newcomer to the village. I'm staying at The Gravedigger's Rest. The local cricket club is holding a fund-raising event today and I was asked to see if you could come and help with the loudspeaker equipment.' He suddenly realised that he had neither been given nor had he asked for the cottage owner's surname. 'I think they want you to do the announcing. They said to tell you that they need you,' he added. 'And that there is a couple of pints of beer in it for you and as many sandwiches as you can eat.'

The cottage's invisible inhabitant blew his nose loudly. It was difficult to tell precisely what this meant. 'Wait there,' was the instruction from above.

Biffo waited for a while and looked around again. The cottage was in a beautiful position. In the distance Biffo could just make out the village cricket ground. A few yards away a fast flowing stream bubbled its way across water-smoothed pebbles. A few minutes later he heard a bolt being pulled back on the other side of the door. Then there was the sound of a second bolt being pulled back. This was followed by the sound of a key turning in a lock. Eventually, the front door swung slowly inwards.

It was very dark inside the cottage, and difficult to see in from outside, but Biffo could just make out a tall, slender figure holding open the door.

'Er...Percy?' asked Biffo. He felt himself blushing and wished he knew the man's full name.

Percy stepped back into the darkness for a moment. 'You had better come in,' he said. He spoke carefully and clearly and Biffo was captivated by the man's deep rich brandy and cigar voice. Percy switched on the light so that Biffo could see where he was going, pointed to a single, elderly armchair in front of an empty fireplace and squinted in what was for him clearly unaccustomed brightness. There was a large, freshly made wooden box on the floor, surrounded by tools and woodshavings. The box was over six foot long and big enough to be a coffin. The man was wearing a pair of pinstriped trousers that had seen much better days. Above the waist he was wearing an off-white vest. A pair of bright red braces hung down from his waist.

Many people become irascible, demanding, unforgiving and intolerant when they have lived on their own for a while. Percy was different. He had been irascible, demanding, unforgiving and intolerant all his life and this may, perhaps, have explained why he had always lived alone.

'What are you making?' asked Biffo, stepping around the box. He thought he was making polite conversation.

'My coffin,' said Percy, without emotion.

Biffo sat down rather suddenly and Percy switched off the light the moment his bottom hit the seat cushion.

'Hope you don't mind if I turn the electricity off,' said Percy. 'The windmill isn't working terribly well at the moment. I've got a battery and an old bicycle fixed up to provide an emergency supply but why waste electricity? You don't need light to talk by, do you?' He disappeared for a moment and when he reappeared he struck a match and lit a candle. 'You don't mind if I shave before we go, do you?' Biffo, who said nothing, felt sure that he had heard the voice before. But he couldn't think where.

Standing in front of the fireplace, and looking into a large, oval mirror hanging on a nail above the mantlepiece, Percy then proceeded to use the candle and a wet rag to 'shave' his face.

Biffo watched this shadowy tableau in astonishment. 'I've never seen anyone else do that!' he said as the room gradually filled with the smell of burning hair.

'I learnt the trick from a fellow who used to have a cottage just over the hill,' said Percy. The candle flickered as he spoke. 'The flame singes the hairs. You can get as close a shave as you can with a blade.'

'But doesn't it hurt?' asked Biffo. 'Don't you burn yourself?'

'I did the first few times I did it,' admitted Percy. 'The trick lies in knowing how to hold the candle.' He finished shaving, dabbed at his face with the wet cloth and then rubbed his fingers over his jaw and chin to check that he hadn't missed any patches of bristle. When he was satisfied he put the candle into a holder. He then plucked a white, collarless shirt from where it was hanging on a nail that had been hammered into the wall.

'What do you do here?' asked Biffo, as Percy struggled into his shirt in the semi-darkness. 'I hope you don't mind my asking?'

'I'm a coppice woodsman,' said Percy. 'Probably one of the last in the country.'

'What's a coppice woodsman?' asked Biffo, feeling indecently ignorant.

'I work with wood,' explained Percy, buttoning up his shirt. 'I take the bark off oak for tanning and I make oak stakes for furniture, beezum brushes and hurdles.' He stopped for a moment to check again that his skin was smooth enough. 'And I'm a charcoal burner too, of course. I burn oak, ash, birch and alder. I make wooden tent pegs for old-fashioned campers and I make walking sticks for the holiday-makers.'

'How long have you been doing this?' asked Biffo.

Percy thought for a moment. 'Nine or ten years I should think.' Satisfied with his chin he went back to fastening the buttons on his shirt. 'I'm afraid I rather lose track of the time out here.'

Biffo was surprised. He had expected to hear that Percy had been a woodsman all his life. He was full of questions he wanted to ask.

'You haven't always lived in the country then?'

'Oh no.'

'What did you do before you became an...er...'

'...coppice woodsman?'

'Yes. Coppice woodsman'

'I was a newsreader,' said Percy.

'Of course!' said Biffo, suddenly remembering and feeling rather stupid. 'Of course. Percy Kempton. I remember now. I remember your voice.'

'That was another life,' said Percy, rather dismissively.

'Why did you give it up?' asked Biffo.

'Couldn't stand it any longer,' said Percy. 'Terrible people in broadcasting. No souls. No spirit. No passion. All veneer and no wood underneath. I woke up one morning and realised that all my problems were created by other people. So I made a deliberate decision to become a recluse. If you don't mix with other people they can't cause you any trouble, can they?'

'I suppose not,' agreed Biffo. 'I was in broadcasting,' he said. 'Until quite recently.'

'You've given it up?' asked Percy.

'I ran away.'

'To Fondling-Under-Water?'

'Yes. I didn't mean to come here. It just, sort of happened that way.'

'Good for you. You won't regret it for an instant. I don't know anywhere in the world quite like Fondling-Under-Water. If you're looking for peace you'll find it here.' Percy went to a cupboard next to the fireplace and took out a collar and a London club tie which Biffo recognised. He fastened the collar onto the shirt, wrapped the tie around his neck and tied it. He did this quickly and surprisingly skilfully for a man who did not look as if he often wore a tie. He then took his jacket out of the cupboard and put that on before slipping his feet into a pair of shoes.

'I hope you don't mind my asking,' said Biffo. 'But why are you making a coffin?'

'It's mine,' said Percy.

'Oh, I'm sorry. What's...er...wrong?'

'Nothing is wrong.'

'No, I mean, are you ill.' Biffo, stopped and hesitated for a moment. 'I'm sorry,' he said. 'Perhaps you don't want to talk about it.' He held up a hand in the dark. 'That's fine.'

'I'm not ill. At least not that I know of,' said Percy. 'But I'm dying nevertheless.'

Biffo frowned, puzzled.

'We're all dying,' explained Percy. 'We all have to go sometime. I'm just planning ahead a little. I'm making myself a decent sized coffin out of decent wood.' He looked at Biffo, as though aware of what he was thinking. 'I'm not worried about dying,' he said. 'I'm not even worried about being old. In fact I rather like being old. I used to be in a constant hurry when I was young. But now that I'm old and have less time left I feel as though I can wait for ever for everything. When I reached middle age I worried about falling ill and dying. Now that I'm old I know I'm not going to die young. I've had a good innings. So I don't have to worry about dying young and being cheated any more.' He brushed his jacket down with his hands. 'Do I look all right?'

Biffo peered into the darkness. 'You look very smart,' he said honestly. The transformation had been remarkable.

'Right!' said Percy. 'We'll just have a drink and then we'll get along to the village.' He reached into a drawer and took out a pewter hip flask. He took the top off the flask and offered it to Biffo.

Biffo hesitated for a moment. He was about to refuse, on the grounds that it was a little early in the day for him, but then realised that this might sound rude. 'Thank you,' he said, accepting the flask and taking a gentle sip. He swallowed and immediately started coughing. 'Powerful stuff.' he said, when he had control of his voice again. He handed the flask back to Percy.

'I'm very impressed that you agreed to come because the village needs you,' said Biffo.

'This village is my family,' said Percy. He held the flask to his mouth and tipped it up. He swallowed several times before lowering the flask. 'These people mean everything to me,' he said. 'They are all I've got. They're a mixed bunch. Some of them are probably outright crooks.' He offered the flask to Biffo who held up a hand, smiled and shook his head. 'Most of them don't take a great deal of notice of the law and not many of them have much of a conscience when it comes to insurance companies and banks and so on but they're loyal, discrete, honest people when it really matters and with people they care about.' He held the flask to his lips again and took another long drink. 'I don't like people terribly much. As a rule I much prefer my own company. But if I needed their help I know they'd give it to me.'

Biffo nodded. He understood.

'Come on then,' said Percy, closing the flask and slipping it into his pocket.

'I came by bicycle,' said Biffo, as they stepped out into the sunshine. He pointed to Miss Box's bicycle, leaning up against the wall of the cottage.

'That looks like Miss Box's delivery bicycle,' said Percy, with a slight smile.

'It is,' agreed Biffo.

'Ah,' said Percy. He locked up his front door and nodded towards the path. 'Shall we walk?'

Together, the former news reader and the former television producer walked along the rocky path to the village and the cricket ground.

~ Chapter 75 ~

AN AD HOC COMMITTEE, CONSISTING of Paddy, Cheesy and Puffy, had arranged a number of events, in addition to the cricket match, to help enliven the Fondling-Under-Water fund-raising day.

The trio had put up notices in both The Gravedigger's Rest and Miss Box's shop inviting villagers to take part in a three-legged race, a sack race, an egg and spoon race and a competition to see who could toss a caber the furthest.

First, there was the problem with the organisation of the tossing the caber event.

Paddy and Cheesy had disagreed on the definition of a caber.

Cheesy, who had seen caber tossing first hand on a visit to Scotland, had at first suggested that they use a telegraph pole but Puffy had insisted that no one would be able to lift a telegraph pole, let alone toss one and that as far as he was concerned no one with functioning brain tissue would consider tossing anything heavier than a salad.

Paddy had expressed some doubts about whether, even if anyone could lift one, they would be able to find a spare telegraph pole lying around in the village. He had expressed the view that they should not steal a telegraph pole since in his view even the authorities would not have a great deal of difficulty in linking up the disappearance of a telegraph pole from one of the roads into or out of Fondling-Under-Water with the sudden appearance of an identical item at a local fund-raising event.

The trio had eventually compromised and agreed that they would use a large, wooden fence post for the caber tossing event. Puffy had reminded the other two that there was a large, unused and slightly rotten fence post buried in the nettles behind the pavilion which would serve this purpose extremely well. 'If we could get the competitors to take the post down towards the river we might be able to get them to throw the damned thing into the water and get rid of it,' said Puffy hopefully.

A number of 'surprises' had been organised to ensure that the day was a memorable success. Itchy erected a net just off the playing area so that spectators (including women and children) could bowl at some of the star batsmen taking part in the match. Spectators would pay £1 for the privilege of bowling three balls at a batsman. The cash incentive would be that they would receive £5 every time they hit the batsman's wicket.

The planned highlight of the day was, however, undoubtedly the fact that Paddy had, through his brother's dentist, arranged for a member of the nearby parachuting club to be dropped from a light plane at 1.55 pm and to float down onto the pitch just in time to shout 'Play' and start the match. In order to serenade the parachutist, and announce his arrival, the Fondling-Under-Water brass band would welcome his arrival by playing 'Those Magnificent Men In Their Flying Machines'.

Refreshments for the day were, of course, being provided by Mrs Betty Cleavidge and the team of butter-knife-twirling ladies who normally provided teas for the cricket club.

Mrs Betty Cleavidge and her tireless team had, in anticipation of the forthcoming match, prepared a veritable mountain of sandwiches, fairy cakes, sausage rolls and jam tarts.

When Paddy told them about the fund-raising events and the expected inflow of spectators and contestants they stepped up their sandwich and cake making activities into overdrive.

These were committed tea time specialists and it never occurred to them to prepare food for a luncheon and for a tea; instead they simply made enough food for two teas. And since they were expecting an unknown number of guests they made as much food as they possibly could.

They chopped several pounds of cheddar cheese into neat, little cubes, bought all the cocktail onions and little sausages that Miss Box could find in her shop, and duly skewered the cubes of cheese, the cocktail onions and the little sausages on little wooden cocktail sticks. They made pasties and sausage rolls and prepared trifles, chocolate cakes, Victoria sponges filled with jam, cream and a dozen other fillings, apple pies, blackberry pies and mixed fruit pies. They baked tea cakes, crumpets, muffins and currant buns by the boxful and, curiously, acquired enough pickled gherkins to satisfy an army of gherkin addicts. (Mrs Betty Cleavidge had once been asked for pickled gherkins by a visiting player. A proud hostess, she had been mortified by her inability to satisfy this request and she had sworn never again to be found short of a pickled gherkin.)

Puffy Harbottle had generously donated two barrels of beer and a barrel of cider to augment the vast quantities of tea and orange squash which Mrs Betty Cleavidge and her team planned to produce.

Mrs Betty Cleavidge had rejected the idea of charging anyone for tea, sandwiches and cakes. The club had always supplied its players and the visiting team with free refreshments and Mrs Betty Cleavidge was a great believer in tradition. However, in an inspired moment of anticipation Mrs Betty Cleavidge had taken the precaution of obtaining a large supply of antacid tablets on loan from Rupert Fitzwalter the local doctor, antique dealer and bookie. Showing rare commercial acumen she intended to sell these tablets at the very reasonable price of £1.50 each to those of her customers who ate their way into gastric disharmony. Puffy, who knew of this arrangement, felt that there was a strong likelihood that this venture could well prove to be the most profitable part of the day. This was no reflection on the cooking skills of Mrs Betty Cleavidge and her team of sandwich makers but was, rather, an acknowledgement of the fact that when people are faced with vast quantities of free food they will invariably eat more than they need or is good for them.

~ Chapter 76 ~

IT WAS TEN MINUTES TO eleven, and just ten minutes before the official start of the festivities, when Percy and Biffo (the latter wheeling his bicycle) arrived at the Fondling-Under-Water cricket ground.

'Percy!' cried Paddy, who was the first to spot the arrival of the former newsreader. 'Thank you for coming!' He shook hands with Percy and started to explain why they needed him.

'My friend has explained it all,' said Percy, waving his free hand in Biffo's direction. 'You're trying to raise money for a new lawnmower.' Biffo couldn't help noticing that Percy's enunciation was not quite as clear as it had been when they had left the cottage. He seemed to have a little difficulty with the word lawnmower.

'We've set up a microphone over here,' said Puffy, pointing and leading the way to a tennis umpire's chair which had been set up just inside the square leg boundary. A microphone was ready waiting on the umpire's table, connected by several long leads to a series of loudspeakers around the ground.

'Splendid!' said Percy. He stood and looked up the steps to the chair. 'Seems quite high up, doesn't it!'

'We thought it would give you a good view,' said Puffy, who had arrived to say 'hello' to Percy.

'Absolutely,' said Percy. 'Marvellous.' He put a foot on the bottom rung, preparing to climb the short ladder to the chair and turned around. 'My new friend mentioned something about a glass of beer?'

'Of course!' said Puffy, hurrying off towards the pavilion.

'It's been a long walk,' explained Percy to Paddy and Biffo. He climbed cautiously into position on his chair

'Quite!' agreed Paddy. He turned and whispered to Biffo. 'He didn't have anything to drink before he left did he?'

Biffo shook his head. 'Just a sip or two from a hip flask.'

'We have to watch him,' whispered Paddy. 'Sober he's fantastic but if he gets tiddly he can be a bit of a nightmare.'

Biffo, not knowing what to say to this, said nothing.

'I say, would one of you chaps fill my flask for me?'

Biffo and Paddy looked up.

Percy was holding out his flask. The top was off and he was holding the flask upside down. It was clearly empty.

'Puffy's bringing you a beer,' Paddy reminded him.

'That's fine for quenching the thirst,' said Percy, with a broad smile. 'But I need something a little stronger for quelling the nerves.' He winked, waved the flask about and then threw it down. Biffo, much to his own surprise, caught it neatly.

'What would you like in it?' Biffo asked.

'Whisky would be nice,' answered Percy. He paused. 'Or brandy.' He cleared his throat. 'Some people drink to forget,' he said. 'I have forgotten everything I want to forget. I drink because I like the taste.'

Biffo turned and started to walk back towards the pavilion. 'We'll have to watch him,' whispered Paddy, accompanying him. He shook his head. 'This may have been a big mistake...'

'Gin will do nicely,' Percy called after them. 'If there isn't any whisky or brandy.'

~ Chapter 77 ~

WHEN BIFFO AND PERCY HAD arrived at the cricket ground there had been no more than a couple of dozen people about. But by the time the little hand on the pavilion clock had reached eleven and the big hand was pointing straight up virtually every house, every cottage and every farm within five miles was empty and everyone had converged on the Fondling-Under-Water cricket ground.

The team players were, of course, in white but many of the spectators – even the women – were wearing white too. Biffo had never before realised that white came in so many different shades.

Even villagers who weren't particularly fond of cricket had come along to see what was happening, to have some fun and to help raise a few pounds for the cricket club. Those who owned an electrical extension cable had turned up because they all knew that their best chance of getting their property back was to help the cricket club raise enough money to buy a new lawnmower. There was also a widespread fear that if the club didn't find the money to buy a new mower Itchy would be on the prowl trying to borrow someone else's equipment. Most people in the village knew what had happened to Puffy Harbottle's lawnmower.

'What's in it?' Paddy asked Biffo, pointing to the pewter hip flask Biffo was carrying back to Percy.

Biffo confirmed that the flask was now full of twelve year old malt whisky.

Paddy looked at the flask and winced. 'Is it neat?'

Biffo looked at him.

'The whisky. Is it neat? Or did you put some water in?'

'It's neat,' replied Biffo. 'I thought he'd prefer it without water. The stuff he had in it when we were walking down here tasted like pure rocket fuel.'

Paddy sighed. 'Would you ask him to announce the egg and spoon race?' he asked. He handed Biffo a piece of paper. 'The names of the competitors and everything else he's likely to need are all on there.' He leant a little closer. 'If you have to fill his flask again I would be grateful if you would try and add some water! A mixture consisting of one third whisky and two thirds water would probably prove helpful.'

Biffo said he would try and then took the flask and the piece of paper across to where Percy was sitting.

'I've brought your flask,' said Biffo, holding the flask up in the air so that Percy could reach down and take it from him. 'I filled it with malt whisky.'

'Jolly good!' said Percy. He handed down an empty pint glass. 'Would you hand that back to Puffy?' he said. 'Perhaps you would ask him if he would be kind enough to fill it up again when he has next got a spare moment.' He spoke clearly; carefully enunciating each word separately.

'Paddy asked if you'd announce the first heat of the egg and spoon race,' said Biffo, holding up the piece of paper he had been given so that Percy could take it.

'Egg and spoon, eh?' said Percy, slipping his flask into his pocket and accepting the piece of paper from Biffo. His eyes positively twinkled. 'Do you know, I don't think I've ever announced the start of an egg and spoon race before!'

~ Chapter 78 ~

THE EARLY HEATS FOR THE egg and spoon race, the sack race and the three-legged race were all conducted without much trouble. Mrs Jack Hobbs was threatened with disqualification for gluing her egg to her spoon and Mrs Herbert Sutcliffe complained that the sack she had been given still contained several pounds of fertiliser. (Her objection was based not on olfactory grounds but on the grounds that the additional weight constituted an unofficial handicap.)

Lord Hepplewhite, who had sat on the local bench for thirty years, and who was always made referee on occasions like this, took the potential sting out of these problems by ruling that Mrs Hobbs' egg should be unglued from its spoon and that Mrs Sutcliffe should be given a fresh and more acceptable sack. In the event it proved quite impossible to separate Mrs Hobbs' egg from her spoon and so she was provided with a fresh egg and a fresh spoon. The replacement of Mrs Sutcliffe's unsatisfactory sack offered no such problems.

The real excitement of the morning took place in the nets where spectators (including women and children) could bowl at a succession of star batsmen from the Fondling-Under-Water team. To everyone's disappointment the visiting professionals had declined to take part in this part of the entertainment. When telephoned the previous evening, their captain for the day, Cyril Player had expressed the players' formal regret and pointed out that they felt that it would be demeaning to their professional status if they were to take part in what amounted to little more than a side show. This excuse did not go down particularly well with the villagers, several of whom remembered that three of the visiting batsmen had made television advertisements for a brand of yoghurt, two of the team were regular guests on a television panel game which was famous for dunking losing contestants in a vat of green goo, while a sixth had acted in a seaside pantomime in which he had been required to wear full cricket gear while running around the stage hitting everyone with a large rubber cricket bat and shouting out 'I'm Batty the village idiot!'.

'Bunch of stuck up snobs,' said Mrs Harborough, who was known for, and proud of, her plain speaking.

None of this mattered much, however, for the event still proved to be an enormous success. The unexpected star turned out to be none other than Lady Hepplewhite; the exquisitely proportioned wife of Fondling-Under-Water's only peer.

'Gosh, isn't it heavy!' cried her Ladyship, when she first picked up a cricket ball. 'What do I do?'

Bill Stickers who was escorting the club patron's wife and trying to keep out of sight as much as possible, explained to Lady Hepplewhite that she had to bowl the ball in the general direction of Jack Hobbs who was waiting some twenty two yards away.

Lady Hepplewhite's first attempt to bowl was so unsuccessful that she didn't want to try again but Bill encouraged her to have another go and suggested that she try bowling underarm. He explained that although unusual this was entirely legal. It was an inspired suggestion. Lady Hepplewhite's first ball whistled underneath Jack Hobbs' bat and removed his leg stump from the ground. Her second ball narrowly missed the off stump. And her third ball bounced off the batsman's foot and removed his middle stump. Jack, limping badly, retired from the nets and Herbert Sutcliffe took his place.

Feeling rather embarrassed at having won £10 when the club was trying to raise money rather than give it away, Lady Hepplewhite insisted on using her winnings to buy more attempts. But things did not go quite according to plan. Twenty five minutes and six batsmen later she walked back to her deckchair clutching £140 in notes and coins.

~ Chapter 79 ~

THE VISITING CRICKET TEAM ARRIVED shortly after one o'clock, just in time for lunch and the judging of the fancy dress competition.

Cyril Rodney Arthur Percival Player and his ten professional playing colleagues arrived at the ground in a flurry of brand new, well-polished, sponsored cars. They unloaded their bored, immaculate, leggy, blonde girlfriends and battered bags of kit under the watchful, and slightly envious, eyes of the Fondling-Under-Water cricket team and their faithful and loyal supporters.

On the whole the professionals were taller, broader and slimmer than the village players. They were all heavily tanned and as they clambered out of their cars and stretched their backs there was an arrogance about their every movement which several members of the local team found strangely disturbing. Most of the professionals wore jeans and casual shirts. One or two wore tailored slacks and blazers. Cyril Player wore a pair of light blue slacks and a blazer with the England badge on the breast pocket. Biffo wondered how he had managed to get hold of the blazer since, according to Puffy, he had never officially been a member of an England touring party.

'Isn't that Michael Hunt?' Cheesy asked Puffy, nodding towards a tall, broad-backed, blond-haired giant wearing faded blue jeans, a dazzling white T-shirt and a pair of designer sunglasses. He spoke in a whisper, partly it seemed through awe and partly through fear.

'I think so,' whispered Puffy.

'Who's Michael Hunt?' asked Biffo.

The other two looked at him in astonishment.

'Where have you been for the last two years?' asked Cheesy, incredulously. 'He's the fastest bowler in England. Some say he's the fastest bowler in the world. He felled a South African with a bouncer eighteen months ago and nearly killed him.'

'I've never had much time to read the sports pages,' admitted Biffo.

'I'm not playing against him,' whispered Cheesy. He started to rub his knee. 'I think my patella just fell off. Or a cartilage turned to powder.'

'Don't be daft!' Puffy whispered back. 'He won't bowl flat out at us.'

Just then the man reputed to the fastest bowler in the world glanced across in their direction. The three of them waved at him and grinned broadly; like schoolboys who have been caught staring at a beautiful woman. Hunt nodded his acknowledgement, without smiling, and turned away and bent his head to listen to his blonde, busty, long-legged companion. He patted her gently on the behind and then, without looking, reached out and took a pen and an autograph book from a small boy. He signed his name and handed the pen and book back to the boy without once looking at him.

'And that's Tom Morton!' said Puffy. 'Over there, with Cyril and Paddy.' He nodded in the direction of another giant. This one had red hair and was taller and broader than Michael Hunt. It occurred to Biffo that if Tom Morton had decided to walk across the M1 motorway cars, lorries and coaches would have screeched to a halt – not to avoid knocking down an innocent motorist but to avoid crashing their vehicles into a mountain of a man who looked solid enough to crush a mere 20 ton lorry into an unrecognisable tangle of crumpled metal.

'Heaven preserve us!' muttered Cheesy, sounding as nervous as though someone had just pointed out Dracula. 'It is.'

'Who's Tom Morton?' asked Biffo.

Cheesy looked at him, as though not really believing that Biffo didn't know. 'The other half of England's best opening attack for decades!' he replied, when he realised that Biffo's ignorance was genuine. 'He was banned last year for threatening an umpire and punching an opposition batsman. But he's still one of the best bowlers in the country.'

The banned fast bowler had joined the rest of the visiting team of professionals at Mrs Betty Cleavidge's groaning trestle tables. The mound of sandwiches and cakes was already beginning to shrink noticeably. The professionals, like locusts, ate speedily and with quiet determination. Most of them didn't seem particularly concerned about what they were eating.

'When does his ban finish?' asked Puffy.

'It's about now,' said Cheesy. 'He's probably come here for a bit of practice.'

'Oh gawd!' said Puffy. 'You know what that means, don't you?'

Cheesy nodded.

'What does it mean?' asked Biffo.

'It means he'll probably want to bowl flat out,' said Puffy.

'He certainly will,' whispered Cheesy, his voice now little more than a croak. 'Look who just got out of that green Rover!'

'The short chap with white hair, in the beige safari suit?' said Biffo.

'No,' said Cheesy. 'That's George Tompkins. He used to play for England. He's a television commentator now. But the one with him – the podgy guy with the beard and the sunglasses – is Bert Dobson one of the England selectors.'

'Oh, no!' said Puffy. 'Tom Morton really is going to have to take this match seriously.'

'I remember George Tompkins!' said Biffo, pleased to recognise a name at last. 'Which one is he?'

'The little chap in the badly-fitting safari suit.'

'He was the best spin bowler I ever saw!' said Biffo.

'He was a wicket keeper,' said Puffy.

'Are you sure?'

'He was a wicket keeper,' said Cheesy, with certainty.

'I remember!' said Biffo. 'He scored 100 against the West Indies didn't he? At Edgbaston?'

'It was against Australia,' said Cheesy.

'At Headingley,' said Puffy.

'Well, I knew he'd scored 100,' said Biffo. He paused for a moment and stared at the man who was almost one of his sporting heroes. 'Wow!'

'Look who's getting out of the Jaguar!' said Puffy.

The other two looked to see who was getting out of the Jaguar.

'The scruffy bloke with the long hair?' said Cheesy.

'Yes.'

'Who is it?' Cheesy asked.

'I don't know,' said Puffy. 'But look what he's just got out of the boot.'

'A bag?' said Cheesy.

'A camera bag,' said Puffy. 'And a telephone lens.'

'Telephoto lens,' said Biffo.

'That's what I said,' said Puffy.

'No, you said telephone lens,' said Biffo.

'Don't be silly,' said Puffy.

'Is he a photographer?' asked Cheesy.

'It's the press,' whispered Puffy. 'The press are here.'

'I think there's another one getting out of that sports car,' said Biffo, pointing towards a short, fat man wearing an army flak jacket and a pair of brown corduroy trousers who was struggling to lift something out of the boot of his car.

'Oh my gawd!' murmured Cheesy. 'This was supposed to be a quiet fund-raising match.'

The short fat man, who had pulled an enormous lens out of the boot of his car, was now wrestling with it and the camera to which it was attached and struggling to fasten the whole thing to an extremely sturdy looking tripod. He seemed to have equipment powerful enough to take close up pictures of moon craters.

'We're going to be famous!' said Puffy, full of wonder. 'Do you think I might get my picture in the papers?'

'Village Batsman Felled By England Star!' said Cheesy gloomily. He wrote out the headline in the air with his finger as he spoke. 'Do you have a helmet?'

Puffy looked at Cheesy as if he'd asked him if he had a wooden leg. 'What do you mean?'

'A helmet. Have you got one?' He paused. 'It's one of those things batsmen wear on their heads to stop them getting killed by bad-tempered fast bowlers who are trying to impress selectors and win back their places in the England side.'

'I know what a helmet is,' said Puffy, rather impatiently. 'But of course I haven't got one. I've only got one pad and my bat's got a bit chipped out of the blade.'

'Have you got one?' said Cheesy to Biffo.

'No,' answered Biffo. 'I don't even have a bat or a pad.'

'I bet we haven't got a helmet between us,' said Cheesy, gloomily. 'They'll kill us all. It'll be a massacre. It'll be the Battle of Wounded Knee all over again.'

'The battle of wounded knee?' said Biffo.

'Cheesy was hit on the knee twelve years ago,' explained Puffy. 'He's never forgotten it.'

'Nine years ago,' said Cheesy. 'It was nine years ago. They broke a bone in my knee.' He pulled a face. 'It hurt a lot. Two other blokes had bones broken too.'

'Who was bowling?' asked Biffo.

'Some tearaway kid playing for another village,' said Cheesy. 'He wasn't half as fast as these blokes are.' He sighed. He started to move away towards the pavilion. 'I'm going to go and write out my will.'

'Don't be daft,' Puffy called after him. He paused and then added. 'You haven't got anything to leave anyone.'

'Do you really think it's going to be dangerous?' Biffo asked Puffy.

Puffy thought for a moment. 'If they start bowling fast I'm going to take guard about three yards outside my leg stump,' he said. 'These blokes don't bowl that wide.' He paused, thought for a moment and grinned. 'But I wouldn't miss the chance of being able to say I'd batted against Tom Morton and Michael Hunt for anything.' He stopped and pointed at Paddy who was hurrying across towards them. 'I think the vice captain wants a word.'

'Biffo!' called the vice captain, slightly breathless and considerably less composed than usual. 'Would you be kind enough to pop over and give Percy this slip of paper to read?'

Biffo hurried off to complete his errand. As he went he noticed that The Fondling-Under-Water Morris Dancing Team had started performing in front of the pavilion.

Eight men in white shirts, black knee-length breeches, white socks and black shoes were jumping up and down and banging sticks in the air. They wore top hats and colourful sashes and had little bells sewn onto their socks. No one was watching them but they were enjoying themselves so much that they hadn't noticed. They probably wouldn't have cared even if they had noticed.

'I see Cyril has brought some heavy fire-power with him,' said Puffy, referring to England's two premier fast bowlers.

'Yes,' agreed Paddy, looking grim.

'Do we know anyone who owns a motorbike?' asked Puffy.

Paddy looked confused. 'Are you thinking of trying to make a quick getaway?' he said, with a rather hollow laugh.

'No,' said Puffy earnestly. 'I wouldn't miss this match for

the world. But I don't have a batting helmet and these guys do tend to bowl rather quickly. It just occurred to me that if I can find someone who owns a motorbike I might be able to borrow a motorcycling helmet.'

'Ah,' said Paddy. 'I see what you mean.' He started to move away. 'I'd better wander over to the pavilion to make sure that everything is going OK with the fancy dress competition.'

'I'll come with you,' said Puffy. 'I'm feeling a trifle peckish. A little light lunch might settle the butterflies in my stomach.'

'Ah, bit of a problem there,' said Paddy, as they headed for the pavilion. 'When I last saw her our dear Betty Cleavidge was in grave danger of losing vital supplies of hair. She says she made enough food for a couple of thousand people but that the visitors are eating everything in sight. She's worried that there might not be anything left for tea.' He paused. 'She asked me to tell our side to hold back for a while.' Paddy scratched his head and looked rather sheepish. 'I forgot to mention it to the others.' He shrugged. 'Nothing like this has ever happened before.' He looked very miserable. Suddenly his face lit up. 'I know someone who's got a moped!' he said. 'Constable Hobbling.'

Puffy frowned. He was puzzled by what seemed to be a rather unexpected turn in the direction of the conversation. 'A moped?'

'You were looking for a motorbike.'

'Of course!' said Puffy, finally understanding. 'And Constable Hobbling, being a law abiding citizen, always wears a helmet. Terrific! I'll go and find him.'

And so while Paddy scurried back to check on the fancy dress competition, and to warn the rest of the team to lay off the sausage rolls and jam tarts, Puffy set off in search of Constable Hobbling.

~ Chapter 80 ~

As PADDY HURRIED TO THE pavilion and Puffy searched for Constable Hobbling the loudspeakers around the ground crackled into action.

'Ladies and gentlemen,' said Percy, his rich, deep whisky, gin and brandy-soaked tones immediately grabbing everyone's attention. 'The Fondling-Under-Water Cricket Club is pleased to welcome Mr Cyril Player of England, Somerset, Warwickshire, Derbyshire, Nottinghamshire and the Fondling-Under-Water Cricket Club, and his team, to the Fondling-Under-Water Cricket Club. The match will begin shortly. Meanwhile, the club captain is delighted to announce that Lady Hepplewhite has kindly agreed to judge the Fondling-Under-Water Cricket Club first ever Fancy Dress Competition. The judging will take place in front of the pavilion and will start immediately.'

Listening to the former newsreader Biffo realised that he could tell which words were supposed to begin with capital letters by the way Percy pronounced them.

In response to Percy's announcement the area in front of the pavilion suddenly began to swarm with fairies (ranging in age from six to sixty), gorillas (ranging in size from enormous to 'just how many people are there in that gorilla suit?') and representations of long dead members of the royal family.

There were three vicars, four wildly underdressed and extravagantly over made up women who looked like ladies of the night (three of them were male and one of them, it later turned out, was not), five famous and instantly recognisable cartoon characters, six movie stars and seven Elvis Presleys.

The only member of the cricket team taking part in the competition was Justin, the wicket keeper. He was dressed, surprisingly convincingly, as a lemon. The main part of the lemon was carved out of sponge rubber. Justin's arms, legs and head, all which poked out from the lemon itself, were painted yellow. He looked so realistic that everyone who looked at him immediately felt the need for a little something sweet.

Meanwhile, the unceasing demand for fairy cakes, jam tarts, cream horns and thick slices of black forest gateau kept Mrs Cleavidge both on her toes and on tenterhooks. As the demand grew so the slices of black forest gateau grew thinner.

Though this was the first time the Fondling-Under-Water Cricket Club had organised one, fancy dress competitions were, Biffo learned from Cheesy, an integral and expected part of most village celebrations.

There was, Cheesy told him, always a fancy dress competition during the summer fête and there was another at the children's Christmas party. Curiously, even the organisers of the autumn produce show ('Biggest Onions', 'Longest Leeks', 'Best Blackberries' and so on) did not feel able to present their event to the public without the additional attraction of a fancy dress competition.

'Every kid in the village has at least one fancy dress costume,' said Cheesy. 'Most of the adults have two.'

He explained that during the fancy dress 'off season' – a period of about six weeks in January and February – there was always much tinkering with and swapping of costumes. He told Biffo that most women in Fondling-Under-Water know how to convert a fairy costume for a nine year old into a tart costume for a 45 year old man using little more (and sometimes less) than a pair of scissors, a few safety pins, a yard of net curtain and an old cushion cover or two.

Cheesy also explained that the fancy dress competition was always judged by Lady Hepplewhite. The current holder of that title, the fifth or possible sixth Lady Hepplewhite, had already done it so often, Cheesy said, that there had once been a rumour that she had put it down on her passport under the heading 'occupation'.

'Are you entering the fancy dress competition?' Biffo had asked Puffy when he had first heard about this aspect of the day's entertainment.

'Me?' Puffy seemed rather taken aback at this. 'Of course not!' he snorted. 'I can make a complete idiot of myself without dressing up as a pirate and hopping around with a stuffed parrot sewn onto my jacket.'

Although, like Puffy, most of the cricket team members had chosen not to take part in the fancy dress competition they were, to a man (and, not forgetting the vicar, a transvestite) gathered around the judging area in order to offer support to Justin. Biffo wandered over to join them in offering Justin thoroughly biased encouragement and loud cheers if he won.

'Damned good costume, Justin!' said Cheesy.

Justin grinned his delight.

'Where did you get it from?' asked Itchy.

'A bloke I know runs a theatrical shop,' replied Justin. 'He's got piles of really good costumes in stock. I'll give you his phone number if you like.'

'You obviously felt a bit fruity when you chose that one,' said Herbert Sutcliffe.

This was greeted with general groans.

'He's got loads of really good fruits,' said Justin, with great enthusiasm. No one seemed to think it odd to stand and listen to a lemon enthuse in this way. 'I could have been an orange, a strawberry, a raspberry, a slice of melon or a banana.'

'Why not a slice of melon?' asked Itchy.

'I didn't want to be part of something,' said Justin. 'I wanted to be a whole fruit.'

'Why didn't you choose a banana?' asked Cheesy, who seemed taken with the idea of a banana suit, and who clearly found it curious that Justin had not also found the idea of dressing as a banana irresistible.

Justin stared at him. 'I didn't want to look stupid,' he snapped, drawing himself up to his full (but not very spectacular) height.

~ Chapter 81 ~

PUFFY FOUND CONSTABLE HOBBLING SITTING on the light roller. His moped was parked nearby with the helmet on the seat. Constable Hobbling was dressed in his blue police uniform. His police helmet was perched on his head. He looked very miserable.

'Can we borrow your helmet?' asked Puffy, coming straight to the point.

The policeman looked up, reached up and grabbed the top of his police helmet with his hands as though worried that Puffy might grab it and run off with it. He seemed alarmed.

'My helmet?' he said. 'What do you want my helmet for?' he demanded. 'You can't have it anyway,' he said. 'It's part of my uniform,' he explained. 'I've heard that an Inspector is coming up today to see if I've made an arrest. If he sees me without my helmet there'll be big trouble.'

'Not that helmet,' said Puffy. 'Your motorcycle helmet.' He pointed to the relevant item. 'We don't have a batting helmet between us.'

'Oh,' said Constable Hobbling. He nodded.

'We can borrow it?'

'Yes, of course.' said the policeman with a shrug.

'You seem a bit down in the dumps,' said Puffy. 'What's up.'

'I'm still worrying about finding someone to arrest,' said Constable Hobbling.

'Oh don't worry about that,' said Puffy. 'If the worst comes to the worst you can always arrest Itchy.'

The constable looked up. For a moment there was hope in his eyes. 'Could I?' he asked, eagerly. Then he paused, thought for a moment, pushed back his helmet and scratched the front of his head. 'But what for?' he asked Puffy.

The landlord shrugged. 'Take your pick,' he replied, with a shrug. 'I expect Itchy's broken most of the laws you can think of.'

Constable Hobbling nodded in agreement and thought about this for a minute or two. Then, his shoulders drooped and with obvious sadness, he shook his head. 'I couldn't do it,' he said. 'I couldn't arrest Itchy.'

'Well you're going to have to arrest someone,' said Puffy.

'I know,' replied the policeman. 'That's why I feel so miserable.'

~ Chapter 82 ~

IT WAS LATER AGREED THAT the judging of the fancy dress competition went well, although it was also generally agreed that it would have been better if the proceedings had not been marred by a small and slightly embarrassing moment when Lady Hepplewhite was about to announce the winner.

Lady Hepplewhite preferred to follow an informal process when judging the winner of the Fondling-Under-Water fancy dress competitions. She would wander around amidst the entrants, select a winner, retreat to a vantage point, usually standing upon a chair, and draw attention to her choice with the aid of a pointed finger.

On this occasion she decided to eschew fairies, animals and cartoon characters and award the winning prize of two bottles of parsnip wine and an armful of rhubarb to one of the four tarts.

'Oh, that one has to be the winner!' said Lady Hepplewhite, standing precariously on a folding wooden chair and pointing out a leggy blonde in fishnet stockings, a pelmet-sized black skirt, a see-through purple blouse and a huge, shoulder length blonde wig.

'Who is the winner?' Biffo asked Puffy who was standing beside him.

Puffy leant forward an inch or two and inspected the winner, who did not yet seem aware of Lady Hepplewhite's choice, but who, from the direction in which Lady Hepplewhite's aristocratic finger was pointing, was unmistakeable.

'Haven't the foggiest,' said Puffy. 'It isn't one of our lads.' He peered again, puzzled. 'It must be a bloke from another village.'

'If that's a bloke I'm a cabbage,' said Biffo. 'That blouse is see through and those aren't balloons.'

They both edged a little closer. The putative winner of the fancy dress competition was talking to Tom Morton. Suddenly she reached up, put her arms around his neck, pulled down his head and kissed him full on the lips.

'They're not and he isn't,' agreed Puffy. Suddenly his voice dropped. 'Oh my gawd,' he said, looking at Biffo. He lowered his voice. 'She's given the prize to Tom Morton's girlfriend. And she's not even entered in the competition.'

'We'll have to do something,' said Biffo, nodding towards Lady Hepplewhite, who had explained her choice to Bill Stickers. The club captain was hurrying off to tell Tom Morton's girlfriend the news that she had won a fancy dress competition she hadn't entered.

'It's too late to stop Bill,' said Biffo. 'Let's have a word with Lady Hepplewhite.'

'What the hell are we going to tell her?' asked Puffy. 'If Tom finds out Lady Hepplewhite has given his girlfriend a prize because she thinks she looks like a bloke dressed up to look like a tart he'll kill us all – one by one and legally!'

'Come with me,' said Biffo, 'I've got an idea!' He ran over to where Lady Hepplewhite was standing, still on her chair, waiting for Bill to return with the winner of the fancy dress competition.

'Can I have a word, your Ladyship?' asked Biffo.

'Not now dear, I'm judging,' said Lady Hepplewhite.

'Your Ladyship this is Biffo Brimstone,' said Puffy. 'He's just arrived in the village. He's playing in the team today.'

'Oh how nice!' said Lady Hepplewhite. She held out a hand. Biffo wasn't sure whether to shake it or kiss it so he did both.

'Lady Hepplewhite,' said Biffo, speaking as fast as he could. 'I think there's been a terrible mistake. Did you just pick that girl in the purple blouse and the black skirt as winner of the fancy dress competition?'

'Now, now!' said Lady Hepplewhite, wagging a reproving finger. 'You may be new to the village but you must learn that I'm not open to bribery or persuasion! I'm sorry if you feel that someone else should have won but I really can't let you interfere with the judging process.'

'No, no,' said Biffo. 'I don't want to.' He paused. 'Well, yes, in a way I suppose I do,' he admitted. 'The problem is that I think you've given the prize to the wrong person.'

'There you go!' said Lady Hepplewhite, wagging a reproving finger.

'Hurry up!' hissed Puffy. 'They're coming!'

'The girl you think is a bloke dressed up as a tart isn't what you think she is,' said Biffo. 'She's not a bloke in drag. She is really Tom Morton's girlfriend and she and he are going to be very piss...annoyed when they find out what's happened. Tom Morton is one of the visiting cricketers. He's a fast bowler who plays for England.'

Lady Hepplewhite looked away from Biffo and back into the crowd. Bill Stickers was now threading his way through the fairies, the animals, the Elvis Presleys, the cartoon characters, Justin's lemon and the assorted players, with Tom Morton and his girlfriend in tow. Tom Morton was striding. The girlfriend was tottering and discovering just how difficult it can be to try and walk quickly on grass while wearing pencil-thin five inch high heels.

'Oh dear!' said Lady Hepplewhite, suddenly going white. 'What on earth am I going to do.'

'Here she is!' said Bill, who had not yet told Tom Morton's girlfriend why she had been picked out of the crowd.

'What's going on?' demanded Tom Morton, clearly preparing himself to get very cross. Since he was normally an angry man this meant simply notching up his anger level several degrees. The press photographers, smelling trouble, had forced their way through the crowd and were grouped around the fast bowler, his girlfriend and Lady Hepplewhite.

'Lady Hepplewhite was planning to pick out a winner for the fancy dress competition,' said Biffo suddenly. Everyone looked at him and he felt himself going slightly weak at the knees. He spoke directly to Tom Morton's girlfriend. 'But when she saw you in the crowd she thought that the Fondling-Under-Water Cricket Club really should have a beauty queen to help us celebrate this occasion.' Biffo smiled. 'Lady Hepplewhite would like you to be that beauty queen.'

'Oh yes, absolutely!' said Lady Hepplewhite, almost fainting with relief. 'Oh yes. It would be just wonderful if you would accept.'

Tom Morton's girlfriend squealed with delight. Tom Morton wasn't the sort of person to squeal. But when his girlfriend was happy he too knew happiness.

'Brilliant!' Puffy whispered in Biffo's ear.

'What's your name, my dear?' asked Lady Hepplewhite.

'Lotti,' said the new beauty queen. 'With an i.' She blushed and curtsied. 'Your Highness,' she added.

'Dotty?'

'Lotti, your Highness.' repeated the beauty queen. There was more blushing and more curtsying.

'Lotti?'

'That's right, your Highness!' beamed the beauty queen. 'Lotti!' This time there was no blushing. But there was another curtsey.

'Of course it is, my dear,' said Lady Hepplewhite. 'Well done! What a lovely name. And you don't need to call me 'your Highness', 'your Ladyship' will do nicely.'

'Thank you your Highness!' The beauty queen curtsied again. She was going up and down more often than a Harrods lift during the Christmas season.

'So, who's the winner of the fancy dress competition?' asked Bill Stickers. Intelligence and tact had never been his strong points.

'The...er winner of the competition is...er...the...,' stumbled Lady Hepplewhite. She looked down at Biffo for help.

Biffo looked around, desperately seeking inspiration. 'The lemon,' he prompted.

'The lemon!' said Lady Hepplewhite, with another great sigh of relief. She smiled sweetly. 'The winner of the fancy dress competition is the lemon!' she declared solemnly, as though announcing the winner of an Oscar for best actor.

The announcement was greeted with much cheering.

It was, Biffo thought later, one of his greatest achievements. In two minutes he had snatched the day from the brink of disaster and made everyone happy. Such joys are not known to many.

At that moment the pavilion clock struck two and the brass band started to play 'Those Magnificent Men in Their Flying Machines' to celebrate the arrival of the parachutist. Thinking that they were late in their musical welcome they played the tune very loud and very quickly.

Unfortunately, the parachutist was nowhere to be seen. Heads were bent back in vain as several hundred eyes searched the skies but saw nothing but swallows, seagulls and clouds. None of these were equipped with parachutes.

'Not yet!' hissed Paddy, running over to where the band was playing and waving his arms from side to side. 'Wait until you can see him coming!'

~ Chapter 83 ~

'I CAN'T PLAY!' INSISTED A tearful Jack Hobbs. 'I can't stand, I can't walk and I certainly can't play cricket.'

The unhappy Fondling-Under-Water opening batsman was sitting in the pavilion with his foot up on a chair. His right trouser leg was rolled up to the knee and the old boot and grubby sock which had been removed from his right foot were lying on the floor nearby. The whole team was gathered around.

'Let me take a look,' said Rupert, the local antique dealer, bookie and doctor. He spoke in his role as village physician though, given the age of Jack's leg, and the long odds against him playing, his interest could have been inspired by his role as an antique dealer or, indeed, his role as village bookie.

He bent down and prodded at Jack's bared limb. 'Does that hurt?' he asked. Jack made the sort of sound a cat makes prior to regurgitating the half digested remains of the previous evening's shrew.

'It's not broken,' said Rupert, confidently. 'But it's very swollen.' He sucked in a couple of litres of air between his teeth and shook his head in dismay and sympathy. 'You're going to have a massive bruise.' He casually pressed his thumb into the flesh at the side of Jack's foot. Jack winced.

'What did you do that for?' demanded the unhappy batsman.

'It's what we doctors do,' explained Rupert. He thought for a moment. 'I'm not entirely sure why,' he admitted. 'But we just do.' He stood up and stretched his back.

'Is that it?' demanded Jack.

'Is that what?' said Rupert, puzzled.

'Is that all you're going to do? Aren't you going to examine me?'

'I have examined you!'

'Not properly.'

'What do you mean by properly?'

'You know,' said Jack. He stopped for a moment, thinking hard. 'A thorough medical examination,' he said.

'What do you want me to do?' asked Rupert, rather impatiently. 'Peer down your throat? Ask you if you were ever dropped on your head as a child? Check you for signs of German measles? A cricket ball hit you on the foot and you've got a bruise!'

'Sorry, doctor,' said Jack, meekly.

'I should think so too,' said Rupert.

'Can you play with a runner?' asked Paddy.

Rupert relented, possibly feeling rather sorry for his tirade. 'But it'll be a big bruise,' he said. 'I dare say that's going to be the biggest bruise I've seen for years.'

Jack looked suitably flattered. Clearly proud, he smiled and quietly thanked Rupert.

Paddy tried again. 'Can you play with a runner?'

Jack didn't even stop to think about the question. He simply shook his head. 'I can't even stand,' he said miserably. 'It's all that bloody woman's fault.'

The silence which followed the realisation that the Fondling-Under-Water cricket team had lost one of its opening batsmen did not last for long, although it was broken in a thoroughly unexpected way when Justin, still convincingly dressed as a lemon burst into the pavilion.

'Can someone unzip me, please?' wheezed the aged wicket keeper, who was, he would have been perfectly happy to admit, far too old to be bursting into anywhere. Until that moment he would have insisted that his bursting into rooms days were long since over.

Since Biffo was standing nearest to the door it was to the village newcomer that the winner of the fancy dress competition offered his back.

Biffo rummaged around at the back of the lemon, found the zip toggle and pulled. Nothing happened. Biffo pulled again, a little harder this time.

'Careful!' cried Justin. His face, legs and arms were still painted yellow to match the lemon costume he was wearing but a red flush was beginning to show through the yellow giving him a rather curious orange appearance. 'Don't rip it whatever you do. The bloke who lent me this costume will kill me if I take it back ripped.'

'It's stuck,' said Biffo.

'It can't be stuck,' said Justin, more in hope than knowledge. He moved away from Biffo and promiscuously offered his back elsewhere. 'Unzip me!' he appealed.

The vicar, who fitted Lettice's tennis skirt remarkably well and who, Lettice had been pleased to see when she spotted him a little earlier, had put on a white bra underneath his white blouse, was the next to try. He pulled at the zip toggle for a few moments without any result. 'I'm sorry Justin,' he said at last. 'It seems to be stuck.' The vicar spoke in a high-pitched voice in a brave attempt to sound in tune with his appearance.

'It can't be stuck!' said Justin, as though addressing a simpleton. 'How can it be stuck?'

'Zips are always getting stuck,' squeaked the vicar. He thought he was being sultry. Those around merely thought he sounded odd.

'I'll go and find a real woman,' said Justin cruelly. 'They're good with zips.' He waddled off, out of the pavilion and down the steps towards the trestle tables where Mrs Betty Cleavidge and her helpers were distributing late luncheons and early teas. Justin was not generally quite so insensitive to the feelings of others but when you are dressed as a lemon and you no longer want to be dressed as a lemon it is sometimes difficult to be tactful. The vicar, hurt by Justin's remark, looked as if he was about to burst into tears. Biffo, feeling sorry for the unhappy clergyman, put his arm around him and patted the distressed cleric on the shoulder. The vicar, encouraged by this display of sympathy, took a small, embroidered handkerchief from his sleeve, forgot himself and blew his nose loudly. It was a very earthy masculine blow, rather than the delicate feminine sniff which he might have attempted had he been properly in control of himself and been able to think about things a little more clearly.

'I still don't understand what happened,' said Paddy, standing beside his injured opening batsman and rubbing his ear. He had been standing rather too close to the vicar when he, or possibly she, had blown his, or quite possibly her, nose. 'How come you were hit at all?'

'She bowled underarm,' complained Jack. 'The ball never left the ground. It was impossible to do anything about it.'

'That's daft,' retorted Len, who, arm in a sling, had come to watch and cheer and, whenever appropriate, to do some appealing from the boundary. 'If it was rolling along the ground all you had to do was leave your bat on the ground.'

'But you couldn't do that!' said Jack, his voice replete with indignation. 'When a ball rolls along the ground it doesn't just roll along the ground; it bounces and jumps all over the place.' He attempted to show what he meant with an illustrative hand movement but he did this rather too energetically and his foot very nearly fell off the chair upon which it was resting. He paled, swallowed hard and paused while he readjusted his leg. 'Of course, it might not bounce around on a really flat wicket but...'

'Sssshhhhh!' said Paddy, shushing furiously while at the same time looking around nervously in case Itchy was within earshot. Itchy was very sensitive about the quality of the pitches he prepared – even in the nets.

'Besides,' continued Jack. 'You couldn't be sure she was always going to roll 'em along the ground. Sometimes, without any warning she'd whirl her arm round and the ball would land half way down the wicket and go whizzing past at ear height. She bowled two damned fine bouncers at me, I can tell you.' He paused. 'Anyway,' he added defensively. 'It wasn't just me who got out to her. She kept getting everyone out.'

Paddy could not deny this. 'That's true,' he agreed ruefully. 'Thanks to her bowling we lost a lot of money on that stall.' He paused, stared at Jack's foot and sighed loudly. 'I hate to think what's going to happen to us when we're up against Tom Morton and Michael Hunt.'

'I'd rather face them than her any day,' muttered Jack, safe now in the knowledge that this was not something he was going to have to do.

'Who's going to open the batting with Herbert?' asked Puffy.

'I will,' said Paddy. 'But we're going to be a player short. Who else can we find to play?'

Outside the Fondling-Under-Water brass band started to play another enthusiastic rendition of 'Those Magnificent Men in Their Flying Machines'.

Everyone rushed to the pavilion windows and door in order to watch the parachutist descend. Unfortunately, there was no parachutist in sight. The band, misled by a circling buzzard high in the sky, gradually abandoned the tune.

'You'd think the damned fools would realise that there won't be a parachutist until there is a plane,' muttered Paddy. A lone trombonist, eyes closed and lost in the pleasure of the moment, continued with a solo rendition of the welcoming music.

'What about Lord Hepplewhite?' asked Cheesy. 'He used to play.'

Paddy, turning away from the pavilion window, shook his head. 'He gave up playing years ago,' he said. 'Apart from the gout, the arthritis, the poor hearing, the bad eyes and the heart trouble he's not in bad condition for a man his age. But despite the operation he's still got that prostate problem, of course, and so he'd have to field close to the pavilion. Added to which there is the fact that his Lordship has a little difficulty in bending.'

The trombonist, realising that his fellow musicians had stopped playing, gradually abandoned his solitary musical welcome.

'Do you play, doctor?' Biffo asked Rupert Fitzwalter.

'Certainly not!' said the doctor, quite firmly. 'I have my hands full attending to you lot. First there was Constable Hobbling's knee. Then it was Franklin's ankle. And then Len's arm. And Jack's foot. You lot don't just need a team doctor – you need your own MASH unit. You haven't got a healthy body between you.'

'What about Arthur Sturgeon?' suggested Itchy.

This suggestion was greeted with the sort of enthusiasm with which Hannibal might have responded if an aide had suggested using three-legged giraffes as an alternative to elephants. Cheesy made a noise like a chicken.

'Who's Arthur Sturgeon?' Biffo whispered to Puffy.

'He's the club scorer,' explained Puffy.

'I didn't know the club had a scorer!' said Biffo, strangely impressed by this minor revelation.

'He's been our scorer since he was a lad,' said Puffy.

'Has he never played cricket?' asked Biffo.

'Just once,' said Puffy. 'We were short of a player for a league match when Justin sprained his wrist opening a jar of marmalade. It was about ten or twelve years ago. Arthur scored nought, bowled one over for thirty four runs and dropped two easy catches. He proved himself to be probably the most uncoordinated human being alive. At the end of the match he went round all the other players asking them how we thought he'd done.'

Cheesy, apparently bored with the chicken impersonation started to work his way through the rest of his repertoire of farmyard animal impersonations.

'What did you tell him?'

'We told him that he had done very well and showed enormous promise but that he was far too valuable as a scorer to play in the team on a regular basis.'

'And he was happy with that?'

'I think so,' said Puffy. 'But for years afterwards he always drove around with his cricket bag in the boot of his car – just in case. We went to the Oval for a day at the Test Match a couple of years ago and Arthur insisted on carrying his cricket bag with him. He said that if one of the England players injured himself they might need someone to stand in for him.'

'Arthur always likes to be prepared,' said Cheesy. 'He was a boy scout.' He looked at Puffy. 'Wasn't that the day when there wasn't any play?'

'There's never any play when we go up to London for the Test Match,' said Puffy. 'I'm not sure that they ever actually play the matches.' He thought for a moment. 'When you're watching the match on television and it rains they always play scenes from old Tests. But when you've paid money and you're sitting there in the rain there's nothing at all to watch.'

'I lost £50 that day,' said Cheesy. 'It's coming back to me now.'

'One thing has always worried me about those old matches they show in black and white on the TV,' said Itchy. 'At the end, when Bradman had reached his hundred or his two hundred, or the match was over, all the blokes in the crowd would throw their hats into the air.'

Everyone agreed that they had noticed this. Cheesy began to perform his impersonation of a pig.

'So how did they all find their hats afterwards?' asked Itchy.

'How did you lose £50?' Biffo asked Cheesy.

'The ground staff spent the entire day taking the covers off and putting them back on again,' explained Puffy on Cheesy's behalf. 'We didn't have anything else to do, and we'd paid for our tickets, so we stayed there and watched them.'

'Since there wasn't any cricket to bet on we had a few bets on how long it would take the ground staff to get the covers on and off,' explained Cheesy, temporarily abandoning the pig noises. He shrugged and thought about it for a moment or two. 'They were quicker than I thought they'd be.'

'Consistently,' added Puffy.

Cheesy nodded but said nothing. The memory of his loss seemed to have depressed him.

'Well, if you don't want Arthur Sturgeon someone think of someone else,' said Itchy, rather grumpily. 'I was just trying to be helpful.' He stopped and thought for a moment. 'And I'm serious about all those hats. How did all those blokes find their own hats afterwards?'

Various other suggestions were made. All were dismissed quite quickly. The village of Fondling-Under-Water seemed to be extremely light on able bodied cricket players.

'Hats are expensive,' said Itchy, when the suggestions had dried up. 'And, besides, a man acquires an affection for a hat.' He reached up, as though to reassure himself that his own head covering was still in place. Comforted, he pulled his floppy white hat down a little more firmly.

There was a long silence.

'Perhaps we should ask Lady Hepplewhite,' suggested Biffo, tentatively.

Everyone looked at him and stared. Biffo felt himself blushing. He didn't know quite why but he felt embarrassed.

'Lady Hepplewhite?' said Cheesy, as though Biffo had suggested inviting the Man in the Moon to pop down for a match.

'She's a woman,' Itchy pointed out. He seemed genuinely surprised that Biffo had not noticed this.

'But Jack himself admitted that her bowling is pretty well unplayable,' said Biffo, dragging courage from some previously unknown source and bravely defending his suggestion. 'Maybe she could add a little something to our bowling attack.' His voice tailed off and he wished he hadn't spoken.

'It's an idea,' admitted Puffy, much to Biffo's surprise.

'We can't have a woman in the team!' said Itchy indignantly.

There was a lengthy silence. It seemed a quieter, heavier, more potent silence than the usual sort of everyday silence that simply doesn't contain any noise.

'Can you think of anyone else we can ask?' asked Paddy. 'It's a little off the wall but it could be a brilliant suggestion.' He looked at his watch. 'Besides, we haven't got all day to find another player. And I don't want to play this match with ten men.'

'You will be playing with ten men if you invite Lady Hepplewhite,' pointed out Len rather pedantically.

Suddenly, a shadow fell across the pavilion.

'Are you chaps ready to start this match?'

Everyone turned.

Cyril Player, dressed in his freshly-laundered cricket whites and ready for action, was standing in the doorway. He was surrounded by a halo of sunshine which gave him a strange, almost mystical look. He flipped a coin with his right thumb, watched while it span high up into the air, and then caught it neatly in his left hand. 'So, do you want to take your two innings one after the other? Or do you want to bat first and last, with us batting in the middle?'

'I think it would be sensible for us to bat first and last, Cyril,' said Paddy. 'It'll mean that your chaps can have a bit of fun with us and score as many as you like. If we take both our innings first you might end up needing to score just half a dozen runs. I'm sure that would disappoint many of the spectators.'

'No point in bothering with the toss then,' said the visitor's captain. He examined the coin carefully and pocketed it. 'That's the coin I used when I captained Surrey in the Bunson & Hodges Cup,' he remarked casually, as though he had only remembered this upon examining the coin. 'What's happening about my benefit collection?' he asked, looking around the pavilion.

'I suggest you get a couple of your chaps to take buckets round while we're batting,' said Paddy. 'We'll get our announcer to ask everyone to give generously.'

'Jolly good,' said Cyril.

'And, of course, I expect you'll have brought copies of your autobiography to sign. What was it called?'

"Running for Cover',' said Cyril. 'I've got a couple of hundred copies in the car. I'll sign them during the tea interval.'

'Splendid.' said Paddy. 'I'm sure they'll be very popular. Meanwhile, we do have one slight problem,' he said. 'One of our opening batsmen has been injured so we're short a player.' He hesitated. 'We're having a little difficulty finding a replacement at such short notice.' He paused and swallowed hard. 'Do you have any objection if we replace him with a woman?'

'No objection whatsoever,' said Cyril. 'You can play eleven women if you like.' He looked at the vicar, dressed in his white blouse and short skirt. 'Is that her?'

'Er, no,' said Paddy. 'That's the vicar.'

Cyril stared hard at the vicar and then back at Paddy and shrugged. 'I'm agnostic, myself,' he said, before heading for the door. He paused at the top of the steps. 'I can let you and members of your team have 10% discount on the price of my book,' he said generously. His studded boots clattered noisily on the pavilion steps as he trotted back out onto the field.

'He called me 'her'!' said the vicar. 'He thought I was a woman!' He was clearly thrilled by this. The melancholy aroused by Justin's caustic comment, had been lifted.

'Who's going to ask Lady Hepplewhite if she'll play?' Paddy asked.

'You ask her,' said Puffy. 'You're the vice captain.'

'Bill ought to ask her,' said Paddy. 'He's the captain.'

'I'm not asking her,' said Bill quickly. 'She's a woman. I don't want to go down in history as the man who brought a woman into the Fondling-Under-Water cricket team.' No one was tactless enough to mention that Bill was about to go down in history as the man who sold the cricket club ground.

'Biffo should ask her,' said Puffy. 'He rescued her from that fancy dress fiasco.'

'She hardly knows me!' protested Biffo.

'That's no problem,' said Puffy.

Outside Lady Hepplewhite was sitting waiting for the match to begin. She was blissfully unaware of the fact that her status was about to change from spectator to player.

~ Chapter 84 ~

WHILE RUPERT HAD BEEN EXAMINING Jack's swollen foot, and assorted members of the team had been struggling to help Justin escape from his disguise as a lemon, Percy had been working hard to keep the spectators amused in what appeared to be an unexpected hiatus in the proceedings.

The fancy dress competition, the egg and spoon race and the three-legged race were all over. And the caber had gone missing. The commentator's task had not been an easy one.

Percy, however, was feeling extremely comfortable in front of the microphone and he was doing his best to keep the crowd entertained. He was treating them to a philosophical monologue.

'Chopping your own wood, fetching your own reeds, thatching your own roof, these are proper occupations for a man,' he said. His rich, oak tones reverberating around the ground. 'We speak of the industrial revolution as though it was something to be proud of. But was it? Men were put into factories and terraced houses were built so that the occupants could be chained, day and night, to their grimy work benches. Machinery destroyed craftsmanship and with it went pride and joy and independence and enthusiasm. All these were replaced with dullness and boredom and dependence and insecurity and fear. Men were turned into servants and as the industrial revolution still goes on it becomes increasingly clear that it is not a revolution of the people for the people but a revolution for the rich. The people should have listened to Ned Ludd and the Tolpuddle Martyrs.'

Percy paused. It had occurred to him that Ned Ludd and

the Tolpuddle Martyrs sounded like a rock group and its lead singer. 'Let's hear it for Ned Ludd and the Tolpuddle Martyrs!' he cried out, to cheers from the crowd around the ground, most of whom did think that Ned Ludd and the Tolpuddle Martyrs must be rock stars.

'What the hell is Percy talking about?' hissed Paddy. The Fondling-Under-Water vice captain was proud of his ability to remain calm when circumstances justified panic but his taut neck muscles and staring eyes indicated that panic was not far away.

Percy paused again. He needed another drink.

~ Chapter 85 ~

'Psst!' hissed Lord Hepplewhite. He curled a finger in Paddy's direction, making it clear that he wanted to talk to him. Paddy excused himself, and stepped over to where the Lord was sitting.

'Have you invited my lady wife to play in the match?'

'Yes, my Lord,' admitted Paddy. 'Jack Hobbs has a bruised food and we're a player short. Lady Hepplewhite did bowl very effectively in the nets.'

'She's a woman!' shouted Lord Hepplewhite.

'Er...yes,' said Paddy. He looked over in Lady Hepplewhite's direction. Lord Hepplewhite's observation was indisputable. Lady Hepplewhite saw the vice captain looking in her direction and waved to him. Paddy blushed, smiled and shyly waved back. 'We had noticed that, My Lord,' he said.

'Had you noticed?'

'We had, my Lord.'

'That's all right, then,' said Lord Hepplewhite, a little calmer now. 'As long as you had noticed.'

'She's a remarkably good bowler,' said Paddy enthusiastically. 'I gather she specialises in underarm deliveries but Jack also says she's got a very good bouncer.'

'Good bouncers, did you say?' said Lord Hepplewhite, cupping a hand to his ear. Without waiting for a reply he nodded his agreement and winked at Paddy. 'You've got a good eye my boy. Exactly why I married her.' He winked again.

Paddy wasn't sure what the protocol was. Would he be considered rude if he didn't agree with Lord Hepplewhite? Or would it be more impertinent for him to agree? He decided to stick with the undeniable and risk impertinence. 'Yes, my Lord,' he said. 'Lovely bouncers.'

~ Chapter 86 ~

MRS BETTY CLEAVIDGE WAS DISTRAUGHT. She needed every ounce of courage she could muster not to bury her head in her pinafore and burst into tears.

Never before in her decades of making teas for the Fondling-Under-Water cricket team had there ever been any danger of the food running out. She felt deeply ashamed and embarrassed. She had long cherished her ability to feed the 5,000, however hungry they might be, but the first tea interval hadn't yet arrived and bald patches were already appearing on trestle tables upon which stores of pasties, pies, tarts, sandwiches and cakes should have been piled high.

Not for one moment did she think of blaming those who had demolished her carefully prepared mountains of food.

It was her job to make sure that there was plenty of food available. And if the food ran out it was her fault. She was not a woman who shied away from responsibility. She had authority over the preparation of food for the Fondling-Under-Water cricket team. And with that authority went responsibility. She was not interested in excuses or explanations.

'Life is simple enough,' she said to the vicar's wife. 'My responsibility is to make sure that there is plenty of food to go round. If there isn't enough food to go round then I have failed those who put their trust in me.'

How could she possibly blame those who had eaten the food she had made? Was not food made to be eaten?

But Mrs Cleavidge was not a weak woman. In a crisis she had unplumbed depths. And from deep within her tortured soul she had garnered every ounce of strength she could find. She was not going to succumb. She was going to make sure that everyone had plenty to eat. And there was only one way to do this.

'Can you manage by yourself for a while?' she asked her most senior assistant, Mrs Stilton; partner, cook, laundress, masseuse and darner to the Fondling-Under-Water star whose name she shared.

Cheesy's wife, whose bust and hip measurements had grown with and matched her age every year since her early 30s (her age, bust and hips had now all reached the commendable figure of 46), was a dependable and hard working sort. Mrs Cleavidge had no hesitation in putting the immediate moment to moment management of the trestle tables, and the tea making, into her capable and experienced hands. Mrs Cleavidge did not delegate easily and she would not have handed over the custody of the urn to anyone else.

Mrs Cleavidge's big problem was that her own cottage, complete with the kitchen which had spawned galaxies of cream horns, jam tarts, Black Forest gateaux, Victoria sponges, mince pies and endless pots of chutney, was three miles away as the crow flies and nearly half as far again for those who do not have wings.

Mrs Cleavidge looked around. The obvious solution was standing no more than a few yards away from her.

'Mrs Counter!' called Mrs Cleavidge. 'May I have a word?'

The vicar's wife bustled over from her post. She had been dispensing plastic beakers full of orange squash to a line of small boys which seemed to her to be endless. (This was because the line of small boys was, indeed, endless. As each boy left the front of the queue clutching his beaker of orange squash he would walk around and join the back of the queue again. This was not because the boys were thirsty but because they were having a competition to see who could collect the most beakers.)

'Do you mind if I use your kitchen?' Mrs Cleavidge asked the vicar's wife. 'I need to rustle up some quick pasties for teatime.'

'Help yourself, dear,' replied Mrs Counter. 'The back door's open. Just let yourself in. But I'm not sure how much food there is in the larder.'

'Don't you worry about food,' said Mrs Cleavidge, unfastening her pinafore. 'I'll pop into Miss Box's shop on the way round.'

And with that she was off.

~ Chapter 87 ~

'AH, THERE YOU ARE, FRANKLIN!' said Paddy, when he saw the Fondling-Under-Water umpire being wheeled towards the stumps.

'What are you doing!' yelled Itchy running across to protest. 'You can't wheel that thing all over the pitch.'

'We'll make sure it doesn't go on the wicket,' said Paddy, with a comforting wave of his hand. Itchy did not seem convinced. 'It's the only way Franklin can umpire,' added the vice captain. He looked down at Franklin and beamed with genuine delight. 'I must say, Franklin,' he said, 'that you are looking very fit and healthy after your accident.'

'How's he going to signal leg byes?' asked Itchy, uncharacteristically putting an oil-stained finger on a problem no one else had foreseen.

'The umpire stands on one leg to signal a leg bye, doesn't he?' asked Franklin, though it wasn't so much a question as a snarl.

Itchy thought for a few moments. 'Yes,' he agreed. 'I suppose so.'

'Well standing on one leg is the one thing I'm really good at,' snapped Franklin.

'I'd like you to meet the visiting team's umpire,' said Paddy, turning slightly. For the first time Franklin saw that behind Paddy there was standing a leggy blonde, wearing fishnet stockings, a pelmet-length black skirt and a see-through purple blouse. She wore a shoulder-length blonde wig.

'This is Lotti,' said Paddy. 'Lotti, this is Franklin Minton, our umpire. He's been in an accident – hence the wheelchair.'

'Pleased to meet you,' said Lotti, holding out a hand. Her nails, which were painted purple to match her blouse, were as long as penknife blades. Franklin took her hand gingerly. He tried not to look at what was on display under the purple blouse. Since he was sitting in a wheelchair and Lotti was bending down towards him this was not easy. There wasn't much else to look at.

'Lotti, who is Tom Morton's girlfriend, has an advanced diploma in physical education,' said Paddy. 'She tells me that she doesn't know terribly much about cricket but she has nevertheless kindly agreed to take an end for this match.'

'I've done theoretical hockey,' said Lotti.

Paddy frowned and looked at her. 'What, er, what exactly is theoretical hockey?' he asked.

'Well the college I attended didn't actually have any sports fields and so we couldn't actually play any of the games we learned about,' explained Lotti. 'So we studied them from a theoretical point of view.'

'Ah.' said Paddy, as though he understood. He didn't understand and didn't really think he wanted to.

'And there can't be a lot of difference between cricket and hockey can there?' said Lotti. 'They're both played with a ball and a stick after all!' She didn't look like the sort of girl who played a lot of outdoor ball games.

'Er, I think you'll find that there are one or two slight differences,' said Paddy, cautiously.

'But I'm sure everything will be OK,' said Lotti. 'Tom showed me how to do this,' she continued, holding a finger up in front of her. 'I'm supposed to do it when he yells 'Howzat?'' She looked around, clearly pleased that she had remembered this complicated manoeuvre. 'Besides,' went on Lotti, proudly and confidently sharing the details of her secret weapon. 'I've brought my camera with me for any difficult decisions.'

Franklin and Paddy looked at her and then at one another but no one spoke.

Lotti took a thin strapped white plastic handbag off her shoulder, reached into it and pulled out an instant camera.

'Here you are!' she said proudly. 'It takes photographs and then prints them out instant...instantan...all at once. Fashion photographers use them all the time.'

Franklin looked at her carefully. 'You're planning to use that,' he nodded at the camera, 'to help you make decisions?'

'Oh yes!' said Lotti. She looked very pleased with herself. 'If there's anything controversial I'll take a photograph and then we'll all look at the print together and you can help me make a decision.' The way she explained things it almost sounded sensible.

No one spoke. No one wanted to contradict Tom Morton's girlfriend.

~ Chapter 88 ~

AT LONG LAST THE BIG match was about to start. The atmosphere was heavy with expectation and excitement. This was a moment for which the villagers had waited for some considerable time. They were keen to see the famous cricketing legends of the visiting side. But they were keener still to see their own local heroes do battle. No one really expected the Fondling-Under-Water players to win. The spectators simply hoped that they would acquit themselves with dignity. After all, every run scored and wicket taken would be a victory against opposition of such imposing calibre.

The visiting captain had arranged his fielders with the skill and precision for which he liked to think he would one day be remembered by generations not yet born.

In his heart he knew that as a batsman his career had been just slightly better than mediocre. As a bowler, he knew that the best that could be said was that he had always bowled a good line and a reliable length. Arthritis in his shoulder meant that his bowling days had been over for some time. He had been lucky to play for England and he knew it. His hope now was that he would be remembered for his captaincy skills.

Four slips, two gullies, a forward short leg and an unusually silly mid on made it clear that the visiting captain was in an aggressive mood. Cyril Player was back where it had all started so many seasons, and so many overs ago. He was determined to show the villagers the titan he had become.

Tom Morton, a gleam in his eye, fire in his belly (he had eaten a particularly hot curry the night before) and a brand new cricket ball in his right hand was pacing out his run up.

Michael Hunt, currently fielding at long leg, was doing vigorous shoulder-loosening exercises to let the spectators and the captain know that he would be opening the bowling at the other end.

Around the boundary edge press photographers were loading their cameras, feeding their motor drives with fresh batteries and sharpening up the focus on their telephoto lenses.

At the end from which Tom Morton was due to bowl Franklin Minton was sitting in his wheelchair with Mr Morton's long-sleeved England sweater draped around his shoulders. Looking around at the array of cricketing talent displayed before him Franklin could, at least until the Fondling-Under-Water opening batsmen arrived at the crease, believe that he was umpiring in a Test Match. Just as some cricketers dream of playing cricket for their country so Franklin dreamt of raising his finger at international level.

At square leg the luscious Lotti, far less impressed than Franklin Minton, was touching up her nail polish just in case she needed to give anyone out. She did not want to embarrass herself, or Tom, by holding up a finger upon which the nail varnish was chipped.

'We have two umpires today,' announced Percy Kempton, helpfully. 'To help you differentiate between the two I can tell you that at one end we have Mr Franklin Minton. He is wearing the white coat. Our second umpire, at the other end, is the lovely Lotti....' There was a pause while Percy flicked, unsuccessfully, through his notes looking in vain for Lotti's second name. 'Our second umpire is the lovely...er...Lotti,' he said again. 'You can identify her by the fact that she is not wearing a white coat.'

Around the boundary edge several members of Betty Cleavidge's sandwich making squad were taking a few moments off from wielding their butter knives to collect donations from the spectators. The buckets they carried were all labelled with small notices stating that money collected would go towards the purchase of a new lawnmower.

And striding out to the wicket were the two opening batsmen for the Fondling-Under-Water cricket club: Herbert Sutcliffe and Paddy Fields. Both wore pads and both carried bats which had lots of red marks down the edges but no marks at all in the middle. But only Herbert, due to face the first ball, was wearing a helmet. Constable Hobbling's motorcycle helmet would be worn by whichever batsman was due to stand in the firing line.

Back in the pavilion, the waiting batsmen fidgeted nervously. There was tension there, and all around the ground.

When Paddy and Herbert reached the wicket they stopped for a moment. Paddy took off one of his batting gloves and held out his hand to Herbert. 'Good luck!' he whispered.

'Thanks Paddy,' said Herbert, removing one of his own gloves and shaking hands with the club vice captain. 'I'll do my best.'

'I know you will,' said Paddy. 'And no man can ask more than that, from you or from anyone.' He had to fight hard to swallow a lump in his throat.

Herbert nodded and walked down the pitch to take up his position in front of his stumps.

'Herbert looks imposing doesn't he!' Biffo said to Puffy in the pavilion. 'Just look at him. Head held high. Eyes looking straight ahead. No man went in front of a firing squad with more courage.'

(Not until it was his turn to bat, and wear Constable Hobbling's motorcycle helmet, did Biffo discover that the design of the helmet was such that it was quite impossible to see anything at all unless one held one's head high and looked straight ahead.)

'Middle and leg, please umpire,' said Herbert, grounding his bat in front of his stumps. In response to Franklin's direction he moved his bat a quarter of an inch one way and then half an inch the other way. When he was thoroughly satisfied he made himself a mark on Itchy's virgin turf.

Franklin turned his head and peered over his shoulder. It was, he discovered, difficult to look behind you when you were sitting in a wheelchair. It hurt his neck and he decided not to do it again. In the distance, far, far behind him he could just see Tom Morton standing motionless on the outfield.

For Franklin, as well as the Fondling-Under-Water batsmen, this was the moment of truth. He hoped he would have the courage to be fair. More significant, perhaps, he hoped he would have the eyesight to see the ball when Tom bowled.

'Play!' he called.

His voice sounded much hoarser and drier than he remembered it.

Franklin had for years warmed the cockles and muscles of his heart by planning his autobiography. (He already had a title. His book was going to be called 'The Umpire Strikes Back'.) He might not have umpired at international level but now he could at least tell his readers that he had told international players what to do and when to do it.

The single four letter word starting the match had hardly escaped his lips when high overhead a small aeroplane flew into sight. It could be heard buzzing away like some gargantuan fly. On the boundary's edge the members of the brass band tilted back their heads as though they were connected together by steel rods. They all wanted to check that there was indeed an aeroplane overhead.

And within the briefest of brief moments a tiny figure, seemingly no bigger than a child's doll, emerged from the aeroplane and started to plummet down towards the little piece of the planet known as Fondling-Under-Water.

This time there was no doubt. This was no buzzard, no seagull, no high-flying swallow or swift. The long-awaited parachutist was on his way. And with enthusiasm more than making up for any lack of ability, talent, training or skill the brass band burst, as they had been instructed so to do, into their much awaited and spirited rendition of 'Those Magnificent Men In Their Flying Machines'.

On dark winter evenings, when there is frost and mist outside and cricket consists of nothing but past memories and future hopes, there is still discussion in The Gravedigger's Rest about whether or not Herbert Sutcliffe was distracted by this sudden and spirited musical interruption.

But the fact is that neither he nor Franklin Minton, nor indeed Paddy Fields, saw Tom Morton's first ball. Travelling at somewhere between 80 and 90 miles per hour it pitched on a perfect length, deviated off the pitch just a fraction and neatly removed Herbert's off stump completely, sending it and both bails flying back towards the wicket keeper.

The parachutist, gliding slowly and silently down to earth, waved at the people he saw below. No one waved back. He thought this very odd. People usually waved and cheered and jumped up and down a lot when he arrived. They were all staring at something that was happening in the field below him.

Franklin Minton, the umpire, had nothing to do. There was no need for appeal or consultation. Herbert Sutcliffe was as out as any batsman can be.

Naturally, Herbert was unhappy about his dismissal, as indeed were his colleagues back in the pavilion. And the scorebook in which Arthur Sturgeon had neatly pencilled in the details of Herbert's innings showed quite clearly that the Fondling-Under-Water opening batsman had been dismissed for nought, bowled first ball by Tom Morton, and that the Fondling-Under-Water team had lost their first wicket without scoring a run.

'And that's the first wicket to fall,' announced Percy Kempton. He peered at the batsman trudging back towards the pavilion but couldn't identify him. He certainly didn't know the name of the bowler. He suddenly realised that he didn't have the foggiest idea which side was batting and which side was fielding. 'For those of you keeping score I can tell you that one of the batsmen is out,' said Percy. He paused. 'And it seems that one of the opposing bowlers has taken a wicket.' He took a nip from his flask and congratulated himself on handling the situation so well. Knowing virtually nothing about cricket, and knowing so few of the players by sight, he had harboured some slight fears about his suitability for the job of cricket commentator. A few sips of sustaining fluid had helped make these fears disappear.

Franklin was suddenly aware that a large figure was blotting out much of the daylight. 'Can I have my sweater?' asked the successful bowler. 'I don't want to get cold while the next batsmen comes out.'

'It's all tied up neatly now,' said Franklin, who liked having Tom Morton's thick, cosy, white sweater wrapped around his shoulders. He didn't want to give it back. He liked being wrapped up in an England sweater.

'I want my sweater!' insisted the fast bowler. He had never been accused of being a polite person. Stubborn, rude, arrogant, bad tempered, vicious – all these things he had been called. But never polite.

'Well you can't have it!' said Franklin. He clutched at the jumper and looked up at Tom Morton defiantly. Tom seethed.

Moments later the parachutist landed gracefully at midwicket. His arrival was greeted with total silence. He looked around, puzzled. Feeling distinctly embarrassed, like a guest who realises he is at the wrong party, and suspecting that he must have been dropped on the wrong field, he quietly cursed the pilot of the aeroplane, collected together his parachute, rolled it into an untidy bundle and trudged off red-faced towards the pavilion hoping that he might find a telephone so that he could ring and ask his mother to come and fetch him.

Tom Morton, now furious, raised an arm to hit the umpire but out of the corner of his eye he saw the row of telephoto lenses at the boundary edge. He wasn't blessed with great intelligence, or sympathy towards the feelings of others, but he knew that even in professional cricket circles it would not do his reputation any good to be photographed knocking over an umpire.

At the back of his mind he even had an idea that knocking over an umpire who was confined to a wheelchair might be even worse than knocking over an umpire who was standing up. And so he didn't hit Franklin. But as he walked away Tom was still seething. Someone called his name and without even bothering to look he automatically put out a hand and caught the ball that had been thrown to him.

He was not a happy bunny.

~ Chapter 89 ~

Percy, like most males who are loosely involved with the world of show business, had always liked cricket, even though he had never really understood what was happening on the other side of the little white fence which invariably, and quite properly, separated the professional players from the amateur spectators.

During his years at the BBC it had been common practice for him, usually together with several colleagues, to totter out of the BBC headquarters in Portland Place and head north across the Marylebone Road, around the edge of Regent's Park and into St John's Wood and Lord's Cricket Ground.

The main attractions were the all day bar and the chance of a little fresh air and sunshine but Percy had never objected to the cricket matches which invariably also seemed to be going on there when he visited.

'I have nothing against cricket,' he once said. 'But the best bit about it is that they let you drink all day long.'

Sipping at his beer, Percy watched Puffy Harbottle take Herbert Sutcliffe's place at the crease

Two minutes later Puffy was back in the pavilion insisting that the ball with which he had been bowled must have been a 'no ball'.

'No one could bowl that fast without overstepping the crease by at least ten yards,' he insisted. 'Franklin must be blind. Sitting in that wheelchair is probably restricting his field of vision.'

By the end of Tom Morton's first over the Fondling-Under-Water cricket club had lost three wickets for no runs.

'If we're not careful this match is going to be all over in twenty minutes' time,' said Justin, watching from the pavilion. The wicket keeper, still dressed as a lemon, turned to Cheesy Stilton, who was buckling on the pads which just a moment or two earlier had been fastened around the previous batsman's legs. 'You'll have to try and stretch things out a bit,' he said.

Cheesy stopped buckling for a moment and looked Justin in the eye. 'Have you any suggestions as to how I might do that?'

'I don't know!' retorted Justin. 'Do I have to think of everything?' He thought for a moment. 'Appeal against the light. Tell the umpire you think that Tom Morton's action is suspect. I'm pretty sure an umpire in the West Indies once called him for throwing. Find a dandelion in the middle of the pitch that needs digging out.'

'There are no dandelions in the middle of my pitch!' said Itchy indignantly. It was impossible to criticise Itchy's wickets within the county without him hearing about it immediately if not sooner.

Wishing to avoid further uninvited conflict Cheesy picked up Herbert's bat and marched out of the pavilion.

At the far end of the ground Michael Hunt was polishing the ball on his trousers and keenly awaiting the arrival of the new batsman. He had already managed to produce a nice red streak down his right thigh. He had been thinking of bowling at half or three quarter pace – just to give the villager players a chance – but Tom Morton's success at the pavilion end had made that an impossibility. If Tom was going to bowl flat out then he had to bowl flat out too. He didn't want to drive home at the end of the day without having taken a wicket. He looked down at the red streak he had produced and rubbed the ball against his thigh a little harder; while he did so he took the opportunity to pick at the seam with his thumb nail.

Fired up by the exchange with the wicket keeper Cheesy was keen to do battle with the opposition. He marched straight to the vacant crease and started to dig a small hole in front of his stumps. He wasn't sure why he was doing this, and he knew it offended Itchy, but every batsman he had ever seen had done it so he always did it.

'How are you feeling?' asked a familiar voice.

Cheesy looked up to see a pale looking Paddy trying to grin at him. Paddy had not yet faced a ball but had had to stand and watch while three of his best batsman had been dismissed. The grin was not convincing.

'Maybe it will rain,' said Cheesy hopefully.

Paddy looked up at the sky. It didn't look as though it was going to rain. There were even rays of sunshine poking through.

'Perhaps we could get that aeroplane which dropped the

parachutist to come back,' said Cheesy. 'We could give him a watering can and tell him to fly round and round in circles.'

'Let's keep that as a back up plan!' said Paddy, smiling at last.

'Are you two playing cricket or would you like someone to bring out a couple of deck chairs, a pot of tea and a plate of cakes?' shouted Cyril Player. He nodded towards the end from which Michael Hunt was waiting to bowl. 'The umpire is waiting,' he said. 'And it's not polite to keep a lady waiting.'

Paddy and Cheesy looked first at him and then at the stumps at the non-striker's end. Tom Morton's girlfriend, Lotti, saw them looking. She smiled at them and waved with her right hand. She was holding her camera in her left hand. Her white plastic handbag was on the ground, leaning against the stumps at her feet.

'Good luck!' said Cheesy.

'Thanks,' said Paddy, walking back to his crease. 'I think I may need it.'

'Are you ready?' called Lotti.

'As ready as I'll ever be,' replied Paddy. He twirled his bat, looked around the field and muttered a short prayer to whichever saint looks after batsmen and lost causes.

Thirty seconds later, on his way back to the pavilion, he handed Constable Hobbling's motor cycle helmet to Helmut Walton.

'Was it the inswinger?' asked Helmut.

'Was what the inswinger?' asked Paddy.

'The ball that bowled you. Michael Hunt has a vicious inswinger.'

'I don't have the foggiest idea whether it was an inswinger, an outswinger or an unidentified flying object,' confessed Paddy. 'I didn't see it at all. One moment I was standing there waiting for him to bowl and the next he was dancing down the pitch with a bloody great grin across his face. When I turned round I could see the wicket keeper wandering around picking up stumps and bails and so I had a pretty good idea I was probably out.'

'Ah,' nodded Helmut wisely. 'I have a theory,' he said. 'I am going down the wicket to rush just before he bowls.'

Paddy stared at him. 'You're going to what?'

'I am going down the wicket to rush just before he bowls,' repeated Helmut.

'You're mad,' said Paddy.

'Yes, that is probably true,' admitted Helmut. 'But this is my theory: the further down the wicket I run the less of my stumps the bowler can see and the more difficult it will be for the umpire to out give me if the ball hits my person!'

Paddy thought about this for a moment. 'I suppose you're right,' he admitted at last. 'But aren't you worried that you'll be hit?'

'Oh no,' said Helmut. He bent a little closer to Paddy. 'I have protection,' he confided. 'I have tucked newspaper under my shirt and another down inside of my trousers.'

'Oh,' said Paddy. He thought about this. 'Oh,' he said again. 'Well good luck then,' he added, before continuing his slow, long walk back to the pavilion. He decided that there might be some sense in Helmut's theory but that he would be unwilling to try it even if he had a full set of the Encyclopedia Britannica tucked under his shirt and a set of London telephone directories stuffed down the front of his trousers.

~ Chapter 90 ~

WHEN PADDY FIELDS WAS DISMISSED and Helmut Walton went out to bat, Fondling-Under-Water had lost their first four wickets without scoring a run.

By the end of Michael Hunt's first over Helmut had shown that, with the notable exception of his wife (whom, it must be said, he loved dearly) he was afraid of nothing and no-one.

When, still five or six yards away from the wicket, Michael Hunt looked up to make sure that he was still heading in the correct direction, he was flabbergasted to see that instead of standing cowering in his crease the batsman, a huge, bear-like figure with a massive moustache, was racing up the wicket towards him.

'He's not supposed to do that!' Hunt just had time to think. But it was too late for him to stop running in and too late for him to hold onto the ball. He was on automatic pilot and nothing, with the possible exception of the sudden erection of a brick wall, could stop him.

Helmut was half way down the pitch, furiously swinging his bat, when the second ball hit him. It bounced off his shoulder, soared over mid-wicket's head and raced away towards the boundary.

'Run!' screamed Helmut, who was still whirling his bat around his head.

Cheesy, who had been trying hard to think of something sympathetic to say to the next incoming batsman had, when he had seen his team-mate racing towards him, assumed that Helmut was merely saving time by running back to the pavilion before he was actually out. The suggestion that they might actually get some runs completely threw him.

As it happened, Cheesy's hesitation did not matter a great deal. The visiting captain's aggressive field placing meant that none of the visiting team was able to prevent the ball racing away to the boundary.

Helmut's unorthodox approach to batting did not go unnoticed.

In some quarters it caused confusion – even consternation.

Franklin Minton, standing, or rather sitting, at square leg, was trying to decide whether there was a limit to the extent to which a batsman was allowed to charge down the wicket and, if not, whether it was permissible for a batsman to shoulder charge the bowler before he let go of the ball. And would the batsman then be allowed to hit the ball if the bowler dropped it?

His umpiring colleague, Lotti, had retreated in dismay when she saw Helmut charging towards her. She had been convinced that he had gone mad and was about to attack her with the big wooden thing he was carrying.

Tom Morton, who was still seething over whatever it was that had made him seethe before (he had forgotten why he was seething but had not forgotten to seethe) was now fuming as well since it seemed to him that once you let batsmen stop being frightened of you they will start taking all sorts of liberties.

But by no means all those who observed Helmut's gallant attempt to prove that attack is the best form of defence were dismayed.

In the pavilion the nine elevenths of the Fondling-Under-Water team who were not actively involved in the game were as close to ecstasy as cricketers can be when their eleven minute old innings has resulted in the loss of four wickets for just four runs.

And Percy Kempton, sitting in front of the microphone, decided that this was the moment to abandon all pretence at impartiality and firmly to nail his colours to the mast.

When he had worked for the BBC he had been taught that commentators must at all times endeavour to disguise any feelings of favouritism to which they might be prey.

'The reporter is an invisible fly forever hovering above the manure of human existence,' an esteemed but long dead producer had once written in a BBC training manual.

But Percy was no longer working for the BBC and Helmut Walton's valiant refusal to lie down and accept defeat had aroused within him strong feelings which he was not prepared to ignore.

'Go get 'em, Helmut!' he roared, all caution thrown to the winds.

On the pitch the contestants were preparing themselves for the next round of a contest which no longer seemed to be following the expected route.

Michael Hunt, a cricketer who would, in an intelligence test, have found it something of a strain to give a block of wood a hard time, had decided that the best way to combat Helmut Walton's aggressive approach to batting was to take an even longer run and bowl even faster. He had, therefore, retreated to the boundary's edge in preparation for his second delivery.

Helmut, on the other hand, had decided to vary his approach. Rightly concluding that his down the wicket charge might have slightly annoyed the England bowler (evidence supporting this conclusion was not difficult to come by – fish or vegetables held a few inches away from Michael Hunt's ears would have been nicely steamed within five minutes or so) he decided, instead, to stay in his crease and simply try to keep out of the firing line.

Meanwhile, Percy was desperately trying to think of something to say.

Football fans are known to turn the names of their favourite teams into slogans at the peep of a referee's whistle or the raising of a linesman's flag. 'Liverpool' or 'Arsenal' they will sing, stretching the appropriate syllables out into a chorus without making the result sound in the slightest bit contrived.

It is not easy to turn the name 'Fondling-Under-Water' into a crowd pleasing hymn but Percy was not about to allow himself to be worried by such a minor consideration.

'Give me an F,' he began, vaguely remembering one of the chants he had heard during a visit to Stamford Bridge and attempting to adapt it to fit the circumstances. 'Give me an O, give me an N, give me a D, give me a...'

At this point Percy rather lost his way and had to stop and think for a moment. Eventually he found a roughly printed score card which he had been given. This made things considerably easier. 'Give me an L, give me an I, give me an N, give me a G,' he continued, using his finger to help him keep track of where he was. The crowd, catching on to what he wanted, started shouting out letters of the alphabet, though since their efforts were not synchronised the result was rather confusing.

After the 'G' Percy paused, unsure about what to do next.

Michael Hunt was also in uncharted waters. He had never actually run as far as he was now attempting to run – not, at least, at full pace – and he was beginning to feel a little short of breath. Fifteen yards from the stumps he felt as though his chest was about to burst and he had to slow down a little. Five yards from the stumps he had to slow down a lot. By the time he reached the stumps at the bowler's end, and was ready to deliver the ball, he had virtually stopped moving. The result was a fairly gentle full toss which Helmut, now standing well back in his crease, had plenty of time to see and to play.

'Give me a little space,' said Percy, regaining his enthusiasm and continuing with exhortations to the crowd. 'A little gap,' he explained.

The spectators who had been following his instructions as faithfully as they had been able were thrown by this exhortation. One man shouted 'little space' and a boy shouted 'little gap', several women simply 'space'.

Beyond the boundary's edge Helmut's wife, watching her husband bat for the first time in her life, and feeling so proud of him that she uncharacteristically vowed to herself that one evening she would, as a treat, let him stay in The Gravedigger's Rest for twice his normal allowance, shouted out 'space'. She followed this by shouting out 'gap' just to be on the safe side.

At the time some critics claimed (and, indeed, there are those who still do) that Helmut's second consecutive boundary shot off Michael Hunt's bowling was even luckier than the first.

But this is akin to hair splitting; an activity to be contemplated only by the slight in spirit and the small in heart. The important thing is that Helmut swung his bat, his bat collided in mid air with the ball and the end result was an immediate doubling of the Fondling-Under-Water Cricket Club score.

The fact that Michael Hunt's third delivery removed Helmut's middle stump could not detract from the magnificence of a breathtaking innings from the winner of a previous season's award for the 'Best Middle Order Batsman of the Second Half of the Season'.

It would have been difficult that day to find anyone in Fondling-Under-Water who did not feel that Helmut well deserved the standing ovation he received from the crowd and his team mates. His innings had lasted for three balls and he had scored eight runs. He was a hero.

~ Chapter 91 ~

THE END OF HELMUT WALTON'S innings marked the high point and the beginning of a sad down turn in the fortunes of the Fondling-Under-Water cricket club.

Biffo managed to get his (borrowed) bat onto the ball but sadly only succeeded in deflecting the latter onto his stumps. Cheesy, determined to go down fighting, skied a ball that stayed in the air long enough for the wicket keeper, by far the youngest and fittest member of the visiting side, to run to deep mid-wicket to take the catch.

The arrival at the crease of the Reverend Counter in his blouse and borrowed tennis skirt caused some consternation among members of the visiting side but it was, perhaps, when he was joined at the crease by Justin, still stuck in his costume and dressed as a lemon, that they began to lose their concentration a little.

Sadly, despite their not insignificant psychological advantage the lemon and the vicar in a skirt failed to add noticeably to the village team's score. (It would be more precise to say that they didn't actually manage to add anything at all.) The lemon, who had been unable to fit Constable Hobbling's motor cycle helmet onto his head but whose vision and ability to hold the bat were both impaired by his costume, was bowled around his lemon coloured legs for a duck while the vicar, who claimed later to have been attempting to play a terribly fine leg glance, was caught behind by the wicket keeper.

Constable Hobbling, who had rather surprised those members of the fielding side who had guilty consciences by toddling out to bat dressed not in cricket whites but police blues, and who had the unique advantage of being able to bat in a helmet which actually fitted his head, played two doughty forward defensive strokes before being controversially given out leg before wicket to a ball from Tom Morton. The finger which gave him out was raised by the delectable Lotti. (Constable Hobbling obtained remarkably little comfort from the subsequent revelation that Lotti had merely been examining the condition of her nail varnish at the time.)

Lady Hepplewhite, took the home side score into double figures when Michael Hunt, overcome by an entirely unprecedented and unexpected attack of gallantry, bowled her a gentle full toss. Mr Hunt was forced to watch in dismay (he also felt deeply betrayed) as Lady Hepplewhite drove the ball firmly through the covers for four. When Constable Hobbling was dismissed Lady Hepplewhite was left undefeated.

When the Fondling-Under-Water first innings finally

closed, just thirty seven minutes after it had started, the village team had scored a not terribly grand total of twelve runs. There had been but three scoring strokes.

The fielding side, the arrogance with which they had arrived now strengthened by the success their skills had wrought, strode towards the pavilion like giants. Not one of them seemed an inch under ten feet tall.

Overcome with a feeling of generosity which he would later greatly regret Cyril Player took out his wallet and casually tossed a crisp ten pound note into one of the buckets which were being used to collect money for the new lawnmower fund. He managed to turn this simple act into a dramatic gesture. The whole event, from the withdrawing of his wallet from his back pocket to the final flutter of the ten pound note into the bottom of the bucket, lasted quite long enough to be seen by everyone within fifty yards of the pavilion steps.

'I think you'll find that this is the first of today's two tea intervals,' announced Percy Kempton, reading from the hand written time table of events with which he had been supplied. 'What an exciting match this is turning out to be,' he continued. 'It's clear that there is going to be a tense finish – so don't go away!'

There was a pause and a slight rustle as he moved one piece of paper out of the way and brought another into vision. 'The Fondling-Under-Water Cricket Club is pleased to announce that during this interval international cricketing star Cyril Player will be signing copies of his new book at a table just in front of the pavilion,' announced Percy.

~ Chapter 92 ~

PERCY'S VOICE HAD HARDLY FADED when another, almost equally loud voice, could be heard just outside the pavilion.

'P.C.Hobbling!'

The voice was so loud and so commanding that everyone in or near to the pavilion stopped talking or eating and turned to stare at the source of the sound. This turned out to be a tall, extremely thin, gaunt-faced police inspector who wore a blue uniform and, to show the world that he was above the rank of constable, a prettily-decorated flat hat. The policeman had an unusually small head (it was, nevertheless, perfectly adequately proportioned for the brain it contained) and the hat, the smallest which the police stores were able to supply, sat a little low and rested on the tops of his ears, pushing them down slightly. This gave him a strange, almost extra-terrestrial look

Constable Hobbling, who had been sitting at the back of the pavilion attempting to soothe his troubled spirit with a cup of tea and a plate of egg and cress sandwiches, rushed forward in obedient response to the call from his superior officer.

As soon as he saw the cadaverous figure who had called his name he slammed his heels together, sprang to attention and saluted.

The impressive effect of this combination of slickly executed movements was slightly diminished by the fact that he had forgotten to remove the egg and cress sandwich from the hand with which he saluted. The resulting impact of sandwich on helmet did not add a great deal to the impression he gave. It didn't do much for his confidence, either. When Betty Cleavidge made an egg and cress sandwich she used plenty of egg, plenty of cress and plenty of butter.

'I'd like a word,' said the cadaverous police inspector. He then performed a neat, one hundred and eighty degree turn and marched away from the pavilion.

Pausing only to wipe the egg and the cress from his ear, his helmet and his uniform collar Constable Hobbling hurried down the steps and followed close behind.

~ Chapter 93 ~

MEANWHILE, BACK IN THE PAVILION, Paddy put away his mobile phone and grinned.

'I have some good news', he said. 'Bill, you'll be particularly interested in this.'

The other players looked at their vice captain. The more

energetic among them raised querulous eyebrows.

'That was my cousin,' said Paddy. 'He's been looking through some old planning files in his office...'

~ Chapter 94 ~

ACCORDING TO THE HISTORY BOOKS the return of Napoleon to Paris, after his exile on the island of Elba, was a time of unprecedented, and subsequently unequalled personal glory.

But when today's historians write the story of our century they will have a new example of personal victory to share top spot with Monsieur Bonaparte's days of triumph.

Mrs Betty Cleavidge arrived back at the Fondling-Under-Water cricket ground less than five minutes after the start of the first tea interval.

It had been decided that since the two teams were between them playing three innings there should be two tea intervals; one after the first Fondling-Under-Water innings and before the only innings the professionals would have, and one after the professionals had batted and before the Fondling-Under-Water players had their second innings.

This simple plan suited Cyril Player very well for it gave him two opportunities to sign copies of his book and, hopefully, to increase the size of his benefit fund.

Mrs Cleavidge, pushing the vicar's wheelbarrow with zeal, determination and a pair of arms which would not have looked out of place if worn by a heavyweight boxing champion, arrived back on the ground eager and ready to fill hungry stomachs during the first of these two intervals. As she arrived she was surprised to see Bill, the Fondling-Under-Water Cricket Club captain, go running off down the lane. She was curious but she had other things on her mind.

'What on earth have you got there, Mrs Cleavidge?' asked the doughty Mrs Stilton, peering at the wheelbarrow.

'Pasties, Mrs Stilton!' replied Mrs Cleavidge glowing with pride and the physical consequences of her exertions.

The distance from the vicarage to the cricket ground is

not a great one for a pedestrian carrying, say, a shopping bag filled with a loaf of bread, a bottle of milk and a pound of tomatoes. But Mrs Cleavidge had made far too many pasties to carry in shopping bags. And a wheelbarrow which is piled high with pasties requires a considerable amount of pushing.

Mrs Cleavidge lowered the handles of the wheelbarrow, pulled back the two tea towels with which she had protected her handiwork for the duration of the journey, and rubbed at her lower back. Quite justifiably she felt very pleased with herself.

'My, oh my,' said Mrs Stilton who had probably avoided considerable disappointment in her life by never having exhibited any inclination to appear on Mastermind or take part in the Brain of Britain competition.

'Good heavens!' said Mrs Counter, the vicar's wife. 'Do you think they'll eat that many pasties?'

'I hope not!' replied Mrs Cleavidge. 'If there aren't some left over I won't know for sure that I've made enough, will I?'

'Quite right, quite right, Mrs Cleavidge,' answered Mrs Counter. 'I hadn't thought of that.'

'Let's get these pasties out of the wheelbarrow and onto a trestle table,' said Mrs Cleavidge, bending down to pick up the wheelbarrow handles again, prior to pushing her pasties across to the nearest table. She paused, with her hands on the wheelbarrow handles and spoke to the vicar's wife. 'I bought all the ingredients from Miss Box but I forgot to pick up any mixed herbs so I rummaged around in your kitchen and found yours. I used the lot I'm afraid but I'll get a replacement jar for you from Miss Box on Monday.'

'Mixed herbs?' said the vicar's wife, looking terribly confused. She thought for a moment. 'I didn't have any mixed herbs,' she said at last.

'Oh yes you did!' said Mrs Cleavidge firmly. 'In that big glass jar tucked away behind the tea caddy.' She bent her arms, lifted the back end of the wheelbarrow off the ground and trundled her pasties across to where Mrs Stilton, having made a nice large space on a trestle table, was waiting for her arrival.

'A big jar behind the tea caddy?' repeated the vicar's wife. She spoke so quietly that Mrs Cleavidge could hardly hear her.

She opened her mouth as though about to speak but closed it again without saying a word. She had gone a very strange colour.

~ Chapter 95 ~

When Constable Hobbling returned to the pavilion his team mates gathered around him, oozing sympathy and understanding.

'The Inspector says that if I don't make an arrest this afternoon I'm going to be transferred to clerical duties at police headquarters,' the village policeman reported, glumly.

He sat down on a wooden chair, put his elbows on his knees and his head in his hands.

The general consensus was that this was utterly unfair, quite unreasonable and generally pretty worrying.

'What will happen to us?' demanded Itchy, rather tactlessly expressing the fear that everyone felt but that no one else had felt able to express.

Constable Hobbling reached out and took a raspberry jam tart from a plate in front of him. He put the whole of the tart into his mouth without even looking at it.

'Will they send us another policeman?' asked Itchy, whose tactlessness knew no bounds.

Constable Hobbling, who was unable to speak, nodded. As a result many worried glances were exchanged. Puffy, as landlord of The Gravedigger's Rest, was particularly concerned. He exchanged worried glances with Biffo, Paddy and Cheesy. He had little doubt that a new policeman would be unlikely to take the sort of sensible, mature and well-balanced attitude towards such delicate and crucial things as licensing laws, as had been displayed so consistently by Constable Hobbling.

The much-loved policeman swallowed and licked his lips. 'I keep telling him that no one here breaks the law,' he said, morosely. 'But he doesn't believe me.'

The members of the cricket club looked at one another. It was becoming dangerously clear to them all that they might well be dealing with a more perceptive and intelligent man than they had at first suspected.

Constable Hobbling reached out and took another jam tart. The trouble with comfort eating is, as many would-be-slimmers have found to their cost, that the comfort only comes when you are actually eating. Eating a jam tart (or a cream cake or a packet of biscuits) may help provide comfort and solace but the minute the tart (or the cream cake or the packet of biscuits) has been consumed the comfort and solace will cease. The only answer is to keep eating.

After a cursory glance Constable Hobbling popped the tart into his mouth. Once again he felt a little better for a few moments. But, sadly, he knew that the relief would not last.

~ Chapter 96 ~

CONSTABLE HOBBLING WAS BY NO means the only person in Fondling-Under-Water to be having a day he would happily forget. Former England cricketer Cyril Player was also having one of those frustrating and disappointing days that deserve to be put out with the rubbish.

Mr Player had begun the tea interval sitting behind several huge piles of his books. He had his pen poised and fingers held ready to scrawl his signature. A notice pinned to the front of the trestle table he had borrowed warned potential purchasers not to ask for personal inscriptions.

Mr Player had brought with him two hundred copies of the autobiography entitled 'Running for Cover' which a skilful ghost writer had written for him. He had also brought three pens. With extraordinary optimism he had even brought with him a notebook so that he could, if he ran out of books, write down the names and addresses of additional purchasers and then fulfil their orders when he had obtained additional supplies from his publisher.

Several people who had read the book had told him how much they had enjoyed it and one day, when things were a little quieter and he had the time to spare, he thoroughly intended to read his autobiography himself.

Things had not, however, worked out quite according to

plan and at the end of the tea interval there had been no discernible change in the height of the piles of books before him. He still had one hundred and ninety nine copies of his autobiography left on the table. And there was plenty of ink left in his pens.

The sole copy which had been sold had been bought by Paddy Field, the Fondling-Under-Water captain, who had bought a copy of Mr Player's book as a gesture of goodwill.

There could be little doubt that so far the visiting professional was considerably out of pocket on the day. Mr Player's hopes for turning the event into a financial success now rested largely upon the collection which it had been agreed he would be entitled to hold immediately after the conclusion of the first tea interval and during the visiting team's innings.

No one thought it necessary to tell him that his prospects of enjoying a good collection had not been enhanced by the fact that Mrs Cleavidge's team of sandwich makers had already been round the crowd once and had, through a potent mixture of charm, cleavage and physical intimidation (wielding a butter knife can build up pretty impressive biceps), collected every available piece of loose change on the ground.

~ Chapter 97 ~

'THIS ISN'T JUST ABOUT GETTING lots and lots of arrests just to show the ratepayers that we're giving them value for money,' said the Inspector to Constable Hobbling.

Towards the end of the first tea interval the Inspector had called the unhappy Constable Hobbling out onto the grass for yet another meeting. The Inspector liked meetings. If he didn't have regular meetings he got withdrawal symptoms.

Constable Hobbling made an appreciative noise and waited for the Inspector to continue. He was looking forward to hearing the Inspector's other reasons why he needed to arrest his friends.

But the Inspector had finished talking and was now busy taking large bites out of one of Betty Cleavidge's special pasties.

If there was another reason for Constable Hobbling to make more arrests (or, to be more accurate, to make an arrest) the Inspector wasn't going to share that reason with Constable Hobbling.

Suddenly Cheesy appeared. He had a plastic beaker filled with orange squash in one hand and a slice of fruit cake in the other.

'I'm sorry to bother you, Constable,' said Cheesy, spraying a fine mist of fruit cake over the village policeman's uniform. 'But I just wanted to thank you for your wonderful work in stopping that burglary the other day. Your quick thinking undoubtedly saved our family silver.' And with that Cheesy wandered off.

Constable Hobbling, who didn't have the faintest idea what Cheesy was talking about just stared in silent horror at his fast-bowling colleague. He was utterly confused by the idea of Cheesy having any family silver to be stolen. As far as he knew Cheesy and his family still ate their meals using plastic cutlery which they had acquired during a Spanish holiday in the 1960s.

'That's the sort of thing I like to hear!' whispered the Inspector, clearly impressed.

Seconds later Itchy Hedrubb wandered over and held out a stained hand. 'Excuse me,' he said, speaking to the Inspector. 'Am I interrupting?'

'Not at all,' said the Inspector, transferring his pasty to his left hand so that he could take Itchy's proffered palm.

'I just want to thank our policeman,' said Itchy. 'I haven't had the chance before, but his swift action saved my little girl from drowning the other day.'

'Really?' said the Inspector.

'He was too modest to stay around to be congratulated,' said Itchy, speaking to the Inspector.

Constable Hobbling stared at him. Itchy's daughter was 22, married and heavily pregnant.

'Thank you, Constable Hobbling,' said Itchy. 'I think I speak for the whole village when I say that we all feel much happier knowing that you're looking after us all.' He then wandered off and disappeared back into the pavilion.

'This is what community policing is all about,' said the Inspector, clearly delighted. He took another huge bite out of his pasty. 'Congratulations!' he said. He waved his pasty about. 'Very good pasty!' he added.

'Thank you, sir,' said Constable Hobbling, brushing pasty crumbs off his uniform.

'Excuse me!' The two policemen turned. 'Do you mind if I have a word?' asked Puffy who had appeared as if by magic.

'This is Mr Harbottle,' Constable Hobbling explained to his superior. 'He's the landlord of our local hostelry.'

'I'm sorry I haven't had chance to thank you for sorting out that little problem the other day,' Puffy said to Constable Hobbling.

'What little problem was that?' the Inspector asked Puffy. Constable Hobbling was glad the inspector had asked the question. He too wanted to know the answer.

'A coach full of football fans stopped at The Gravedigger's Rest,' explained Puffy. 'They had been drinking on the coach and they were a bit the worse for wear. For a moment I thought we were going to have some trouble. But Constable Hobbling had seen the coach pull up and he came in and sorted things out.'

'You didn't have any trouble?' asked the Inspector. He put the remains of his pasty into his mouth.

'None whatsoever,' said Puffy. 'Some men have that special quality that enables them to win the respect of others,' he went on. 'And Constable Hobbling has that special quality in spades.'

'I'm glad to hear it,' said the Inspector.

'Thank you again,' said Puffy to Constable Hobbling. 'We're all grateful to you.' Like Cheesy and Itchy before him he then wandered off back in the direction of the pavilion.

'Would you like another one, sir?' asked Constable Hobbling, who couldn't remember ever feeling quite so embarrassed.

'Another one?' said the Inspector. 'You mean there are more people in this village who think you're a combination of Robin Hood, the Lone Ranger and Albert Schweizer?'

'No, no,' said Constable Hobbling quickly. 'I meant another pasty.'

The Inspector looked around. 'Do you think that would be possible?' he asked. 'I wouldn't want to have to, you know, exert any undue professional pressure on anyone.'

'Oh no, sir, nothing like that will be necessary,' said Constable Hobbling, heading off confidently towards the refreshment area. 'I'm sure I'll be able to get you another pasty.'

It was a close run thing. Only by prising three quarters of the last pasty out of the eager fingers of Itchy Hedrubb was Constable Hobbling able to make good his promise.

'What happened to the rest of it?' asked the Inspector, examining the damaged pasty suspiciously.

'I'm afraid a small piece broke off when the catering assistant was handing it to me,' apologised Constable Hobbling, who rightly felt that the Inspector would probably enjoy his pasty more if he did not know that the missing segment had already begun its journey through Itchy Hedrubb's intestinal tract.

~ Chapter 98 ~

UNLIKE CONSTABLE HOBBLING, MR PLAYER had not attempted to ease his disappointment with food. He wanted to keep his fingers clean lest any stickiness mark the books before him.

However, Tom Morton and Michael Hunt had, between them, consumed no fewer than five of Betty Cleavidge's freshly baked pasties and had enthusiastically recommended them to the rest of his team. They were, they had both declared, the tastiest pasties they had ever eaten.

By the time the first tea interval had ended the wheelbarrow was empty. Every single one of Mrs Cleavidge's pasties had been devoured with relish (and, in many cases, a large dollop of Mrs Cleavidge's home-made chutney).

All the members of both teams except Cyril Player had eaten at least one, as had the two umpires.

Mrs Cleavidge was very pleased with her emergency endeavours to feed the flannelled multitudes (though, naturally, disappointed that she had not made too many).

There had been a few pasties left over for spectators to

enjoy and one of Mrs Cleavidge's eager helpers had taken a couple over to Percy Kempton's table. Even the visiting police inspector, who had come to Fondling-Under-Water to have firm words with Constable Hobbling, had consumed and enjoyed a pair of pasties.

There was just one person on the field who was not delighted with the success of Mrs Cleavidge's pasties. There was one person who was not looking forward to the forthcoming proceedings.

As the Fondling-Under-Water team strolled out onto the field, and the two batsmen who were destined to open the batting for the visiting team strode out to join them, Mrs Counter, the vicar's wife, sat in a dark corner of the pavilion nervously chewing her handkerchief.

~ Chapter 99 ~

ALTHOUGH IN EVERY OTHER RESPECT the Reverend and Mrs Counter were thoroughly law-abiding citizens they had, ever since they had studied together at University, shared a liking for an occasional puff at a home-made cigarette.

They both found that an occasional evening spent sharing a roll-your-own or two helped them to escape from those aspects of twentieth century life which managed to break through and touch (contaminate might be a more appropriate word) the lives of the residents of Fondling-Under-Water.

Being well aware of the known links between the smoking of tobacco and the development of cancer, heart disease and other serious disorders they preferred to relax by smoking marijuana – a substance which they regarded as infinitely less toxic than the stuff subsidised with such enthusiasm by politicians. They found that it helped them to relax very effectively.

This was not an activity which they regarded as risky for, generally speaking, the residents of Fondling-Under-Water did not feel oppressed by the law in the same way that residents of some parts of London, Birmingham or Manchester might feel oppressed by the law.

Nevertheless, since marijuana is an illegal substance, illogically and unscientifically classified (through a bizarre historical quirk) in the same general category as heroin and cocaine, the vicar and his wife kept their supplies in a plain glass jar which was half hidden away behind the tea caddy.

It is generally agreed that marijuana helps those who smoke it (or otherwise consume it) to relax and forget some of their most pressing anxieties.

What is less well known is that, as with most drugs, the precise effect that marijuana has – and the end result – depends very much upon the state of mind of the person using it.

At the tea interval which followed their disastrous first innings the Fondling-Under-Water batsmen were feeling depressed and miserable. They had not, in truth, expected to win their match against the professionals – but nor had they expected to be dismissed for a total that looked more like a shoe size than a cricket score.

Consequently, Mrs Cleavidge's marijuana-packed pasties were just what the doctor would have ordered for the Fondling-Under-Water players if he could have done so without being arrested, disbarred, discredited and generally sent to bed without any supper. In order to play at their best the Fondling-Under-Water team needed to relax a little and lose their inhibitions. Some of Reverend and Mrs Counter's special herb was just what they needed.

The visiting professionals, on the other hand, were feeling worked up and ready to decimate the local amateurs.

For them tension was as much a part of their necessary stock-in-trade as a set of stumps, a ball and a pair of bats. They thrived on tension and pressure. They fed on stress in the same way that small boys thrive on crisps.

Despite the fact that they were playing a village team of amateurs all of them wanted – indeed needed would perhaps be a better word – to win. And so they definitely didn't want – or need – to be relaxed.

Next to a potent laxative a healthy dose of marijuana was the last thing the visiting professionals needed in their tea time pasties.

~ Chapter 100 ~

EVEN THE LEAST DISCERNING SPECTATOR would have found it impossible not to notice a considerable difference in the demeanour of the players who took the field after the first of the afternoon's two tea intervals.

Before the first tea interval the home side batsmen had walked out to take their chances with Tom Morton and Michael Hunt with the same sort of level of enthusiasm which Anne Boleyn probably showed when lumbering off to keep her final appointment with the state authorised axe man.

But, after the tea interval, Paddy Fields and the Fondling-Under-Water Cricket Club team walked out onto the field as though they did not have a care in the world.

They appeared, indeed, to be looking forward to their forthcoming adventures on the cricket field. They were full of utterly unexpected enthusiasm. They laughed, they joked and they gaily threw the ball to one another. (Even the fact that the person to whom the ball had been thrown invariably missed the catch didn't seem to worry them in the slightest.)

At the boundary's edge this change of heart was, by some cynics, put down to the fact that the Fondling-Under-Water players would no longer have to face the bowling of Tom Morton or Michael Hunt.

But not all of those present that day subscribed to this point of view.

Sitting in the pavilion, and taking a few moments well earned rest, Mrs Cleavidge and her team of butter knife twirlers felt, with not a little pride and with more justification than most of them (the exception being the vicar's wife) could possibly know, that it was the magnificent tea they had provided which had given their team such an unexpected and potent mixture of *joie de vivre* and fighting spirit.

'It was your jam tarts which perked them up,' Mrs Stilton said to Mrs Hedrubb.

'Oh no,' said Mrs Hedrubb modestly to Mrs Stilton, 'I'm sure we can give the credit to your sponge cake. No one makes a sponge cake like you do.'

'I think we both know the real reason why the team looks so happy,' whispered Mrs Stilton, sycophantically. She nodded in the direction of Mrs Cleavidge. 'It was Betty's pasties that made the difference.'

'Oh yes, of course,' agreed Mrs Hedrubb, nodding enthusiastically. Her several chins nodded with her.

'Oh yes, yes,' said Avril Showers, the policeman's paramour.

'Absolutely,' agreed Mrs Stickers. 'The pasties were very, very popular.' She blushed, as she always did when she spoke in public. Some people thought she blushed because of her hormones but she knew that wasn't true. She had always blushed.

'Yes, I think you're right,' said the wicket keeper's mother. 'It must have been the pasties.' The wicket keeper's mother was so old that she still thought of America as a colony but she knew which way was up and which side to butter a piece of bread.

Mrs Cleavidge beamed with pride and nodded her thanks to her acolytes but, within seconds, the glorious moment was rather spoilt by the vicar's wife.

'Oh no, I don't think so,' said Mrs Counter rather too quickly and much too loudly.

They all turned round and stared at her.

'Oh?' said Mrs Cleavidge. 'Do you not? Well I'm sure you have a point. Your cheese and tomato sandwiches always go down well and I know your husband appreciates those tiny little onions you bring.'

The vicar's wife opened her mouth to speak but all she could manage was a passable imitation of a goldfish.

'By the way do tell your husband how nice I think he looked today,' said Mrs Cleavidge sweetly. 'That little white skirt fit him very well.'

'What I meant to say,' said the vicar's wife, blushing as red as a tomato, 'was that I don't think it was any one particular food that made the difference.' She swallowed hard and looked around but encountered nothing but blank faces and slightly raised eyebrows. Mrs Cleavidge ruled the cricket teas with an iron will and had a tongue that could cut flesh at twenty paces. 'I'm sure that Mrs Cleavidge's pasties were an absolute favourite,' Mrs Counter blundered on, 'but I just, er, didn't, er...think that it was perhaps only the pasties which have er...although I could, of course, be wrong about this because they were very popular, very very popular...' Slowly the unhappy Mrs Counter lost heart and gave up. She put her handkerchief back into her mouth, from whence she wished she had never taken it, and carried on chewing. It was a paper handkerchief and it did not take well to this sort of rough physical treatment.

'Excuse me,' said the police Inspector suddenly appearing in the pavilion doorway. 'I'm sorry to bother you, but do you have any of those pasties left?'

~ Chapter 101 ~

'WHERE WOULD YOU LIKE ME to field today, skipper?' Herbert asked Paddy Fields with unusual politeness.

'Oh anywhere you like, Herbert,' replied Paddy with a broad smile. He waved his arms around in a series of magnanimous gestures and spoke to the rest of the team. 'Just spread yourselves about a bit,' he said with a chuckle.

He felt far too comfortable and confident to worry about field placings.

Naturally, everyone stayed as close to the wicket as they could so that they would not have to walk too far at the end of each over.

Norman Soames and Cecil Kipling, the opening batsmen for the visiting side, wandered out towards the business area of the cricket ground and looked around them.

'Aggressive field placings,' commented Norman.

Cecil, who felt a little strange and had had to concentrate hard to make sure that his right and left legs moved alternately, paused for a moment and looked around. In addition to the wicket keeper, and the opening bowler pacing out his run up, there appeared to be four slips, two gullies, two leg slips and a silly mid on. 'Very aggressive,' he agreed. The wicket keeper appeared to be a lemon. Cecil wondered if something he had eaten could possibly have disagreed with him. He looked away from the lemon. 'There are two women fielding,' he said, referring to Lady Hepplewhite, who was fielding at fourth slip, and the vicar, who was just a yard or so away from her in the gully.

'No, I don't think so,' said Norman. 'The one with the sticking plasters on his legs is a bloke in a skirt.' He paused and thought for a moment. 'I think someone said he's the local vicar.'

'Oh,' said Cecil. 'That's all right then.' Something didn't seem quite right but he couldn't quite think what it was.

Constable Hobbling, who had finished measuring out his run up, marked Itchy's precious turf with the heel of his size twelve boot. He checked the strap of his helmet to make sure that it was tight enough. He had thought about taking the helmet off while he was bowling but had decided that the visiting inspector would almost certainly not approve of this. He didn't want to upset the visiting inspector. He felt a warm and utterly unexpected rush of affection for his senior colleague.

'What did you say that bloke in the skirt has got stuck on his legs?' asked Cecil, who was rather short sighted.

Norman squinted at the vicar's legs. 'Looks like sticking plasters to me,' he replied.

'Oh!' said Cecil.

'Shall we start soon?' called Franklin Minton.

'I'm ready,' replied Constable Hobbling.

'We're all ready,' said Paddy, looking around. The other fielders all nodded. Several of them held their hands out in catching positions to indicate their readiness.

'Why has he got sticking plasters stuck all over his legs?' Cecil called down the wicket.

'Dunno,' replied Norman. 'Maybe he cut himself shaving.'

'Ah,' said Cecil, nodding wisely. 'Probably.'

'Are you two ready?' Franklin asked the two batsmen.

'Definitely,' replied Norman Soames, walking down to the lemon's end of the pitch, to receive the first ball of the innings.

'Haven't you forgotten something?' asked Franklin, rather drily.

'What's that?' asked Norman, stopping in the middle of the pitch and looking back up the wicket towards the umpire.

He thought hard but could not think of anything he should have said or done that he hadn't done or said.

'Your bat,' said Franklin, pointing to the space the missing bat would have occupied if it hadn't been forgotten. 'You haven't got a bat,' he explained.

Norman looked down. Franklin was absolutely right. His newly-whitened pads were neatly buckled around his legs and he was wearing expensive batting gloves which he had designed himself and which bore a facsimile of his signature, but his hands were empty. He had indeed forgotten to bring his bat with him.

'You daft beggar!' said Cecil Kipling, pointing a finger at his colleague and laughing out aloud.

Norman looked at Cecil and frowned. There was, he felt sure, something about his batting colleague that wasn't quite right. He thought hard and long. 'You haven't got one either,' he said, at last. The accusation was perfectly accurate and this time it was his turn to laugh.

Cecil examined his own hands. It was true that they too were batless.

'What the hell is going on out there?' demanded Cyril Player, standing beside the rest of his team outside the pavilion.

'It looks like Norman and Cecil have forgotten their bats,' said Peter Wodehouse, of Northamptonshire, Glamorgan and Surrey.

Everyone, except the captain, felt that the fact that the two opening batsmen had gone out to bat without their bats was the funniest thing they had seen for a long time. There was much chuckling and giggling among the visiting team members.

On the third man boundary Tom Morton and Michael Hunt, who had been given buckets so that they could collect money for their captain's benefit fund, were giggling like teenage schoolgirls. Apart from two buttons, three pebbles, a badge and a five penny piece their buckets were empty but they didn't care. They didn't have a care in the world.

Their captain had selected them for this task for two reasons. First, since they were the number ten and eleven batsmen he felt it unlikely that their presence at the crease would be required. And second they were, with the exception of himself, of course, the two best known players in the visiting side. But his two representatives were not doing much to improve his bank balance.

The visiting captain didn't think that the batsmen's failure to take their bats with them was funny at all. He thought it was distinctly unprofessional. He tried to point this out to the rest of his team. 'Would anyone giggle if a doctor went out without his stethoscope or a policeman without his truncheon?' he asked. The response was simply more chuckling and more giggling.

Incensed, Cyril glowered at the gigglers and glared at the chucklers before grabbing two bats and marching straight out to the middle with them. He knew that he was not a humourless man – he had been known to tell jokes himself when speaking at dinner engagements – but going out to bat without a bat seemed to him to be distinctly lacking in any comedic quality.

While the two batsmen waited for their captain to arrive with their bats Helmut Walton and Lady Hepplewhite helped Justin Wilson, the wicket keeper who was still zipped firmly inside his lemon costume, to get back onto his feet. The hapless wicket keeper had laughed so much he had fallen over and his attempts to stand up had simply sent him rolling around the field in large circles.

~ Chapter 102 ~

ONCE THE TWO BATSMEN WERE properly equipped, and the fielding side had managed to settle down a little, Franklin looked around the field to check that everyone was ready. He then called 'play' and thus began the visiting team's first and only innings.

To say that things started badly for the professionals would not for one moment convey the full scale of the disastrous first half an hour.

Constable Hobbling's first ball was a very slow full toss which even a mediocre village player would, under normal circumstances, have fully expected to send whizzing off towards the boundary.

But when Norman saw the ball coming towards him he suddenly started to giggle uncontrollably. He walked down the wicket, took his left hand off his bat and used it to point at the ball before falling to his knees with tears streaming down his face. By this time the ball had passed him by, had missed the stumps by about a yard and had, much to everyone's surprise, been caught by Justin the wicket keeper.

Responding to loud cries of 'Stump him!' from his team mates Justin panicked (panicking was one of the things he did best) and hurled the ball away from him as though it was a hot potato.

Puffy, who was fielding in the gully, caught the ball and threw it to his vice captain Paddy Fields. Alone among the trio Paddy had the presence of mind to walk to the stumps and use the ball to knock off the bails.

'Howzzaaaaaaaaaaaaaaaaaaat?' cried Constable Hobbling, dancing a little jig in front of Franklin Minton.

The umpire raised a finger and the visitors had lost their first wicket.

The next batsman, S.J. Honeypot (of Warwickshire and Somerset) retained his composure long enough to edge Constable Hobbling's second ball to the wicket keeper. Much to everyone's surprise Justin held onto the catch. Justin was probably more surprised by this than anyone else. Catching and holding onto the ball were skills he was still working on.

'What happened?' asked his replacement, Thomas Winston, as they crossed in the middle of the field.

'I was bowled by the policeman, caught by the lemon and given out by a man in a wheelchair,' said S.J. Honeypot accurately but glumly. 'But I was distracted by the woman fielding at fourth slip and the vicar in the skirt fielding in the gully.' He shook his head sadly. 'She's got nice legs but his are covered in bits of sticking plaster.'

'Never mind,' said Thomas. 'Look on the bright side.'

'What bright side?' asked S.J. Honeypot.

Thomas, who hadn't anticipated the question, thought about this for a moment or two. 'You can go and have a sit down,' he said at last. 'And there are some jam tarts left,' he added, knowing S.J.'s weakness.

'Oh whizzo!' said S.J. Honeypot, brightening up considerably. He wished his fellow professional good luck and walked back to the pavilion with a broad smile on his face.

Thomas Winston, the incoming batsman, hit the first two balls he received from Constable Hobbling for four each and at the end of the first over the visiting professionals had scored eight runs for the loss of just two wickets.

And that was probably the high point of the visitors' innings.

~ Chapter 103 ~

CHEESY STILTON HAD THOMAS WINSTON caught by the vicar before he had added any more runs to his score. And, in his second over Constable Hobbling dismissed Cecil Kipling, who had managed to remain at the non-striker's end for so long that he forgot that he was standing at the business end of the wicket. He was bowled while leaning nonchalantly on his bat, standing two feet to the left of his stumps and watching with utter fascination as a little fluffy white cloud wandered slowly across the sky. When Franklin Minton explained to him what had happened he burst out laughing.

It was at this point that the professionals' captain strode purposefully out to the wicket to join Kenny Lillywhite, a visitor who was yet to inconvenience Arthur Sturgeon, the scorer.

It is fair to say that Cyril Player was not a happy man. The day was not turning out as he had hoped or expected.

He had hoped that he would, on his return to Fondling-Under-Water, be treated as some sort of prodigal son. He had expected his hand-picked team of skilled professionals to show the amateur players of Fondling-Under-Water the size of the gap between village cricket and professional cricket.

And he had hoped and expected to add a sizeable sum of money to his tax free benefit fund.

In contrast to these hopes and expectations the day had so far been packed to the brim with disappointments. Only one villager (and that was Paddy Fields who had clearly made the purchase as a gesture of goodwill) had taken the trouble to buy a copy of his autobiography.

Moreover, he was pessimistic about the chances of Tom Morton and Michael Hunt managing to part the villagers from any of their loose change. On reflection it seemed to him that he might have chosen the wrong players for this vital task.

Worst of all his team now seemed to be treating the whole afternoon as a bit of fun. Since the tea interval they seemed to their captain to have lost their edge. They were all clearly having a jolly time and they were doing far more laughing than was good for any team of professionals. Mr Player did not regard cricket as a game or even a sport. It was a job and Mr Player regarded jobs as serious things.

And so, like any good general, Cyril Player had decided to lead his men from the front.

Despite comments which he knew had, in the past, been made about him in one or two of the cricketing magazines he felt that he was not an unintelligent man and while walking out to the crease he had formulated a plan. It was a simple plan but he had always believed in simplicity. He would, he had decided, thrash the impudent locals, score 200 in no time at all, declare and then dismiss them for another derisory score. In this simple way he would win the match convincingly and be able to leave Fondling-Under-Water with his head held high, even if his pockets were as empty as they had been when he had arrived.

Alas, as the hapless Mr Player would have known if he had been a more sensitive and observant individual, fate has a regrettable tendency not to take too kindly to plans. However noble the intention may be it is, all too often, the appointed function of fate to stuff a thick-pointed stick into life's delicate machinery.

The Fondling-Under-Water opening bowler, Constable Hobbling, had, after his stirring opening spell, been rested and when Cyril Player reached the crease he found that the vicar had taken the ball and was polishing the ball on his skirt and preparing to bowl his first over.

Despite his immense experience, and the many years he had spent as a professional cricketer, this was the first time that

Cyril had found himself being bowled to by a hook-nosed, transvestite leg break bowler with eight bits of sticking plaster decorating his pink and hairless legs.

It was also the first time he could remember playing in a match in which the wicket keeper was dressed as a lemon.

Despite all this Cyril had little difficulty in concentrating on the task ahead. He was a professional doing a difficult job and he was also far too unimaginative to be disturbed by any of these relatively unusual features. He took guard, made a firm mark on Itchy's pitch and prepared for the vicar's first ball.

The vicar's first ball, which was a trifle shorter than he would have liked, landed a foot or so outside the leg stump and failed to turn. Mr Player had plenty of time to plan and execute his first scoring shot and he watched with some pride as the ball, sweetly struck in the centre of the bat, raced away towards the boundary. There was clearly no need to run. Four runs were in the bank.

The vicar's second ball was a better length and was much better directed. It even had a small amount of top spin added to it and when it bounced it kept low. None of this threatened Mr Player who had always regarded himself as one of the best players of spin bowling in the country. He drove the ball back down the wicket and watched with satisfaction as it shot past the vicar's outstretched fingers.

'Run!' yelled Cyril, scampering down the pitch as though his life depended upon his reaching the other end as quickly as possible. He ran, head down, without even looking up to see if the batsman at the other end had heard him and was responding. He knew that Kenny Lillywhite was a reliable professional.

Not looking up to check that Kenny was running in his direction was a mistake.

'What?' said Kenny Lillywhite, normally such a reliable professional.

When the captain's call awakened him from his reverie he had been looking at the grain of the wood in his bat and thinking how beautiful it was. He looked up and saw his captain, a fierce look on his face, racing towards him as though he was being chased by a pack of man-eating wolves. Or, since Justin was leaping up and down in excitement at the far end of the pitch, a single man-eating lemon.

'Run!' screamed his captain. 'Run!'

At this point Kenny lost his self control and panicked. It wasn't his fault. The pasties Mrs Cleavidge had baked contained a large portion of marijuana and the drug affects different people in different ways.

He threw down his bat, the very bat which, just a moment earlier, he had been admiring so keenly, and started to run.

Unhappily, he did not run towards Mr Player, a direction which would, under the circumstances, have been far more appropriate, and which would have taken him to the safety of the crease at the other end of the pitch. Instead he ran in the same direction that his captain was running.

Since he was already starting from the end towards which the captain was running this meant that he ended up running towards the pavilion. Since he was a fit and well-trained professional he ran quickly and within ten yards he had overtaken the vicar who was chasing after the ball.

Within moments Kenny had overtaken the ball too.

When the captain arrived at his destination he realised with horror that he hadn't seen Kenny Lillywhite running past him in the other direction, as is the normal procedure in these circumstances. He looked around and to his astonishment saw his batting partner running off towards the pavilion.

'Kenny!' he yelled. 'Where the hell are you going?'

Kenny stopped dead in his tracks, allowing the ball and then the vicar to overtake him again. He turned round and it occurred to him that his captain looked rather cross. Indeed, he felt that the word 'angry' might be more appropriate.

Kenny tried to explain but found it difficult to put his feelings into words.

'Hurry up! yelled Paddy Fields to the vicar.

The vicar slowed down for a moment and looked behind to see what was happening. When he stopped one of his false breasts popped out of his bra and slipped out between the buttons of his blouse. The vicar caught the errant prosthesis just in time as it headed earthwards.

'Get the ball and throw it!' shouted Paddy.
'What?' called the vicar.
Paddy repeated his instructions.
'Get back here!' shouted Cyril to Kenny.

Kenny was not entirely convinced of the wisdom of this but he was now far more frightened of the captain than he was of the invisible pack of wolves or the highly visible lemon. And so he started to run back towards the stumps which he had so recently abandoned.

Cyril Player now had a difficult decision to make. Should he stay where he was and hope that Kenny Lillywhite would be able to make it all the way to the wicket keeper's end before the vicar could throw the ball back to the lemon? Or should he run back towards the set of stumps he had just left, leaving Kenny a shorter distance to run?

He was trying to make a decision about this when the vicar stopped, swooped, picked up the ball, turned and threw in towards the wicket keeper. Unfortunately, instead of throwing the ball, which he had picked up with his left hand, he threw the false breast which he was holding in his right hand.

'I was flustered,' he explained for several years afterwards. 'It was a mistake anyone could make.'

When the silicone breast hit him on the back of the neck Kenny finally lost all self control. He had no idea what it was that had hit him but he didn't like the feel of it. There was an unpleasant squelchy sort of feel to it – as though it was perhaps an alien of some kind. A small alien but an alien. He didn't like the idea of being used as target practice by anyone but he was especially averse to be being attacked by aliens, however big they were or were not. He threw himself on the ground and tried to make himself into as small a target as possible.

If Cyril Player had been a weaker man he would have probably sat down on the grass himself. He may even have burst into tears. But he was not a weak man and he did neither of those things. Instead he tried to work out who would be run out if he stayed where he was.

While Cyril Player was thinking, the Reverend Counter, who had realised what he had done, was screaming in horror.

He raced up to the spot where Kenny Lillywhite was crouching on the ground waiting to be captured by aliens, dropped the ball he was holding, picked up his missing bosom and thrust it back inside his blouse without even bothering to dust it off. Only when this was done did he feel whole again.

It was then that he became aware of the instructions being shouted at him. The general consensus of opinion seemed to be that he should throw the ball to the wicket keeper as quickly as he could. Eager not to disappoint his colleagues he responded to this widespread appeal by doing exactly what everyone wanted him to do.

The throw was a good one. It hit the middle stump, just below the bails, about a second before the desperately diving Cyril Player threw himself at the crease.

And about a second after that Franklin Minton gave the visiting captain out.

At the vicar's insistence Mr Minton and the scorer later decided that, whatever the laws of cricket might say, Mr Player had been stumped – thus giving the vicar the honour of taking the wicket. Cricket historians believe that this was probably the first and only time that a batsman had been bowled and stumped by the same player.

To everyone's astonishment the Polaroid photograph taken by Lotti, who had shown admirable presence of mind while umpiring at square leg, proved conclusively that the umpire's decision had been a sound one.

After Cyril's dismissal the professionals struggled slightly more than a little.

A trembling Kenny Lillywhite retired hurt for a while but returned to the crease after being subjected to what could most appropriately be described as a 'firm talking to' by the captain. He later told his chum Cecil Kipling that he didn't really want to resume his innings but that going out to bat again was the only way he could escape from the captain's vitriolic tongue. He was dismissed when he mistimed a square cut and was caught by Constable Hobbling off Cheesy Stilton's bowling.

Peter Wodehouse, once described by Wisden as the greatest off spin bowler to have come out of Walsall for a good twelve months, was given out l.b.w. by a surprisingly confident Lotti. A quicker ball from Cheesy Stilton had caught Mr Wodehouse on the knee and loud appeals from the two gully fielders had weighed far more heavily with Tom Morton's girlfriend than Mr Wodehouse's protestations that the ball had been too wide and too high.

'Those two gentlemen had no direct interest in the dismissal,' Lotti told the unhappy batsman as he paused before starting the long trudge back to the pavilion. 'If the bowler had appealed I would have ignored him but when two objective observers came to the same conclusion I had to take their views seriously.'

Mr Wodehouse had surprised some spectators and delighted all members of the press contingent by bursting into tears and having what could only be described as a tantrum when he reached the pavilion steps.

~ Chapter 104 ~

DAVID PORTER AND CLIVE WOODWRIGHT had constructed the foundations for a promising looking partnership, and had contributed 29 runs to the visitors' surprisingly meagre total, when Paddy Fields decided that the time had come to unleash his secret weapon: Lady Hepplewhite.

It had been a long time since either David Porter or Clive Woodwright had faced a bowler with two X chromosomes and they were neither of them happy about it. They held a short meeting in the middle of the pitch to discuss the problem.

'We're going to look right pillocks if we're bowled out by a woman,' muttered David Porter with a thoroughly uncharacteristic giggle. He was an experienced and canny Yorkshireman with a pair of exceedingly hairy eyebrows and a permanent scowl. His ability to intimidate his opponents was legendary but this afternoon he was extremely relaxed and nowhere near as combative as usual.

'What do you suggest?' asked Clive Woodwright, a solid but slightly-built journeyman cricketer who was in his twilight years with Lancashire County Cricket Club.

Mr Clive Woodwright was a competent batsman and a competent medium pace bowler but no one had ever accused him of being an intellectual. He had once spent four summers working on a crossword puzzle torn from a copy of the Daily Mirror.

Mrs Cleavidge's pasty had done nothing to sharpen the quality of his intellect.

'You stay down that end and just try to block,' said David. 'I'll stay at the other end and try to get myself out when either the policeman or the tall bloke in a skirt is bowling.'

'Right ho!' agreed Clive, automatically prodding at the wicket with his bat before returning to his crease. He felt calmer and more relaxed than he had felt for years and decided to try to remember to play more village cricket in the future.

However, at the business end of the wicket Clive Woodwright was having difficulty in concentrating. When the bathukolpian Lady Hepplewhite came bouncing in to bowl her first ball he simply didn't know where to look. He was hypnotised by the jiggling evidence of her bountiful XX chromosome status. In the end he turned his head away completely, lost sight of the ball and was clean bowled by a slow delivery which never left the ground and skidded underneath the bottom of his bat.

With the remaining balls of her over Lady Hepplewhite succeeded in dismissing both Tom Morton and Michael Hunt in the space of just four deliveries. They were both clean bowled by balls which hardly left the ground between leaving Lady Hepplewhite's delicate hand and arriving at the stumps.

Much to the astonishment of the spectators neither player seemed to mind at all. Tom Morton congratulated her Ladyship on her good form and Michael Hunt, who had eaten no less than three of Mrs Cleavidge's pasties, seemed to be inexplicably amused by the fact that when he was dismissed both bails had fallen off the stumps and onto the ground.

'How did you get out to that?' demanded the furious captain when Tom Morton returned to the pavilion. 'The ball never even bounced!'

'How could you see from where you were?' demanded

Tom. 'I tell you it bounced. It bounced at least eight times!'

At the end of the innings David Porter remained undefeated.

To everyone's surprise the professionals had been dismissed for a mere 64 runs. The Fondling-Under-Water Cricket Club, the home side, required a relatively modest 53 runs to win.

'You played like complete buffoons!' complained the visiting captain in the dressing room a few minutes after the end of the innings. His eyes were nearly popping out of his head with rage. He glared at them all, one by one. 'Do you want to let a bunch of village yokels make you look like idiots?' he demanded.

'If it makes them feel happy and good about themselves then that's fine by me,' said Tom Morton, who was leaning against the wall with one arm around Lotti, his girlfriend. He had a strangely calm and satisfied smile on his face. It was a side of him that neither she nor anyone else had ever seen before.

'Cricket isn't about winning or losing,' said Michael Hunt quietly. 'We should be using the sport – and whatever skills we may have – to help strengthen our relationships with our fellow men.'

'And women,' said Cecil Kipling, who suddenly realised that he secretly felt disappointed that he hadn't been bowled by Lady Hepplewhite.

'Yes, and women,' agreed Michael Hunt.

'I'm disappointed that I didn't get bowled by Lady Hepplewhite,' said Cecil Kipling, who suddenly realised that secrets were a burden he didn't want to carry. It would, he thought, have been a wonderful thing to have been bowled by a woman.

'I don't know what's got into you lot today,' muttered their captain. 'I think you've all lost your minds.'

'It would have been a wonderful thing to have been bowled by a woman,' said Cecil Kipling wistfully.

'Where are those collecting buckets?' the captain asked, ignoring Mr Kipling.

Michael Hunt pointed to the far corner of the dressing room.

'There's isn't much in them, I'm afraid,' said the fast bowler. 'The people around here don't seem to have much money.'

Cyril walked over to the buckets and looked in. The two buckets contained two buttons, five pebbles, a badge and a five penny piece. It was not what he had hoped for.

Fired by a potent mixture of frustration, anger and the knowledge that his all efforts had resulted in a net financial loss for the day, Cyril kicked the two buckets over so that the buttons, the pebbles, the badge and the five penny piece were scattered across the floor.

The five penny piece rolled to a halt a few inches away from Kenny Lillywhite's left foot. Kenny looked around, and then, confident that no one was watching, bent down, picked up the coin and slipped it into his pocket. It wasn't a very big fee for a day's work but his mother had always taught him that if you look after the pennies the pounds will look after themselves. Besides, his father had been born in Glasgow.

Cyril set his jaw and pulled himself back together. The day was not yet over. He would show these damned amateurs. They were going to get the biggest hiding any cricket team had ever received.

~ Chapter 105 ~

'So, how's it going, Constable?' asked the Inspector.

'Pretty well, on a personal level,' said Constable Hobbling proudly. 'I think I can be safely said to have done a little towards cementing relationships between the force and the village. My moped helmet has been of great comfort to the other players in the team.'

He vaguely remembered having read somewhere that the Chief Constable regarded relations with the public to be one of his priorities. 'The team seems to be doing better than expected.'

'Team?' said the inspector, puzzled. He had been under the impression that Constable Hobbling was Fondling-Under-Water's lone warrior in the ongoing battle against crime.

'The Fondling-Under-Water Cricket team.'

'Ah yes. That team,' said the inspector. 'I was enquiring about your search for someone to arrest.'

'Not quite what you would call a complete success just yet, sir,' admitted Constable Hobbling rather miserably. 'But I have hopes. High hopes. Maybe someone might get a little rowdy later on.' He cleared his throat. 'Would a drunk and disorderly do, inspector?' he asked diffidently.

'A drunk and disorderly would do very well,' agreed the inspector. He looked around and bent closer to Constable Hobbling. 'Meanwhile, as what I think you might call a backstop, have you looked around the vehicles?' he asked conspiratorially. The inspector was not normally inclined to help his underlings but the pasties he had consumed had given him a surprisingly satisfied feeling. He felt curiously at peace with the world. It was, for him, a strange feeling.

Constable Hobbling admitted, with some reluctance, that this was not something he had tried.

'There's bound to be one with a lapsed tax disc,' advised the police inspector. 'Or maybe even a bald tyre or two,' he added brightly. The inspector winked and touched the side of his nose with his right forefinger. It was not a gesture he had ever made before. It was something he had once seen in a film and it seemed vaguely appropriate. Then he did something that (on or off duty) he hadn't done for over a decade: he smiled.

Constable Hobbling recoiled automatically and backed away. He didn't like being smiled at by the inspector. It gave him an uneasy feeling. He looked around nervously, he had heard about the 'good cop/bad cop' routines favoured by the city slickers. But the inspector was by himself. Constable Hobbling wondered if there was any such thing as a one-man 'good cop/bad cop' routine.

~ Chapter 106 ~

IT WAS GENERALLY AGREED AMONG the members of the press who were present at the ground that day that Tom Morton's first over of the Fondling-Under-Water second innings was the slowest he had ever been seen to bowl. There were those among the experts who claimed that he was bowling slower than Constable Hobbling or Cheesy Stilton – neither of whom would have had the temerity to describe themselves in public, in daylight and without having consumed a relatively large quantity of alcohol, as genuinely 'fast' bowlers.

Herbert snicked Tom's first ball through the slips for two and edged his second past the wicket keeper for a daring single.

After the third ball, which Paddy had blocked with a straight bat and a surprising amount of confidence, Cyril marched over to his premier fast bowler, stood in front of him with his hands on his hips. 'What the hell are you doing?' he hissed. He had froth on his lips and looked as if he was about to have a nervous breakdown.

Tom looked at him, and frowned. 'Don't let yourself get so upset,' he said. He raised both hands, palm up, in a calming gesture. 'Stay cool,' he urged.

'Why are you bowling so slowly?' demanded his captain. 'My granny could bowl faster.'

Hearing his colleague being insulted Michael Hunt walked over and stood next to Tom.

'I don't want to hurt any of these blokes,' protested Tom, lowering his voice so that he would not hurt their feelings. 'They seem a nice bunch and they're only amateurs.'

'Do you want them to beat us?' demanded their captain. There was clearly no doubt in his mind that this question was intended to be rhetorical but to his astonishment Tom simply shrugged. 'What if they do?' he said. 'It doesn't matter.' He smiled.

Cyril stared at him for the best part of a minute without speaking. 'It doesn't matter!' he said, at last. 'It doesn't matter? Do you really mean that?'

Tom thought about this for a while and then nodded to indicate that he did, indeed, mean what he had said.

'Well, I think it does matter!' snapped the captain. 'Finish this over and then take your sweater. You won't be bowling again in this match.'

Tom, who felt more relaxed than he could ever remember feeling before simply smiled. 'OK skipper!' he said.

'If he's not bowling then neither am I,' said Michael Hunt firmly.

~ Chapter 107 ~

AND SO, INSTEAD OF FACING two of the finest fast bowlers in the world, the relieved Fondling-Under-Water batsmen found themselves having to deal with an attack which could perhaps most accurately be described as half-hearted.

'We can win this match,' muttered Paddy to Herbert when they met in the middle of the pitch to calm their nerves by prodding at a few imaginary bumps.

Herbert was rather alarmed by Paddy's confidence. 'Do you think so?' he said, rather weakly. He had never been an optimistic man, nor a man to whom confidence came naturally. The idea of defeating a team of professionals was not one he could readily come to terms with. Breaking the bank at Monte Carlo would have seemed a more realistic – and realisable – proposition. Moreover, it didn't seem right. Amateur cricketers simply weren't supposed to beat professionals.

'We've got 22 runs on the board and we haven't lost a wicket!' Paddy pointed out, with thinly-disguised delight.

Herbert felt beads of sweat breaking out on his brow and was bowled next ball by a slow full toss from David Porter.

'Oh, I say,' David said as Herbert walked past him on his way back to the pavilion. 'I'm sorry about that. The ball slipped.' He seemed genuinely apologetic.

For a while the visitors, led by their determined captain, succeeded in holding back the Fondling-Under-Water amateurs.

But the end came in an unexpected way after Helmut had walked down the pitch and hit the first ball he received as hard and as high as he could over mid off's head.

Thomas Winston, who was fielding at mid off at the time, ran backwards to position himself underneath the ball but suddenly realised that the ball wasn't going to travel as far as he had thought it would. He was leaning forwards with arms outstretched, when the ball crashed through his fingertips and landed on the grass.

Under normal circumstances few cricketers would have found this incident amusing. But how many cricketers take the field after consuming Mrs Cleavidge's special pasties?

When the ball landed at his feet and he realised that he had missed it Thomas suddenly started laughing.

'You missed it!' cried Cecil. And then he started laughing.

'He missed it!' said S.J. Honeypot to Tom Morton. And they both burst out laughing too.

Soon ten elevenths of the visiting side were helpless with laughter. The sole exception was, of course, Cyril Player who did not see anything at all funny in a fielder failing to take a straightforward catch.

'Throw the ball!' yelled Cyril

Thomas Winston looked at his captain, picked up the ball and threw it to Kenny Lillywhite who threw it to David Porter who threw it to Clive Woodwright.

Meanwhile, Helmut and Paddy carried on running.

'How many...puff...puff...how many's that?' a breathless Paddy eventually asked Franklin Minton.

'Seven,' replied the umpire.

'How long...puff...puff...can we keep doing this?' asked Helmut, one run later. He was sweating profusely and beginning to look rather flushed.

'As long as you like,' replied Franklin.

'Can I...puff...puff..have a runner?' asked Paddy when the shot had gained them eleven runs.

'No, I don't think so,' said Franklin.

'Throw the ball to me!' screamed Cyril, jumping up and down in frustration. Michael Hunt threw the ball to David Porter who threw it over the captain's head to Kenny Lillywhite.

'They're still running!' said Tom Morton, who had finally gained control of himself and stopped laughing. As soon as he'd said it he started laughing again. He caught the ball and threw it to Michael Hunt who threw it to Thomas Winston.

'They're still running!' said Clive Woodwright.

'How many is it now?' shouted Kenny Lillywhite.

'Twelve!' replied Franklin Minton.

'Twelve!' said Kenny, with tears streaming down his face.

'They're still running!' cried Michael Hunt, pointing to the two batsmen and collapsing to his knees, with tears of laughter dripping off his chin.

Moments after the home side had completed a historic victory a furious and red-faced Cyril Player brushed aside reporters and photographers, climbed into his sparkling, sponsored motor vehicle and, with wheels spinning wildly, left without bothering to wait for the three team members he had brought with him.

Two days later, after unconfirmed reports that he had, suddenly and apparently without provocation, attacked a small boy with a bat, an announcement was made that Mr Player was receiving treatment at a private clinic and, after taking professional advice from the team's resident psychoanalyst, had decided to retire from professional cricket.

Several newspapers subsequently reported that the small boy, posing as an autograph hunter, had with feigned innocence asked Mr Player if the batsmen had stopped running yet.

Chapter 108 ~

THE FONDLING-UNDER-WATER CRICKET TEAM and their supporters were still celebrating when Damien Washbrook's Mercedes purred into the car park at the Fondling-Under-Water cricket ground.

A huge lorry pulled up behind the saloon. On the back of the lorry there sat a prefabricated building.

'My first instant house has already arrived!' said Damien, climbing out of the Mercedes.

'I suggest you send it back where it came from – or find somewhere else to erect it,' said Paddy, walking across to him. 'You can't put it here.' The rest of the cricket team followed Paddy.

'What do you mean I can't build here!' sneered Damien. He waved a bunch of papers. 'I own this piece of land. And I've got planning permission. I'm going to put 87 residential dwellings here.'

'You can't,' said Paddy.

'I can!' insisted Damien defiantly.

'I'm afraid not!' said Paddy.

'Oh yes I can,' said Damien, beginning to look worried.

'Oh no you can't!' said Puffy, Biffo, Cheesy and Itchy in unison.

'It's no good at all you lot trying to get clever with me. I can build on this land and by jove that's what I'm going to do!'

Edwina, who was wearing a bottle green suit with matching green shoes, moved closer to her man.

'I suggest that you take a good close look at the document that gives you planning permission,' said Paddy.

Paddy had a certainty about him which disconcerted the lawyer. He went a little pale, flicked through the papers he was holding, picked one out and gave the remainder to Edwina to hold. 'There isn't a problem is there?' she asked, looking anxious.

'No, of course not!' said Damien. 'They're just trying to get us worried.' As he spoke his eye was flicking through the document he had pulled out.

'It's all absolutely fine!' said Damien to Paddy. 'I'm a lawyer. I know all about this sort of thing.'

'Have you looked at the date when the document was signed and stamped?' asked Paddy.

'What of it?' asked Damien.

'It's very important,' said Paddy. 'Especially when you read it along with clause 26.'

Damien went back to reading the document which gave him permission to build on the land he had bought. Suddenly all the colour drained from his face and he went a sickly, deathly grey.

'What is it?' demanded Edwina, realising immediately that something was wrong.

'When the local planning committee gave the previous owner permission to build on this land there were special circumstances,' explained Paddy. 'The permission was given on the understanding that if no buildings were erected within two years then the planning permission would be revoked.'

Edwina licked her lips. Despite her make-up she too had now gone a very unhealthy colour. 'Is that true?' she asked. Damien staring in disbelief at the piece of paper he was holding, nodded. 'It seems to be true,' he whispered. Only those standing immediately next to him could hear him.

'You fool!' cried Edwina, lifting her fists and attacking the lawyer. 'You bloody stupid fool!'

'The only thing you can use this land for is cricket,' said Paddy. 'Do you want to start your own team?'

'You idiot!' screeched Edwina. 'The land is worthless!'

'It's not exactly worthless,' interrupted Bill Stickers.

Everyone turned and looked at him. 'You could probably get eight or ten thousand pounds for it at auction,' said Bill.

Damien put his head in his hands.

'But I'll give you a chance to double that,' said Bill. 'If you sell the land back to me now – today – I'll give you twenty thousand pounds for it.'

Damien lifted his head out of his hands and looked at Bill suspiciously.

'I want to be generous,' said Bill. 'But the offer only stands if you sell the land back to me now. Today. If you wait until tomorrow I'll pay you ten thousand at the most.'

Damien sighed and seemed to shrink. He was thinking about how he was going to explain all this to his brother.

'Don't listen to him!' said Edwina.

'Twenty thousand today or ten thousand tomorrow,' said Bill.

'Will you make it thirty?' asked Damien.

'Twenty,' insisted Bill. 'It's a generous offer for a piece of land with a large damp patch and no planning permission.'

Damien sighed. 'OK,' he said, weakly.

'Sensible chap,' said Bill. He pulled a rumpled bundle of papers out of his left hand trouser pocket. 'It just so happens that I've got a contract here.' He delved into his right hand trouser pocket. 'And I've got the cash here.'

Moments later Bill Stickers was £20,000 poorer. But he didn't give a fig about that. He had rescued The Fondling-Under-Water Cricket Club ground. He was prouder and more excited than he had been on the day when he'd won the Lottery.

~ Chapter 109 ~

'I JUST CAN'T BELIEVE IT,' said Damien miserably. He stood for a moment by the side of his Mercedes and stared at the cricket ground. Edwina, white-faced, climbed into the passenger seat and fastened her seat belt. 'All that money lost so that a bunch of village idiots can play cricket!' said Damien. He opened the driver's door but still didn't get into the car. 'Bloody stupid game anyway.' he said sourly.

'What did you say?' demanded Cheesy.

'I said that cricket is a bloody stupid game,' said Damien, gaining courage from his misfortune.

Cheesy and one or two of the other players moved forwards belligerently but Constable Hobbling was way ahead of them. In three quick strides he was standing beside the solicitor and had his hand on his collar. 'I arrrest you!' he said. He suddenly realised that he didn't know what to say. He seemed to remember that he was supposed to give some sort of warning. 'Anything you say will...'

'...I know, I know,' interrupted Damien irritably. 'Just what do you think you're arresting me for?'

'You said cricket is a bloody stupid game,' said Constable Hobbling.

'Don't be daft!' said Damien. 'You can't arrest me for that.'

'Look around,' said Constable Hobbling.

Damien looked around.

'What do you see?' asked the policeman.

'A lot of very bad tempered and slightly stupid villagers.'

'You upset a lot of people,' said Constable Hobbling. 'That's behaviour likely to cause a breach of the peace. You're nicked.'

It took a moment for this to sink in but a moment later there was a huge cheer.

The loudest cheer came from the Inspector. 'Well done, lad!' said the senior policeman, walking forwards and shaking hands with Constable Hobbling.

~ Chapter 110 ~

FOR A WHILE THERE WAS a little confusion after Constable Hobbling had arrested Damien Washbrook. A large proportion of the confusion was caused by the fact that the village constable had never arrested anyone before and wasn't absolutely, entirely sure what to do. When someone is arrested it is usually the arrestee who is nervous and slightly agitated. On this occasion things were reversed.

'What do I do now?' Constable Hobbling whispered to the Inspector. He took a large handkerchief out of his trouser pocket and mopped his face. It had been a long, hot, hard day.

'Take him to the station,' explained the Inspector.

'But how do I get him there?' asked Constable Hobbling. 'My moped hasn't got a passenger seat.' The unhappy policeman looked at his watch. 'And there isn't another bus until Monday morning.' Tactical and strategic problems were already beginning to take away the pleasure of his first arrest.

'You could borrow a car,' suggested the Inspector.

'That's a bit difficult,' said Constable Hobbling, apologetically. He shuffled about a bit and mopped his forehead again. 'I don't have a driving licence,' he admitted at last.

The Inspector thought about this for a while. 'Ah!' he said. And then because it was the best thing he could think of to say he repeated it. 'Ah.' he said again.

In the end they decided that Constable Hobbling, phutphutting along on his tiny-engined moped, would lead the way to the nearest police station. Damien Washbrook, driving his purring Mercedes saloon, would follow. And the Inspector, driving his official police car, would bring up the rear and make sure that Mr Washbrook didn't make a break for it and choose the life of a fugitive instead of facing his punishment at the hands of the law.

The journey to the police station was a slow one, made slower by the fact that in order to get up the hills Constable Hobbling had to climb off his little moped and walk. Behind him, on each occasion, the Mercedes would purr patiently and the police car would whine its protests.

'Excuse me!' said a voice no one recognised, as the procession left the cricket ground. A large percentage of The Fondling-Under-Water Cricket Club turned round. A small, rather rotund man in a plaid shirt and faded blue jeans was standing behind them with a plastic clipboard in his hand. 'Where do you want these prefabs putting?' he asked.

Cheesy looked at Itchy and Itchy looked at Puffy and Puffy looked at Biffo. None of them spoke.

'I've got one. There's another 86 coming,' said the driver. 'Where do you want the damned things putting?'

'Are these the buildings which were ordered by Mr Damien Washbrook?' asked Biffo, as though they were expecting several deliveries of prefabricated buildings and he didn't want to get them mixed up.

The man in the plaid shirt looked at his clipboard. 'That's him. Are you him?' There was now a long queue of lorries building up behind the leader of the pack.

'No,' said Biffo, managing to suppress a little smile. 'I'm not Mr Washbrook. I'm afraid that Mr Washbrook has just been arrested and is currently being escorted to the local police station.'

The lorry driver in the plaid shirt scratched his head. 'So what the hell am I supposed to do with all these buildings?'

'Have you got Mr Washbrook's home address?'

Once again the lorry driver consulted his clipboard. This time he turned the board round to show Biffo the address that was written down as Damien's home address. Biffo recognised it immediately. It was the address he had shared when living with Edwina.

'In the absence of any alternative instructions I suggest that you deliver them to Mr Washbrook's home,' said Biffo. 'There's quite a large driveway and a large garden. The ones you can't get into the driveway or the garden you'll just have to leave in the road, on the verge or on the village green.'

The lorry driver smiled his thanks at Biffo and left.

~ **Chapter 111** ~

'That was brilliantly done!' said Puffy to Bill Stickers as they stood and watched the small procession, led by Constable Hobbling, begin its journey to the local police station.

'It was Paddy's idea,' said Bill, suddenly overtaken by an exceptional burst of modesty.

'But why did you offer him twice as much as the land is worth?'

'Because I didn't want the cricket club land to be in a stranger's hands for a moment longer than necessary,' said Bill. 'And because I didn't want him to have time to think up some fresh scheme,' he added. 'Paddy thought he'd be unable to refuse the chance to cut his losses.'

'So you've got the land back – and you're £80,000 ahead!' said Puffy. 'Not a bad day's work.'

'The cash will come in very handy,' said Bill. 'The wife and I can buy a little cottage and stay in the village. I'm going to open a little barber's shop. To be perfectly honest I've missed it. I'm looking forward to getting the scissors in my hand again.' He made a snip snip snip movement with the first two fingers of his right hand. 'But the cricket pitch doesn't belong to me,' said Bill. He handed the papers he and Damien had signed over to Paddy. 'I bought the land back on behalf of the cricket club.'

Paddy looked through the papers he had been given and clapped Bill on the shoulder. 'Thank you Bill!' he said. 'That's a very generous gesture.'

'I didn't want to be tempted again,' said Bill honestly.

'As vice captain,' said Paddy, 'I think I can speak for the rest of the team and the club when I say that I hope you will continue to be our captain, chairman and president.'

There was a murmur of approval for this.

A tear appeared in a corner of Bill's left eye. He raised a hand and quickly wiped it away. 'I'm very touched,' he said, his voice breaking. 'It's been a long day. I feel very tired,' he added. 'And emotional.'

'You need a drink,' said Puffy.

'So do I!' said Cheesy, Paddy, Herbert, Helmut, Justin and the vicar in unison.

It was this that reminded Biffo that his friend Streaky Bacon would be at the pub that evening to record the first in his series of quiz programmes.

~ Chapter 112 ~

WHEN THE VICTORIOUS FONDLING-UNDER-WATER CRICKET TEAM, closely followed by Lord Hepplewhite, Mrs Cleavidge and her tea ladies, the brass band, the Morris dancers, the parachutist (who was still waiting for his mum to fetch him), the inimitable Percy Kempton, Franklin Minton and Laetitia Anne de Tomatso, walked round the corner and arrived at The Gravedigger's Rest they found Streaky Bacon standing on the front doorstep doing what looked like the sort of jig a man might dance if, perchance, he suddenly found himself forced to stand on top of a hot stove while not wearing any shoes.

Two huge television vans were parked outside the pub, and alongside the vans were two Volvo estate cars, three BMWs, Streaky's Porsche and several other large and expensive-looking vehicles. The excitement on the cricket pitch had been so great that none of the villagers had heard any of these vehicles arrive.

'Where on earth have you all been?' Streaky demanded, pointing to his watch and giving an excellent impersonation of a man on the very brink of a nervous breakdown. 'You should have been here three hours ago for rehearsals!'

'We've been playing cricket!' said Itchy, surprised that anyone, even someone from London, should ask such a stupid question. 'We won!' he added with a big, self satisfied grin.

'Where?' demanded Streaky.

'Where what?'

'Where were you playing cricket?'

'On the cricket pitch,' said Itchy patiently, but clearly surprised at the extent of the ignorance exhibited by visitors from the capital city.

'Yes, but where was the cricket pitch?' asked Streaky trying not to become violent. Why, he wondered, were people who lived in the country so irredeemably stupid.

'Just over there,' said Itchy, nodding in the direction of the cricket pitch. He moved to a small window in the hallway. 'You can see it from here,' he said, pointing to the now deserted cricket pitch.

'You were there?'

'Up until about five minutes ago.'

'Why didn't someone tell me?' demanded Streaky. 'You're due on air in seven minutes!' he said, interrupting himself and pointing to his watch again. 'Never mind about all that, let's get you all into the pub!'

Biffo looked at his friend, clearly puzzled. 'Is the programme live?' he asked him.

'Of course it's live!' said Streaky, now almost crying. 'Do you think I'd be in a state like this if it was recorded?' Biffo had never seen him so upset. Suddenly full of remorse for snapping at his friend he started to apologise. 'I'm sorry,' he said. 'I don't know what's come over me.' He took a deep breath and tried to settle himself. 'They wanted it live because they say it makes the whole thing more exciting.'

'Don't worry about it!' said Biffo. 'I'm sorry we're late.'

Streaky started to pull people into the pub by their arms and then paused to look at his watch again. 'Six minutes to show time!' he yelled. This did not make people move any faster but it did make them panic a little.

'I really thought it was going to be a recorded programme,' said Biffo, genuinely apologetic. With similarly unimpressive results he too then started to try and hurry people into the pub.

Puffy and Lettice, who had managed to make their way to the front of the crowd on the walk round to the pub, picked their way gingerly in between several cameras and microphones and a vast array of lights, and their various human attendants, and stepped carefully over and between a tangle of cables connecting the cameras and microphones to the vans outside the pub. Eventually they reached the bar. Once in position they started pulling and pouring as though they were entered in some sort of Olympic competition for bar attendants.

Two tables had been set up at the far end of the room, with four chairs behind each one. Four people were sitting on one set of chairs. They had notepads and pencils, a water carafe and four glasses in front of them. A girl in blue jeans and a pink shirt rushed constantly from one to the other. She had a comb in one hand and a box of make-up and tissues in the other. First, she dabbed a bead of sweat from a nose, then she coaxed an errant hair back into a position, then she repaired a make-up crack caused by too broad a smile, then she dabbed a bead of sweat from a forehead. The other table was similarly equipped but the chairs behind it were empty.

Someone, presumably one of Streaky's production assistants, had lit a log fire in the hearth and the blazing fire had boosted the temperature in the bar to an uncomfortable level.

Voluptua Bradshaw, Streaky's girlfriend and the presenter of the programme, was holding a large, old-fashioned microphone in one hand and sitting on a stool with a thick clipboard on her knee. She was wearing a shimmering, strapless blue dress that looked curiously out of place in a well-used English public house. She looked terrified and appeared to be talking to herself as she tried to remember what it was that she had to say.

'Who are your team members?' asked Streaky as thirsty and weary sunbaked villagers tottered weakly into the pub. Being regulars most of them negotiated the step and the beam without difficulty.

'Me, Paddy, Puffy, the vicar, Biffo, Herbert, Constable Hobbling, Bill...,' began Cheesy, responding to Streaky's question.

'No, no, no, no, no! You can only have four members in your team!' cried Streaky. He looked up towards the newly replaced and decorated ceiling as though searching for divine guidance, or, at the very least, a little inspiration. There was still a smell of paint in the air. 'I knew this was going to be a disaster.' he muttered to himself, wringing his hands. He looked at his watch again. 'Five minutes!' he yelled above the noise in the bar. Puffy and Lettice were serving beer and gin as rapidly as they could to the cricket team, the tea ladies, the brass band, the Morris dancers, Franklin Minton, Percy Kempton, the parachutist ('Can

I just have a small glass of diet lemonade please?') and the rest of the village. All were trying to order their refreshments at once.

'I want four team members representing The Gravedigger's Arms!' said Streaky loudly.

'Rest,' said Biffo.

'I can't!' said Streaky. 'How can I possibly rest? I don't have time to rest. I've got to panic. If I don't panic who will?'

'No, it's The Gravedigger's Rest,' explained Biffo calmly. 'I thought you'd want to get the name of the pub right.'

'Oh I'm sorry,' said Streaky, swallowing hard and trying to regain control. He rolled his hand into a fist and hit himself firmly between the eyes. 'Don't worry about me,' he said. 'I think I'm losing my mind,' he added.

Suddenly the crowd which was moving into the pub parted and Voluptua came struggling through. 'I can't go on!' she cried, tears trickling down her cheeks. 'I can't do it!'

'Can't do what?' demanded Streaky.

'I can't do it!' said Voluptua. She threw her arms around Streaky's neck and collapsed sobbing into his arms.

'I'll go and find four people for the pub team,' offered Biffo. He hurried over to the bar and used the brass foot rail to lift himself a few inches higher than the crowd around him. 'Mr Bacon, the producer, represents Better Television – the company which has so generously helped restore the pub to its former waterproof state – and he would like four volunteers to represent The Gravedigger's Rest.'

'At what?' whispered Puffy, leaning across the bar and nudging Biffo's elbow. 'Tell them what its all about.'

'Oh, yes, thanks,' whispered Biffo to Puffy. He raised his voice again. 'It's a sort of trivia quiz thing,' he explained. 'There are, as you can see, four visiting celebrities and there are supposed to be four people representing the pub.'

'What sort of questions are they going to ask?' asked Cheesy.

'I don't know,' replied Biffo, stumped. 'Sort of, well, trivial ones I suppose.'

'Are there any prizes?' asked Itchy.

'I don't know,' said Biffo. 'Probably.' He looked around

for someone to ask. 'Are there any prizes?' he asked a short girl with curly blonde hair who was standing next to one of the cameras.

'I think so,' said the girl. 'There usually are.'

'Four minutes!' cried a tall, red-haired girl in black jeans and a black T-shirt. She was wearing headphones with a small microphone attached and seemed to have temporarily taken over the job of panicking. She did it very well. Streaky was still trying to comfort Voluptua who appeared to be having the nervous breakdown Streaky had seemed about to have.

'Yes,' said Biffo, answering Itchy.

'Then in that case I'll volunteer,' replied Itchy instantly.

'Can we have more light on the celebrities?' asked one of the cameramen, pointing to the corner of the pub were the celebrities were sitting. An electrician moved some lights, knocked over a table and some drinks and bumped into Mrs Cleavidge who spilt half a glass of port down the front of Mrs Counter's best frock.

'I'll have a go,' said Justin.

'You can't be on television,' said Puffy, from behind the bar.

'Why not?'

'Because you're still dressed as a lemon,' said Puffy. 'I'm not having this pub represented by a lemon.'

'That's not fair,' moaned Justin, who seemed terribly disappointed. He sat down on a vacant bar stool and put his yellow head in a yellow hand.

'You can have a drink on the house,' said Puffy, in compensation. 'Any drink you like as long it's half a pint of bitter.'

'Oh thanks!' said Justin, cheered by Puffy's generosity. 'I'll have half a pint of bitter. If that's all right with you.'

'Don't worry about it,' smiled the vicar's wife to Mrs Cleavidge. Now, more than ever, she wished she'd gone home at the end of the match.

'We don't mind having a go,' said Lady Hepplewhite, raising one hand and clutching her husband to her with the other.

'Great!' said Biffo. 'Thanks. Would you go and sit down at that empty table, please? There doesn't seem to be all that long to kick off. We need one more.'

Puffy handed Justin his half pint of beer.

'I'll have a go,' said the vicar gamely. The Reverend Hubert Counter was having a wonderful day. And now he was going to get a chance to appear on television.' On the spur of the moment he decided to begin his television career with a new voice. He started to experiment with something which seemed a little sexier. 'It'll be so exciting!' he said.

Biffo looked at him. 'Fine!' he said. 'Thanks.'

'Hey!' protested Puffy.

'Do you want to volunteer?' asked Biffo.

'No!' said Puffy, holding up a hand as a sign of defeat. 'What do I care?' He hesitated. 'Does anyone watch this damned programme anyway?'

'Look at this way,' said Biffo, reassuringly. 'You've got a new roof and new ceilings. Your customers are all locals and most of them are in here. What have you possibly got to lose?'

Puffy thought about this and then smiled. 'When you put it like that,' he said. 'Not a lot.'

A peer, a peeress, a transvestite vicar and a barely literate groundsman might not have been everyone's ideal choice to represent the village pub in a televised quiz programme but with less than four minutes to go before the programme was due to start Biffo did not feel that setting up a selection panel was entirely appropriate.

'It's not fair I can't be on the team,' complained Justin.

'You can be first reserve,' said Biffo. 'In case anyone drops out.'

'Oh,' said Justin. 'Thanks.' He grinned proudly.

The four contestants hurried over to their table and sat down. The make-up girl, who was still fussing around with the four celebrities, rushed over to see what she could do to help.

'Who are the celebrities?' asked Lettice in a whisper.

'I don't have the faintest idea,' Puffy whispered back.

'Three minutes!' cried the tall red-haired girl. She had stopped panicking and now sounded and looked very calm. A moment later Voluptua, who neither sounded nor looked calm, was escorted by Streaky back through the bar to the stool which she had so recently vacated. Her hair was a mess, one of the shoulder straps holding up her dress had slipped down over one shoulder, mascara had run down her cheeks and she was sobbing. Streaky stayed with her for a moment and then left her to the attention of the make-up girl who had abandoned Lord and Lady Hepplewhite, Itchy and the Reverend Counter without so much as laying a powder puff on any of them.

'Is she OK?' Biffo asked his former television colleague.

'Oh, she'll be fine,' lied Streaky. He rushed off to berate a cameraman who was eating what looked and smelt like a bacon sandwich though it was not easy to understand how he had managed to obtain such an item.

'Who are the celebrities?' Biffo asked the redhead.

'The tall, bald one on the far left in the orange corduroy jacket, the silk shirt and the pink floppy bow tie is Sir Ramick Hobbs. He's terribly important at some University or other and he's our token intellectual.' The redhead examined him closely. 'Didn't you used to work at Better Television?'

'In another life,' replied Biffo.

'And you don't know who any of these celebrities are?'

'I produced the arts programme,' explained Biffo. 'I've vaguely heard of Sir Ramick Hobbs but he never appeared on any of my programmes. Who are the others?'

'The vast cleavage next to him belongs to Bobby Sox. She had two hit records a couple of million years ago and is married to a 19 year old footballer who earns £2 million a year. She says she's only 29 but if she is then she was minus three when she had her first record in the charts. She's been married five or six times and always writes a kiss and tell book afterwards but she describes herself as a born again feminist.'

'The stupid-looking bloke on her right is called Deadly Dave – sometimes billed as The Darlington Destroyer. He claims to be a boxer. He's wearing dark glasses because he had a big fight last Saturday and lost for the sixth or seventh time in a row. I've lost count. He doesn't seem to be a terribly good boxer and by all accounts he's not a very nice person but everyone loves him because he has a very clever manager who's successfully positioned him as a permanent underdog. As you know the British hate winners and love underdogs.'

'And the girl on the far right? The plump one who looks about 18.'

'You really, really don't know?'

'Haven't the foggiest.'

'Honest?'

'Honest.'

'You are out of touch aren't you. That's Amanda. She isn't plump she's grotesquely fat and she isn't 18 she's only 17. She's the obligatory TV chef. Every celebrity panel has to include at least one chef these days. The government's probably passed a law about it. She's sponsored by two big meat packers and her ratings are incredibly high. Streaky only managed to get her for this programme because her agent was tickled pink by his name.' The redhead checked the stop watch which was fastened to her clip board. 'Two minutes!' she called, raising her voice to make this announcement.

'Do you think she'll make it?' asked Streaky anxiously, now back at Biffo's elbow. He nodded in Voluptua's direction.

Biffo looked at him, looked at Voluptua and then looked back at Streaky. 'No.'

'What am I going to do?' begged Streaky. 'Where the hell can I find another presenter?' He put his thumb into his mouth and bit it. 'I should have brought a spare, shouldn't I?'

'What about Percy Kempton?' asked Biffo.

Streaky took his thumb out of his mouth and looked at his friend. 'Percy Kempton? Is he here?'

'Sitting over there,' said Biffo, nodding towards Percy.

'There is a god!' cried Streaky. 'Is he drunk?' he asked. 'Oh, what the...what does it matter. Thank you, Biffo!' he said, hurrying across to Percy's table.

Miraculously, the make-up girl had restored Voluptua's hair, dress and make-up to its pre-sob state. When she was satisfied with Voluptua she rushed over to the pub's panel and headed straight for the vicar. Her yelp of despair could be heard across the room. 'We can either take this stuff off or just put a lot more on and hope everyone thinks you've been in a car accident and you're still waiting for cosmetic surgery!' she said, looking at the vicar's make-up.

The vicar, slightly startled and not a little hurt, looked up at her and fluttered his eyelashes without saying anything. With a deep, weary, sigh the make-up girl reached into her pocket and produced a large tube of foundation cream. With one slick, practised movement she twisted the top off the tube and proceeded to spread a thick layer of cream over the vicar's face.

Suddenly, the red-haired girl was waving her arms to attract Voluptua's attention.

'Break a leg, darling!' cried Streaky from where he sat at Percy's table.

'Quiet please!' called a stocky, middle aged man in a pair of baggy blue jeans and a much darned sweater. Like the redhead he was wearing headphones fitted with a microphone and carrying a clipboard. He held the clipboard high to make it clear to everyone that as the owner of a clipboard he was an important person who needed to be obeyed. The talking and laughing died to a dull whisper, enlivened by the occasional chink of glass on glass or glass on table.

The redhead used her fingers to count down from ten to one and then, when just one finger was left, she pointed at Voluptua in a single, generous, emphatic movement that seemed to galvanise the neophyte presenter into action.

~ Chapter 113 ~

THE FORMAT OF THE PROGRAMME was devastatingly simple and the plan was that Voluptua would begin the proceedings by introducing the two teams.

It is difficult to imagine a simpler and less adventurous beginning but things did not go quite as smoothly as Streaky had hoped, or indeed as they had rehearsed. The first problem was that Voluptua didn't know the names of the pub team and had to ask them to introduce themselves.

The second problem was that Voluptua came from a family of enthusiastic royalists. Her father and mother lived in a two bedroom terraced house in an unpronounceable and rarely visited Welsh seaside resort and the only pictures their home contained were of members of the Royal Family. At the age of four Voluptua had been taught to curtsey every time she passed the portrait of King George which hung in the hallway.

It is, in consequence, perhaps not surprising that she became extremely flustered when she found out that she had a peer and a peeress on the panel. Her confusion was compounded when the vicar lost his head and, despite using the peculiarly high pitched voice he had prepared, introduced himself as the Reverend Hubert Counter. Although he quickly corrected this error, and reintroduced himself as Hermione Counter, Voluptua's fragile confidence was damaged beyond repair. She threw the microphone she was holding onto the bar in front of Puffy and fled, tears flowing, towards the open arms of her lover and mentor, Streaky Bacon.

Percy Kempton did not hesitate for a moment.

Unburdened by the attentions of the make-up girl (who, brave creature, tried to dab at him with her powder puff as he strode past) Percy picked up the abandoned microphone and continued where Voluptua would have left off if she had ever started.

Ignoring Voluptua's bizarre disappearance in the knowledge that if he ignored it the viewers would soon forget it had ever happened ('never explain, never apologise and never pass wind – from any orifice – within range of a live microphone' had been the vivid and unforgettable instructions he had received when he had first entered the then romantic and mystical world of broadcasting) Percy perused the questions on the clipboard as he talked and walked and smiled his way to the corner where the two teams sat waiting for the action to begin.

At the start of the programme the four celebrities had been rather smug and cocky. In contrast Lord and Lady Hepplewhite, Itchy and the vicar had begun to wonder about their wisdom in exposing themselves to what suddenly appeared to be the prospect of national humiliation. The celebrities had done their best to make the amateurs feel uncomfortable.

But now the situation was reversed. The celebrities were now more nervous and uncertain than the four representatives of The Gravedigger's Rest. The celebrities had begun the festivities comforted by the belief that they knew what to expect but the sandy foundations upon which their confidence had been built had been washed away by Voluptua's flood of salty tears.

'What's your name?' demanded Percy, bending down and breathing beer and gin fumes into Amanda's face.

The chubby chefette tried to back away but her chair was up against the wall and there wasn't anywhere to go. She opened her mouth but nothing came out.

'Nil points for the so-called celebrities,' cried Percy. There was a roar of approval from Len who, since he had been unable to play cricket because of his broken arm, had kept his other arm active by drinking a good deal.

A squeal of protest came from the celebrity panel.

'You can't do that!' protested Bobby Sox. 'That's...' she struggled to find the words she was looking for, 'that's unfair.' Len laughed a lot. Very loudly. There was much cheering from the audience.

'Rubbish!' said Percy. He peered at her. 'Who are you?'

'I'm Bobby Sox!' said Bobby Sox, sharing her teeth and cleavage with the camera and the viewers.

'Where on earth did you get such a silly name?' asked Percy.

Bobby Sox glared at him. Her mouth was smiling but her eyes were not.

'I don't see...'

'No points!' cried Percy. 'No points for the daft biddy with the vast cleavage. What's the score?'

'The celebrities have nil and The Gravedigger's Rest team has one point,' said the girl keeping score. 'But you've asked the celebrities two...er... questions and you haven't asked The Gravedigger's Rest team any questions at all.'

'Right!' said Percy. He turned back to his clipboard, studied the questions for a moment or two then shook his head and sighed in disgust. 'These are really boring questions,' he said, tossing the clipboard aside. The board landed on the floor, the clip sprang open and the papers it had been holding scattered far and wide.

This made Len laugh again. He laughed very loudly and when he laughed everyone else laughed with him.

'Who is that?' Streaky Bacon whispered to an aide. 'Get his name. Sign him up. I want him in every show I ever make.'

'Tell me,' said Percy, addressing Itchy. 'Have you ever heard of any of these silly beggars on the celebrity panel?'

Itchy did not own a television set, didn't like to admit to his ignorance, and feared that the celebrities might be disappointed by the truth. But he was, if nothing else, an intrinsically honest man, unless the circumstances suggested otherwise, and so he hesitated and then shook his head. 'I'm afraid not,' he confessed.

'One point to the home team!' said Percy, without a moment's hesitation.

'Hey!' protested Sir Ramick Hobbs indignantly. 'Why did they get a point for that?'

'Are you suggesting that the gentleman was lying?' demanded Percy, swivelling round towards him, slightly unsteadily.

'Well no, not at all,' laughed Sir Ramick, fingering his bow tie rather nervously.

'Then he must have given the right answer,' said Percy triumphantly.

'But it seemed a funny sort of question,' protested Sir Ramick weakly.

Percy scratched his head. 'You didn't think the question trivial?'

'Well yes, absolutely. Of course it was trivial. That's exactly my point.'

'You're a buffoon,' said Percy. 'When the delectable Voluptua introduced this programme I distinctly remember her describing the show as dedicated to trivia.'

'Ah yes, but there's trivia and there's trivia,' complained Sir Ramick weakly.

'Balderdash!' said Percy. He paused, staring at Sir Ramick's jacket, shirt and bow tie. 'Who chooses your clothes?'

'I beg your pardon?'

'Who chooses your clothes?'

Sir Ramick hesitated. 'I do.' He looked down.

'Do you think you look good?'

Sir Ramick thought about this for a moment. 'Well, yes, I think I do,' he said.

Percy turned to the audience. 'Do you think he looks good?'

There was a chorus of 'No'. Len shouted loudest. And then he laughed a lot too.

'You're wrong,' said Percy bluntly. 'You look a complete idiot. And you don't get any points. Would someone get me a drink, please?'

'What do you want, Percy?' responded Puffy from behind the bar.

'Whatever you've got, Puffy,' replied Percy, 'But a lot of it. I can feel flashes of sanity breaking through and with that comes a desperate fear that I'm in danger of sobering up.'

~ Chapter 114 ~

AT THE END OF THE programme the celebrities had gained just two points. In contrast to this pitiful showing the local team, representing The Gravedigger's Rest, had accumulated an impressive twelve points.

Lord Hepplewhite had correctly identified his wife's bra size. Itchy Hedrubb had gained three points by naming the groundsmen at three leading Test Match grounds. (No one had known whether or not he was correct but Percy had ruled that he was and since Percy had appointed himself sole arbiter of right and wrong that was that.) Lady Hepplewhite had accurately explained how to make a Bloody Mary and had identified Deadly Dave's left humerus. The Reverend Hubert Counter (a.k.a. Hermione) had named all twelve disciples, hummed the opening bars of Beethoven's Fifth Symphony and explained the difference between a camisole and a chemisette.

It had, in sporting terms, been what is customarily known as a rout.

With ninety seconds of the programme left Voluptua Bradshaw bravely returned to the fray, holding a piece of paper upon which Streaky had carefully written down a short ad lib.

'The producer has asked me to remind you all that at the beginning of this series it was announced by Better Television that any team which managed to defeat our celebrities in a round of 'Celebrity Trivia!' would receive a genuine replica plastic statuette of myself,' here, to great cheers, Voluptua held up a genuine replica plastic statuette of herself, 'and £1,500 worth of bedding plants from Digwell Garden Supplies.' She smiled, winningly, at the four members of the winning team.

'Excuse me,' said Itchy, instantly. 'But could we change our prize?'

A look of panic spread across Voluptua's face. She looked down at the sheet of paper Streaky had given her. It made no mention of an interruption from Itchy. 'Er...'

'Of course you can!' said Percy, magnanimously, stepping into the breach.

'It's just that I happen to know that Digwell Garden Supplies also make a very good ride on mower,' said Itchy speaking very quickly. 'And if the rest of the team don't mind,' he looked at the other team members who instantly made it clear that they had no objection at all to switching their bedding plants for a lawnmower, 'and if it's all the same to you and Better Television I think we could really do with the ride on mower because...'

Percy looked across towards Streaky who was nodding enthusiastically. The producer had just received a telephone call from Mr Buttress telling him that the preliminary reports showed that the programme had achieved record viewing figures.

'No problem at all!' said Percy, happily. 'The lawnmower is yours!'

The red-haired girl made a winding up movement with her right arm. Percy put an arm around Voluptua, turned her towards the camera and hissed 'Smile and wave!' into her ear.

They both smiled and waved. Everyone else smiled and waved back at them.

Behind the bar Biffo found himself putting his arm around Lettice. He felt her snuggle against him. And then he felt her arm around his waist. He looked down. She looked up. They kissed.

Biffo's second innings was going well.

~